*"ADRIENNE," KRISTIAN MURMURED.
"OH, GOD, MY WILD, SWEET ADRIENNE.
DO YOU KNOW HOW LONG I'VE WAITED FOR
THIS?"*

They were locked in embrace. Kristian's lips rained soft kisses on her cheeks and ears and neck. She could feel the length of his body along hers, his hard, insistent masculinity.

She clung to him. Her knees felt weak, and a warm melting had begun to spread like butter through her belly and thighs. Never with any man had she felt like this. It was as if she could give up her entire self to him, let him do with her whatever he wished . . .

Slowly, luxuriously, Kristian stripped the clothes from her body, until the rose faille gown lay crumpled on the floor and she was stretched naked on the bed, her body bared to his gaze. Only the Passion Star remained, glowing barbaric at her throat, for she would not let him remove that. It was a part of her, especially tonight, and she could not let it go . . .

the Passion Star

by

Julia Grice

WARNER BOOKS

A Warner Communications Company

For Lee, with all my love

Names of some actors and actresses mentioned in passing—such as Fanny Davenport, Bijou Heron, Adelaide Ristori—are quite real. Theaters mentioned in the book really existed. However, cast members of *Melissa Charles* or the *Passion Star* are fictitious, as are all other characters in the book. The reader might be interested to know that, as far as I am aware, grease paint was not invented and used widely until after this book closes.

I would like to thank Dr. Ron Peterson for his medical advice, and John K. Payne for assistance with problems of the plot, as well as others who were generous with suggestions. A special thanks goes to Douglas Alden Peterson and Roni Tripodi, for their encouragement.

One

Prologue

Paris, France, 1849.

Outside in the streets of Paris it was cool and misty, the moisture magnifying all sounds. A street vendor hawked fish, her voice piercing. A carriage rumbled by. Horses' hooves clattered on cobblestones, and iron wheels screeched. From somewhere came the liquid shout of a mother scolding her child.

But inside the little *pension* it was all very quiet save for the stirrings of the dying woman. She lay on a feather mattress, propped up by a dozen pillows; her breathing had grown irregular and she gasped for breath.

Her yellow-white hair streamed out around her face on the pillow. It was soft and lustrous, its strands as shining as if they had captured sunlight. Once she had possessed a stunning beauty, her cheekbones high and carved, her eyes full of slanted fire. Very little carmine or rouge had been needed to heighten the loveliness of that face for the stage.

Now nothing was left of her beauty but her hair, and not even death could remove its luster.

"I'm dying, Solange," she whispered in French to her younger sister who crouched beside the bed, silent tears running down her cheeks and into the corners of her mouth. "Dying . . . dying . . . God, it isn't fair!"

"Oh, surely you are not. Not yet," Solange protested. "I've sent for the doctor, and he'll bring more medicine for you, and clysters, and more leeches to bleed you. . . ."

"Bleeding! That won't help me now. Nothing will. God, Solange, oh, God, I wanted to live for Martin. He needs me . . ."

"*I* need you," whispered Solange. "Oh, please, Adrienne, don't die. . . ."

Chapter 1

Glasgow, Scotland, 1871.

"Ah, Addie, stand still, will you, daughter?" Solange McGill's voice was weary. "I'll never get this bodice fitted properly if you keep wriggling about like a puppy!"

Gray light filtered in through the window of the dingy flat, bringing with it the shouts of the children playing outside in the Close. Sounds always echoed here in the poorest part of Glasgow, where the ancient stone walls wound about like a maze, blocking off sun and air.

But Adrienne did not hear the shouts of the children, some of whom were her own brothers and sisters. Instead, excitement surged in her like a fist clenching in her belly. She fidgeted impatiently while her mother pinned and basted the dress she was to wear for the audition.

She felt like jumping up and down, like racing to the window to shout out to the quarreling children with their dirty faces and legs. She, Adrienne McGill, was different, not like them. *She* was going to do something with her life. She—

"Addie, will you stand still? *Oui,* even Tessie can stand more quietly than you, and she is only eight. And you a big girl of eighteen, old enough to be married by now with a baby or two!"

Addie. It was a nickname which Adrienne hated. Each flat syllable was dumpy and ugly, making her think of fat women in shapeless dresses. Why, she wondered, could no one remember to call her by her full name? Adrienne was a beautiful name, belonging to her aunt, who had been a famous French actress.

Obediently she turned as her mother worked. *Maman*'s hands, still scabbed from winter chapping, prodded at the gray taffeta gown. The dress had once been worn by *Maman* to church. Now *Maman,* sacrificing her one good gown, had carefully turned the hem and scrubbed away the stains which had marred the bodice.

For today Adrienne would wear the dress to audition at the Brittania Music Hall. And if she got the job—

Again the excitement boiled in her. She, Adrienne McGill, would no longer do sewing with her mother. Instead, she would be an actress. She would sweep upon the stage to receive the wild applause of the audience. They would clap and call for her, they would throw bouquets of spring flowers upon the stage, hyacinths and jonquils—

"Ouch!" Adrienne jumped as her mother's basting needle jabbed too close to her ribs; the daydream ebbed. *"Maman,* I know you are a good seamstress, but do you have to sew me, too?"

"Ah, Addie, I'm sorry. I was thinking of other things, I'm afraid." Solange was a transplanted Parisienne, and her voice still held the liquid French accent.

Now her roughened hand held up a small mirror. "Turn, child, turn, so that I can see how the underarm seam looks."

Adrienne peeped at her own reflection. Oval face, high cheekbones, full, wilful lips, slanted eyes full of merry blue fire. Her hair, however, was her most striking feature. It was the color of palest ale when sunlight shines through the glass that holds it. Men and even women would stop to stare at her as she walked past them in the street. Once, an old woman had reached out to stroke Adrienne's curls with gnarled old fingers.

"Lovely," she had murmured. "Hair like a fairy princess, like spun gossamer . . ." Then she had crossed

14

herself and scurried away, mumbling as if she had seen something wicked.

Now Adrienne heard *Maman*'s voice, rich with pride. "Oh, they'll stare at you in this dress! The cloth is so fine, see how it catches the light?"

Adrienne sighed and let her mind wander away from her mother's talk. Again she imagined herself an actress, making a grand entrance in an extravagantly beautiful gown, sumptuous with lace and flounces. It was a game Adrienne played on her way to market, or to buy more thread for *Maman*. She was not a girl who sewed with her mother, but a countess, perhaps, like Aurelia Prendergast, for whom *Maman* sewed fine petticoats and corset covers.

If you were beautiful, surely anything wonderful could happen to you.

She frowned, thinking of what had happened yesterday, which was not so wonderful. She had been hurrying along the narrow Close at 165 High Street, when Jaimie McAndrews had jumped out and grabbed her. Jaimie was seventeen, short and broad of shoulder. His family lived in the flat across the Close by the stone stairs. As children, they had played together in the gutters, or stolen fruit from the market. But now Jaimie seemed dull and heavy, already worn down by a man's labor in a nearby ironworks.

"Addie, Addie!" Jaimie had shouted. He had whirled her into his arms and pressed her against the rotten wooden shutters of a window. Then he had pushed his body against hers so urgently that she had felt the hard bulge of his maleness. She had been frightened—not by Jaimie, hadn't she known him since they were children?—but by something in herself.

You could not grow up in the worst area of Glasgow in the last third of the nineteenth century without being aware of sex. Prostitutes lurked in the narrow, alley-like wynds, waiting for customers or entertaining them behind stairways or privy sheds. Men and women fought, and the sounds of their lovemaking carried out into the dank stone corridors. Once a girl had been raped in the Close outside the flat, her cries piercing with terror.

Yes, Adrienne knew that something happened between men and women. And now, as her mother pulled and tugged and basted, she felt the color rise to her cheeks. What would it be like? she wondered. To feel *that* part of a man inside your own body? Would it be wonderful, as some of the girls had whispered? Or would it be ugly, a quick invasion marked with fighting and cries, as usually seemed the case here in the Closes?

She didn't know.

"Addie, turn," her mother commanded. "What will they say at the Brittania if you slump like that? Lift your arms! Higher, please. And do stand still. How many times must I mention it?"

"Perhaps a hundred?" Adrienne could not help smiling. Of all the eight children, even Devin, who was five and gravely ill, she herself was her mother's favorite, and she knew it.

"Ah, *oui,* you are pert, aren't you, daughter?"

But Solange, pausing to tug again at the lower seam of the right armhole, said it with pride. "You are so like *her,* full of spirit and temper. My sister Adrienne was a real woman, Addie. There was life in her, a spirit that could never be quenched!"

"Yes, *Maman.*"

Adrienne had grown up on stories of Adrienne La-Rivière, the beautiful and notorious French actress who had died mysteriously, murdered, it was said, by a rival. Adrienne had been named after her and fed, from babyhood, on tales of the Parisian stage. For Solange had been, briefly, a wardrobe mistress for the Théâtre de l'Odéon, having been given the job by her sister.

"You will have a life like hers one day," her mother mused, her voice inflected with the rich, thrilling timbre imparted by a daydream often repeated.

"I hope not! I don't wish to be murdered!"

Solange made a swift, Gallic gesture. "Hush! Don't joke about death, my darling. Ah, *oui,* I saw it all at the Odéon. They would come to me to have their gowns fitted, all of the lovely ones. Adélie, Colette, Marie. But my Adrienne was the most beautiful one of all. So like you, my Addie. The men would flock back to the dressing

16

room to see her, to bring her flowers and take her out for supper. She had a hundred admirers, but one in particular —*oui,* he was special. He was grievously hurt in a carriage accident just before she died. . . ."

The rough, sore hands tugged at a thread. Then firmly Solange turned her daughter and began to work on the other side. "*You* are beautiful, Addie, lovelier than any girl at the Odéon. Your face is like a profile on a coin. Pure and cool, and yet wicked, too. Impish and desirable . . ."

Adrienne lowered her arms, feeling her face go suddenly hot.

"Child, child, will you lift your arms! Yes, Addie, you have the looks. Your face has good bones. Your hair is stunning. And there is a quality about you. I've known it since you were a baby. Ah, *oui,* how I've prayed that some sweaty, dirty man would not snatch you up and ruin you!"

Adrienne thought of Jaimie McAndrews, and shivered. Then a cough sounded from the other, small room of the flat. It was a child's cough, wheezing and painful.

Both women stiffened. Then Adrienne caught her breath and ran into the next room.

Her little brother Devin lay on his pallet by the soot-blackened stove, five years old, thin and wasted and feverish. Mrs. McAndrews, who sometimes acted as midwife, said that he had consumption, and fed him tonics and possets and made him poultices for his chest. But still Devin got no better. Recently he had begun to cough up blood-streaked mucus and to complain of ear pain and difficulty swallowing.

"Devin?" Adrienne said now, going to him and taking his hand. "Devin, are you better?"

The big eyes, bleak with suffering, looked up at her. A hand stroked his right ear. "Better," he repeated. "Will you tell me a story, Addie?"

"Of course I will, Devin. As soon as *Maman* finishes fitting my gown. Did you know I'm to try out at the Brittania tonight? Perhaps I'll become a famous actress. Would you like that, Devin?"

"Will you be famous tomorrow, Addie?"

17

Adrienne smiled. "No, not tomorrow, little brother. But perhaps the day after that!" She pulled him to her and hugged him. "You lie still, Devin, and rest. Tomorrow I'll bring you home some milk and eggs, something good for your chest. Would you like that?"

But, exhausted, Devin had already fallen into a half-doze, his face nearly as pale as the laundered linens on which he lay.

"*Maman!*" Back in the other room, Adrienne's whisper was choked. "*Maman,* he's worse today. Today he fell asleep while I was still talking to him. I'm afraid—"

"And so am I, child. But it's good milk and eggs and fish which will help him more than anything. If your Papa were not drinking so much these days—"

Mother and daughter glanced at each other. Jack McGill, who at twenty-five had been handsome and dashing enough to steal Solange away from Paris, was at forty-five a sodden drunk. He sought in Scotch whisky relief from the intolerable burden of being the father of eight and living off the High Street. The ancient warren of stone buildings, due soon to be torn down, was crammed with people. Sometimes there were as many as a dozen to a room, a thousand to an acre. Most were Irish immigrants, or countrymen from the Highlands or Lowlands who had come to work in the textile mills, iron foundries and engineering works of Glasgow. All were poor.

The racking cough sounded again, and Adrienne stiffened. "Milk," she whispered fiercely. "*Maman,* I'll get it, I promise, not only for Devin, but for all of us. And I'll get eggs and meat. I swear it! I'll bring all my earnings home to you, I won't save even tuppence for myself."

"Of course, child. You're a generous girl, and a good one. God knows I've needed your help with the lacework and sewing. But I've heard there might be a job for you at the Brittania and I'd hoped—perhaps it's really time at last—"

Solange's voice rose, took on fullness. "The man said you're just what's needed, and God knows it's a start. You're destined, Addie. I really believe that. Destined..."

Adrienne bit her lower lip. *"Maman,* are you sure—"

"Hush, child, and listen. I've taught you to sing. You must take deep breaths and do your very best, and don't let them stop you. *Oui,* there'll be other girls trying to take the job away from you. Don't let them. Fight for yourself. Let them see your talent, the greatness that is in you. As it was in *her.*"

"Maman . . ." Adrienne squirmed under the firm pushing of her mother's hand. *"Maman,* are you really sure? Perhaps I'm not destined at all. I know I can sing—I've danced and sung for pennies in the High Street, but . . ."

She hesitated, trying to put her thought into words. Her mother's voice, rich with promise, had created a shining edifice. Yet perhaps that was all it was. *Maman*'s imagining, a shining spiderweb of a dream, and no more. She would arrive at the Brittania and there would be no job for her. They would look her over and laugh and send her away and the dream would be over.

Her life would go on as before. She would continue to sew lace collars and petticoats with *Maman.* In a year, she would be married to Jaimie McAndrews or someone like him. A year after that would come the first baby. She would have many babies. Eight, nine, or even fifteen, like Jaimie's mother, who had a gaping black hole in the front of her mouth where she had lost her teeth. "Each bairn takes away a tooth. Except for greedy Jaimie, who took two," Mrs. McAndrews said sometimes, her sunken mouth twisting.

"There," Solange said with satisfaction. "Walk across the room, Addie, and hold your back straight. I want to see what you look like."

"Maman! I—"

"Oui, that dress will suit you very well. Of course, you'll have to pinch your cheeks and lips to give you some color. Or I can find you some carmine—perhaps it wouldn't hurt to try that, just a bit. It's what actresses use."

Actresses.

19

Adrienne turned to gaze at her mother's shining eyes, at the belief in them.

She drew in a deep, shivering breath. *Tomorrow,* she thought. Tomorrow there would be time to think about the bad things, of Mrs. McAndrews and sewing collars for the rest of her life.

For now, for today . . .

It was early afternoon. Adrienne ran an anxious hand along the bodice of the gray taffeta gown. Then, lifting its hem to protect it, she stepped out into the Close. Her mother's last-minute admonitions echoed in her ears.

"Remember, Addie, don't let them stop you. Because they'll try to, they always do. Just keep telling yourself that you can do it. You're destined, Addie. Destined, as *she* was."

It was cold outdoors. A chill April moisture filled the air. Adrienne shivered, wishing she had worn her old black shawl. But Solange had decreed that the shawl was too shabby to go with the dress. Her daughter, she maintained, must look as elegant as possible. If it was cold, then she must just suffer.

Adrienne hurried between the narrow stone buildings, wrinkling her nose at the odor which rose from a nearby dung-heap, where precious horse manure was stored until needed. She headed toward the arch which opened onto the High Street, emitting a halo of light like the exit of a tunnel.

The Closes and their thoroughfares—Rottenrow, Drygate, High Street—were the heart of this most ancient sector of Glasgow. Narrow alleys or wynds, so tight that a wheelbarrow could scarcely squeeze through them, connected the Closes, which were courtyards fifteen to twenty feet square. Leaning in on all sides, oppressively near, were the walls of the surrounding three- and four-story buildings, their gray old stones cutting out most of the afternoon light.

A faint gleam of sun shone off a pair of men's trousers hung from a pole extended from a fourth-floor window. More poles held looped strings of laundry. Ancient doors opened onto the narrow yard. The floor of the Close itself was paved with uneven cobbles. A gutter ran down its center, in which swill and waste water flowed.

Adrienne caught her breath in distaste as she skirted a spatter of moisture where someone had tossed out a pan of water.

Some people got used to it, she knew. Lived here until they no longer saw the squalor, or smelled the dung-heaps. But she had been taught to read and write by *Maman,* had been instilled with all the airs and graces and manners which *Maman* could recall from the Parisian stage. She had spent four years at the Catholic school, while *Maman* did mending for the nuns. She had even read penny novels, given them by Countess Aurelia. So she knew what the other world, the world of rich and pampered ladies, was like . . .

"Addie! Addie! Where you be goin'?"

The voice startled her. Adrienne whirled about, catching up the taffeta gown so that it would not brush the paving stones and their filth. A broad-shouldered but short figure was silhouetted at the entrance to the High Street.

"Addie, I say! Where'd you get that fancy dress? And where you be going, eh?"

It was Jaimie McAndrews, come to plague her again, and probably to push her up against the wall for another kiss. Quick anger pushed through Adrienne.

"Never you mind where I'm going!" she called, her high, rich voice carrying in the Close like the peal of a bell.

"Aw, you can tell me. Goin' out to get a job, are you? Your Ma was sayin' to my Ma—"

"Never mind what my *Maman* said! It's none of your business! And don't call me Addie!" she cried out, as the stocky seventeen-year-old swaggered in her direction. "My name isn't Addie. How many times do I have to tell you? It's Adrienne!"

Jaimie grinned. "It's Addie to me, it's Addie to everyone, and it always will be. Nothing you can say will change that, me girl. Aw, come here, will you?" he added, as Adrienne tried to edge past him. "I want to talk with you."

"Talk with me? As you did yesterday? I don't call that talking! I call it—"

"You call it what?" Jaimie's smile revealed crooked but white teeth. He leaned against the damp stone wall, effectively blocking her passage.

"That dress," he added. "It makes you look pretty, Addie. You look . . ." He moved his big hands inarticulately. "You look . . . different. Not like us. Swell."

"I am different," she retorted airily, "from the likes of you, anyway! Please move, Jaimie, so I can get by. I have something important to do!"

Adrienne's eyes darted exasperatedly about her. A wooden bucket, half-filled with stagnant water, sat by one of the ancient doors. She edged toward it.

"Addie, Addie! Come out walking with me. We'll go over to Nelson Street, there's a shop there sells the swellest chocolates. I could get us some if you was to look careful and watch your step—"

"Do you mean steal some sweets?" She was scornful. "Not me, Jaimie McAndrews. I have better things to do than that. As for you, if you don't move that big lummox body of yours out of my way, I'm going to dump water all over you."

She reached downward and grabbed the bucket of water. Hefting it by its two handles, she managed to brandish it in his direction without sloshing any onto her dress.

"Oh! Will you, Addie? Will you indeed? I'll see if you will—I'll see! Mayhap I'll pour water over *you*—"

He dodged suddenly toward the pail. Their fingers met over one of the two wire handles, and for an instant they struggled. Then the pail tipped, spilling water over the taffeta dress.

Adrienne let out a cry of dismay. She jumped to her feet and began to pelt down the Close toward its exit, her boots skittering wildly on the cobbles. Belatedly she remembered her hem, snatched it up, and kept on running.

"Addie! Addie!"

"Oh, go to hell, Jaimie McAndrews!" She skidded out of the doorway and into the safety of the High Street.

The High Street was as it always looked, a grim thoroughfare, treeless, and lined with sooty four-story buildings. A few carriages and barrows raised dust in the street. An old woman in black trudged along with a basket of bread from the baker's, giving the water stain on Adrienne's dress a sour look as she passed.

Adrienne flushed and bent over, trying to repair the damage. Carefully she blotted the moisture with a discreet portion of petticoat, until the fabric was not so obviously damp.

Then she drew a deep breath and began to sail down the walk, letting her skirts swish out behind her as if she were Aurelia Prendergast. She lifted her shoulders, tilted her chin, and let herself feel the role. She was no longer Addie McGill, she was Countess Aurelia, rich and pampered . . .

"Addie, come back!" Jaimie bellowed.

"I won't! I'm going to go to the Brittania Theater and become an actress!"

Maman's dreams, *Maman*'s burning, excited eyes, even Devin's cough, all seemed jumbled in her mind now. She felt giddy, whirly. She felt as if she could spin around and around, shocking the glum dray driver who clattered by.

"No one can stop me!" she called. "Not you and not my Papa and not anyone!"

"Addie—"

"And my name is not Addie, it's Adrienne! Do you hear me? I'm Adrienne!"

The Brittania Theater was located on Trongate, a typical Glasgow business street with its bleak rows of soot-blackened buildings, each topped by a bristle of chimney-pots. Dominating this setting was the tall, rococo Tron Steeple, and the Tontine Building, a new hotel decorated with stone arches, gargoyle faces, and large cement balls.

23

Adrienne hurried past the Tontine Building, barely glancing at it. She shivered as the damp April wind whipped down the thoroughfare. Her boasts to Jaimie forgotten, a sick excitement now squirmed in her belly. Soon, she thought, very soon now she would have her chance. Her chance at the theater, at the golden life *Maman* had pictured so vividly.

They had to like her, oh, they had to!

As she passed the Old Equitable Loan Company, an old man came shambling around the corner. He pushed a two-wheeled barrow in front of him. Boxes and bags were piled high on it, seeming almost ready to tumble down. The old man himself was thin and wizened, white whiskers fuzzed on sunken cheeks. His eyes were frightening, coated over with a strange, milky-white film.

Yet despite this, he seemed to notice her almost at once. The filmed eyes turned sharply in her direction.

Resolutely, Adrienne stopped him. "Do you know where I should go to audition for the Brittania? My *Maman* said—"

"Aye, no plays there this time of day, me girl. Nor music-hall shows, neither." The old man spat onto the cobbles.

"Please, then, is there somewhere I should go?"

"I' there." He gestured toward a stone archway wedged between two shops. This led, Adrienne knew, to the warren of wynds and closes behind the business area.

"I' the wynd is the stage door." The whitish eyes focused on her with a curious intensity. "That's where ye go. Aye, women like you have to use the back—it's good enough for ye."

"Women like who?" Adrienne demanded. "What do you mean?"

"Why, actresses." He spat a thick gob of phlegm onto the paving-stones. "She-spawn of the devil! Mistress of Beelzebub, fornicatress, trollop—that's what ye are. Ye and your like—whores! Harlots! Trulls!"

The old man, filthy in his bundled layers of clothing, pulled aside from the fullness of Adrienne's skirts, as if touching her might contaminate him.

She stared at him, furious and hurt. She could feel her face begin to redden. Her temper, always fierce, began to sweep her up in its force.

"Actress!" she cried. "Yes, I'm an actress—or I wish to be! But I'm not . . . like you say!"

Two women carrying market baskets had turned to gawk, for Adrienne's voice had strong carrying qualities, and now her anger made it even more powerful. "I tell you, I'm not a— I'm not any of the things you say. I'm as respectable as anyone!"

But the old man only spat again, derisively. Then he grasped the handles of his barrow and began to push it in front of him. The two women nudged each other and laughed.

Adrienne picked up her skirts and ran toward the archway which opened into the wynd, her cheeks flaming with shame. She dashed through its portal and leaned against the ancient stone wall. Her heart slammed under the gray taffeta.

How dare that old man speak to her so? How dare he act as if she were no better than a prostitute! In all the years of daydreaming, *Maman* had always spoken of actresses in a special, reverent way, as if they were some rare and magical breed set apart from the rest of womankind.

And yet—Adrienne's brain spun perilously. Hadn't Papa beaten her each time she had spoken of wanting to go on the stage, until finally she dared not mention it to him? Hadn't Papa and *Maman* quarreled often about that? Hadn't even Mrs. McAndrews jibed at her, telling her she would go to the devil if she followed her mother's wishes?

Spawn of the devil. Whore . . . whore . . .

Adrienne stepped back from the wall. Dully she looked about her. The narrow wynd was like a hundred others, with its cobbled gutter, stacked piles of rotting wood, its tumbledown privy and abandoned wheelbarrow.

But the sign, *Brittania Stage Door,* projected from a building half-way down the wynd. Adrienne sucked in a sharp breath. She thought of *Maman,* waiting at home to

25

hear how the audition came out. Of Devin, waiting for the milk and eggs she could bring him. *Will you be famous tomorrow, Addie?*

Slowly she smoothed down the damp place on the taffeta dress. She straightened her back and lifted her chin high. Then, her movements as deliberate as those of a lady of quality, she walked toward the stage door.

Chapter 2

Ghostly voices echoed against damp stone.

"Well, and where is she? Where is the little one? Damn, I need someone little, a creature who can contort herself properly! Peronne, I don't know why you persist in sending me these huge lummoxes of country girls who can barely squeeze into their corsets, let alone a box!"

Adrienne let the stage door creak shut behind her. She drew a quick, frightened breath. She saw that she was standing against a stone wall. It loomed several stories high above her into darkness, punctuated at odd intervals by slit-like windows. From somewhere came the frank stench of a privy.

Her heart was slamming, and she swallowed hard to rid herself of a thick lump in her throat.

Again the quarreling voices penetrated her nervousness.

"You are a fool, Peronne, if you think that you can foist off a barnyard slut on me, Xenos Shane! Do you think that such a one would set off the Passion Star? Do you?"

"N-no, sir."

"Then look sharp, and find me someone who will! Immediately, do you hear me?"

Adrienne craned her neck to look about her for the speakers. She was standing in a huge, looming enclosure, whose roof seemed to stretch endlessly above her into darkness. High above her hung an odd assortment of ropes, wires, pulleys, and other large objects, all of which

27

looked perilously as if they might tumble down at any moment. An odd odor, like rotting animal flesh, pervaded the theater and mingled with the privy stench.

The voices rose, then lowered to a mutter. Adrienne shivered, wrinkling her nose at the unpleasant smell. She wrapped her arms tightly about herself, against the vault-like cold which seemed to ooze from the very pores of the stone walls. She wished now that she had worn her shawl, shabby as it was. Anything would be better than this deathly chill.

And, she thought, moistening her lips, it was as if ghosts roamed here. Talking ghosts . . .

"Well? And who might you be?"

"Oh!" Adrienne jumped violently.

A man strode from behind a painted panel. He was short, only a few inches taller than Adrienne herself. Yet his voice was so huge and booming that it made him, too, seem large. He was in his fifties, with gray-white hair combed back from his face in a flaring crest. He had a hooked nose and wet, too-red lips. The cut of his black suit was as theatrical and flamboyant as the man himself.

"Well?" he repeated.

"Me? Are you speaking to me?"

"Yes, it's you I'm addressing, and not the Center Door Fancy." The man twisted his mouth, using the strange phrase almost deliberately, as if he knew full well that she would not know what it meant.

Adrienne felt a flush rise from the neckline of her dress. "I—I'm Adrienne . . . Gill." Some impulse made her drop the first syllable of her last name. "I've come here to audition."

"Oh?"

"Yes. But I thought—where are the others? The other girls who were to try out? *Maman* said—" She faltered.

"*Maman?*" The deep voice, so out of place in the short, pear-shaped body, boomed upward to the roof. "You call your mother *Maman,* then, in the French way? Are you French?"

"No. *Maman* was born in Paris and worked once as a

wardrobe mistress at the *Theatre de l'Odéon*. She taught me French, though I do not speak it well. I went four years to the Catholic school here, while *Maman* did sewing for the nuns. I took singing lessons with Lady Prendergast's daughter. I am as well educated as anyone," she added proudly.

"I see. And where do you live?"

"I live off the High Street," she admitted.

Xenos Shane's face showed distaste. "You come from that rat-warren, then? That disgusting pile of stones and filth? I don't understand how people can live like that—in such dirt."

Shame rushed through her, hot and ugly. She wanted to cry, to run away. Instead, she drew herself up. "Most of them can't help it," she told him defiantly. "They'd live elsewhere, if they could. Anyway, *I'm* clean. *Maman* was strict about that. And I can sing, and dance, too. I have danced for pennies in the Close—I was very good, they all said, and—"

She saw that he was looking at her hair now, the way they all did, staring at her long curls, the color of new ale lit from behind by sunlight.

"You asked about the others," he said, interrupting her. "I sent them all home. Dairymaids, that's what they were. All big rumps and bosoms and fat thighs. Quite unsuitable."

She, however, was suitable, the man's look seemed to say. Very suitable indeed. Adrienne squirmed as his eyes moved across her body. It was as if he were inspecting every seam *Maman* had sewn, and the flesh beneath the gown as well.

"I was not brought up to hear talk like that," she said stiffly.

"You, a girl from the Closes?" The man laughed. "Don't be prudish, my sweeting. You have a good voice, girl, it'll carry well, once you've trained it. It has a good deal of color to it. Your hair, of course, is stunning. As for your other attributes, they'll do well, too. Even if you're a bit small for an actress." His eyes judged her. "Of course," he added thoughtfully. "That dreadful dress has got to go."

29

Dreadful dress! Adrienne felt a stinging indignation. She thought of *Maman*'s hard work on the gown, the hours she had spent restitching each seam, then pressing the yards and yards of taffeta with a flatiron heated on the stove, all of it done in perspiring haste so as to get Adrienne ready in time.

And now this man—this squat, ugly, arrogant man —dared to tell her that *Maman*'s work was ugly!

"My gown is beautiful," she told him stonily. She tossed her head. "As for you, I don't even know who you are!" She heard her voice rush on, quite unable to stop it. "Besides, there's a bad smell in this theater—it smells rotten!"

The man with the booming voice laughed. "Ah, quite a temper you have, my sweetmeat." He moistened already-wet lips. "The odor, my dear, is the sizing they use in the scenery paint. I believe it consists of animal skins simmered to a jelly. A noisome stench, but a very necessary one if we are to have stage sets."

"Oh—"

"Well, we'd better get started. The others have already gone home. As our friend, Peronne, the stage manager, is also about to do, before the evening show. By the way, we'll have to hurry if we are to have you outfitted."

"Outfitted?"

"Did you think that I would let you go on in that monstrosity of a dress? Don't you know that the gaslights would fade it all to nothing? Gaslight requires strong colors and strong make-up. I think . . . yes, red for you. Red should do just fine. Lucky that my wife has a costume which should fit you. You're almost the same size as she is."

"Your wife?" Adrienne, forgetting her temper outburst, tried to take all of this in. "A costume?"

"You see, my sweeting, my wife, Frances, usually assists me. She sets off the Passion Star very nicely." Xenos Shane's glistening eyes appraised her. "Unfortunately, she has been taken with some female troubles and can't help me. Therefore, it has fallen upon me to look about for some young creature such as yourself to fill the need."

Some young creature such as yourself. Why did those words fill her with such unease? There was something dark to them, Adrienne thought wildly. Something secret and unsavory.

"I don't know—" She began to edge away from him.

"You asked who I am. Well, I'm Xenos Shane, lately of New York City. You have heard of me, I presume?" He gave her a mock bow, executing it with sardonic flourish. "The well-known magician, famous here in Glasgow, in Edinburgh, in London, and in glorious Pittsburgh. My act is renowned—the Disappearing Appassionata—"

"The what?" In spite of her unease, Adrienne could not suppress a giggle. "What did you say?"

Xenos Shane scowled. His white brows beetled together in the center of his nose.

"I said Appassionata. Don't laugh, girl, or I'll have you tossed out on the dung heap you came from." The full lips twisted. "Yes, Miss Gill, you are going to be my Appassionata, my wild and lovely beauty gowned in a dress the color of flame. You will be the center of all men's eyes, and then you will vanish in a flash of smoke. What do you think of that?"

Xenos Shane led Adrienne down a narrow stone corridor to her left. The hallway, lined with battered wooden doors, was strong with the privy stench and the smell of sizing. But, as the magician hurried ahead of her, he did not seem to be aware of the smell. Adrienne wrinkled her nose and tried not to think of it either.

"Here," Xenos Shane said. He pushed open one of the doors. "There is a gown in there. Put it on and let me see how you look in it. And hurry, will you? We must have time to rehearse before tonight. It is vital."

"Yes. Yes, of course."

The room was small and squalid. Plaster had fallen off the walls in huge chunks, most of it still lying on the

31

floor, unswept, along with crumpled tins, soiled bits of rag, a filthy rabbit's foot, a candle stub. A gas fixture on the wall badly needed cleaning.

There were two pieces of furniture, a rickety table and an old wooden chair. A grimy white pitcher and basin occupied the table, and a wavy mirror caught Adrienne's image, reflecting back a frightened face.

A row of hooks bristled from one wall, and from one of these hung a red silk gown. Dubiously Adrienne reached for it and held it up to herself.

The gown, of a fashionable cut, with yards of flounces, ruching and ribbons, was indeed a fiery red. But it was in desperate need of cleaning. The bodice was marred by water and food marks, the armpits were circled with perspiration stains, and some of the flounces were ripped. A boned hoopskirt, hanging from a hook by a ribbon, was in similar condition.

Adrienne regarded both in dismay. The thought of putting such a dress next to her own body made her shudder. Her own gray taffeta was at least clean, and surely it was prettier, too, if not so fashionable. But Xenos Shane had said something about the gaslights, she remembered.

Well, she could endure this filthy dress, couldn't she, for the sake of Devin? For the money she would be paid, the milk and fish and eggs she would be able to buy?

She looked at herself again in the mirror, imagining that she was Adrienne La Riviére. She struck a pose, one arm outflung dramatically. *Vraiment, this gown, I really can't abide it, I must have something new, in peau de soie. . . .*

Adrienne sighed. She began to fumble with the fastenings of the gray taffeta. Outside in the corridor she could hear Xenos Shane pacing about. Yet each time he passed the dressing room, his steps seemed to pause.

She hesitated. Then she lifted up the wooden chair and propped it against the door.

Five minutes later, she stood in her petticoats and worn corset cover. Carefully she stepped into the hoop skirt and tied its bands at her waist. Then, holding her

32

breath against its acrid smell, she settled the red silk dress over her shoulders.

The gown buttoned in back, and Adrienne began to struggle with its small jet buttons. How she wished *Maman* were here to help her! But *Maman* was not here, she reminded herself. She was alone in this horrid theater with Xenos Shane, and if she could not reach the buttons herself, then Xenos would have to help her with them, for there was no one else. And she did not want that man's hands on her. She did not want him to touch her at all.

"Have you found the dress? Do you wish assistance?" The heavy, theatrical voice boomed against the corridor walls.

"No! I'll be all right. I . . . I'm nearly done now."

Actually, there were still about a third of the jet buttons left to go. Adrienne strained to reach them, her face furrowed with effort.

"Well, wash your face when you get the dress on, my sweeting." The voice was full of a mocking laughter. "You've a smudge on one cheek. You look as if you might have slept on that dung-heap of yours."

"I never—" She bit off the words and leaned toward the mirror. Through smears of powder and grease, she stared at herself.

There *was* a smudge of dirt on her face, she noted with horror. It must have happened in the wynd when Jaimie had been chasing her. Had she really arrived at the theater, not only with water on her gown but with dirt on her face? No wonder Xenos Shane had stared at her so!

She scrubbed at the spot, using a corner of her petticoat, for she had no handkerchief. Then she rubbed at the rest of her face, too, until her cheeks were flushed. Adjusting the gown, she saw that its neckline was very low indeed. It plunged downward to reveal the shadows at the top of her breasts, and the cleft between them.

"Are you coming, Miss Gill? I've told you, we have much work to do. You're as ignorant as a kitten, and I must be sure you're competent before tonight. Much depends on it."

"Oh, very well!" She burst out of the dressing room. "This dress!" she cried. "Must I really wear it? The color doesn't become me, and it isn't even clean. It smells!"

Xenos Shane scowled. "Oh? So it does? And just who do you think you are, young miss, to tell me that you don't like the costume you are to wear? Do you think that the noses beyond the footlights are going to be able to smell you? No, my sweet, they can only see you, and lucky they'll be to do that. That hair of yours, like the tassels of Indiana corn—"

The gnarled, moist hands were suddenly at her back, fumbling at the jet buttons. Adrienne stood rigidly as the magician finished the buttoning. Through the sleazy silk, she could feel the heat of his hands.

"You'll do as I tell you," the magician said. "And you won't complain. I think, my little sweeting, that you possess entirely too much temper. You'll have to curb that if you wish to work with me."

The hands closed tightly about her shoulders, squeezing her flesh hard. Then, almost as suddenly as he had grabbed her, Xenos Shane released her.

"Very well," he added. "You will wear this. It is part of the act, and it is one of the reasons I hired you. I think your looks will set it off well."

He held up something which dangled from a golden chain, and glittered blue.

"But . . . what is it?" Adrienne's voice was a whisper. Her anger over the dress was quite gone now in her fascination with the jewel.

"It's the Passion Star, of course. What do you think of it?"

Adrienne caught her breath. The stone, nearly two inches long and one and a half inches deep, held a deep blue luster the color of sky at twilight. Set within its huge oval was—there was no other word for it—a six-legged star. Each of the star's spreading legs reached nearly to the edge of the stone. Their points seemed to wink and glitter at her, holding in their depths a mystery.

"It's beautiful," she breathed. "What sort of stone is it?"

Xenos Shane smiled. Evidently he was pleased that

she, too, found the jewel fascinating. He twirled the chain about, until the gem itself rested in the cavity of his palm.

"It is a star sapphire," he announced proudly. "I've traveled a bit since I left New York; I bought this twenty years ago near the town of Chantabun on the Gulf of Siam. They have many ruby mines and sapphire deposits there, and this was one of their finest—nearly three hundred and fifty carats, which makes this stone one a king would be proud to own. In fact, one did." The magician chuckled. "For all the good it did him."

Adrienne's eyes studied the sapphire, its sprawling star set in the midst of cold, pure blue. Not even the greasiness of Xenos Shane's palm, the twisted deformation of his fingers, could mar the luster of the gem. And there was something about the stone which seemed to draw her to it. As if—yes, as if somehow her fate was linked to it.

But how could that be?

Xenos Shane's voice went on. "Did you know, Miss Gill, that the ancients said if you rub a sapphire on your tongue, it will make you wise and articulate? The stone also gives great protection against poison. Although it seems that it does not give immunity against the other powers of passion."

Adrienne looked up. "What do you mean?"

"Why, I'm afraid that this stone here has a very bloody history indeed. It seems that a great king bought it for his beautiful young wife. He gave it to her to wear, for she was a jewel to him, an ornament to his life. And then one day he found her with a lover, and, of course, his anger knew no bounds. And she—she was proud. She would not beg, nor would she plead. So . . . he had her executed."

"Executed!" Adrienne recoiled in horror.

"Yes, my dear. It is one of the uglier features of the Orient. Those who commit adultery are executed as punishment for their crime. It is a marvelous deterrent." Xenos Shane was grinning at her.

"But to kill her! Why, that's terrible!"

"Terrible, perhaps, but true. Her husband, the king,

35

commanded that she wear this stone, the one he had given her, to her death. She had no choice but to wear it. She died very bravely, it is said, her lover's name on her lips."

"Oh—"

Adrienne could almost see it all: a lovely, dark-haired girl with firm lips and set chin, walking to the ax, this blue sapphire glittering at her throat. How she must have hated wearing it! How her heart must have cried out in agony for her lover!

Dazedly, she realized that Xenos Shane was still speaking to her.

"After her death, the king could no longer bear the sight of the Passion Star. He sold it in the bazaar. I bought it, perhaps in exchange for certain other items which I shall not mention to you now. Nevertheless, I took the stone with me. Now it is here in Scotland and I use it in my performances. Audiences, especially the women, are fascinated with it. As they are always enthralled by the girl who wears the stone."

Xenos' hand extended. Slowly he tilted up Adrienne's chin, until she had no choice but to look at him. For one long moment he held her eyes locked with his.

"Yes, my sweetmeat, tonight you will wear the Passion Star like that other beautiful, doomed girl. And you will fascinate our audience. I will see to that. And then perhaps later, after the show is over, you will fascinate me. What do you think of that? Eh?"

Chapter 3

It was, of course, the smallness of her body which had really prompted Xenos Shane to hire her. Adrienne became aware of this only moments after the rehearsal had begun. One strong flare of gas jetted up from the center of the row of footlights, hissing eerily. A stock stage set depicted ancient temple ruins, and the theater itself, empty now, yawned in front of them.

To her surprise, the magician had four assistants, who filed through the stage door shortly after the gas was lit. They were black men, she noted with amazement. They ranged in height from well over six feet to less than five feet, the last one a slight boy of twelve or so, with skin the shade of coffee mixed with cream. The youth gave Adrienne a shy grin. All were naked, save for white loincloths and turbans wrapped about their heads.

"Former slaves, all of them," Xenos Shane told her with pride. "They were starving when I brought 'em here from South Carolina, and willing to do anything. They're a novelty here in Scotland; they get plenty of attention, and they like that. And I treat them well. As long as they behave themselves, they have nothing to worry about."

Was there menace in what he said? Some hidden meaning? Again Adrienne shivered. Surely at least part of that message was meant for her.

Well, she didn't care. As soon as the performance was over, she would collect the pay he had promised her, and she would run home to *Maman*. She would appear onstage with the magician just this one night. . . .

The first segment of Xenos Shane's act consisted of what he called the "Magic Palanquin." In it, Adrienne, borne regally by the four ex-slaves, was carried on stage lying in an elaborately carved litter. Its ornate, draped roof was supported by four poles, its red velvet curtains drawn back.

"This one is easy enough, but it always amazes them," declared Xenos. "I wave a sword and Cuffy here—" He gestured toward the tallest black. "Cuffy draws the curtains and then opens them again quickly. You, my dear, have completely disappeared. And, naturally, the audience is amazed. Where could you have gone? My four Nubians have been holding your litter aloft on their shoulders all of this time; there is nowhere you could have fled without being seen. Ah, it is a mystery."

Adrienne stared at the magician, at the gleam of his eyes, the quick, nervous gesture with which he pushed back his crest of silver-white hair.

"But obviously it isn't a mystery," she said. "There must be some way you cause me to vanish."

"Yes, my sweetmeat, there is."

He went on to explain that the four poles which supported the roof of the palanquin were hollow, and contained pulleys and ropes.

"When Cuffy pulls the curtain, he also raises the double bottom and you are simply lifted to the roof of the canopy. All you have to do is to make yourself very small and conceal yourself until the curtains are drawn again and you can reappear."

Adrienne gazed at the litter. It looked fragile, with barely enough room for a child to hide. She felt her mouth go dry with a sudden apprehension.

"But . . . this isn't big enough," she whispered.

Xenos Shane grinned. "Oh, yes, it is. I had this litter especially made in a wagon shop in London. Notice, the shadows on the moldings have been carefully painted and exaggerated to make the palanquin seem small. Actually, it is big enough for you, if you contort yourself properly and make sure that the hem of your gown is wrapped about your body, with the hoop collapsed, so that it doesn't drag down and betray our secret."

Tricks, Adrienne thought. Floors that lifted, and hoop skirts that collapsed. She had not been hired as an actress at all, but merely as a prop for Xenos Shane's magic. She was no more important to him than the palanquin itself, or the four perspiring blacks.

"I see now," she remarked grimly, "why you did not want to hire the plumper girls."

Xenos Shane gave an explosive, sputtering laugh.

"Yes, my dear. One does not ask a Great Dane to do the work of a terrier. Now, let us try it. When you have been lifted to the roof, you must hold your body just . . . so. You must let your bones and muscles relax and become fluid. You must think of yourself as a wet rag, a rag that can be compressed and squeezed small, and then smaller still. Become flat, if you can. Flat!"

Then followed the long, tense moments of rehearsal. Over and over, Adrienne was carried onstage, the litter swaying on the shoulders of its four bearers. Time after time Cuffy, the tallest of the black men, closed the curtains and the false bottom of the palanquin rose, pressing Adrienne against its thick, dusty top.

The cloth which lined it was fusty with age, and smelled of mold. It seemed to press unbearably toward her. She stirred her hands, thrusting at the curtains in mounting panic. What if they forgot she was here? What if the ropes failed, or there wasn't enough air, if she perished here, dying of strangulation?

She couldn't breathe . . . couldn't breathe. . . .

"Stop wriggling about!" Xenos Shane ordered. "You're shaking the whole litter and everyone will know you are up there. Not to mention the fact that your gown is dragging out in plain sight for all to see."

"Just let me down!" She was choking on dust. "I don't like it up here, I can't breathe! There isn't any air! I feel as—as if I'm trapped!"

Her heart was slamming, her lips were dry, and it took all of her will power not to kick and scream and pound at the curtains which bound her.

Was there a chuckle of amusement?

"Some do have that reaction," the magician said. "My wife did, at first. Why didn't you tell me that you had it, too, you little fool? Well, it's too late now. You're hired, and I need someone, and you must endure."

Adrienne thought of Devin, of the money needed to buy him proper food. Of Adrienne LaRivière, the passionate French actress whose spirit and vitality had, according to *Maman,* carried her through many of life's trials.

But, she wondered defiantly, had Adrienne LaRivière ever been stuffed into a box without air?

Well, it didn't matter, she told herself. Her right hand went unconsciously to the Passion Star which Xenos had given her to wear, the sapphire cool and smooth against the skin of her breast. She *would* endure this. She would think of other things—pleasant things—and she would get through this ordeal somehow.

She was Adrienne LaRivière, arriving in Paris on the train, accompanied by twenty trunks stuffed full of costumes and wigs, and five maidservants to dress her. At the station to meet her was a huge crowd, all of them cheering and screaming. And she, Adrienne, swept forward to meet them, blowing them kisses, laughing and crying in her joy that they loved her so much.

"Adrienne," they were calling. *"Adrienne, we love you . . ."*

Grimly, Adrienne made the fantasy last a full twenty minutes, until Xenos Shane had pronounced her efforts satisfactory. Then they began to work on his next offering, an act he called the "Cassadaga Propaganda."

"This is a rare manifestation of spirit activity quite amazing and horrifying," he intoned in the deep, booming voice which filled the whole theater. "Reaching as it does into the misty outer world, about which we know so little."

A small, beautifully-crafted cabinet had been placed on a sheet of glass, and then the glass balanced on the backs of two chairs. With a flourish, Xenos opened the silk-lined cabinet, showing it to be empty. Then he tossed into it two tambourines and some bells.

He shut the door of the cabinet, and immediately the instruments began to play. Then they flew out of the top of the cabinet to land, jangling, on the stage floor.

- "I know by now that there is a trick to this one, too," Adrienne said dully. She was only glad that this act—whatever it was—required no more of her than to stand beside Xenos and smile.

The magician gave her a sharp look. "Of course there is a trick. Everything in life has its devices, its secrecies. Surely you know that, Miss Gill? If not, you are soon to learn."

The trick to the Cassadaga Propaganda, it seemed, was simple enough. The smallest of the ex-slaves, twelve-year-old Elijah, was suspended from concealed wires at the back of the cabinet. Like a little monkey, he seated himself cross-legged on a tiny shelf which protruded from the rear of the cabinet. Deftly he reached his hand through a hidden opening in the silken lining of the cabinet and handled the objects within.

The audience did not even know he was there.

"The boy is bright and deft with his hands. But it's lighting which makes this trick work and conceals the wires," Xenos told her. "And what do you think of it, Miss Gill? Do you find it amazing? Does it frighten you and fill you with wonder?"

How self-mocking he was, she thought. His eyes seemed to rake over her body, glittering in the light of the hissing gas jet.

"No," she said. "How can it be magic when you have that boy there to shake the tambourines and write upon a tablet?"

"Ah, but that is the secret. *You* know it is a trick, because you have seen the underpinnings, so to speak. But the audience has not. They too 'know' it is a trick— yet they cannot see how I accomplish it. So they at once know and do not know, they believe and yet do not believe."

"As long as I don't have to stay trapped in a tight little box for very long, I don't care what they believe," Adrienne said, sighing. "What other tricks are there for me to learn?"

Xenos Shane scowled. "Patience, my girl. Now, while you are standing poised . . . so . . . I will explain to the audience the story of the Passion Star, and I will let them gawk at its flash and color. After that we will embark on the *pièce de résistance,* the spectacle which I alone invented and which has brought me fame across two continents—the Burning Appassionata."

"Burning? You said nothing to me about any burning."

"Didn't I? So I didn't."

"But—" She licked her lips. "What do you expect me to do, then? Surely not . . ."

Xenos Shane gave his deep, booming laugh. "Do you mean, my sweeting, that you don't relish the thought of being cremated alive? Ah, but you needn't worry. It is but an illusion. A frightening one, but still only an illusion."

"Then—"

"Wait, and I will explain."

With a flourish, the four ex-slaves rolled out a large screen, its three sides and floor forming a giant box. In the center was a four-legged table. Four candles burned in a candelabra placed beneath the table. A cylindrical cloth —rather like a long bag—hung suspended from a cord above the table.

"You simply stand on that table, Miss Gill, and I jerk the cord, *so.* I lower the cloth over your head until you are completely concealed. I demonstrate to the audience that the table is clear, the floor is. clear, there is no way you could jump down without being seen."

Xenos Shane's wet eyes roved possessively over the bodice of the red silk gown Adrienne wore, touching upon the sapphire which gleamed opulently at her breast. He cleared his throat.

"Then—it's very simple—I fire a pistol and—poof —the contents of the cloth burn. You are cremated. When the hideous destruction is finished, I raise what is left of the cloth to reveal nothing more than a skull, a charred jewel, and a pile of bones—yours."

"Mine! You don't mean—"

Xenos Shane reached behind him, and from the shadows near one of the wings extracted a black leather box. From it he pulled out a white object which glimmered in the gaslight.

Adrienne gasped. The object was a human skull, with several missing front teeth, yellowed and grinning.

"My dear girl, didn't I tell you that all of life is but a trick? A ruse, a charade, a sham?" Xenos Shane gestured toward the table. "Underneath that pretty little table and converging at its center are actually two large mirrors. You think you see four table legs and four candles—actually, you see only two of each. When the screen drops over you, you simply slip through the trap door in the table top, and put the bones and some fireworks on the table. When you hear the pistol fire, you ignite the fireworks and slip behind the mirrors.

"The trick is simple, ingenious, and maddening for the audience, who feel sure that, heinous as I am, I cannot sacrifice a live victim *every* night. Yet try as they might, they cannot imagine how I can fool them."

Another trap, Adrienne thought dully. Another small, enclosed space into which she must crawl.

Beads of perspiration sprang to her forehead. She could already feel moisture sliding down beneath the armholes of the red gown. No wonder, she thought in mounting panic, the silk dress was so stained and shabby. Was Xenos Shane's wife, too, afraid of being trapped and suffocated? Did she, too, perspire in terror?

"What's wrong?" Xenos Shane asked it sharply.

"N-nothing."

"Your face looks as bone-yellow as poor old Yorick here. And we can't have that. I'll have Elijah show you about your make-up before we go on tonight. Some carmine on your cheeks should help matters."

A hand gripped her upper arm, digging into her flesh with such viciousness that Adrienne nearly cried aloud.

"Buck up, my sweeting. You're going to show off that sapphire for me whether you wish it or not. I need you, do you get it? I need you to go on with me tonight. It's too late for second thoughts."

43

The music-hall show—all thirty acts of it—was due to begin soon. Adrienne stood at the back of the same dressing room she had used before, marveling at the change in it.

Before, the room had been empty, the rows of hooks on the wall vacant. Now the hooks were full of clothes, and the room was full of women. They swarmed about in various stages of undress, the skirts of their petticoats sweeping the floor and taking up nearly all of the space.

Girls preened in front of the soiled mirror, spitting on their fingers and wiping a clean place so they could see themselves. They scrubbed at armpits with damp rags, or buttoned each other up the back. They curled each other's hair in crimping-pins, or pinned it over rolls and puffs. They giggled and chattered and quarrelled. They traded bits of music-hall gossip, or talked about "turns" a few would take at other theaters this night. Their scents filled the air—musk and attar of roses and the delicate reek of female perspiration, of butter and grease and burnt cork.

Somewhere a door slammed. A man laughed. Out in the hallway dogs yapped and there was the sharp slap of footsteps. More doors slammed. Male laughter rose from what must be the men's dressing room next door.

"Excuse me, dearie."

A plump woman in her fifties pushed past Adrienne toward the mirror. She had the jowly, dewlapped face of a bulldog, and wore an improbable costume of purple velvet and drooping peacock feathers. "Crowded here, ain't it, love?"

"Yes. Could you tell me—"

"Ah, dearie, don't tell me *you* are old Shane's Appassionata tonight? You got to be by the looks of that dress. Poor Frances! How she hated being stuffed into boxes at his beck and call. Poor thing, I often wondered *was* she his wife at all. Being as dark as she was, well—"

Winking, the plump actress shoved aside two other girls and created a space for herself at the mirror. She took a glass jar out of her reticule and began to grease its contents over her face.

Adrienne sighed. She wondered what she should do

now. Xenos Shane had said something about make-up, and she knew he wished her to wear it for the performance. But he had not supplied her with any, and at the moment she did not even know where he was. Out in the corridor, she assumed, or in the men's dressing room, along with the Passion Star, which he had removed from her neck as if he thought she might steal it, she recalled indignantly.

If only she had not promised *Maman* she would bring home milk and meat! If only Devin were not so ill, if *Maman* were not so shining-eyed with hope and pride, so convinced of Adrienne's destiny!

A strange sensation stabbed its way through Adrienne's throat and chest. It was a feeling of vast and desperate loneliness. *Maman,* so immersed in her dreams of beautiful actresses and glamorous costumes, lived in a world of fantasy. *This* was the real world, the world of sweat-stained gowns and privy smells and chattering girls who ignored you as if you weren't even there.

And yet, was it possible? Was it even remotely possible that Adrienne McGill might one day be famous? That people would remember her name and revere it, and love her because she could bring them happiness?

A ragged theater poster, printed in black lettering, had been tossed carelessly to the floor. To distract herself, Adrienne stooped and picked it up.

New Brittania Palace of Varieties, it proclaimed in elaborate lettering. *Trongate Street. Fresh faces and favorites this week! Doors open at 7:15, Overture at 7:45. Most expensive engagement and first appearance in Glasgow for six nights only, the Wondrous Xenos Shane, who will frighten and terrify with his Burning Appassionata and Spirit Magic!*

Reading this, Adrienne felt her heart suddenly lurch. She herself was to be the Burning Appassionata! It was she about whom the poster spoke!

Feeling oddly exhilarated, she read on, down to the long list of names headed by the word *Programme.* Quickly her eyes skimmed the names of the other acts. Frank Maura, Equilibrist. Prof. Wingfield and his per-

45

forming troupe of dogs. The Sisters du Cane. Millie Zara. Peggy Pryde.

And all of them, presumably, had "fresh faces" with which to delight the music hall crowd, of whom Adrienne was beginning to be thoroughly frightened. Last September, *Maman* had scraped up the pennies for herself and the four oldest McGill children to attend the Brittania. They had sat in the gallery with the noisy working folk, who had cheered, laughed, joked, and swilled down the drinks they had bought in the lobby, clapping noisily at the "turns" they liked the best.

Now it would be she, Adrienne, whom they would watch, she at whom they would whistle and call.

Adrienne let the poster drop from her hand and flutter to the floor. No one even turned to look. The other girls went on chattering, fighting for places in front of the mirror with good-natured humor.

Just then the battered door burst open and Elijah, the small black boy, entered carrying a wicker basket. The girls clustered in front of the mirror gave him an incurious stare, then turned back to their talk. One, clad only in corset and petticoats, the tops of her breasts showing, did not even bother to cover herself.

It was as if, Adrienne thought in bewilderment, they did not even consider him male at all.

The boy came up to Adrienne and whispered, *"He* sent this for you. He said if you don't wear it, he'll be angry with you. This all belongs to Frances. He said you could use it, if you are careful."

Adrienne took the basket and peered into it. Some of its contents were common household articles, others had been a part of *Maman*'s tales of the theater. Still, it seemed strange to see them all assembled—a pat of butter, a box of rice powder, a small envelope, matches, half a dozen corks, a candle, a knitting needle, a rabbit's foot, a linen towel.

"I don't know what to do with any of these," she whispered to Elijah.

The boy's eyes, dark and lustrous in his creamy face, gleamed.

"I do, Miss. I've been in lots of dressing rooms and

46

watched the ladies, and I helped *her* to do it, too. I can show you just what to do."

"Can you?" Adrienne was too grateful for help to care that it came from a child.

"Sure, I can. Look. First you've got to rub this butter all over your face, it's better for your skin than that lard that some of them use. That's what *she* says, anyway."

Hesitantly, Adrienne dipped a forefinger in the soft yellow butter and began to cream it onto her face.

"Does Frances enjoy being the Burning Appassionata?" she asked after a moment.

"She cries," the boy replied briefly.

"Then why does she do it? She shouldn't have to if she doesn't wish it! To lie cramped up and trapped in a small space like that—"

"She has to. He makes her." An odd expression had crossed Elijah's face.

"I'm sure of that," Adrienne said grimly. "But can't she run away?"

"She a slave, too," the boy said. "She just whiter-skinned, that's all. Here, miss. Take this here towel and rub off the rest of the butter. Then rub this on your cheeks. It's powdered vermillion, and will make your cheeks rosy and pretty."

As Adrienne fumbled with the little envelope, Elijah took it from her and began to rub the carmine into her cheeks himself. His fingers worked deftly, as if he had done this often before. His tongue shot out to moisten his lips, and he worked with professional concentration.

Perhaps, Adrienne thought, Frances had made a pet of him. Certainly it seemed that way. And Elijah was a winsome boy, whose cheerful face would ward away loneliness. She felt an abrupt kinship with the missing Frances, and almost forgave her for the fact that the red silk gown was so shabby and smelly.

With one of the matches, Elijah lit the candle. Then he took the knitting needle and held it over the flame until it was blackened with soot.

"You stand still, now," he ordered. "Stand still and don't sneeze, or I might poke out your eyes."

Obediently, Adrienne stood frozen while Elijah took the pointed knitting needle and lined her eyes just back of the lashes. She waited while he burned a cork and darkened her eyebrows, managing this operation with delicate skill. He added more of the red powder to a dab of butter and worked it into a paste, which he applied to her lips. Then he took the rabbit's foot and dusted rice powder all over her face.

"Here, you can look now," he said at last. He reached into the bottom of the basket and produced a small hand mirror—a clean one, Adrienne noted with pleasure.

"Oh!" She stared at herself in shock.

Before, when she had seen her own face in the dressing-room mirror, it had been pale, its color washed out by the gas jet which burned on the wall. Now her skin tones were warm and natural. Her eyes were large and lustrous, her brows curving wings. Her high cheekbones were ruddy, as if she had spent a day in the sun. Her full lips held the suggestion of a pout.

And—her eyes fastened upon the reflection greedily—the red silk gown gave to her body a sensuousness she had not known it could possess. The silk cloth clung to the lines of her breasts, accenting their fullness. Her waist was tiny, lithe, the skirt flaring out again, with the aid of the hoop skirt, to a fashionable bulk.

She narrowed her eyes at herself. Then, unconsciously, she struck a pose which the Countess Aurelia might have used. Aurelia Prendergast, for whom *Maman* had done fine sewing, had once been a famous beauty, acclaimed for her graceful bearing. But she, Adrienne, was surely a beauty too. The mirror told her so. Her own heartbeat, quickened with pleasure, told her, too.

"Oh, Elijah!" she gasped at last. She stared at her bare, creamy neck. She was sure that the gleaming Passion Star would add the finishing touch. "I can't believe this is really me!"

"It is. And you are beautiful," the boy pronounced.

"Am I?"

"You are even prettier than Frances," he told her.

48

Chapter 4

"And so the beautiful young queen was cremated upon her funeral pyre, the lovely and faithless body going up in flame and at last subsiding to embers, with only this stone, the Passion Star, remaining to recall her memory. . . ."

Xenos Shane's flamboyant voice reached into the back rows of the Brittania. It caused a hush to fall on the noisy audience.

At her cue, Adrienne stepped forward. She lifted the sapphire in both hands and moved it so that it glittered in the footlights. She could hear the sighs and *ahs* of audience reaction, and it was true that the sapphire seemed to possess a presence, an allure all its own.

From the corner of her eye, she could see Shane posturing grandly, his face coated with make-up. A sweetish smell came from him, an odor she knew well, for she had smelled it often on her father. Xenos Shane had been drinking.

She stared downward at the row of white-hot gas jets. These were marked off with a guard chain to protect costumes from the open flames—a very necessary precaution, *Maman* said, for theater fires were common, and women's voluminous skirts presented a real hazard. Beyond the footlights, the theater itself was a vast, shadowy void in which white blurs of faces could be seen peering from box seats, and beyond them row after row of more white faces.

Like cabbages, Adrienne thought with a fresh surge of panic. Cabbages lined up in a row at the market.

". . . and so, dear audience, this rare and precious stone of *five hundred carats* was brought to Glasgow by myself, purchased direct from the hands of a grieving king who told me that he could no longer bear the sight of it and all that it signified. . . ."

With a start, she realized that Xenos had launched into his introduction for the Burning Appassionata.

". . . and now, my friends, I am going to demonstrate to you a phenomenon without parallel in the physical world, a spectacle so amazing and stupendous that you will go home amazed and horrified."

Xenos gestured toward the wings. Elijah hurried onstage carrying a small, velvet stool, on which Adrienne might stand in order to mount to the table. The three-sided wooden screen had been rolled out and waited in readiness.

"My lovely young Appassionata herself will be a part of this spectacle; will, in fact, be a *very* integral part . . ." Xenos Shane chuckled, and the audience began to stir and murmur in anticipation.

Carefully, artfully, the magician raised the excitement of the music-hall patrons. With a flourish, he lit the candles in the candelabrum, concealing with his body the fact that he only lit two.

Feeling her knees tremble so violently that she feared she might fall, Adrienne mounted to the table top. She turned to face the footlights. It was as if she were moving in some strange nightmare, she thought wildly. The harsh, glaring footlights, the hundreds of faces beyond them . . .

They were all looking at her.

At the red silk gown which clung to every line of her body, its low neckline revealing the curves of neck and breast. At her pale hair, carefully braided and looped so that its strands gleamed in the gaslight. She felt almost naked. And yet there was a curious pleasure, too. The audience liked her, she knew they did. And she felt a bond with them, a bond strong and compelling.

For now, for this moment, she was theirs. . . .

She was only half-aware that Xenos Shane had finished lighting the candle and now grasped the cord which was attached to the cylindrical cloth suspended over her head.

"You'll go through with this, my sweeting. Or I'll toss you onto the dung heap from which you came."

The hiss which came from the corner of the magician's smiling mouth was so malevolent that Adrienne could not believe she had really heard it at all.

She waited, trembling, for the cloth to begin lowering over her head.

Adrienne crouched in the small escape-box hidden behind the converging mirrors. Her knees were tucked almost up to her chin, her head screwed to the left. The sides of the box pressed around her. The shouts of the audience seemed magnified, a giant, headless roar.

Only inches away from her head, she knew, cotton was burning, ignited by a substance Xenos Shane had referred to as "quick-match." It was a witches' brew of chemicals, he had told her, and one touch with a rod covered in cotton which had been dipped in sulphuric acid would ignite it. Now she could smell the acrid odor of burning, hear the roared delight of the audience.

They had liked her. She had sensed it, the strong feeling radiating up from the theater with almost physical intensity. And now they loved the thought that she was being cremated alive. They knew the trick couldn't be real, and yet they hoped that it was.

Long seconds passed, and still the noise of the crowd did not abate. Cramps shot up and down Adrienne's legs, knotting her calves. Her hands were shaking violently, and she took long, slow breaths, trying to control her panic. Why was it taking so long? Why hadn't they yet rolled the wooden screen offstage? Had they forgotten her?

The crowd sounds died down a fraction. She could hear Xenos's voice, and knew that he must be lifting away the cloth to reveal the yellowed, grinning skull, the human bones, the charred replica of the Passion Star which she had placed upon the table before slipping through the trap door.

Perspiration ran down her forehead. It trickled between her breasts and thighs. She could hear the sounds of cheers and clapping, a huge roar that seemed to roll on and on, like a giant thunderstorm. A storm of voices . . .

As if for solace, her hand crept to her throat, to the smooth roundness of the star sapphire. A young girl had once worn this stone bravely to her death. . . .

The roar was abating. She felt the sudden movement of wheels, a draft of chilly air. The wooden frame rolled over an unevenness in the stage floor.

Hands reached in for her.

"You can get out now, miss." Elijah's soft voice prodded at her. "It's all over. *He's* waiting, he wants to see you."

Adrienne waited backstage for Xenos Shane, gazing about her with curiosity. A strange apparatus bristled with valves and handles, operated by a boy sitting on a stool. Did it control the gas jets? she wondered. Nearby, performers waited to take their turns. One was the woman who had spoken to Adrienne in the dressing room. Now, decked in her gaudy costume and a red wig, she stood knitting a blue sock, her needles moving deftly, exactly as if she were any ordinary housewife.

"Well, where is it? I want it back, miss. And immediately."

The voice came from behind her. Adrienne whirled about to see Xenos Shane, still in stage make-up.

She stepped back from him, startled. "What do you wish back, sir?"

"Why, my sapphire, of course. Did you think I planned to let you take it home, my sweetmeat?"

Before Adrienne could move, the magician's hands had already gone to the back of her neck and were unfastening the clasp of the pendant. She could feel the damp, unpleasant sensation of his flesh against her own.

"Very well," she said sullenly. "I didn't want to wear it anyway."

Xenos Shane smiled. Again she smelled the sweetish odor of brandy on his breath.

"I think you did. I think you wanted to wear it very much indeed. You're fascinated by this gem, aren't you, Miss Gill? The legend, the romantic story. Ah, you are so very young."

He grimaced and lifted the sapphire in his palm, holding it so that the six-sided star gleamed. Then, with a flourish, he dropped it into his breast pocket. He patted the pocket as if to secure it there.

"Well, that's that, isn't it? Now, come along with me, there's something I must get for you."

Her pay? Adrienne hoped that that was the case. Obediently she followed him toward the dressing-room corridor, deserted now. They passed the dressing room she had used earlier, and the two men's rooms, heading instead for the last door.

This proved to be a small enclosure with white-washed stone walls. Evidently the room was used for storing props, for it was lined with shelves containing a motley assortment of items: rickety chairs, papier mache stones, bundles of lathe, gaudy cloth flowers—even, to Adrienne's horror, a stuffed cat.

A small gasolier flickered on the wall. Flaring shadows shot up the walls, making the cat look as if it breathed.

Adrienne suppressed a scream. "Oh—that cat!"

"Don't worry, he's stuffed. I'm only here to retrieve my bottle—I hid it here while I took my turn onstage. I don't trust that Cuffy, he knows where I keep my things, and he's watered down my flask twice."

The magician began to poke among a pile of folded cloths and rags. Finally he extracted an amber glass flask of brandy. He uncorked it and tilted it hungrily to his lips. Adrienne could hear the avid sounds of his swallowing.

Shane moved closer to her, his breath quickened.

"Want some brandy, my sweeting? It'll work miracles for those fears and megrims of yours. Now, Frances—" His tongue slurred slightly on the word. "She would not take any. Foolish woman, she doesn't know the good it would do her. But *you* know it would help. Now, don't you, my girl?"

Adrienne said it quickly. "I don't need any brandy. All it does is to make my Pa sick and mean."

In the distance, they could hear applause, the sound of a drum as an acrobat did his turn.

"And," Adrienne hurried on, "It's my pay I want now. You promised me. You see, I told *Maman* I'd bring home some food, some milk and eggs."

"You won't do all that on one day's pay, girl." The magician took another swig from the brandy bottle, wiping his mouth with the back of his hand. "Fact is, you won't bring home any pay at all if you only work one night. I don't pay little girls who run off on me. Why should I? Here, have some brandy."

He thrust the brandy flask toward her.

"Please—" Desperately she shoved it away. "Please, I don't want any. I want to take my pay and go home. I . . . I don't wish to work for you any longer."

"Ah! Is that so?" The magician's hand began to caress her back.

"Yes! It's so! And please take your hands off me, Mr. Shane! Just because you hired me does not give you any right—"

She stumbled backwards, nearly tripping over a stored bundle of lathing. She grabbed for the door latch with both hands. It did not budge. She twisted and pulled at it frantically. Panic swept through her. She was trapped here in this small room with Xenos Shane—

"Sorry, my sweetmeat, there's something wrong with that latch. It's done that before. I'll have to speak to Peronne about it."

He was behind her now, one hand cupping her breast, kneading it up and down as if it had been bread dough. Adrienne clawed into his hand with her fingernails.

"Ouch! Damn you, you're a vixen, aren't you?" But he did not let go.

54

"Please," she begged. "Please, let me out. And give me my pay."

"Ah, your money." He was still behind her, his arms pressing her to him with surprising strength. "Didn't I introduce you to the stage? Didn't I allow you to be my Appassionata, to wear a fabulous jewel the likes of which you, a dirty little street girl, could never have known? You should thank me, my dear, not ask me for crass money. You should consider yourself lucky—"

"Lucky! I hated being your foolish Appassionata! I hated your shabby tricks, being shut in your boxes—"

"Hush," he said. "And try this." He pressed the flask into her hand, and then his fingers closed over hers, forcing the flask upwards toward her mouth.

"That's it. Ah, that's it. Take a swig now, why don't you? It'll do you good. Relax you, make a woman of you."

Adrienne had not realized that the magician's hands could be so strong. Inexorably they pushed the flask toward her lips. Then she felt the hard shove of glass against her lips. Fiery liquid dribbled into her mouth. Then it gushed, pouring over her tongue until she had to swallow or choke.

She swallowed.

Fire burned down her throat, followed by a quick warmth spreading outward through her veins.

"Please," she begged, gasping. "Please—open the door and let me out—"

"Not yet, my sweetmeat. Not just yet."

Again the magician forced up the bottle, ramming it against Adrienne's mouth and yanking back her head, so that she had no choice but to gag down the fiery liquid. Brandy splashed down her bodice, sending up its aromatic fumes.

"Drink," Xenos Shane muttered. "Drink, damn you, you little harlot. That hair of yours—like sunlight it is. Where on God's earth did you get it? Ah, you thought you could get away from old Xenos, did you? Thought you could escape him . . . well, you can't, my sweeting. You can't. . . ."

More brandy, poured into her mouth as if she had

been a dog. Her head wrenched backwards by the hair, she had no choice but to swallow.

Again she felt it, the warmth rushing through her, spreading down her veins like soft, warm oil.

"No," she muttered. "I want to get out—to get my pay and go home to *Maman*—"

"So soon? Oh, my sweeting, must you go yet? There is much, so much I can teach you, so much you must learn."

Again Xenos thrust the flask of brandy at her, and Adrienne found that this time her hand reached for it. The alcohol soothed its way down her throat. She took another long swallow, noting with wonderment the effects of the brandy.

Gauze, she thought dreamily. A curtain as soft as the silken undergarments which *Maman* sewed for Aurelia Prendergast seemed to fall over the surface of her mind, covering up her fear and disgust. The cramped little property room, lit by its one fitful gas fixture, seemed to grow larger, to appear almost cozy.

And now even Xenos Shane no longer seemed as frightening. His thick, flamboyant features appeared softer now, and his hooded black eyes seemed now very wise, to hold secrets which only he could teach her. . . .

She didn't know how much time had passed. She felt hazy, unreal, removed from what was happening. Yet in some strange way she was a part of it, too. Was this really herself, Adrienne McGill, stretched out naked, her nipples erect as Xenos' hand spread liquid fire across her skin? She wanted to moan deep in her throat, to cry out in abandon.

And yet—

She felt a squirm of fright. Hadn't she heard the cries of the girl who had been raped in the Close? Ugly, piercing, terrified cries they had been. Yet, she thought in confusion, it was as if the brandy were a shield, protecting her from such thoughts, covering her fright like a layer of smooth silk.

"Here." Xenos pushed the bottle at her. "One more

sip, little sweetmeat. Ah, you like that stuff, don't you? Ah, yes, it's just what you need, it always works, doesn't it?"

His voice was thick, husky, oddly exciting. Obediently Adrienne took another swallow of the brandy, feeling again its potency, the soft, lazy warmth of it, smoothing away terror.

And now she could feel him over her, his hands urgent.

"No— Please, no, *Maman* said— I must not—"

"Your *Maman* will not know, will she? Why should she know unless you tell her? Ah, there is much old Xenos can teach you. . . ."

A dream. This wasn't real. Surely it wasn't. It was all a soft, hazy, brandy dream.

He pressed down on her, fumbling now at the buttons of his pants. Her hands, flailing blindly at his chest, met the pocket into which—was it only minutes ago?— Xenos had thrust the Passion Star. She knew it was the same pocket, for she could feel the oval shape of the stone, the metallic give of its golden chain.

"Girl—girl—oh, God—"

Underneath the warm glow of the liquor, Adrienne was aware that the magician's hands were caressing her back, her buttocks, the soft, inner flesh of her thighs.

"No!" She tried to twist away from him.

"Ah, girl, you don't know . . . there . . . there . . there . . ."

A rough finger probed between her thighs. Then, before she could react in shock, something hard rammed at her, splitting her with pain. An object hard, fleshy and throbbing, thrust deep within her, withdrew and then thrust again.

Adrienne arched her back, gasping. She could smell Xenos's body, the scent of his perspiration, the make-up he had used on his face, the burnt cork and carmine. These were sour, acrid odors, yet they held a curious excitement. Or was it only the brandy in her, lending everything its soft glow?

"No— Oh, please, Xenos, please! Don't—"

Things were happening to her, strange things with almost a pleasure to them—a horrid, forbidden pleasure. For she could still feel Xenos inside her, drawing in and out of her with a growing sweetness—a sweetness which she did not want to feel, for this was wrong, wrong . . .

"God—oh, God, my sweeting, you like this, don't you? I can tell, you like it, you like it. . . ."

He writhed over her. His voice was husky, incoherent, pouring out hoarse cries which made little sense to her. Desperately her hands pushed at the immovable male chest which pressed down on her. Her mind struggled to shield itself behind the brandy haze, behind the fuzzy curtain which blocked sensation, erasing pain and fright.

This was a dream, she thought in dull amazement. None of it was real. It had come—all of it—from the glass flask which now lay beside them on the floor, tilted on its side.

The hardness, the delicious hardness, moved within her. It pulled in and out, its sensation growing. Somehow her hands continued to fight, to flail at him. Her fingers brushed for a second time the shape of the sapphire and this time her hand darted into the pocket and closed down upon the smoothly perfect roundness of the sapphire. It was as if her fingers moved completely independently of her thoughts.

"Oh, God! Oh, you little sweetmeat, you whore— oh, Jesus—"

Xenos's hands were clamped around the round fullness of her buttocks, kneading them with frantic urgency. His breathing was quick, hoarse.

The stone seemed to slide out of its pocket almost by itself, its motion aided by the thrusting movements of the man. Her fingers felt the coolness of its chain, the texture of the stone's ornate setting.

Now Xenos convulsed over her. His body jerked as he thrust deeper into her, filling her. He uttered a thick, choking gasp, and then it happened.

The sweetness which had been gathering in her suddenly drew itself into one aching, hot ball of flame and exploded. Mindlessly she felt herself burst apart into arcs

58

of pleasure. Spinning, flying upward, totally out of control. . . .

"Sweeting . . ."

He was resting all of his weight on her, sagging down on her until she felt as if she could barely breathe.

Abruptly the silken curtain of the brandy was gone, ripped away as abruptly as *Maman*'s scissors slashed out the sleeve of a dress. Reality seeped in. What had happened? In God's name, what had happened?

She thought in dull horror of the sordid rapes that occurred within the stone walls of the closes. She herself had been raped. As for Xenos, he was an ugly, brutal man, and he smelled of sweat and lard and stale clothing. How had she seen him—even for a moment—as anything other than what he was?

She thought of her father, Jack McGill. Was this what his whisky did to Papa? Smoothed over the ugliness in his world and made it bearable? Erased the pain and fear so that they could be endured?

Rapidly she pushed the notion away and gave Xenos a shove, a hard one.

"Get off me!" she managed to cry out. "Get away!"

Obediently the magician rolled aside. She sensed that the mania in him—what strength there had been— was quite gone now. He was spent, harmless.

She gathered her feet beneath her and sprang up. The brandy haze was totally gone from her now, leaving her mind cold and clear. Now her thoughts were filled with revulsion, and with the beginnings of a hard, burning anger.

"I want my pay," she heard herself demand. "I worked hard, and I want what's due me."

Xenos Shane made a hoarse noise almost like a snore.

"I said I want my pay," she repeated. She had not known that she could be so determined. It was as if she were a different person now, a new, adult Adrienne.

"All right, girl. Dammit, if you insist . . ."

Xenos rolled on his left side and fumbled in his

disarrayed clothing. He pushed a coin at her without looking at it, then rolled on his back, eyes closed.

"Tomorrow, Miss Gill. Come back tomorrow and you can be my Appassionata again, eh?"

But she did not even hear him. She was already at the door of the little room, clawing at the latch with hands grown mercilessly strong. When it did not give, she thrust her shoulder against the wall, and then the latch released, and she nearly fell forward as the door opened. She ran into the hall.

She fled in the direction of the stage door, her disordered gown flapping at her back. Several performers, standing in the wings, turned to stare at her as she skidded past. One of them snickered.

Had they known? she wondered furiously. Had they somehow all known? There was a twisting pain in her chest, an ache of rage and hurt. She knew it would never quite go away again.

She would never know how she managed to stumble home through the dark wynds and streets. Some instinct of self-preservation made her stop in a Close, cavernous with black shadows, to make a crude toilette. She fastened the red silk gown in back as best she could, then dipped the hem of her petticoat into water pumped from a courtyard well.

Fiercely she scrubbed away the stage make-up, rubbing her skin until it was nearly raw. She combed her fallen hair with her fingers, pinning it back up with the few pins which still remained.

Then, shivering against the night chill, she slipped out of the Close again. She moved quietly in the shadows, so as not to be seen by the footpads and gangs of reckless youths who roamed these streets after dark.

On the broad thoroughfare of Trongate, a carriage rattled past her. Its occupants, four drunken young men, called out loudly to her. The driver slowed his vehicle at their command, evidently hoping to stop and pick her up.

They thought her a prostitute, Adrienne thought

with mounting dismay. It was the garish red gown, the fact that she wore no bonnet, shawl or wrap, and was out alone at this dangerous hour.

The carriage had nearly halted now, its horses tossing their heads restlessly. Adrienne quickened her footsteps. She darted around a corner and into the nearest wynd, through an aperture too narrow for the carriage to enter. She dashed inward and crouched in the shadow of a building, praying that no one would decide to pursue her on foot.

Long seconds passed. She waited, frozen, her heart pounding loud in her ears. She heard shouts, groans, the crash of smashing glass as someone tossed a bottle out of the carriage and onto the paving stones. There were the sounds of someone vomiting. Then, thankfully, there was the clop of horses' hooves as the vehicle moved on.

She ran on again, a sob catching in her throat. Lamplight glimmered fitfully from a few windows, and once she heard cries coming from a doorway. Was it someone being beaten, or raped, or only giving way to despair or grief? But she dared not stop. She could only stumble on, impelled by her own terror.

When at last she reached the Close at 165 High Street, she was exhausted. Her body was shivering violently from cold, and from shock. As she climbed the flight of worn stone steps which led to the flat, she saw that *Maman* had kept a lamp burning. In fact, she saw with growing puzzlement, lamps were lit in both of the flat's two rooms.

She pounded on the door. After what seemed a very long time, she heard the lock rattle and the bolt slide. *Maman,* wearing a water-stained apron, stood silhouetted against the lamplight. Deep wrinkles were furrowed from her nose to the corners of her mouth.

"So you're back, daughter."

Adrienne, who had been about to fling herself into her mother's arms, paused. Beyond Solange's shoulder, she could see that all of the children, save Devin, of course, were still up. They sat in a row on a cot near the fireplace, even the baby, Thaddeus, who was not yet two.

Their faces looked solemn, and tears had made paths on eight-year-old Tessie's cheeks.

The fire had gone nearly out, Adrienne noted, too, with that same careful, observing part of her mind. And this was unusual, for her mother always kept the fire hot when Jack McGill was expected home. Her father was a man to demand his comforts, and his wife, afraid of his temper, usually obliged him.

"Yes, *Maman*," she said. "I'm back."

"What kind of job did you get, Adrienne?" *Maman*'s voice was quiet, strange.

"I . . . I was a magician's assistant. I was the Burning Appassionata." Adrienne's voice caught. "He shut me in a box, *Maman*. I—I felt I couldn't breathe. I thought I would die there, I was so very frightened."

"Then you didn't sing?" The customary lilt of excitement in Solange's voice when she spoke of Adrienne's talent was quite gone.

"No. No, *Maman*, I didn't sing. But—look what I brought home."

She reached into her bodice and pulled out the coin Xenos Shane had given her, looking at it for the first time. It glimmered up from the palm of her hand.

Adrienne gasped, and heard her mother's answering indrawn breath.

"*Maman!* Look, it's a sovereign!"

A sovereign, worth one pound, would buy far more than a few pieces of meat. It would feed a family.

"Child . . ." Solange passed a weary hand in front of her eyes and shook her head, as if she did not comprehend fully. "Addie . . . Daughter, there is something I must tell you."

"Yes, *Maman?* What is it?"

"It's your brother, Devin. He . . . Devin died tonight, child. He hemorrhaged and died. There wasn't anything I could do to save him."

Shock slammed through Adrienne.

"No! No, it isn't true, it can't be!" She pushed past her mother and rushed into the next room, the soot-dimmed room where Devin always lay on his cot by the iron stove.

He was still there, she noted with relief, a slight mound underneath the clean, quilted coverlet.

"No, *Maman*," she began in a rush. "You're wrong; Devin can't be dead. He's just sick, that's all. We'll call a doctor—we'll take him to hospital—"

Adrienne fumbled inside her bodice and pulled out the Passion Star. It dangled from her hand, its blue deepened almost to black in the flickering lamplight. The six-legged star in the center of the sapphire gleamed richly.

"*Maman,* look! We have the sovereign, and we can sell this. We'll buy a doctor for Devin, we'll buy him milk and meat. We can take him to the country where it's green and he can get well."

"Child, child." Maman had followed her into the room. Now her words were infinitely weary. "Addie, look. I have laid him out. Can you not see it?"

Adrienne paused, swallowing. Then she took a step closer to the cot where her brother lay so still. Trembling, she pulled away the quilt which covered him.

Beneath it, Devin lay utterly still, his delicate body now even more infinitely fragile, his face and hands colored a waxen white. Instead of his usual frayed nightshirt, he wore his best clothing, a clean, mended shirt, a pair of trousers sewn by *Maman* from a pair of Jack McGill's.

"*Maman . . .*"

She did not even realize that she had said the word. She could not stop staring at Devin. There was a feeling in the room, a strange, chillingly empty feeling, so strong that she could sense it in every shivering pore of her skin. And yet it was as if Devin were somehow no longer there. As if the thing which had made him Devin, her beloved small brother, had completely gone.

She took a step closer to the cot. And now she saw them. The pennies laid carefully on his eyelids in order to hold them shut.

Pennies . . .

Addie, look. I have laid him out. Can you not see it?

"*No!*" Her voice was almost a scream. "*Maman . . . Maman . . .* he can't be . . . not dead . . . he—he—" But there were no words. Of all the children, Devin had been *hers*. It had been she who had carted him about, who had told him stories and brushed his curly, red-gold hair.

Now *Maman*'s work-worn hand touched Adrienne's arm. Wearily, she took the Passion Star from Adrienne's unprotesting hand. It lay in her own chapped palm, looking exotic and out of place.

"This stone, this jewel. Where did you get it, Addie?"

The children had come to the doorway to stare at them. The baby, Thaddeus, had begun to whimper, his thumb in his mouth. In the cot Devin lay still, so very still. The pennies laid upon his eyelids were obscene.

"Why, it—it is the Passion Star, *Maman*." Adrienne's voice was high. It was as if her words belonged to someone else. This wasn't real, she thought wildly. In only a few moments, she would wake up. She would be in her bed with Tessie and Jeannie, and it would all be merely a harmless bad dream.

"The Passion Star?" *Maman* asked flatly.

"Yes, that's what he called it. It's a star sapphire. See? The star has six points. See how they glitter? I wore it onstage for my part in the act. He said a beautiful queen wore it when she was executed for . . . for adultery."

Maman was staring at her. Her eyes traveled over Adrienne's body, over the red silk gown with its bedraggled flounces and perspiration stains, over the hair which had begun to stream again out of its ribbons and pins.

"Addie. You stole this, didn't you? He would never have given it to you otherwise." *Maman*'s voice was low, terrible.

"Maman, I—"

Then Adrienne stopped. *He forced me,* she wanted to sob out. *He locked me in a room and made me drink brandy and did frightening things to me. . . .*

But she said none of these things. Instead, she stood very still, her body trembling, her eyes fixed on the small mound beneath the quilt which was Devin, the brother she had loved.

Solange laid the sapphire down on the battered table, strewn with scraps of cloth and ribbon, where she had been sewing. Her movements were very slow. Adrienne saw the worn, sagging body, the back bent from years of close sewing, the face scored by wrinkles. How tired *Maman* was! And the dreamy excitement in her eyes had been extinguished like a stove ember gone out.

"Addie, you must take this jewel back to the Brittannia immediately."

Adrienne's breath caught. *"Maman,* you don't understand. I can't take it back. I can't!"

"You must." A note of urgency had sharpened Solange's words. "Don't you see, child? That man, that magician, must already have the police on you! If they come here, if they find you, you'll go to jail!"

Adrienne stared at her mother. She felt strange, as if she were a new person, someone entirely different from the young girl who had left the flat this afternoon for the Brittannia. So much had happened. Xenos Shane, Devin . . .

She was no longer that same eager girl. That Adrienne was gone forever. In her place was someone new and hard, someone who could choke back her grief for Devin and reach out for the Passion Star, closing her fingers on it and thrusting it back into her bodice

"I can't take it back, *Maman,* and I won't. And I won't go to jail."

She lifted her chin defiantly.

"Perhaps you will be all right—if you take it back and beg for mercy," *Maman* said.

"No! I won't give it back, and I won't beg. *He* doesn't deserve to have it, anyway. She wouldn't have wanted him to, she died so bravely. . . ."

"She?" Solange wearily pushed her hair back from her eyes. It was as if the gesture took enormous effort. "Daughter, what are you talking about? *Mon dieu,* if you don't give it back, they will come. They will find you somehow. Addie, you can't stay here. Oh, child, you are a thief, a felon. Don't you see that? You stole."

"Yes, I did."

Adrienne did not recognize the heavy, flat voice that

65

came out of her throat. Or the anger—hard, adult anger—that poured through her.

"Child . . . child . . . you must leave here, you must go before you are caught. Before the police come!"

"Then I'll leave."

"Adrienne . . ." The mother looked bewildered. "I named you after *her*. You carry her name, you were going to be an actress. You were destined. I had it all planned, I planned it so carefully. . . ."

Adrienne's chin rose, and her lower jaw thrust out stubbornly. She glanced toward the bed where Devin lay, his face waxy. Then she looked toward the door where the other children still watched.

"*Maman.* Take the sovereign and use it to buy food for the others, for Tessie and Thaddeus and the rest. They are hungry, too."

A mixture of expressions crossed Solange's face. Grief, pain, fright, love. She started toward her daughter.

"*Maman,* I'll go now," Adrienne went on thickly. "I don't know where—perhaps I'll take the train to London. But I can't stay here any more and I'll never be back. I—I'm dirty, he said. I come from a dung heap. I'm dirty, and I'm a whore."

Solange's face twisted, and the work-worn hands gave a small, protesting gesture, like a cry. Tears glittered in her eyes.

"Never!" Her voice was fierce. "Not my daughter—ever. My Adrienne will never be anything other than what she is, a good girl, a warm and loving girl."

"*Maman*—"

Tears ran down Solange's cheeks now, making crooked paths. "Go, then, if you must. Go and earn your living as best you can, honorably. But, Addie . . . take the sovereign with you. At least you'll have that. You can buy food. And—and may the love of God go with you."

"*Maman* . . . oh, God, *Maman* . . ."

Then they were in each other's arms, and Adrienne pressed her face into her mother's breast for the last time. But she could not cry. Her eyes were dry and burning. And inside her bodice, next to her bare skin, she could feel the cool power of the Passion Star.

Chapter 5

The sun was high in the sky, obscured by a bluish haze of wood and coal smoke. Adrienne trudged through the streets of London, her mind in a state of whirling panic. Brewer Street, Glasshouse, Piccadilly, Jermyn Street, the names meant nothing to her. She walked unseeingly past the hansom cabs, the women shoppers in their full hoop skirts.

A lemonade vendor jostled her, a ragged woman selling umbrellas gave her a sharp look. A milkman's cart plunged perilously close to her, and as it pulled away she could hear the curses of its driver.

Her flight to London had quickly plunged into disaster, for her money had been stolen on the train.

It had happened while she was sitting in the crowded third-class carriage next to a large family overflowing with babies, half-grown boys and huge boxes crammed full of lunch. Somehow, her small chatelaine purse must have fallen to the floor. Perhaps one of the boys had taken it, or the thin-looking woman who had pushed into the car at a later stop. At any rate, the purse was gone—disappeared into the seething railway crowd as if it had never existed.

I'm dirty, and I'm a whore.

Never! Not my daughter—ever. My Adrienne will never be anything other than what she is, a good girl, a warm and loving girl. . . .

Now only the Passion Star remained, because it had been stuffed into Adrienne's bodice instead of carried in

67

the purse. As she walked, she found that her hand kept traveling to her breast, to touch the small bulge the stone made there. It was as if it were a talisman.

Like an echo of her own confusion, the London streets were choked with traffic: carriages, drays, carts, hackney cabs. In Oxford Street and in the Strand, hundreds of vehicles fought each other for space. Irritable drivers and pedestrians shouted at each other, or choked on clouds of dust and dried horse dung.

There were horse-drawn omnibuses painted in bright colors and pasted with advertisements. Hansom cabs darted in and out, two-wheeled, precarious, their drivers perched on a seat in back.

Adrienne trudged on, half-aware of the city's smells, of a sense of boiling, burgeoning life: the stench of horse dung and ammonia, the odor of coal smoke, of chemicals. The scent of a purfumery, a soapmaker, a paper mill.

But it was only the smell of hot coffee and roast potatoes wafting out from a coffee stall which at last woke her from her stupor.

She had had no breakfast and no noon meal. She had no money to buy food, and nowhere to sleep tonight. And the only clothing she possessed was contained in the small canvas bag which she had lugged about with her all day. Its handles had made blisters on her palms.

She stopped at a small, green square to creep into the shade of a tree to rest. Wearily, she spread her skirts and sat down upon the grass, throwing the bag beside her. In the square, birds gave their liquid trills. Distantly she could hear the clatter of horses' hooves on pavement, the cry of a chestnut vendor, a child's excited laugh.

What was she to do now?

She sat with her arms clasped about her knees and drew quick, frightened breaths. Her belly was growling with hunger. The realization sank into her that she was stranded here in London without resources. She had no friends, nowhere to go. And she certainly could not return home, for the police would be searching for her.

All she had was the Passion Star, carefully tucked now into the front of her serviceable blue dress, where it would be safe.

Impulsively, she pulled the sapphire from its hiding spot. She held it in her palm, savoring the smooth warmness where it had lain against her skin. In the filmed sunlight, the stone seemed to wink up at her mockingly.

Was this, she wondered, her punishment for having stolen it? To be stranded here alone in London without money or resources? Was Xenos Shane, somewhere in Glasgow, laughing uproariously at the trick fate had played on her?

A more sobering thought came to her. Had the Glasgow police guessed that she had bought a train ticket to London? Were they even now searching for her here? The Passion Star, she remembered with growing fear, had been well-known. Its loss surely would have been mentioned in the Glasgow papers.

Panic climbed her throat like acid. She looked down at the sapphire, tracing with a fingertip the perfect, oval shape of it.

How much was it worth?

Surely a stone of that size must be immensely valuable. Even Adrienne, innocent of financial dealings as she was, knew that much. She caught her breath. The sapphire might be worth hundreds of pounds—perhaps even more. Enough money to support herself, to send something home to *Maman* and the children.

And yet—to sell the sapphire . . . A curious pang pressed at Adrienne's throat, a feeling of haunting regret. A beautiful young woman had worn the Passion Star proudly to her death. Perhaps it still held remnants of her emotions, her love and terror.

Still. . . .

Adrienne bit down hard on her lower lip. She had spent most of the day walking the streets of London in blind panic. She had thought only of her predicament, her fear, her grief over Devin. She had passed hundreds of shops without going in to see if there was a job for her. She had even passed a music hall. A blind busker had been playing his violin outside its door, while a little black mongrel dog sat with a cup fastened to its collar.

What had she done to help herself? Nothing.

Now, as she touched the sapphire again, her fingertip trembled. Beautiful as the Passion Star was, it also represented money.

Half an hour later she had found a pawnshop situated between a milliner's and a gunsmith. She could feel her body tremble, from hunger and fear, as she pulled open the door.

A small brass bell jingled as she entered. The shop had the fusty odor of clothes stored away too long, and as Adrienne stepped inside, she could see why. A battered wooden counter and glass display case held a bewildering array of objects—watches, small pieces of jewelry and glassware, brooches, cameos, hair ornaments. A cabinet against the wall was piled high with stacked clothing, blankets and hats.

Among these objects puttered an old man of about seventy-five. His face was as wrinkled as a dried apple, his eyes small raisins. He looked up at Adrienne sourly.

"Yes, yes, yes? And what is it you want?"

"It's this." She held out the Passion Star. It gleamed in the dusty light, looking beautiful and exotic and totally out-of-place, the gleam of its six-legged star bewitching. The old man drew in a sharp breath.

"You wish to sell that?"

"Yes."

"Ah, you are short of funds just now?" Reluctantly the pawnbroker tore his eyes away from the jewel to inspect Adrienne. His glance missed nothing, from the dusty blue foulard dress to the look of desperation on her face.

"Yes, I am."

"Then you are in the right place." The pawnbroker fumbled in a drawer and drew out a jeweler's glass. For long moments he turned the sapphire over and over, examining it with the minutest of care. Once he glanced up at Adrienne, frowning.

"Well?" she asked. "How much will you give me for it?"

The wrinkled old lips pursed. "You speak with a Scots burr, my dear. Could it be that you come from Glasgow?"

Glasgow! Adrienne felt herself begin to shake.

"I've had a telegram about a stone like this—from Glasgow, it was, from a detective agency. It seems the stone is well-known and there's been a big hue and cry over it."

A wash of icy fear poured through Adrienne. So it was true then. Detectives *were* after her—they had even sent telegrams to pawnshops in London! Was the Passion Star really that valuable? Did Xenos Shane want it back that much?

Again the old man's raisin eyes darted her a sharp look. "Of course, if you were to give this sapphire to me, there'd be no questions asked, and I wouldn't have to reply to that telegram, would I?"

"Give it to you?"

"Why, yes. My dear, you stole an important stone, a royal star sapphire. Did you think no one would notice, or care? Did you think you could just sink into the life of London like a stone?"

The old man chuckled at his own joke, the wrinkled face creasing even more. "Ah, no, my dear. There are detectives after you—and easy you'll be to find, too, with that hair of yours. It's like a yellow beacon, lighting their way to you."

"No," she whispered. "I—I'll hide."

"Where?" Again he laughed. "Girl, you're as visible as a peach in a barrel of milk." Greed made the old man moisten his lips. With a trembling hand, he set the Passion Star down on the glass case in order to adjust his magnifier. "Ah, this is a lovely one, and no mistake about it. Such quality!"

Adrienne seized her chance. Her hand darted out and scooped up the sapphire.

"Wait! Wait, miss! You can't leave yet, I haven't appraised the stone! I could help you. We might come to an agreement—"

But Adrienne did not even hear him. She was already out of the shop, slamming its door behind her until the brass bell jangled.

The stage door of the Oxford Theater swung open and shut as the music-hall performers left for home. Their make-up scrubbed away, they jostled each other, or called weary good nights.

Adrienne pressed back against the brick wall to let two plump women pass. Discouragement seeped through her, and she could feel tears hot at the backs of her eyelids. Her belly was growling unmercifully.

It was nearly eight hours later. She had pulled a wide bonnet over her hair to hide its luster, and had trudged the streets of London until her legs shook with exhaustion. The Alhambra, the Canterbury, Gatti's, the names of the music halls had all formed a blur in her mind, a mixture of laughter and disbelieving faces and refusals.

At Gatti's, they had told her to get herself a costume and some humorous songs. At the Alhambra, they had cut her off in the middle of her first song. At the Canterbury, the stage manager had tried to put his hand on her breast.

Now it was late, past eleven, and the manager here at the Oxford had laughed at her for arriving to audition in the middle of the show. Was she completely ignorant, that she knew no better?

But Adrienne, awed by the huge mirror which hung at the back of the Oxford's stage and reflected the entire theater in its glitter, had begged that he listen to her sing. For some reason, he had softened.

Closeted with him in a small dressing room, uncomfortably aware of the delicious odor of the beer and chops which were even now being served to theater patrons, she had sung a French song which *Maman* had taught her. It was a yearning love song, and her voice had trembled from weariness and tension.

"Dearie," the manager had told her at last, "you're not suited, not for singing, anyway, although your voice is rich enough."

"But—"

"Best go back home and find yourself a husband and settle down, like a sensible girl."

Now, as she drew a deep breath, steeling herself to leave the theater for the uncertainty of the streets again, she heard a voice beside her.

"I could have told you there was no work here, you little fool. Times are poor, even for seasoned performers. When will you green girls ever realize that?"

She turned to see a man in his late forties, with rumpled black hair heavily streaked with iron gray. He wore wire-rimmed glasses and his full mustache was streaked with gray as well. He had strong, well-carved features, and would have been good-looking save for the bitter, almost surly, expression he wore.

"But I need the work," she protested. She noted that his black broadcloth suit was of an excellent cut, and immaculately pressed.

The man threw back his head and laughed dourly. "Needing work isn't enough, as even the newest of ballet girls should know. And in the music-hall world, even a pretty face can't help you if you haven't the talent to go with it—as evidently you don't."

"I do have talent! I do!"

"For singing?" The man's lips, visible under the salt-and-pepper mustache, twisted. "I heard you, you know. The manager didn't think you could sing, and neither do I. Of course—" He stared at her speculatively, and seemed about to say more.

"But I can sing!" Her voice was shaking, near tears. "I've sung for pennies often—and they always clapped and begged for more!"

"You're very lovely, my dear. Perhaps that is why they clapped. As for your audition, you only got that because you begged for it so charmingly. It does help in that case to have a pretty face and healthy body."

His bitter comment was made even more stinging by his acid tone.

Adrienne felt herself flush. She was weary—so tired that she could barely stand. She was weak with hunger. And now this unpleasant man was trying to hurt her with his sharp words.

"I do have talent," she repeated stubbornly.

"Talent? Perhaps so. Certainly you have a voice which carries well and has good body and resonance. And you have a—a presence, a glow about you, something which makes people look at you and notice you. But your

73

singing—ah, it's laughable. Your voice is no better trained than that of a street girl selling eels. You don't have an act, you don't even have a costume."

The man looked pointedly at Adrienne's blue foulard, dusty and grimy from her day on the London streets.

Adrienne reddened. "But my song was one which *Maman* taught me, one which she heard at the Odéon. She said that in Paris they—"

"Paris is not London, and it is definitely not the Oxford."

The words were spoken harshly. It was as if he hated her, Adrienne thought in stung surprise. Yet how could that be? He had never seen her before tonight.

"You're not being fair!" she began.

"Am I not? I would say that I am merely being accurate." He turned and moved past her, pushing open the stage door. He had a limp in his right leg, she noticed, as he moved into the alley. She remembered what he had said about healthy bodies. Was it his bad leg which accounted for his bitterness, his surly, hateful words?

Well, whatever it was, he had disappeared down the alley now. Surely she would never see him again.

Adrienne hesitated at the stage door, unwilling to leave the gas-lit backstage—which smelled tantalizingly of beef chops, kidneys, and oysters—for the uncertain darkness of the streets. But at last she drew a deep breath and stepped into the cluttered alley, thankful at least for the cold night air which did not smell of food.

There was a dustbin against the brick wall to her right, and aimlessly she walked in its direction. A stray dog was pawing through its contents. The animal, thin, starving, its sides caved into its ribs, looked as hungry as Adrienne felt.

As she passed it, the dog paused warily, and cringed, as if afraid she might kick him.

"Are you hoping that they threw some of those kidneys into that dustbin?" she whispered to it. "Oh, I wish I had something to give you. You're starving away to nothing, poor thing."

The dog stared at her, ears cocked. Then he resumed his pawing through the dustbin. For one wild moment, Adrienne wished that she could join him. Perhaps there were scraps of bread, of mutton chops and ham. . . .

But she controlled herself and walked on. She was hungry, yes. But, whatever state she had come to, she had not yet sunk low enough to root through garbage.

Dispirited, she left the alley for the street. She did not know what to do now. The theaters were all closing, and around the corner long lines of carriages had pulled up to wait for patrons. Their drivers gossiped over lighted carriage lamps, the horses flicking their tails restlessly. Poorer patrons already thronged down the walk, their voices raucous.

She saw, too, a girl sidling along the walk, her head turning as if she searched for someone. She was no more than eighteen, Adrienne's age, and she wore a garish bottle-greene gown, the neckline cut so low that it revealed the cleft between her breasts.

The girl hesitated. Then, suddenly, she seemed to make up her mind. Swaying her skirts provocatively, she walked up to a pair of men and said something to them in a low voice. One of them put his arm around her.

Adrienne stared, her heart beginning to pound. She had seen enough prostitutes in the Closes and wynds of Glasgow to recognize this one for what she was. The sight filled her with a cold, breathless terror.

What did it take to turn a woman into a prostitute except hunger and desperation and nowhere to sleep for the night?

The girl in green blended into the crowd with her customer and disappeared from view. Adrienne walked on, her steps quicker now. She felt suddenly very alone, very exposed.

"Eh, little lady, and what 'ave we 'ere?" Three working-class youths, full of swagger and laughter, had turned as she walked by them. Now one, with woolly blond hair, grabbed at her arm.

"Please—let me go!"

"Aw! Say, you're prettier than anythin' we seen at the Oxford—or at the South London, either. Whyn't they hire the likes of you, eh? Give us boys a treat!"

The woolly-haired youth clapped another one's shoulder, and all three gave hearty, beery laughs. They smelled of chops and cigar smoke.

They were only boys, no older than Jaimie McAndrews and probably meant her no real harm. Adrienne knew this, and yet she knew also what a dangerous position she was in. If they should choose to follow her, she had no real place to go. Hampered by her long, heavy skirts, she would never be able to outrun them. And there were three.

"Please," she repeated. Her mind worked quickly. "Please, I . . . I must meet my husband here on the corner. He'll be angry if I am late."

"Yer husband! Aw, I don't believe you've got one. Not a girl as pretty as you! Sure you're not an actress?" The blond youth leaned toward her, sliding his arm fully about her waist.

Adroitly Adrienne twisted away from him. "Well, I do have a husband. And—yes—there he is now."

Lifting her hem, she plunged forward into the crowd, scanning it desperately for a man who would fit the role of "husband." And then she saw him, the embittered man who had spoken to her in the theater. He limped slowly among the crowd, his hands in his pockets, shoulders slumped.

Adrienne swept in his direction as if she had been Aurelia Prendergast, or one of the grand ladies she had glimpsed so often on the High Street in their fine carriages. She extended her arms confidently.

"Darling!" Her voice was low, full, rich. "Darling husband, where have you been?"

As the man stared at her, astonished, she smiled up into his eyes. "And where are you going? I've been waiting and looking for you!"

Chapter 6

"And what, pray, is the meaning of this?" The man glared down at her, his eyes narrowed. "I haven't a wife, nor do I want one."

"I'm sorry." She clung to his arm. "It's just that I needed a husband just now. Three young men seemed about to take me home with them."

She had tried to speak lightly, yet her voice was shaking.

The man hesitated, his right foot dragging. "Well, then, what did you expect, venturing out at this hour of the night without protection? A woman alone is considered fair game, you know that."

"I . . . I suppose she is."

"And," he added harshly, "if you wish my services as an escort, you'll have to walk more slowly. My knee is giving me quite a bit of pain, and certainly isn't up to galloping after a young filly such as yourself."

"Oh . . ."

Obediently Adrienne slowed her steps and released his arm. Her cheeks stung again at the anger in his tone.

"I didn't realize I was walking so fast," she snapped. "And why don't you like me? What have I ever done to you that you should speak to me as you did in the theater?"

"How did I speak to you?"

"Why, as if I were a—a nothing! *Less* than a nothing!"

The man with the gray-streaked mustache paused, then resumed his steps, the limp more pronounced than ever. "You, my dear, are not at fault, I suppose. It is the sex you represent which irritates me. Women!" He grimaced.

"I am *myself,* not 'women,'" she replied crossly. "And you've no right to hate me just because of what some other woman did to you."

"Oh?" For the first time, the man seemed to soften. He smiled at her. "Well, I'll reserve judgment on you—for the time. Meanwhile, to where do you wish to be escorted? I assume that is why you rushed up to me with a wifely gleam in your eye."

"I haven't anywhere to be escorted," she admitted.

"What?"

"I—I have nowhere to go."

The man's face looked a question, and Adrienne hesitated, remembering the contempt on Xenos Shane's features when he had learned where she lived in Glasgow, her own hot shame. *You come from that rat-warren, then? I don't understand how people can live like that—in such dirt.* Surely this man, too, would be repelled. And if he learned that she was a thief as well . . .

Swiftly, her mind began to work. Hadn't *Maman* told her she had a vivid imagination? Now she must use it. She must never let anyone know where she had come from, or how she had acquired the Passion Star. Ever.

"I am a runaway," she began hesitantly. That would explain why she was here in London alone.

"Oh?"

"Yes, I am the daughter of—of a countess. I cannot tell you my real name, or where I lived before, but I had to run away because of my—my stepfather. You see, he is a heavy drinker, and when he had had too much to drink he would beat me."

Parts of that statement, she reflected bitterly, were nearly the truth.

"I came here to London on the train," she rushed on. "Unfortunately, my purse was stolen, and I have no money."

The man inclined his head mockingly. "And cannot you send a message to your mother that you wish to return home? Surely she would send you the necessary funds."

Adrienne lifted her chin as Aurelia Prendergast might have done. She was already sinking into the drama of the lie, and had nearly begun to believe it herself.

"I cannot go back," she whispered. "My stepfather . . ." She let her voice waver. "He . . . he made improper advances to me. . . ."

"I see. And now you are utterly on your own."

"Yes."

"And looking for male companionship, I presume?"

"Companionship?" she repeated numbly.

"Yes. Why else would you have stopped me as you did? Well, you couldn't have shown worse judgment. You've come to the worst cad in London—as a dozen women would be happy to tell you. A *roué*, a dilettante, a wastrel—at least that is what certain people would like to think."

Now the man with the mustache took her arm, holding it rather closer to his side than Adrienne would have liked.

"Have you ever heard of a remittance man, my dear? That is exactly what I am—or will be in three days' time. You see, my family considers me a blotch upon their pure name. They wish only to be rid of me, and, in fact, are willing to pay well to do that very thing."

Adrienne stared at him. She had read enough romantic novels to know vaguely what he was talking about. Some well-to-do families solved the problem of the "black sheep" in their midst in the simplest of ways. They paid him a regular stipend to stay away, the farther away the better. Many such "remittance men" emigrated to the United States or other foreign countries.

"And what is it you have done?" she blurted out as they walked. "In order to be treated that way?"

"Done?" He inclined his head toward her, a savage look crossing his face. "I have done much, my girl, much indeed. I am an actor, and a dilettante. I collect things:

79

old coins, jewels, Chinese art, and women. Ah, I have well earned my stipend, let me assure you. And soon I shall be off to New York to spend it in fine style."

They were passing a small chop-house now, its doors and windows set back beneath striped awnings. The smell of roast goose and pheasant drifted out, crisp and greasy, from behind its doors.

Adrienne could not help herself—she slowed her steps. A sudden wave of giddiness seized her, a powerful spasm of hunger that gripped her belly.

"Would you . . ." she began, flushing. "Could you . . ."

"Could I what?"

"I'm hungry," she admitted.

"Well, you little fool, I don't have clairvoyant powers. I can't read minds, you know. Why didn't you say so?"

They ate clear turtle soup, boiled salmon with lobster sauce, and pigeon and peas, all dishes new to Adrienne. She ate hungrily, savoring the rich flavors. There was French wine, too, hearty and red, to set her head awhirl, so that the chop-house seemed to glow with warmth.

His name was Barrett Kendall, she learned. He was the third son of a prominent London physician, and the crime for which he was being paid his remittance was that of impregnating a seventeen-year-old girl. He had offered to marry her but the girl's family, aware of Barrett's reputation as a drinker and womanizer, had declined in horror. Their daughter's honor was ruined; they would not compound the disaster by coupling her with a limping actor.

"You are an actor?" Adrienne took another sip of wine, feeling its tingle in her arms and legs, its silky glow.

"Yes, I've been stage-struck since I was a boy." Barrett's voice had lost some of its bitterness, and as he ate, his eyes roved appreciatively over her. "I've been in the theater for twenty years now. I do character parts to perfection."

To her astonishment, he launched into the broadest

of Lancashire accents, his face and manner assuming the very aspect of a hunchbacked and none-too-intelligent old farmer.

Adrienne giggled.

"I can do anything," he boasted. "Listen to this: '*Massa George, dat's all pas' an' gone now. I's right at de doh, goin' into de glory . . . oh, Massa George . . . look . . . look . . Dere's Massa St Clair and li'l Eva . . . I's comin', I's comin'. . . .*'"

His voice had become older, weak and fawning. Its accent was the soft, slurred tones of the blacks Xenos Shane had used as his assistants.

"Do you know what play that is from?" he asked her abruptly, in his normal tone of voice.

"No."

"It's from an American play called *Uncle Tom's Cabin*. That was one of the very last speeches, when an old slave named Uncle Tom is dying. I have played him often when the play ran here in London. He is one of my specialties."

"Oh? I've never talked with a real actor before."

Barrett grimaced. "Well, you are speaking with one now. I've played most of the theaters in London, and now, unfortunately, I've been reduced to doing the music halls." The man's face again assumed its bitter expression. "Since my accident, that is."

"Accident?"

"Yes. It seems that my hackney cab met an omnibus middle of Piccadilly and the result was people and horses all over the road. I was lucky; I only tore a cartilage in my knee. Two women were killed and a boy's skull was smashed by the shoe of a horse."

He brushed away Adrienne's gesture of sympathy. "I was on crutches for well over a year, and saw the finest physician in London—my father. He performed surgery without result, save that I nearly died of infection. Now my knee is permanently injured. I am in constant pain with it. Perhaps that is why I was foolish enough to try to drown my sorrows with an overly-young miss. I don't know."

There was a silence, broken by the clatter of dishes

in the chop-house kitchen, the murmur of other diners. Adrienne toyed with her wineglass.

"And what will you do there in America?" she asked. America, she was thinking, was so very far away. An ocean away.

"Why, with my remittance checks to support me, I will get a job as an actor. Failing that, I will teach. I know the theater better than anything else."

The waiter began to clear away their dishes, performing this act with a condescending manner which made it clear what he thought of Adrienne and her dusty gown.

"Could you teach me to act?" Adrienne asked thoughtfully, when the man had left.

A boastful expression crossed Barrett Kendall's face. "I could teach *anyone* to act—even a woman of little talent. I am a superb teacher, and when I set out to do something, I accomplish it."

"*I* have much talent," she whispered. "I know I do." The wine she had drunk seemed to glow and shimmer in her mind. She had quite forgotten that Barrett Kendall was sharp and sarcastic, that he plainly seemed to dislike her, and indeed all women.

Barrett's lip curled in scorn. "Talent? Destiny? Every girl feels she has that! Well, perhaps you are one of the lucky ones. By your singing, I would doubt it. Yet there is a presence, something about you . . . You are different, Adrienne, different from the others, although I cannot say exactly how."

He paused for a very long time. Then he laughed bitterly. "Talent? Ah, my dear girl, it's drive you must have. Drive and determination! That will carry you farther than mere talent, it is what will make you great. To keep on going, no matter what, to let nothing stop you, nothing at all . . ."

Barrett's eyes bored into hers. His hand had crept across the table to squeeze her own. His touch was hard, muscular, his fingers pressing hers almost painfully.

As she stared at him, a shiver ran through her. For one wild moment she had a feeling of foreboding, of apprehension. There was something wrong about this man. Something evil.

And yet had he not told her that he could teach acting, that he could make a person of even little talent into an actress? If he could do that with a woman of no ability, what might he not accomplish with her, Adrienne? For she did possess talent. She knew she did, she felt it deep in her bones.

She forced her eyes to meet Barrett Kendall's. She gave him her prettiest, most winsome smile.

"Will you please teach me to act, Mr. Kendall?"

Adrienne rode beside Barrett Kendall in the hansom cab, listening to the clop-clop of the horse's hooves, the jingling of the bridle and trappings. The streets at this late hour were nearly deserted, the night air, seeping through a crack in the window, was cold, and she shivered.

What had she said? What had she done, or promised? That moment in the chop-house, when she had asked Barrett to teach her to act, now seemed dreamlike, unreal. An impulse, no more.

And yet . . . she did wish to be an actress. To learn whatever she had to know, do whatever she had to do. She had not known the depth or intensity of her desire until now.

They rode in silence until they reached their destination, a small, shabby hotel near Grosvenor Square. When the cab stopped, Barrett tossed some coins to the driver, then descended with difficulty, wincing as he bent his right knee.

"Well?" His voice was irritable with pain. "You'll have to manage to get down by yourself, my dear. My knee does not permit gentlemanly behavior."

So she hopped down from the cab, managing her skirts as best she could, and stood staring up at the decaying facade of the hotel, four-storied and sleazy, with awnings bristling out at street level. A carriage rattled past them, and its driver called out to the driver of the hansom. Then he glanced back at Adrienne and whistled, his meaning unmistakable.

Adrienne felt the slow color rise to her cheeks.

"You must marry me," she said quickly. "I won't go in that hotel with you otherwise."

"What!" Barrett Kendall stared down at her.

"I said you must marry me first. I'm not a street girl or a prostitute, no matter what those cabmen might think."

"Marry you!" He grasped her arm and began to pull her in the direction of the hotel. "You are a fool, girl! Oh, I was married once and then widowed ten years ago, and a happier widower there never was. If you think I plan to repeat such a mistake again, and with a chit who harbors ambitions to be an actress—"

She stood stiffly on the walk, her fists clenched. "I have the capacity to be a great actress, Mr. Kendall. I know I do, I can feel it. Oh, I don't know anything now," she went on painfully. "I'm ignorant, I can't even sing, I know little about the stage. But I can learn. I'm a very quick learner."

"A quick learner!" Barrett threw back his head and laughed. "Well, well, that much is good to hear, at least. And what, young woman, makes you think that I want to saddle myself with a creature like you? Merely that I might have the great privilege of teaching you to act?"

Yet, she saw, his eyes were fixed on her face keenly.

"I don't know," she replied dully.

"Well, then."

"But if I were only given a chance . . ."

"And obviously you think your chance has come along in the person of myself."

Adrienne bit her lip. The roseate wine glow was quite gone from her now, and she only felt cold, and rather lost and discouraged. A man came striding down the street, glancing back at them over his shoulder, and Adrienne shivered, instinctively drawing closer to Barrett.

She heard Barrett's voice go on. "Don't you realize how much you are asking, girl? Hours of time, hours of labor! And time is worth money, you know, even my time. Oh, you are an opportunist, aren't you, my little Miss Gill? Perhaps even more so than I am!"

Yet, to her astonishment, Barrett Kendall leaned

closer to her and took her arm, holding it tightly to his body. He looked down at her, his eyes half-closed.

"Yes, I suppose I am an opportunist," she admitted. Something made her reach into her bodice and pull out the Passion Star. She held it out under the glow cast by a nearby gas light. "But look," she added. "You don't have to worry about being paid for your time. I can pay you to teach me—with this!"

Barrett Kendall let out his breath in a long, slow exclamation of surprise. Slowly, reverently, he reached out and took the sapphire from her. He held it in his hand, turning it around and around, weighing it.

"Ah . . . so beautiful. God, how beautiful. This is a royal stone, and no mistake. It must be nearly three hundred fifty carats—yes, I'd say that at least. And what a perfect cabochon cut, a boon to any collection. Did you know, Miss Gill, that those stars are caused by tubular cavities set parallel within the stone?"

Barrett limped toward the gas street light and stood examining the sapphire. "It's got to be the one," he declared at last. "It's got to be."

"The one?"

"You know what I'm talking about, Miss Gill. You stole it, didn't you? You're the girl with the pale yellow hair who's wanted as a felon—it's been in the papers, you fool!"

She stepped backward from him, frightened by the intensity in his face. "I—I did it because he forced me, don't you see? And *she,* she never would have wanted him to have it, he was evil. . . ." She caught her breath. "Anyway, what does it matter? The Passion Star is mine now."

"Providing you aren't caught." Barrett's voice was dry.

"Yes."

His hands caressed the stone. "Your hair," he muttered. "It's tell-tale, isn't it? Daughter of a countess or not, it doesn't matter. Sooner or later, they'll spot you and imprison you."

"Unless," Adrienne said, "I go somewhere else—to the United States, perhaps."

For long moments their eyes met and locked in challenge.

At last Barrett spoke. "So you think, then, Miss Gill, that your future as an actress is worth as much as a stone like this, a stone of unimpeachable quality and rarity? You really think that?"

She spoke levelly. "Yes."

"And you are willing to work hard, to work desperately hard, until you hate me and hate yourself, and loathe the very thought of being an actress, and yet not give up?"

"Yes."

"You are prepared to become the wife of an irascible man with a game leg, a remittance man being sent across the Atlantic as a blot upon the name of his family? A man who, moreover, although he may desire your body, will never love you?"

A long hesitation, but at last Adrienne replied, "I am."

"You don't long for silly, romantic love, then, Miss Gill? For some handsome man who will come along and sweep you up into realms of ecstasy?" A sardonic expression twisted Barrett's face.

"No." She thought of Xenos Shane's violation of her body. "No, I don't want love. I don't need it."

"Very well. Then come along, my dear. I will secure you a room in this most palatial establishment here. Then tomorrow we will seek out the proper authorities and we'll be married just as you please."

Barrett's hand closed around the Passion Star and he started to put it into his pocket.

"Not yet," Adrienne said. Again their eyes locked. She reached out and plucked the sapphire from his grasp. "This stone is my surety, Mr. Kendall. When we are married, then I will give you the Passion Star. But not before."

Chapter 7

Dear Maman, Adrienne wrote. *I am in London now and I am going to be married and go to the United States. It all seems like a dream, a wonderful dream. . . .*

Barrett had settled her in a small hotel room, filled with ponderous, dark furniture, including a huge mahogany wardrobe, well-nicked and scratched by previous tenants. The Turkish rugs on the floor were worn nearly threadbare, and the narrow window looked out upon a mews lined with carriage-houses.

But to Adrienne the room seemed luxurious. She reveled in the roominess of the soft feather bed, the novelty of sleeping alone instead of with two small sisters.

Barrett engaged a dressmaker and a milliner to outfit her for the voyage. Adrienne had deliberately "lost" her satchel containing the few clothes she possessed. One look at the threadbare gowns the bag contained and Barrett would be sure to guess that she was no more the daughter of a countess than was the hotel chambermaid. So she had blurted out explanations which he had seemed to accept.

Anyway, she assured herself, what did it matter now? Soon she would be sumptuously dressed in every respect. Four gowns were being hastily sewn for her, two for traveling and two more, much more elaborate, for the stage. To Adrienne's intense pleasure, several bonnets, fashionably trimmed with lace, tulle and silk flowers, were also being made up.

"Oh, they're going to be beautiful!" she told Barrett joyfully when the milliner had left after completing the first fittings. "Everything is—the bonnets, the gowns. And even the names of the material sound like music— grosgrain, *crêpe de Chine,* duchesse lace—"

She swept grandly about the small hotel lobby, managing an imaginary train as she had seen Aurelia Prendergast do.

He scowled at her. "One would think that you had never worn pretty clothes before. As for me, don't look at me as if I were your benefactor, because I'm not. You are buying all of these fripperies for yourself, and make no mistake about it. Our marriage is strictly a business arrangement, no more."

Adrienne, her arms still holding the "train," froze. For a few brief moments she had allowed herself to take pleasure in the joy of having new gowns. But now that pleasure had seeped away like dishwater into the gutter.

"You needn't make it quite so plain," she snapped.

"And why shouldn't I? Let's face facts. You bought me, Miss Gill—and I was willing enough to be bought. So let's have no more of this soft-eyed gratefulness and simpering. The truth is that you are an escaped thief and felon. You wish to flee the country and to become an actress. I can help you to do both. It's as simple as that."

That night Barrett took her to the theater and they saw Adelaide Ristori as Lady Macbeth.

"From now on, my dear, you must take every chance to observe a true mistress of the craft," he told her at intermission. "It's not enough merely to repeat lines by rote. You must observe, experience, remember. Absorb all of life through the very pores of your skin, so that when the time comes, you will be able to give it back, larger and more magnificent than before."

Adrienne nodded. Her imagination was caught by Barrett's words. Somehow he made it all seem possible— a reality almost within her grasp. For that alone she would try to have affection for him.

Several times during the course of the play, his hand brushed against her own, and once it touched her knee. Adrienne swallowed hard. The thing that men and women did in bed together . . .

But quickly she pushed the thought away. Although he was not unattractive physically, she felt distaste for Barrett, with his salt-and-pepper mustache, the unhealthy pallor of his skin.

But perhaps, she told herself as they left the theater, it would not be as bad as she feared. After all, he was middle-aged, in his forties. Perhaps he would not demand much of her. . . .

Two days later they were married. Adrienne wore one of her new dresses, an elaborate afternoon costume of white tulle and Malines lace, with a trained skirt puffed all the way to the waist and trimmed with a deep flounce. The dressmaker and her three assistants had worked for four nights in order to complete it on time.

As she stood beside Barrett, the words of the marriage service droning in her ears, Adrienne felt a chill of apprehension. Was she doing the right thing? To marry a man whom she barely knew . . .

Yet what else was she to do? The pawnbroker had been right. Her hair was a distinctive pale gold, instantly recognizable. If she stayed here in London, she would surely be caught and put in jail. Moreover, even if she were not caught, she had no job, no money, no clothes other than the ones which Barrett had purchased for her.

Barrett shifted his feet, giving a little wince as his injured kneecap locked. Adrienne pressed her lips tightly together. The sound of *Maman*'s voice seemed to echo in her mind. *You are beautiful enough, as lovely as any of them. . . . You're destined, Adrienne. Destined . . .*

That afternoon, on the tide, they boarded the *Thermopylae*. According to Barrett, who was this night in a talkative, expansive mood, the ship had been built by Hood's of Aberdeen. Even with her sails furled, she was a graceful sight, with her four slender masts, her perfect lines and proportions. Her figurehead was a Grecian warrior, and her hull was painted green and emblazoned with a gilded yellow stripe. She carried twenty passengers.

Adrienne and Barrett were given the second sitting for dinner. At the appointed time, with Adrienne nervously dressed for the occasion in one of her new gowns, they went to join their fellow passengers in the dining saloon. This was a room paneled in rich, dark mahogany and gleaming with brass fittings. The dining table, also made of dark wood, was equipped with brass tubing around its edge to keep food and dishes from sliding off in rough seas. It was illuminated by a large skylight set in the ceiling immediately above the table.

The saloon was filled tonight with the steamy odor of stewed chicken, and Barrett told her that the ship carried live pigs, sheep and chickens to be slaughtered for the table as needed.

A plump woman, dressed in brown faille, was seated across the table from them.

"I'm Nettie Harper," she volunteered. "My husband, George, felt too ill to come to table tonight, but I am sure you will meet him soon. He is consumptive, and was advised to take the sea air for his health."

"The fresh air is considered to be most helpful," Adrienne said in her best Aurelia Prendergast manner. Inwardly, she thought of Devin. If only Devin had been able to take the sea air . . .

The other passengers joined the general conversation, and Adrienne looked about at her traveling companions. They were a varied collection of people: a man in a cleric's collar, a widow and her half-grown daughter, a pair of thin, spinsterish women, a portly physician.

Barrett and the physician, a Dr. Mawson, immediately struck up a conversation—it seemed that Barrett wished advice on his knee. The seat on Adrienne's left was empty, and just as the steward began to serve their first course, the door of the dining saloon burst open.

"You are late, my man," Dr. Mawson looked up from his conversation with Barrett to remark testily. "It's a wonder they will seat you at all—some ships are fussy about such matters."

"Indeed?" The tardy passenger, a man in his late

twenties, shrugged. His eyes flicked over the doctor, casually dismissing him as he seated himself in the empty place.

Adrienne turned to gaze curiously at her seat-companion. He was tall, and carried himself with easy grace. His close-cropped hair was curly, the color of new honey. He had a square-chinned face with high, carved cheekbones and somber eyes set beneath ridges of bone. His mouth was full and sensual, drawn now into a firm line.

Yet there was a withdrawn quality about him, too, a tension visible in the angle of his chin, the set of his mouth. He looked, Adrienne mused, like a picture of a Roman warrior she had once seen in a book: at once fierce and dreamy, arrogant and thoughtful.

The deep-set eyes, she also noted with quickened heart-beat, were staring at her. They were a blue as intense as that of the star sapphire which she wore now at her breast, beneath the fabric of her gown.

"Well?" he asked her suddenly in a low voice meant only for her ears. "And do you like what you see?"

"What? I—I didn't mean . . ."

He stifled a smile of amusement. "What is your name?"

"I am Adrienne Kendall," she murmured. "My husband, Barrett Kendall, the actor, is seated on my right."

"Ah, your husband."

But her companion did not glance at Barrett, but instead focused his intent gaze on her. For a moment their glances held and locked. There was, Adrienne realized in confusion and dismay, almost a physical connection, some force which leaped from him to her and back again, infinitely disturbing.

The steward was serving the soup.

"I'm going to be an actress, too," Adrienne blurted. "My stage name will be Adrienne Gill."

"Indeed? It is an uncommon name, is it not?"

She began to explain about Adrienne LaRivière, but was interrupted by Mrs. Harper, who had opened her mouth in an O of surprise.

"An actress! Oh, my, really! I think it's shocking. A

married woman, working in the theater? It's a wonder your husband permits it."

Whore, daughter of Magdalen. Adrienne felt hot anger. But before she could formulate an indignant reply, the man on her left fixed Mrs. Harper with a cold, blue look.

"Actresses, my dear madam, are just as respectable as any other woman, including yourself."

"Oh!" Mrs. Harper drew herself up, her double chins wobbling. "And who are you, I might ask, sir? An authority on the matter?"

"No. I merely express my opinions, for good or ill, as the case may be."

Mrs. Harper's face left no doubt as to her feelings on the matter. "And your name, sir?" she asked.

"I am Kristian King," he said after a moment's hesitation. "I am a writer, and hope to use my time at sea profitably."

"A writer? Indeed!" Mrs. Harper's lips pressed tightly together. Pointedly, she turned to speak to the cleric on her left, snubbing Kristian.

"Well." Kristian King, making a wry face, had turned back to Adrienne. "It sees that we are both anathema here today—you as an actress, I as a writer."

Adrienne could not help giggling. "I'm not really an actress yet. I merely hope to be one."

"Oh?"

"Yes, my husband is going to teach me."

"If your husband is Barrett Kendall, then he will do an excellent job," Kristian said slowly. "If you are sure that is what you want."

What had he meant? Did he mean to ask her if she was sure she wished to become an actress, or had he meant something else, something which had to do with Barrett? The fierce blue eyes were fixed upon her, and again Adrienne felt that strangely thrilling connection between herself and this man, a shivering, melting feeling that seeped through her bones like warm oil.

But just then Barrett turned to her to ask a question about the voyage, and the moment was over. General conversation resumed, and Adrienne had no more chance to speak to Kristian King.

But she was acutely aware of him sitting next to her, his eyes somber and yet speculative, too.

Their cabin was small, paneled in dark walnut, with shining brasswork and a little brass rail on the top of the built-in dresser, in order to keep objects from sliding about. Bunk beds were built into one narrow wall. An oil lamp glowed fitfully. From somewhere came the noisy creak of timbers, and the slap of sails.

It was their first night aboard the *Thermopylae*.

"Well," Adrienne said nervously, looking about her. In daylight, the cabin had appeared barely wide enough to accommodate her full hoop skirt. Now it seemed not much larger than the hidden boxes which Xenos Shane had used for his magic tricks. "It's very small, isn't it?" she asked. "I mean, for the two of us."

"All cabins are small. And you may as well get used to these quarters, as we will be working here."

"Working?"

"Surely you did not expect to spend this voyage idly strolling about the deck and flirting with your admirers?"

The look Barrett gave her was sharp, and she knew that he had not missed her conversation with Kristian King. "We will begin our labors immediately, and by the time we reach New York, I hope to have you groomed for at least a small role in a play."

"Really?" Adrienne could not conceal her delight.

"I am a superb teacher, my dear—the best there is. I could turn any girl—even a street hawker—into an accomplished actress. So why not you?" With a twist of his lips, Barrett had effectively squelched her joy. "And now, my dear, please give me the collateral for this arrangement," he added. "Your dowry, so to speak. The Passion Star."

With reluctance, Adrienne reached into her bodice. She pulled out the star sapphire. It gleamed back at her, blue and lustrous. For a long moment she gazed at it, thinking of the beautiful girl who had once worn it to her death.

"Well, don't stand there daydreaming. Give it to me now."

Adrienne hesitated. Her fingers closed about the stone, savoring its cool smoothness, the raised edges of its decorative gold setting.

And so the beautiful young queen was cremated upon her funeral pyre, the lovely and faithless body going up in flame and at last subsiding to embers, with only this stone, the Passion Star, remaining to recall her memory. . . .

I could teach anyone to act, even a woman of little talent. . . .

Adrienne felt herself tremble.

"Here!" With a quick, despairing motion, she thrust the jewel at her husband. "Take it, then, Barrett, if you insist."

"I do insist. Ah, thank you, my dear. Thank you."

She turned abruptly from him and gazed out of the small, brass-trimmed porthole at the misty blackness of an April night.

"Turn to me, then, damn you, girl. Turn to me! Open your arms to me! Aren't you my wife now, you little bitch? Haven't you given yourself to me in the bonds of holy wedlock?"

Barrett Kendall's voice was full of a lashing savagery. The oil lamp flickered, the ship swayed on the rising tide, and they struggled together on the edge of the lower bunk. Adrienne wore a cambric nightgown, sewn with rows of Chantilly lace, and Barrett wore—she had hardly dared to look—a long white nightshirt which flapped dismally about his thin legs. As her husband lunged close to her, she could smell his odor of sour perspiration, hair pomatum, and laundry starch.

Xenos Shane, she remembered with growing fear, had smelled of perspiration, too, and of stage make-up. . . .

Barrett's hand closed upon her knee, moist, demanding.

With a shudder of horror, she pushed him away.

"Ah—what do you think you're doing, girl? Pushing me off as if I were some backstage dandy?" Barrett's voice trembled with rage. "You're my wife now, or had you forgotten so quickly? You made a bargain with me!"

"A b-bargain?" she stammered. "I gave you the Passion Star, and you agreed to teach me to act. To—to take me to America."

"For free?" Barrett edged down the thin straw mattress of the lower bunk toward her. Her eyes were drawn to his legs, thin and hairy, the damaged knee thankfully covered by the fabric of his nightshirt.

"Yes, I did agree to teach you. But implicit in our agreement was the fact that you would . . . perform certain wifely duties."

"I didn't—"

Adrienne faltered. A shiver of horror raced through her. She had brought all of this upon herself. Hadn't she sought—even begged—marriage to this man? He had warned her plainly that he might desire her physically but could never love her. And she had assured him that she didn't mind. She had plunged right ahead to make the bargain that gave her what she needed—escape, a destiny as an actress. And she had pushed out of her mind what keeping her end of the agreement would entail. Oh, it wasn't fair!

"I didn't let myself think of that," she whispered, shamed. "Otherwise I couldn't have done it."

"Good God, girl!" He stared at her. Then in a moment she heard the rustle of the mattress and Barrett was up and limping across the cabin. In the half-darkness she heard the squeak of the top drawer of the dresser. There was the clink of glass and then he was back. In his hand he brandished an amber flask, with a glass handle and a sheaf of wheat embossed upon its side.

"Drink some of this," he commanded.

"What is it?"

"It's whisky, you little fool. The finest Scotch whisky. Evidently I was in error. I should have plied you like some reluctant young virgin. Go on, take some!

95

Drink. You'll need something to fortify yourself for physical contact with me."

Never had she heard a man speak with such bitter, self-mocking hatred. This was a nightmare, she thought wildly. Two strangers locked together in a small room from which there was no escape. She just prayed that it would be over with soon. That he would take whatever it was that he wanted and leave her alone.

"Well? Aren't you going to drink? Sorry I can't offer you a civilized glass, my dear, but it seems that in the frenzy of packing I overlooked that amenity."

Reluctantly Adrienne groped for the flask in the flickering half-darkness created by the oil lamp. Xenos Shane, too, had insisted that she drink. . . .

She sat stiffly, holding the bottle in her hand, unable to bring herself to lift it to her lips. She was aware that Barrett had turned down the wick of the lamp until its flame flickered out. Darkness swept into the cabin, so thick and close that Adrienne could almost feel it touching her face. Like a black shroud, she thought in growing panic. Smothering her. . . .

"Go on," her husband commanded. "What are you waiting for? Take a swallow."

"I—I don't want to."

"Perhaps not, but it will do you good. Whisky, the easer of men's cares, the friend of the despairing!"

The second swallow went down more easily. She could already feel the first one taking effect: a tingling, languorous ripple up and down her arms and legs.

How strange, she thought dreamily, that both Xenos Shane and Barrett had given her liquor. It was as if it were medicine, or some magical potion which could change her. . . .

And it was true that she could feel the softness beginning again in her veins, the warm, oily easiness which could block out fear and make it endurable.

She took the third swallow willingly, forcing down the burning liquid and waiting for the lift it would bring her, the ease.

"Ah," Barrett said. "That's much better. Whether

you're pleased with your bargain or not, Adrienne, you're still my wife. Mine, my plaything, my obsession." His laugh was soft, bitter. "Mine to teach, to train. To make great."

The bunk moved as he sat down again beside her. She could hear his sharp, indrawn breath as he bent his bad knee. She sat very still, her body wooden.

His hand crept up her thigh. Instinctively she pulled back, uttering a little cry.

"Do I fill you with such revulsion?" Barrett's hand tightened on the tender flesh of her inner thigh, moving toward her genitals. His fingers pinched her flesh until pain arrowed through her.

"Ouch! Oh, don't, that's hurting me."

"Is it?"

Seconds passed, or was it slow minutes? Barrett's urgent fingers pulled at her nightgown, finding her nipples. And then his mouth pressed on hers. Avid, licking, sucking. He was biting at her, pulling and hurting her tender flesh.

Or did it hurt? It was as if the whisky she had drunk were a shield, a barrier between herself and this thing which was happening now. She felt dizzied, as if the darkness whirled about her in wide, rocking circles.

"There. Ah, there." Barrett's voice came from very far away, hardly real at all. His hands explored her roughly. His mouth continued to do things to her, sucking, urgent things which caused her to shiver deep inside.

"There, my girl, that is much better. You must stimulate the man in me. That is what I wish you to do."

Somehow she was gulping down more of the whisky, its flame warming her body until Barrett's mouth, his groping hands, all seemed far away, until she could lie there on the bunk and not scream out with revulsion.

"Lie back," she heard him mutter. "Yes. Yes, that's it. Lie back, you bitch, and move your hips. Yes, yes, that's it . . . move them . . . open yourself wide for me."

Pain. A pounding violence.

Five minutes later, it was over. Barrett ordered her to crawl into the upper bunk, saying curtly that his knee pained him. Adrienne obeyed him. With trembling fingers, she pulled her nightgown down over bruised, aching nipples. Barrett had bitten at them unmercifully. But she had not known. The soft curtain of whisky had prevented her from feeling much pain.

She felt it now. Her breasts ached and throbbed from the punishment they had been given. Her thighs hurt, too, and the area between her legs. She lay huddled underneath the rough woolen blanket and felt the protection of the whisky melt away from her, as if it had never existed at all.

Barrett began to snore.

For a long time Adrienne lay sobbing silently, feeling beneath her the ceaseless movement of the ship. Her last thought before she fell asleep was of *Maman*'s voice, rich with dreams, with shining, brilliant promises.

"No, no, no! Say the lines again, but with an increase in the volume of your voice and a lowering of the pitch. Do you hear me, Adrienne? You are not on the streets of London selling dried fish or chestnuts! You are an actress now, and you must train your voice to be flexible. *You* must control *it*, and not the reverse!"

"But I am controlling it!" she protested.

"You are not. At the moment you are doing just about as well as a fishwife. But the final nuances, the real control—no, you haven't grasped that yet, and I am beginning to doubt that you ever will."

Adrienne flushed with anger. She glanced down at the dog-eared playbook, from which she had just repeated the lines from *Romeo and Juliet* for at least the fiftieth time. Or was it the sixtieth? She had lost count long ago.

It was three days later. Three days of intense work spent in the cramped cabin with Barrett, save for meals taken in the dining saloon, or short strolls on deck.

The nightmare of sex with Barrett had not repeated itself. For this Adrienne was profoundly grateful. It was as if, having shown the "man" in himself and asserted his mastery over her, Barrett felt no further interest in her.

Now, she thought bitterly, she had become for him no more than a piece of raw wood to be carved into exquisite shape. And if at first some rough hacking with an ax were required, then Barrett would do that, too, without regard for her feelings.

There were times when she hated him with a burning rage. There were other moments when she acknowledged to herself that she had been incredibly lucky to have stumbled upon such a teacher. Fanatic, sarcastic, hard-driving, with a nervous stamina that far outlasted her own, Barrett seemed obsessed with the idea of turning her into a great actress.

Greatness. It had been *Maman*'s dream, and her own.

So she pushed down her hurt, her fury, and her exhaustion, and gave back to him the ceaseless labor that he demanded.

Their day began immediately after breakfast, and continued almost until midnight. The worn copy of *Romeo and Juliet* was her instruction manual. Over and over, until she wished to scream from the monotony, they worked on her voice. On her control of volume, pitch and rate, of timber and quality.

"Adrienne!" Barrett's face would redden in blotches, his mustache twitching. He would rap her on the head with the playbook until her eyes stung.

"You are not a fish vendor, my girl, you are an actress! Can you comprehend that? I wish you to use a chest resonance, and to speak with the words forming near your lips, not back in the middle of your mouth. Do as I ask, please, if you are capable!"

"I *am* capable!"

She would blink back tears of humiliation.

"And for God's sake, don't blubber!"

"I am not blubbering!"

"Aren't you? You wanted this, didn't you? You sold yourself for this very opportunity. And now that you have it, your eyes fill with water at the slightest reprimand."

"I am not crying," she muttered.

"Aren't you? I see baby tears trickling down." Barrett's hands gripped her shoulders, shaking her back and forth as if she were truly a wooden doll without sensation. "There is a chance, girl, a chance. . . . God help me, I saw it in you from the first, that night at the Oxford. It is in your voice, your manner, the very way you hold your body, as if you are a great lady and yet also a wanton. Fascinating! And now you are my wife. You've put yourself under my tutelage, and I insist that you work—I demand it!"

"All right. I'll work harder." She pulled away from him and went to the porthole to stare out at the sun glittering on the sea. She tried to hide the bleak despair she felt. She didn't wish him to see her humiliation, or her homesickness, so raw and strong now that at night she huddled under her blanket choked with silent sobs.

Maman. Tessie. The other children. Poor, dead little Devin. And now she herself was a hunted felon, sailing far away to America, to a new and frightening life with a man she barely knew. Would she ever see her family again?

But quickly she pushed such thoughts from her mind. Of course she would see *Maman* again! Someday perhaps she would return to Glasgow. And when she did, she would be a famous actress, like Adrienne LaRivière, Adelaide Ristori, or the renowned Rachel Felix. She would return wearing a fabulous gown, her neck and wrists encrusted with expensive jewelry. She would carry trunk after trunk, heaped with costumes, wigs, furs, jewelry. She would be followed everywhere by admiring crowds. And she would make it up to *Maman* for everything. For the hard life she had led, for Devin's death.

Afternoons they spent working on physical technique, the skilled movements of the body which an actress must know. Evenings they read from scenes, working over and over, until Adrienne trembled from exhaustion.

"The novice," Barrett said in his harsh voice, "is almost always subject to a wriggling of the feet and a constant twitching of the fingers. She is excited. She is constantly thinking of the fact that she is onstage before an audience. She thinks her own thoughts instead of the thoughts of the character she is playing. That's wrong. You must have control, Adrienne. Control over every muscle and movement and thought, every nuance of your personality!"

There were many things to learn. Changes of level, when she would raise her head slightly, or perhaps rise from a reclining position on the floor to sit gracefully on a chair. There were hundreds of ways, she discovered, to move from one area of the stage to another. There were gestures—a whole gamut of them—and facial expressions to learn.

"Over again!" Barrett would shout irritably. He would rap her with the playbook, or tug at the fabric of her sleeve. "Do it again, and this time please concentrate! You keep repeating the same arm movement like a puppet. You have made Shakespeare seem repetitious because your gestures are repetitious."

Defiance surged in her. "But I *am* expressing anger, am I not? How else should I—"

"Think, girl, just think! Use your imagination, assuming that you have one."

"I do have one!"

"There are times when I doubt it."

So she would push back her fury and repeat the scene until Barrett pronounced himself satisfied.

"Well, you are progressing," he told her at last. They had spent a day so long and tiring that Adrienne felt gray from tiredness.

She regarded him silently.

"I cannot guarantee you will be a superb actress," he went on. "But at least by the end of this voyage you will be competent."

"Are you giving me a compliment?"

"You may take it as you wish."

She felt the blood rise to her cheeks—whether from tiredness or pleasure, she did not know.

"Why did you marry me, Barrett?" she demanded

suddenly. "Surely it was more than just to gain possession of the Passion Star. The way you have been working me, shouting at me, pushing me almost beyond endurance— it's as if you are obsessed!"

Barrett Kendall gave her a long look. The salt-and-pepper mustache seemed to twitch. Finally he jerked away from her and limped to the porthole, where he paused to stare out at the choppy swell of the Atlantic.

"I am a bitter man," he said at last. "Perhaps you have noticed that. Many years ago I had an unhappy marriage with a woman who hated me. I have had many liaisons with women, and most of them ended disastrously —witness my present disgrace as a remittance man. I was nearly killed once in a duel, did you know that?"

He laughed without humor. "I was shot in the right hip. Sometimes that wound still troubles me, when the weather is damp."

Silence grew in the cabin, punctuated by the sounds of a busy ship: pounding feet as a crewman ran to trim the sails; timbers creaking, someone shouting, a bleat from one of the sheep the ship carried for food.

"I drink too much and too often," Barrett went on. "I have used cannabis and opium. I am in constant pain from my knee and I have headaches—they are migraine, my father informs me. He also says that I am choleric— easily irritated, and perhaps prone to apoplexy."

She was puzzled and almost touched at Barrett's frankness. This was a far different man from the one who had violated her on her wedding night, who had shouted at her and rapped her over the head with the playbook.

"But . . . what does this have to do with your marrying me?" she asked hesitantly.

"Nothing. And yet everything. I am not young, Adrienne. My knee is permanently damaged. My health is not the best. I have little real future on the stage now, and I know that." Barrett's voice caught. "Perhaps you could say that I am a man who likes to be in control. A man with ambitions he must fulfill in whatever way he can."

He was looking at her strangely. Adrienne shifted her feet, her fingers tightening on the playbook she still held.

This was the nearest Barrett had ever come to explaining himself to her. She was still not sure that she understood him. But she felt oddly closer to him than she had done before.

Chapter 8

It was dawn of the fifth day. Adrienne had awakened early after a night full of restless dreams. In them, once more she had been in the close at 165 High Street, running away from Jaimie McAndrews, who chased after her, his mouth open to reveal a black, ugly hole where his teeth had been . . .

Now she stood at the rail of the *Thermopylae*, staring out to where a few faint, gray streaks illuminated the horizon. How strange and eerie the dawn sea was, she mused. For at the horizon the water simply met sky and merged with it, leaving no clear definition. There were only the swelling waves, each one topped with a white froth scarcely visible now in the half-light between night and day.

She leaned forward, focusing her eyes on a thin slice of moon still visible. In its dim light, there was a feeling of loneliness and foreboding. Adrienne sighed and pushed away the thought of Barrett still asleep, his body a mound beneath the rough gray woolen blanket. Instead, she tried to think of *Maman*. What was her mother doing at this very moment? Was she now up with the baby, Thaddeus, stirring his gruel over the stove? Or was she beginning to gather her sewing together for the day's painstaking work?

Maman, and Glasgow, seemed very far away here on the open sea.

A breeze came sweeping from the horizon, and

Adrienne shivered, pulling her shawl about her shoulders. From somewhere amidship she could hear sailors talking to each other in sleepy voices. Pots and pans clattered in the galley.

She heard a footfall behind her, and turned, startled. Kristian King loped toward her, broad shoulders swinging easily beneath his well-cut suit. In the indistinct light she could see his curly, close-cropped hair, the somber, square-chinned face.

In spite of herself, her heart had begun to pump faster.

He walked to the rail near her and stood looking out at the horizon.

"This is just false dawn," he remarked after a moment, as if they were continuing a conversation begun hours before. "The real one will come along in a moment and it will be spectacular. The sea is mysterious, and she is never more awe-inspiring than at dawn."

"Yes," Adrienne whispered. "I feel that, too. Don't you think there is something almost frightening about it? It's all so very big. There are no trees or houses or buildings, nothing to make it seem ordinary and commonplace. The sky meets the water and . . . and that's all there is."

Kristian gave her a long look, then nodded. "You have very acute perception, Mrs. Kendall."

"Please, call me Adrienne."

"Adrienne, then." He gave her a brief smile, and she noticed that a dimple cleaved his right cheek. For long moments they stood in companionable silence, listening to the swelling roll of the combers, the splash of water against the side of the ship.

"Were you having trouble sleeping, too?" he asked her at last.

"Yes, I had some bad dreams," she admitted. "I awoke early and I just couldn't stay in that cabin any longer. I—I don't like enclosed places."

"Oh? Doesn't that husband of yours let you out on deck other than in the morning? I've seen you. Each day, precisely after breakfast, he leads you around the deck four or five times, exactly like a pet dog. And meekly you follow him, gazing only at him, hanging upon his every word as if it were pure gold. Is he really all that fascinating?"

"Yes!" She said it defiantly. "As I told you, Barrett is teaching me to act. He was quite well known in the British theater and now we are going to America, where we will appear in New York."

The sky had begun to lighten, the gray clouds at the horizon taking on tinges of pink. Adrienne tightened her shawl about her shoulders against the dawn wind.

"New York? The theater? That's what he talks to you about on your morning strolls?"

"Yes. He tells me about people like Rachel Felix. She was French, you know. Barrett says he saw her act on one of her tours in England, during the Great Exposition of 1851. He says her acting was superb, that she would *jouer le mot,* that is, she carried through each phrase with a gesture appropriate to it—"

"Oh?" Again the dimple flashed, and the blue eyes held amusement. Adrienne stifled a twinge of irritation.

"Yes, when she referred to Hippolyte's head in *Phèdre,* she would actually touch his head. Thus, even though she played in French, those in the audience who spoke only English could understand her. And—"

Kristian gave a soft laugh. "Very well," he said. "I will admit that your husband is indeed fascinating—or at least that he has charmed you enough to turn you into a little parrot. But how much of what you have just told me do you really understand?"

Angrily she turned to him. "I understand all of it, of course. Do you think I am stupid? Barrett is teaching me many things. By the time we reach New York, I'll be ready to assume a role in a stage play—he has said so!"

She slapped the two fringed ends of her shawl together, and moved away from the rail, intending to go below.

Kristian caught her arm. "Don't leave yet. Look at that, will you? The edge of the sun is just at the horizon. In a moment it will rise to spill red fire into the water, and the glow of its burning will transcend everything."

107

In spite of herself, Adrienne stopped, captured by the beauty of the word-picture which Kristian had painted.

"Yes," she whispered.

He was looking at her now, the blue eyes intense, and again she could feel the physical force which radiated from him to her. She caught her breath, almost frightened by the feeling this man could give her.

"You are beautiful," he said softly.

"What?" She stared at him.

"I said that you are lovely—as beautiful as that fiery sunrise in your own way. Perhaps sometime when you are taking your daily constitutional with your keeper—ah, I mean your husband—you will deign to turn and give me a smile."

"He is not my keeper!" she began indignantly. But before she could finish her sentence, Kristian had turned to look out over the rail again.

"I often come on deck to watch the sunrise," he said in a low voice. "A dawning is a symbol of hope. And at this time in my life, I am drawn toward every possible semblance of hope."

What had he meant? And why was there such a tension in the way Kristian looked and stood and spoke? Adrienne stood very still, trying to quell the absurd pounding of her heart.

This was ridiculous, she told herself, gazing downward at her hands trembling together on the ship's rail. To feel so stirred by a man who was not her husband, a mere shipboard acquaintance whom she would never see again once they reached New York. . .

When at last she raised her eyes to look at the sea again, it was brushed with delicate strokes of flaming orange.

She returned to their cabin to find Barrett seated on the lower bunk pulling on his shoes.

"Where have you been?" he demanded irritably. "When I awoke I was quite startled not to find you here."

"I was on deck walking about. I didn't sleep well, and I felt restless and wished to see the sun come up."

"If you were that restless, you should have lit the lamp and spent the time memorizing your lines. I've told you, I want the entire play memorized by tomorrow, Adrienne, and unless I am greatly mistaken, you are still stumbling in some of the parts."

"Am I?"

She walked to the bureau and stood unwinding her shawl. Automatically she folded it and put it away. She felt as if her very thoughts were shivering, or singing, or—

Kristian King had called Barrett her "keeper," she thought confusedly. He had . . . yes, he had laughed at her. But he had also said that he often came on deck to watch the sun rise. Perhaps he would be there again tomorrow.

She could feel the red rise to stain her neck and cheeks.

Barrett rose and limped toward her. He unfastened his coat as he came. Adrienne, still by the bureau, watched him come, a sudden unease plunging through her. Thus had her husband looked in the cabin on their wedding night when he had . . .

Barrett's eyes glittered. "Ah, Adrienne, you are mine, did you know that?"

"Of course. Barrett, please—"

His arms slid around her, his hands roughly seeking her nipples.

"Mine, my dear. When we first came aboard, it was dark, and I did not have the opportunity to savor you as I should. Women are like fine wine, mellow and hearty and full of marvelous body."

She stood rigid. "I—I don't understand what you mean. Barrett, I thought you wished me to work. You wanted the play memorized. . . ."

"So I do. And you will work, never fear. But for now, there is something else we must do. I must uncask the new wine and see if it has begun to age properly."

Adrienne found her powers of motion and began to

109

edge backward along the paneled bulkhead toward the cabin door. Wildly she thought of Kristian King, of his intense blue eyes, the exciting way he had been able to capture her in his gaze. He had called her beautiful.

Despair overwhelmed her.

"Barrett, no—please."

But it was too late. If Barrett Kendall heard her protests, he paid no attention to them. She felt herself being pushed against the wall, cornered by the wiry strength of this man she had married. His hands fumbled at her bodice.

Then she was caught in nightmare again, in the terror of hands pulling at her, punching and kneading her flesh.

"So you are here," Kristian said.

"Yes."

Adrienne stood at the rail of the *Thermopylae* in the exact spot where she and Kristian had stood the previous morning. Over their heads, stays creaked, and a sailor clambered in the rigging, shouting in a hoarse voice to someone farther astern. It was dawn again. Pink clouds lay fluffed along the horizon like balls of Aberdeen wool.

Adrienne drew a deep breath, trying not to think of the black-and-blue marks which marred the tender areas of her breasts near her nipples, the dark bruises along her thighs and belly. What had occurred between Barrett and herself was surely a bad dream, no more. And like all nightmares, in the light of day the menace was diluted. You could almost pretend it had never happened. Almost . . .

Now, against all reason, she felt a ripple of happiness run through her. Again Barrett had been asleep. She had managed to creep out of the upper bunk, pulling on her clothes as silently as she could, her heart hammering in her chest. If her husband were to awaken and catch her . . .

But Barrett had not varied the regular sounds of his snoring.

And now here she was on deck with Kristian, feeling

oddly joyous and free. She stole a sidelong look at him. He was hatless, his honey-colored hair blown by the wind into disorderly curls, so crisp that she ached to touch them.

"Oh, I do love the dawn," she sighed.

Kristian looked at her. "And from where did you watch the sun rise? Before your marriage, I mean?"

She hesitated, thinking of the stone walls of the close, the dung heap with its pungent animal odor. Of *Maman*'s tired face, and Devin lying so still and silent on his cot, pennies over his eyes to hold them shut.

She had vowed never to let anyone know where she came from, ever again.

"I . . . I am the daughter of a countess," she heard herself blurt. The lie came more easily than she had expected. "I cannot give you my real name because I am a runaway. I had to leave home because my stepfather—" She lowered her eyes discreetly, "made improper advances to me."

Kristian nodded, looking surprised. "Did you have friends, then, who helped you?"

"Yes. I lived with them for a time, until I met Barrett."

As before, with each word, the lies began to seem more plausible. Surely, she assured herself, all of it might really have happened. She might actually have been born the daughter of Aurelia Prendergast. And Aurelia's husband did have a glowering visage, ugly enough to be the most wicked of stepfathers. And her own father, Jack McGill . . . She pushed away the thought.

"So then you met and married Barrett Kendall and lived happily ever after," Kristian mused.

Adrienne shifted uneasily. "Now it's turn about," she said hastily. "From what place did you watch the sunrise before you embarked on the *Thermopylae?*"

"From an earl's house near Stratford. When there was time, anyway. I was tutor to his six sons."

She saw Kristian's hands, which had been loosely clasped over the rail, clench into fists. His jaws, too, had tightened, his mouth becoming a straight line. Even the dimple in his right cheek was now a slash.

"You were a tutor, then? I thought you said you were a writer."

"I did both." His voice was sharp. "And I would prefer not to discuss it, if you don't mind." The blue eyes challenged her. "Don't you have some things, Adrienne—if that is indeed your real name—that you would prefer to keep secret?"

Adrienne thought of Xenos Shane, of the Passion Star. "You are right. I—I do have secrets, but I won't tell you what they are."

His dimple flashed briefly. "I don't expect you to. And I don't plan to tell you mine."

There was a long silence, broken only by the ship's noises—the shouts of seamen, the ringing of the watch bells, creaking of timbers and stays, the ceaseless wash of water against the bow of the *Thermopylae*. The pink clouds were growing lighter, shot through with yellow-gold bars of sun.

"Yes, Adrienne is my real first name," she said at last, softly. "My stage name is going to be Adrienne Gill. Do you like it?"

He smiled. She noticed that his teeth were appealingly uneven. His smile was one that crinkled his eyes and lit up his whole face, giving it warmth.

"Yes, I like it very much. So you really do intend to be an actress?"

"Yes! I think I have talent, and Barrett has virtually said so himself." Her voice rushed on. "Did you know that I was named after my aunt, a beautiful French actress called Adrienne LaRivière? She was very spirited and headstrong. *Maman*—my mother, that is—never tired of telling stories about her."

"Yes, I've heard of her. I'm very much interested in the theater myself—French, English, and American."

The blue eyes were fastened upon her so intently that Adrienne felt a soft, swooping pull in the center of her belly. She shivered with excitement. How? she wondered How could this man make her feel like this, so warm and flushed and giddy?

"I suppose I should get back to our cabin," she said

at last, regretfully. "Barrett was . . . angry yesterday when he found me gone."

"He objects to your taking a short stroll alone?"

"Yes. There are times when I feel as if I'm not real to him at all. I feel like a wooden doll whom he must carve into a perfect shape, a masterpiece—"

"Why did you marry him, then? An older man like that?"

She hesitated. "He is not so very old. And, you see, I—I had to marry him."

Kristian's eyes questioned.

"I . . . I had to leave my friends. My money was stolen on the train and I was stranded alone in London without resources. And then when I went to the music halls to apply for work I could not get hired."

Kristian scowled. "Are you telling me that you married Barrett Kendall because you had no money? As a convenience?"

"He knows everything about the theater," she said angrily. "He said he could teach me. And I want to learn. You see—"

"I see, all right!" An incredulous expression had twisted Kristian's face. He moved away from her, his body tensing. "Barrett is well known in London as a philanderer, a womanizer and worse. His family has disowned him. That is the sort of man you have attached yourself to. You sold yourself to him like any street girl, didn't you, Miss Adrienne Gill or whatever your real name is?"

"It wasn't exactly like that!"

"Then how was it, Adrienne? Why *did* you marry such a man?"

"It—it isn't any of your business!" she flared. Angry tears pricked at the backs of her lids. "You have no right to speak to me in this way, Mr. King, none whatsoever! And now I think I shall go down to my cabin. My husband is waiting for me."

"Your *husband*. Ah, yes."

With dignity, she started to sweep past Kristian, her skirts brushing the deck. But as she passed him, he

113

caught at her arm. She was shocked to feel the angry, shaking tension in his grip, as if his body expressed a deep fury which could not be told in any other way.

"Go, then, girl." His words were savage, his face a grim mask. "Go back to your old man, then, your teacher, your keeper. And enjoy him, won't you? Enjoy him to the fullest!"

It was evening. The oil lamp, safely bolted to the dresser top, cast its flickering shadows up the paneled bulkheads of the cabin. The ship had begun to pitch and heave, and at dinner the captain had talked gloomily of a storm coming up.

Each night at dinner, fewer of the passengers had appeared. Both Harpers had succumbed to seasickness, as had the two spinsters. Tonight only four diners had been present: Adrienne, Barrett, Kristian King, and Dr. Mawson.

The food had consisted of fried mutton, mashed turnips and boiled carrots, a combination which did not contributed to the ease of Adrienne's own stomach. Conversation, too, had been strained. As usual, Barrett had monopolized the talk, regaling them all with tales of the London theater. Dr. Mawson had seemed fascinated, Kristian had heard him politely, and even Adrienne, weary as she was, had listened with interest. Barrett had a bitter, almost cruel way of emphasizing the vanities of the actors of whom he spoke.

It was as if, she thought, he secretly hated them and wished to point up their flaws.

As they were leaving the dining saloon, she felt Kristian's eyes on her. "Your husband's stories were very pointed," he murmured. "His tongue is sharp, and it lashes away at the innocent most painfully."

"Yes—"

Barrett's arm tightened on her own, and then they were in the companionway. She could sense her husband's displeasure.

"Come along," he ordered her sharply. "There is work to be done, Adrienne, or had you forgotten?"

Back in the cabin, it was as if the dinner hour, and her brief glimpse of Kristian King, had never happened.

For the dozenth time, she began Juliet's speech. *"How art thou out of breath, when thou hast breath to say to me that thou art out of breath? The excuse that thou dost make in this delay . . ."*

Suddenly she threw down the playbook. "Barrett, I can't do it any more. I'm tired, exhausted. I must stop for today."

His eyes glittered at her. "You cannot quit yet. It's still early. We have much work to do on this scene and on some others before I will pronounce myself satisfied with the day's labors."

"And what of me?" She was trembling with her defiance. "It's no use, Barrett. I can't work any more tonight. I feel as if my skin had actually turned gray with exhaustion." She gave a short, weary laugh. "And I think I am getting seasick."

"Seasick! I forbid it!"

"And how will you stop me?" She felt like giggling wildly. "Barrett, we've been working for eight days now without stop, save to eat and to walk for a short time about the deck. I can't keep it up any longer. I need some time to rest."

"Rest! And didn't you inform me that you were willing to work hard? To do everything you must in order to become an actress?"

"Yes, but I didn't know——"

"And now you complain because I keep you to your word."

"Of course I'm not complaining. But——"

"You made a bargain with me, you little bitch. Despite your high-born background you were penniless, a felon, a thief with something to trade. You traded it."

She stared at Barrett, at the twisted expression on his face, the fanaticism in his eyes. For the first time, real hatred for him rose in her.

"You don't understand!" she cried. "I am a human being, Barrett, not a——a wooden doll that you can carve and polish as if it didn't have any feelings! *I* have feelings! I'm tired! I'm homesick! I want to walk on deck, to stand looking out at the sea as the other passengers do, to—to have fun! I—I even wish to be seasick in peace and privacy!"

"And to meet your writer friend on deck at dawn?" Barrett's voice was a whipcrack.

For a long instant they faced each other. Adrienne could see the twitch of Barrett's mustache, the pale unhealthiness of his face, the glitter of his gray eyes. How had he known? she wondered dully. Had one of the crew seen them on deck? Or had Barrett himself followed her?

"Yes." She said it stonily. "Yes, that, too."

"You are a whore, then." Never, not even on their nightmare wedding night, had she seen Barrett so angry. "Oh, I saw you staring at that man in the dining saloon, hanging on his every word, making a spectacle of yourself and me!"

"I didn't! *You* did most of the talking. Kristian only said a few words to me, it was an ordinary conversation—"

"I should have known better! All women are alike! And I thought you would be different." Barrett brandished the playbook as if it were a weapon. "You with your pale hair, the color of sunlight, of magic. You with your abilities, your marvelous stage presence. You said you would submit to me and my teaching. . . ."

She gazed at him, electrified by what he had said. *You with your abilities, your marvelous stage presence* . . . Then she *did* have talent. A great deal of it. A trembling, excited rush of blood suffused her face. She felt like singing with the triumph of it, like dancing about the cabin.

She did have acting ability. Barrett had said so.

Some day, perhaps very soon, she would be a star.

There was a crash as her husband threw the playbook across the cabin, where it slammed against the wall. Quickly Adrienne forgot her elation and came back to reality. He is mad, she thought. In his own way, he is quite, quite mad.

"I did nothing wrong with Kristian," she told him quickly, moistening her dry lips. "One morning I awoke early and couldn't sleep, so I went on deck. I met him there by accident, that was all."

"Accident?"

She faced him. "Yes, it was accidental, that first time at least. And on the second time we just talked quietly—about the sunrise. I assure you it was all very innocent. After all, am I not married to you?"

"Indeed you are, my little trollop, and I'll ask you not to forget it. It is I to whom you owe your allegiance, not some young rake of a writer who only wishes to get you in bed!"

"That's not so! Kristian has never—"

"Hasn't he? Hasn't he, my dear?"

Slowly Barrett approached her, his right leg dragging, his face paler than she had ever seen it. He was like an angry child, she realized in growing panic. A child who has had a toy snatched from him and can only think about getting it back, broken or whole.

He was going to take her again, she knew, as he had done the other two times. Quickly, savagely, painfully, as if she were truly a doll made expressly for his pleasure.

"Barrett." She edged backward, saying his name slowly, fighting for time. "I think I made a mistake in marrying you. A terrible mistake."

"Perhaps. But a bargain is a bargain, isn't it? You did marry me. And now you're obligated to me. And there's certainly nowhere you can run away here on the ship, is there? Unless you wish to leap overboard."

She stared at him, struggling not to weep.

You don't long for silly, romantic love, then? For some handsome man who will come along and sweep you up into realms of ecstasy? Barrett's words, spoken days ago in London, seemed to hang before her.

"I—I hate you, Barrett! I hate every minute of being in bed with you and I always will! I loathe you!"

She had said it.

She had spoken the thing which had festered between them these days aboard the *Thermopylae*.

Barrett uttered a choked, animal cry. Then he lunged toward her. His hands clenched her shoulders as he spun her toward the bunk.

It was dawn again. Faint light glimmered through the porthole, casting a round disk of paleness on the floor. Nearby, the playbook lay crumpled where Barrett had thrown it the night before. The entire cabin reeked of whisky, for Barrett, after satiating himself with her, had taken a flask to bed with him. Now he lay in the lower bunk, his bad knee propped up, snoring noisily.

Cautiously Adrienne stirred in the upper bunk, praying that its slats would not creak. She rubbed at her burning eyes.

Another day had passed. She had lain awake all night, afraid to move for fear of waking Barrett. During the night the high seas had grown into a storm, and the ship's noises—timbers groaning, the crash of water, the slap of sails and stays—had provided a frightening counterpoint to her own bleak thoughts.

In marrying Barrett Kendall, she had made a dreadful and irrevocable mistake.

Afraid of being captured as a felon, she had been drawn to the safety which Barrett represented, and greedy for the training he could give her. So she had sold herself—and the Passion Star—to him. Now she was legally bound to him for the rest of her life.

She moved restlessly. A sudden, bubbling noise from the lower bunk froze her for a moment. Then, when Barrett still did not wake, she sat up and tossed aside the blanket.

Cautiously she lowered herself from the bunk, moving as lightly as she could.

Barrett did not stir.

She fumbled for her clothing, pulling the garments on as best she could, managing the hooks and buttons with difficulty. Once she stumbled against the bulkhead, and again she froze. But Barrett snored on, his breath wheezing in and out in bubbling gasps, and she knew that he must be deeply asleep.

118

She groped in the bureau drawer for her shawl. As she did so, she felt her hand close over something hard. Puzzled, she felt again, and when she heard the slosh of liquid, she knew what the object was. Barrett had evidently hidden a second flask of whisky among the piles of clothing in the bureau.

She hesitated, then pulled out the bottle. *Whisky,* she thought. That soft, warm curtain which could blur all the rough and ugly edges in her mind. She felt her fingers close around the cork, wrenching it out. And it was without surprise that she found herself tilting the flask upward and taking a long swallow. Just one, she told herself. Just one. . . .

Fire seared the inside of her mouth and throat. Then a slow, sultry warmth began to spread along her veins.

She stood swaying in the darkness of the cabin, feeling the ship roll beneath her feet. Somewhere overhead, footsteps pounded, and a crewman shouted. Bells began to ring, signaling the end of a watch.

Fleetingly, she thought of her father, Jack McGill, of the glazed look his eyes had taken on when he had been drinking. Then she pushed away the thought. She tipped up the flask and took another long swallow. This time she waited expectantly for the fiery thrill along her veins, the veil which would drop between her and her thoughts, making them easier to bear. . . .

Five minutes later, she had groped her way to the cabin door and then she was in the companionway, pitching and tossing, clinging for balance to the rope lines attached to the bulkhead.

"Miss, you shouldn't go on deck just now. The seas are high and it's no place for a woman."

Adrienne turned, startled, to see the second mate, bundled in oilskins, his face wet with sea spray. Evidently he had just completed his watch and was going below.

"But I won't be long."

"Better not, miss. Can be dangerous up there."

But she twisted past him, scrambling up the damp wooden steps and struggling with the heavy hatch.

On deck, the force of the storm reached out to grab

her. The deck, covered with slippery wetness from the giant waves which crashed against the bow, rocked perilously. Stays groaned and whined, timbers screeched, and overhead two crewmen struggled grimly in the rigging, buffeted by the wind and looking as if they might be blown into the sea at any moment.

Adrienne staggered to the starboard rail and clung to it. She felt the wind grab at her gown and yank at the ends of her shawl, nearly ripping it off her shoulders. Huge waves, many of them larger than the *Thermopylae,* swelled and rolled and crashed. There was a wildness, a raw, surging force about them which met some answering chord in Adrienne. She stood with her mouth open, tasting the wet salt spray, and felt a wild kinship with the storm.

Gradually she became aware that she was not alone. Someone else stood at the rail only ten feet away, his face turned upward to catch the full brunt of the spray-laden wind.

It was Kristian King.

He seemed completely unaware of her presence. Clad in a dark coat, now water-soaked, he braced himself against the turbulent roll of the deck. He was hatless, and his hair, damp, curling, had been blown back from his temples by the wind. His mouth was set, his face seemingly carved from stone. Yet there was a fierce exultation in his eyes.

"The storm!" she shouted at last to him. "Don't you love it? Isn't it wonderful?"

Kristian turned. She could see his startled look, as if she had jerked him out of some absorbing thought.

"What are you doing here, Adrienne? In this heavy sea! You must be mad—this is no place for a woman!"

"That's what the second mate said, too," she told him firmly, "but you are both wrong."

The ship lurched sickeningly as a huge wave crashed against the bow, surging tons of water aboard. Kristian grasped Adrienne's arm to support her. The feel of his hand was strong and warm.

"For God's sake, Adrienne. Your gown is getting soaked. You should be down in your cabin where it's safe."

She lifted her chin. "Perhaps I don't wish to be safe."

His mouth twisted in the beginnings of a smile. "You are a wild creature, aren't you?"

She felt his arm tighten about her, bracing her against the pitch of the ship. A soft shiver thrilled through her, a shiver that had nothing to do with the storm, or with the whisky she had drunk in the cabin.

"I can't swim, can you?" she shouted to him over the noise of the storm.

"No—but then most sailors can't swim a stroke, did you know that?"

"Really?"

"You see, it wouldn't do a seaman much good if he did know how to swim. Usually, it would only prolong his agony."

"Agony?"

"Yes. Life is hazardous for a sailor; a man might be blown from the rigging, or washed overboard by the force of a wave. In heavy seas, it's almost impossible to turn the ship about to search for a lost man. And if the captain, by some superhuman effort, does manage to do so, the waves have already tossed the man too far away, or he has already drowned."

"Oh." She bit her lip, some of the exultation of the storm gone for her now. To think of drowning in those vast, rolling waves, to sink downward in this foaming froth . . . she shivered convulsively.

"The sea can be brutal," Kristian said. "My father was a sea captain and died off Cape Horn when I was sixteen. It storms there, violently, and there are murderous seas, so high that the waves sweep right over the deck of a ship, taking everything in their path, including men. My father was one of those men."

Kristian's mouth twisted. "I often think of him, and wonder what it must have been like, to fall into that icy water and to know that you were already dead. That your mates, no matter how they wished it, could never turn the ship back for you."

"Oh, Kristian, I'm so sorry."

"Don't be. It happened many years ago, and surely

121

my father is at peace by now. Even if I am not," he added, in a voice so low that it was almost blown away by the surging wind.

She stared at him, puzzled. "What did you do after he died?" she wondered at last.

"I lived with my mother until she died of a tumor. Then—thank God I had been educated—I went to work as a tutor, to support myself until—"

Abruptly Kristian stopped. His lips were compressed into a thin line.

"Until what?"

"Until I had to leave," he said harshly. "Don't pry into what doesn't concern you, Adrienne."

He grasped both of her shoulders, propelling her in the direction of the companionway. "The storm is worsening. You had best go below to your cabin and to your husband."

"No—I don't want to."

"Nevertheless, you had better. It's dangerous up here, and growing more so."

"No," she repeated stubbornly. "I don't wish to go below . . . to him."

Somehow tears had begun to roll down her cheeks. She clung to the rail, her body rocking under the force of the rolling deck.

He was looking at her. "Adrienne. Oh, God, Adrienne."

Then, as if he were driven and could not help himself, his arms went around her again. He pulled her to him, so tightly that she could feel the strong pounding of his heart. She felt the soft seeking of his mouth on hers, at first tentative, then stronger. Searching, demanding, forcing her lips open until she responded in answering passion.

They clung together. It was as if a flame arced through their bodies from one to the other, burning between them, until Adrienne felt as if she could bear no more.

At last, reluctantly, Kristian released her. Adrienne stood swaying.

"Darling, this is insane. I shouldn't have touched you. You're married to someone else."

"Yes . . ." Tears stung her eyes, and an aching hurt pushed at her throat. "Yes, Kristian, I'm married, but I don't wish to be. I made a mistake—"

"A mistake?"

"You don't know!" she cried wildly. "Oh, Kristian, you just can't know. I hate him, I really do! I can't . . . I can't be with him in *that* way, I just can't!"

Another wave rolled toward the ship. Kristian gazed at her, his face carved into grim lines.

The sun had risen, rain-washed, obscured behind an ominous gray scurf of clouds until all the world seemed a backdrop of gray. The air was full of moist spray and now it had begun to rain. Hard pellets of water drove toward them to sting their faces.

Yet neither of them made any move to go below.

"Adrienne, why, why did you do it? Marry that old man!"

"You don't understand, Kris—" she began.

"Kris? Why do you call me that?" To her surprise, Kristian's mouth twisted bitterly.

"Why, it's just a nickname."

"Well, I don't like it, and I don't want you to use it again," he said harshly.

"Very well. I'll call you Kristian, then, as you wish." She caught her breath. "But still you don't understand— about Barrett, I mean."

"I think I can understand a great deal." Again she could sense the anger in him, frightening in its intensity, like the storm. "For all of your beauty, Adrienne, you're an opportunist, aren't you? That was why you married him, that limping old man so full of himself and his own cruel words. You wanted to use him, didn't you? For your own purposes, whatever they were."

Adrienne could feel her face growing stony. Her cheeks were burning. She felt as if the storm, and the whisky she had drunk in the cabin, were whirling together in her brain.

"Kristian!" Impulsively she threw herself toward

123

him. "Kristian, just hold me. . . . Oh, God, I was a fool to do it, a fool! If only I'd waited until I met you . . ."

She clung to him, pressing her body into his as if it were her only haven.

For a moment she felt him respond to her, straining toward her as his arms clasped her tightly. Then, suddenly, he pushed her away.

They stood looking at each other, their breath coming fast. Droplets of rain stung their faces. Adrienne put up one hand to brush aside the tendrils of hair which slapped at her cheeks.

"You may have been a fool," Kristian said at last, harshly. "Undoubtedly you were. But you did make a choice. Go back to your marriage, girl. Perhaps it can still work. You must give it a chance."

She looked at him, at the tender lines of his mouth now hardened, his eyes so intensely blue. There was a tightness in her chest. It was as if cords of pain were pulling taut there, one by one.

"I won't go back to him!" she cried. "I won't! Oh, I hate him—and I hate you, too. I never want to see you again, Kristian King. Ever, ever!"

"Oh?" His mouth mocked her. "I thought you wished to see me very much indeed."

A wave crashed on deck, washing water in their direction. Adrienne's hand rose. She struck Kristian's face with the side of her palm. The mark of her fingers was red on his face.

Kristian's eyes blazed at her. His dimple was an angry slash, his face savage.

"How childish you are, Adrienne Gill. Slapping my face like a little girl caught up in a tantrum, because I've said something you didn't care to hear. Well, the truth is that you *are* married—whether you wish to be or not. I had no right to meet you here on deck as I've done, or to kiss you either. I regret both. And now I suggest you go below. The storm is worsening, and we're in real danger of being washed overboard."

"Oh!" She yanked her shawl tighter about her shoulders. She felt like bursting into wild tears. "Oh, I don't care if I am washed away! Perhaps I should jump!"

Kristian's laugh was dry. He was gazing at her with an odd expression, as if there was something about her which he did not quite understand, or even like.

"Jump?" he asked softly. "On the contrary, my dear, I doubt if there is anything which would make you throw yourself overboard—even love. You're a pragmatist, Adrienne Gill. A realist. And realists generally survive for a very long, long time."

Chapter 9

Adrienne rested her palms on the windowsill and leaned forward, staring hungrily at the busy street scene three stories below.

New York. It was a city of ceaseless horse traffic, redolent with the smells of manufactories and breweries, of horse droppings and coal smoke, of cooking cabbage and street dust. Directly below her window, two ragwomen squabbled. A fruit vendor cried out her wares. A hansom cab, its horse splendid with trappings, sped past.

And spread out before her—almost as if placed there expressly for her temptation—were the stores and shops of this huge city: jewelers, clothiers, watchmakers, milliners, stationers, dressmakers, the sellers of boots and shoes, of goods of all sorts.

A whole world of opulence and glamor which she had never tasted, had not even dreamed existed until now.

They had been in New York for two days. And Adrienne, thinking of Kristian King in misery and longing, felt as if each hour had been endless. Why, why, had she slapped him? It had been a foolish, a reckless thing to do. For he had left the ship without speaking to her further.

He was gone. And she would never see him again.

The knowledge was an ache in her, a hurt all the more surprising for its unexpectedness. She had never felt anything like this before, this pain, this choking feeling

127

which filled her throat like a huge ball of unshed tears.

Dully she accepted Barrett's order to stay in the hotel room to work on her voice exercises. Why not work? she asked herself grimly. Kristian was gone—disappeared into the vastness of New York, to do whatever it was he had come here to do. He had dropped from her life as if he had never been in it. She had been a fool to love him, a fool to think, even for a moment, that he might love her back. As Barrett had pointed out so scornfully, it had been a shipboard romance, no more.

Now it was ten o'clock of a bright, hard morning at the end of April, and Adrienne, taking a break from her voice exercises, had wandered to the window to gaze at the street below. Anything, she told herself bleakly, to take her thoughts off Kristian. . . .

The millinery shop directly across the street from the hotel had caught her attention. A huge glass case had been moved outside the shop and onto the sidewalk. Inside it she could see hats—a bevy of them, extravagant concoctions of ribbons and ostrich feathers and lace and velvet. Hats fit for a countess, she told herself, hats of which *Maman* had never seen the like—

"Well?" Behind her Barrett's voice cut through her revery like the sharp knife which *Maman* had used to bone fish. "And what are you doing, my dear wife, mooning out of the window like some common girl?"

She swallowed. "I've been working all morning, until my voice is hoarse. Now I'm looking over at that millinery shop. And the cabs—they look so grand as they rumble by. Oh, I would like to ride in one!"

"And where would you go, pray tell? Out gawking and gazing like a green ninny from the country? Surely you are superior to that! And there is work to do. Lines to memorize, voice inflections to get down, your accent to improve—"

"But, Barrett. I have been working—for days now! While we crossed the Atlantic I labored twelve, even fourteen hours a day. And I've made excellent progress, you've said so yourself."

"You've progressed, yes. But not far enough."

"But it's just for one afternoon," she pleaded. "That's all I ask, Barrett! I've never been to New York. I want to see it, to explore, to buy a new bonnet—"

"Good God, girl, must you be as empty-headed as any little fishwife? New bonnets, indeed! I want you to stay here in the room. I have much to do and arrange for us. I'll be back soon enough. If I am not, ring and have a meal sent up to you."

"But Barrett—"

She half-ran after him in frustration. It was unfair that he should be able to venture into this wonderful city while she should have to stay cooped up in the hotel like a prisoner!

But before she could begin to tell him so, he had limped to the dresser to take something wrapped in linen out of its top drawer. He stopped to examine the cloth wrapping. Then he thrust the small bundle into his pocket, checking to see that it rested there safely.

The Passion Star. Of course, Adrienne thought with a sinking heart. What else would Barrett handle with such care? And what did he intend to do with it? Surely he didn't plan to sell it!

She rushed forward impulsively and blocked his exit.

"Barrett, just what do you mean to arrange? Where are you going?"

Her husband's mouth twisted. "My plans for the day are none of your concern."

She thought of the sapphire, its deep, twilight blue, of the girl who had worn it to her death so bravely, and felt a wrench of anger that she could barely control.

"But, Barrett, it is my concern if you have the Passion Star with you! It's mine, my stone—*I gave it to you!*"

"If you gave it to me, then it is mine, not yours." He smiled at her triumphantly.

She edged back against the heavy hotel door. She could feel her heart begin to beat in slow, uneven thumps.

"But . . . you can't mean to sell it," she whispered.

His eyes avoided hers. "You forget, Adrienne, that

you gave this jewel to me in exchange for services rendered."

"Yes," she cried. "But you told me you were a collector. That night at the music hall you told me that, I thought you wished to add the Passion Star to your collection. I thought—"

Barrett's eyes mocked her. "Ah, yes, Adrienne, I am a collector. Didn't I boast to you of my Chinese snuff bottles, my Derby porcelain? But, unfortunately, there are times when even the most inveterate collector must have capital. And I fear this is one of those occasions. My remittance check is pitifully small. There will be much to spend it on here—travel, costumes, hotel bills, railroad fare—"

"But you can't take it!"

"Can't I? You just stay here in the hotel, Adrienne, and let me handle these things. It isn't your concern now. And if you'll kindly stand out of my way so that I may pass?"

She did not move.

Barrett shifted his good leg. "The Passion Star was your bride price, so to speak. Now it's mine, to do with as I will. And if I choose to sell it, I will."

She stared at him, her eyes dilated to their fullest. The Passion Star was *hers,* the price of her destroyed innocence, its purchase confirmed by her flight and exile. No enforced bargain could change that. Barrett might force her to let him use her body—might drive her to live out his dreams of stage triumphs that he could not fulfill himself. But no strength of his or promise of hers would part her now from the gem that had become a vital part of her being.

"You are not going to sell the Passion Star." The husky depth of her voice startled even Adrienne. She hurled herself against Barrett and snatched the gem from his grasp.

To her surprise, he staggered backward, wincing and letting out a cry of pain.

"My knee," he muttered. "Christ, girl, you knocked me off balance—my bad knee . . ."

Still blocking the door, Adrienne thrust the Passion Star into her bodice. She stared at her husband, a sick trembling racing through her body.

"This pendant is special to me. In a way, it *is* me. I may be your wife—God help me for that—but I will not let you take the Passion Star to a pawnshop and sell it for a fraction of its worth!"

Her husband's eyes darted around the room. There was a fine sheen of perspiration on his forehead. "You little bitch," he whispered.

Adrienne lifted her chin. "If I am a bitch," she said slowly, "then you helped to make me one. Barrett, I swear this. If you ever sell the Passion Star—if you even attempt to do so—then I will tell the world how you treated me on our wedding night, how you brutalized me as if I had been an animal. Is that the way you treated your other women, too? Is it, Barrett?"

She saw his lips press together.

She went on hurriedly. "And I'll also tell the theater world why you came to this country, and where you get your income—from a remittance check!"

She saw that she had reached him. Barrett's face, already pale from bad health, had blanched a sickly white.

"You wouldn't, you couldn't." His voice pleaded. "Adrienne, you don't know how gossip can spread in the theater. It's a small world, really, a tight little world. Talk travels like the pox! They'd laugh at me, all of them!"

"Then let them laugh."

"But to have them poking fun at me, making me their butt—girl, you don't know how vicious they can be!"

"As vicious as you are when you speak of your fellow actors? Oh, I understand well enough." Adrienne had not realized that she could speak so icily. Had it been those days of training with Barrett aboard the *Thermopylae* when she had discovered depths of ability within herself which she had not dreamed she possessed?

She heard her own voice go on in that same cold tone.

"I made a mistake in marrying you, Barrett, a dreadful mistake. I see that now. But it's too late. I am married to you, God help me, and there is nothing I can do now to change that. But I *can* change other things."

"What do you mean?"

She drew herself up. "You will continue to train me to become an actress, as we agreed. But there will be no more sleeping together. No more of—what goes on between a man and a wife."

"No more? But you are my w—"

A wild, angry power flowed through her, filling her with strength. "I am your wife from now on in name only!"

Barrett's tongue darted out to touch his lips. Drops of perspiration shone among the gray-black hairs of his mustache.

"If that's the case, my dear little whore-wife, then you must intend someone else to take my place. Who could it be? Your fine ship-board romance, Kristian King?"

She could feel herself tremble.

"No!" she snapped. "There's no one!"

He scowled at her. "I could leave you, Adrienne. Did you know that, you little fool? I could desert you here in New York, and let you fend for yourself as best you could. To ply your trade," he added scornfully. "Whatever profession you could muster."

Whore. Harlot. Trull. Like the memory of a nightmare, the old man's voice seemed to ring in Adrienne's mind. She faced her husband, feeling her heart pound in sickening lurches.

"No, Barrett, you won't desert me." She forced her voice into the full, rich tones that he had taught her. "You're a failure at acting, aren't you? A failure! Otherwise why would you be here in New York at all, worrying about money and thinking of pawning your wife's jewelry? Yet you grabbed at the chance to teach me. Why? I've been wondering about that and now I've come to a conclusion. I think you wish to make me the actor you can never be."

Barrett's face was white.

"I'm right, aren't I?" she pressed on relentlessly. "You value me—because of what I might become. So you will continue to stay married to me under whatever conditions I set—because it's only through me that you can ever be great."

"You bitch! You damned, calculating little bitch! I knew I should have left you in London—damn you!"

Then Barrett, in a burst of petulant strength, yanked her away from the doorway. He pushed past her, staggering on his bad leg, and slammed out of the hotel room.

Five minutes later, her heaving breath calmed somewhat, Adrienne leaned once more at the windowsill. She gazed downward at the ceaseless parade of landaus and buggies and horsecars, wondering where Barrett had gone. Was he headed for a theater somewhere, to make contacts for them, as he had said he would do? Had he sought out a drinking-saloon? Or was he with a woman?

She supposed it didn't really matter. In a way, Barrett was like some of the toughs she had encountered in the alleyways of Glasgow. Like bullies, there were people who would dominate others—until challenged. Then they would submit to a superior will.

Well, she thought grimly, she knew now that her will was strongest. Barrett *was* necessary to her. For all of his twisted ways, his sarcasm, his hatred of women, he was a gifted teacher of acting. Under his tutelage she had already learned much, and could learn a great deal more. Without him, she would not know where to go, or how to get started in the theater. Without him, she would have no chance.

As she pondered, Adrienne's eyes had fastened upon the street below. A movement caught her eye. Two young women, wearing fashionable gowns, were passing almost directly beneath her window. Behind them, burdened with packages, plodded a uniformed maidservant.

Adrienne's eyes followed their progress greedily.

Clothes, she thought with a lift of excitement. She

stared at the packages, wondering what was in them. One was obviously a bonnet-box; other parcels, wrapped with brown paper and string, were more mysterious. Whatever their contents, they held something wonderful, Adrienne was sure. Perhaps a lace-trimmed nightgown, as fragile as spider webs. Velvet or grosgrain ribbon to trim a mantle. Sumptuous fabrics, to be made up into ballgowns . . .

The three disappeared from sight around a corner. Adrienne sighed. She cupped her chin in her hands. How long would she have to stay here in the room? Given the rage in which he had left, she was sure that Barrett would be gone for many hours. And today she did not relish the thought of sitting here alone while, on the streets of New York, people rode in luxurious carriages or shopped.

She straightened up with sudden resolve. Why did she have to remain here in the hotel only because Barrett had told her to do so? She wasn't his prisoner! And especially not now, when the balance of power between them had shifted.

Besides, she assured herself quickly, she was to be an actress, was she not? As such, she would need fashionable clothing. Barrett had mentioned this several times, telling her that actresses were expected to provide their own costumes in the latest styles.

If this were the case, then surely Barrett would not object if she were to equip herself for her new career. If she shopped now, it would save time later, when he had arranged parts in a play for them and they were in a hurry.

Besides—she had rushed to the mirror now and was examining her own reflection, her cheeks reddening in growing excitement—besides, she *had* to go out. She couldn't possibly remain here in the hotel for another moment, not while New York waited for her.

She hurried about the room, combing out her hair until its pale strands glistened, then pinning it into the chignon, puffs and side-curls she had seen once in a ladies' magazine. From the wardrobe she selected her most elaborate bonnet, a creation adorned with a spray of flowers and black lace. Under it, her pale blond hair showed alluringly.

She shrugged into a new, blue mantle and fastened its front buttons. Then she spun out in front of the elaborately carved hotel mirror, and curtseyed to the girl who looked back at her.

How eager that girl looked! And yet . . . how regal, too. Adrienne narrowed her eyes at herself. Surely she looked grand enough to be the daughter of a countess. Unconsciously, she straightened her shoulders, arching her back proudly. Thus had Aurelia Prendergast stood. Thus had the countess swept about the room, her carriage proudly graceful. . . .

On her way out of the room, Adrienne paused in sudden dismay. She had no money. No money at all.

Tears of consternation sprang to her eyes. To have no funds in a city like New York, where stores and shops abounded on every side—it wasn't to be borne, not today.

Five minutes later she had ransacked the large bureau where she and Barrett had stored the clothing from their trunks, and had unearthed seven pennies and a half-dollar. Hidden among Barrett's clothing had also been two finely made amber glass whisky flasks, each one embossed with the raised seal of the maker. Both had been full, the corks still in place.

She thrust the coins into the small cloth purse she carried and again headed toward the door. How much would a half-dollar buy? It was about the size of a florin, a two-shilling piece—surely not much. But blithely she pushed away her misgivings. It would buy something.

Twenty minutes later, she was strolling along Fifth Avenue and yearning into the shop windows, wishing that *Maman* could be here with her, to see and admire, too. At last she found herself standing in front of a large department store.

Bedesco's, said the sign painted in huge white letters on the brick front of the building. *Dry goods, sundries, ladies notions and dresses. Finest Quality.*

A woman emerged from the wide wooden front

door, bearing an armload of packages. Adrienne drew a deep breath, caught the door before it had closed, and went in.

The store was large. Its walls, pillars, and molded tin ceiling were all painted a brilliant white. Shelves and counters bristled with a dazzling array of goods, everything arranged, whenever possible, in symmetrical pyramids. It would almost be a shame, Adrienne thought in wonderment, to buy one of the shining jars of perfume or unguents, and spoil the carefully stacked designs.

A network of metal tubing ran upward from each counter to a track along the ceiling. Adrienne saw a salesclerk, dressed in sober black with a white apron, push money into a metal cylinder. The tube whizzed it upward; minutes later, it flew downward again. Smiling, the clerk took out the change and gave it to her customer, as if this mechanical miracle were the most ordinary thing in the world.

Adrienne wandered about, feeling as if she were lost in a wonderland. Awed, she touched objects—alligator purses, tortoiseshell bands for the hair, gauze cravat bows and Swiss muslin breakfast caps, trimmings and ribbons, buttons made of crochet and jet and bugle.

She paused to look at a hammock, slung on display from two hooks in the ceiling. She wondered what *Maman* would think of such an object. When had *Maman* ever had time to lie down and rest? No, *Maman*'s days had always been filled with work. And when she did leave the crowded, two-room flat, it had been to enter the gloomy, moisture-laden stone Close, which reeked of slop water and animal dung. Where in such a world would there have been a place to hang a hammock?

"Miss? You are interested in purchasing that fine hammock?"

"I—"

"That, of course, is only a display model. We have others on the second floor in our storeroom, and I would be happy to get one for you."

"Oh, no, I really couldn't—"

"Well, then. If you are only looking . . ." The salesclerk's face expressed scorn and disapproval. "Then, if you'll excuse me, I have a charge customer to help."

"Oh."

Adrienne backed away. She felt her face flame as if she had been caught doing something unspeakable. She did not know what a charge customer was. And she did not belong here in this grand store—not really.

Or did she? Surely things were different now! Wasn't she Adrienne Gill, the daughter of a Scottish countess and soon to be an actress? She caught her breath, gave the salesclerk a haughty look as she imagined Aurelia Prendergast might have done, and turned away.

At the far end of the store was a counter displaying lace collars. Adrienne paused to look, drawn by the lacy delicacy of the fichus, confections so laden with frills that it seemed as if no human woman could really wear such things.

Again she was forced to think of *Maman,* plying her needle all day in the dank little flat in Glasgow. *Maman* had never owned such a lovely neckpiece in her life, or even dreamed of doing so. She had only sewn them. Yet here were fifty extravagant collars here in this department store in New York, arranged on a counter top in almost military precision.

"May I help you today?" A clerk came forward. But where the other salesperson had been unpleasantly intimidating, this one looked friendly. In her mid-thirties, she had wide brown eyes and chestnut hair pulled back from her face in neat, looped braids. Like the other clerks, she wore a black dress and starched white apron. A watch was pinned to her bodice front, its chain looped at her waist. A neatly lettered name-tag pinned to her collar proclaimed her to be Miss Fanny Pepper.

"Perhaps." Adrienne could not help smiling at the woman. "Could you tell me what these are?"

She pointed to a display on the lower shelf of the glass case. Small, oval, lace-encrusted objects were arranged in rows, looking as if they could have no other function than to be beautiful.

"Those?" Fanny Pepper laughed. "Oh, those are

shoe rosettes. Aren't they funny, with all that satin and lace? Can you imagine really wearing them? But women do. They wear them to balls and fancy dress parties. Me, I think such fripperies are fit only for the stage."

"The stage?" Adrienne looked up with interest.

"Oh, yes, indeed." Fanny Pepper leaned forward. As she did so, the sleeve of her sober black dress knocked askew the arrangement of collars. "Oops! I'd better set this right before old Mrs. Carlson sees me. We've got to keep these things absolutely straight or she docks our pay, the old witch."

"You said the stage," Adrienne prompted, amused at the woman's light-hearted cheer.

"Yes, well, you might not know it to look at me, but I had a part as an understudy once in *The Black Crook* and even got to dance for two weeks before the play closed. They had four hundred and seventy-five performances! They were a French ballet troupe, fifty dancers stranded here when the Academy of Music burned down, and a musical play was written for them, with dancing. Oh, it was wonderful! We shocked the whole city, we did."

The chestnut-haired clerk smiled happily. "Of course, I haven't danced much since then. I twisted my ankle last fall and had to quit. Now I'm training it, and exercising, and hope to be back on the boards soon, God willing, before I grow too old."

She exhaled a gusty sigh.

"But you work *here*," Adrienne breathed.

"Oh, yes." Fanny Pepper shrugged. "Well, I have to eat, don't I? I have the nastiest habit of wanting my bacon and eggs regularly."

Adrienne, forgetting that she had come here to shop, stared at the other woman in fascination. "I'm going to be an actress," she volunteered. "At least, I hope I am."

Fanny Pepper gave her an appraising look. "Well, you do have the looks for it, I'll say that. That hair of yours is so striking, you'd be remembered, that's sure. And you've a good, rich, carrying voice. It'd be heard in the back row of any theater. Could be you'd do all right. If you could get a part, that is."

"Will that be hard to do?"

"Oh, yes. I've been trying for six months to get a decent role. Of course, I hear that Wallacks is casting this week again, and there are always the road companies. If you don't mind running yourself utterly to exhaustion and playing every opera house from Podunk to Kalamazoo."

"I wouldn't mind. I'd do anything to be on the stage!" Adrienne said it intensely.

"Anything?" Fanny's mouth grew sober. "Well, there are some who would go that far, yes, indeed. But me, I won't. That's why I'm here at Bedesco's selling lace collars and shoe rosettes."

"Oh." Adrienne shifted her feet uneasily. Quickly she picked up one of the collars, holding its intricate lacework in the palm of her hand. Surely Barrett could not object if she bought just one lace collar. It was so small. . . .

"What is a charge?" she blurted out. "I heard a clerk say that and I wondered what it was."

"Why, a charge is when you give your husband's name and the store sends a bill for what you buy," the clerk explained.

"Oh, then I'll do it." Adrienne thrust out the lace collar. "I'll have this one, and—and that one over there, the one with the ribbons. My husband is Barrett Kendall, of course, and we're staying at the St. Denis. Have the bill sent there, please, along with my packages."

She was Aurelia Prendergast, imperious countess ordering a few small items out of a limitless purse. "And I believe I will buy a wrap to go along with these. Over in the other aisle I saw a cashmere mantle, that was really very pretty. . . ."

By the time Adrienne emerged onto the sidewalk again, she had spent a sizeable amount of Barrett's money and was giddy with the excitement of it. Let him scold her if he chose! Surely when she modeled the wraps for him, and unwrapped the length of satin *merveilleux,* he would approve. And if he should not . . . well, she didn't care. She could control Barrett. Hadn't she proved that earlier today?

She walked back to the hotel, imagining herself dreamily as the star of *The Black Crook,* hearing in her mind the thunderous applause. The sidewalk was full of pedestrians—businessmen in black broadcloth suits, ladies in sober walking dresses, a vendor of hot roasted chestnuts, a blind beggar singing for coins.

It was as she turned a corner that Adrienne glimpsed a tall man with honey-colored hair and an easy, graceful, loping walk. And—yes—when he turned his face to one side she saw the carven cheekbones, the somber eyes set beneath ridges of bone. . . .

"Kristian!"

She lifted the hem of her gown and began to run along the sidewalk, darting past two middle-aged matrons, who turned to stare at her curiously. It was seldom that a lady raced along the pavement in such abandon.

"Kristian!" she shrieked. "Oh, please, *please* stop!"

But Kristian, if indeed it was he, continued to stride through the crowd, not even turning to see who had called him.

Frantically, Adrienne raced forward, her fingers clutching at the fabric of her gown so that she would not trip on its voluminous folds. She skidded among the black-clad men, the women with their string shopping bags.

"Kristian! Please, I didn't mean it—I didn't mean to slap you! Please, just stop and talk to me—"

On the contrary, dear Adrienne, I doubt that there is anything that would make you throw yourself overboard —even love.

Kristian had said that to her. But surely he had not meant it. He couldn't have, he had only said it out of the depths of his anger. Because she did love him. She knew it now, knew it in the depths of her bones, in her flesh and heart and mind and brain . . .

"Kristian!"

But the man had disappeared. Adrienne stood alone on the sidewalk, buffeted by the crowds of passersby. A great pain, like animal claws, seemed to tear at her heart.

Chapter 10

"And what, pray tell, are those?"

Barrett Kendall's voice was full of scorn. He pointed to the pile of parcels which Adrienne had placed on the bed after they had been delivered by Bedesco's.

"Those are my purchases, of course."

She regarded him coolly. It was seven o'clock. She had just finished a meal brought up to her by a black-clad waiter: roast beef and poached haddock in wine sauce, served on a tray set with shining silver and cutlery, a starched linen napkin twisted into an elaborate cone. She had spent most of the meal pretending that she had always dined in such luxury.

"I see that," Barrett said. "And just exactly what did you use for money?"

"I charged them," she admitted.

"Charged!"

"Yes, I told them at the department store that you were—that we were staying here at the St. Denis. They sent the bill here."

"Here! My God, Adrienne, don't you realize—" Barrett bit off the words. Then he limped to the bed and began riffling contemptuously through the packages. "Collars!" he exclaimed. "A mantle, for Lord's sake. And satin! Do you think that I am made of money?"

"I bought them because of my career," she told him defiantly. "You said that I had to provide my own costumes, did you not?"

Somehow, subtly, the balance of power between

them had again shifted. Barrett grabbed up the lace fichu from its wrappings and stood wadding it in his hands, as if he would like to rip it in two. Then, with a sudden, vicious motion, he flung it across the room. It landed at the base of the ornate mahogany dressing cabinet, whose interior held space for towels, glasses, brushes, even a chamber pot.

"Adrienne, why do you think I wanted to sell your precious Passion Star? For the pleasure of it? I need the money, you damned little fool! Our passage on the *Thermopylae* took most of my remittance. Our hotel bill—if I am lucky enough to be able to pay it—will take the rest."

She stared at him. Her heart was sinking. Already the fine meal she had eaten seemed to churn unpleasantly in her belly.

"But—" she began.

"What is wrong with you?" he interrupted. "You imperiously order me not to sell that damned sapphire, then you go out and spend money like some silly matron half-crazed with the idea of twenty dollars in her purse."

Adrienne gazed at him, remembering the desperation of being stranded in London with no money. She thought of the flat in Glasgow, of *Maman's* hands, reddened and ruined with hard work. In the department store, for a few hours, she had been able to forget such things. . . .

Barrett's voice still prodded at her. "You married a man living on the edge of financial disaster, my girl. A remittance man, as you were so very kind as to point out to me. So don't make the disaster worse by profligate spending!"

Adrienne said nothing. She could feel the deep wash of blood spread up from her neck to her face. She stood staring at the empty dinner tray, the array of crystal goblets, the delicate English porcelain plates, all of them bulwarks against poverty.

Barrett limped to the dresser, jerked open a drawer and produced one of the flasks of whisky. From the dressing cabinet he took two glasses. He sloshed liquid into them.

"Well, my dear, here it is. Demon whisky, the panacea for all of man's troubles. Drown your sorrows, girl—or celebrate, I don't care which."

"Celebrate?" she asked dully.

Barrett raised his glass and drained off its contents in one swallow. "I've gotten us parts in a play. That's what you wanted, isn't it?"

She stared at him, not touching her glass. "You got me a part?" she whispered.

"Yes. You're to be Eliza in *Uncle Tom's Cabin*. It isn't the prize role, of course—that one is Eva, that gushingly sweet, simpering child. Topsy is a good part, too, if you can play humor. But Eliza isn't bad, and I took the liberty of assuring Dustin Cerny, the manager, that you'd do splendidly."

"But . . . I'm to be in a real play? In *Uncle Tom's Cabin?*"

"Yes. Good God, girl, don't act as if I'd parted the sea for you! This is a road company, cheap, slapped-together, running on sweat and borrowed money. We'll be traveling all over the United States, playing opera houses in towns so small that no one has ever heard of them. But it will be experience for you. Besides, it was all I could get."

Barrett poured himself another glass of whisky, his hand shaking.

Adrienne gazed at him, still trying to absorb the news. A part! A real role in a real production! Absently she lifted her own glass and took a swallow. The alcohol, pungent and fiery, burned its way down. She coughed and choked.

"But they haven't even seen me," she said at last, recovering. "How do you know they even want me?"

"They want you, all right. Their Eliza is very pregnant and they're desperate for a replacement. And I'm to be Uncle Tom—I've played the part before, it's a specialty of mine, and I'm the best damned Tom they're ever going to get and they know it. I told them you came with the bargain."

"Oh."

So they didn't really want her; they had merely taken her because Barrett had forced them to. Still, it was a role, Adrienne assured herself. It was a chance. And surely she could prove herself . . .

"I assured them your background, as the daughter of a countess, is impeccable," he went on. "As for your experience, I told them you'd played Juliet in London, Glasgow and Edinburgh, where you received thunderous applause."

"Juliet? But I only practiced the role aboard the *Thermopylae!*"

"Do they have to know that? I assure you, the role of Eliza is very easy. You won't even have to wear blackface. Eliza is supposed to be the wife of a slave, but the playwright is careful to announce that she only has a 'few drops of Negro blood' in her veins. Which means that she looks as white as you do."

"I can't believe it." Still carrying her glass, Adrienne sat down heavily in one of the ornate chairs.

"Well, it's true. We'll travel until we're gray with weariness, until we don't know what city we're in, and don't care. As for your damned collars and satin and wraps and God-knows-what-all, you'll have to take them all back. Eliza wears a simple dress, not fripperies—you won't need them. Unless, of course, you wish me to go out and sell that damned sapphire of yours."

"No!" Her hand flew to her bodice where the Passion Star still rested. "No, I won't let you sell it. I don't care how poor we are."

Barrett grimaced. "We're poor, all right. In fact, we may just have to slip out of our room here at the St. Denis in the middle of the night. Like thieves." His expression was bitter. "Like thieves and felons. What do you think of that, Miss Adrienne Gill?"

Dear Maman, Adrienne wrote. *I have a role in a real play. I am to be Eliza in* Uncle Tom's Cabin! *Barrett says there are dozens of such road companies touring the country, and we are to be one of them. I have sat up for two nights memorizing the lines and the stage business, with Barrett's help. Thanks to him, I will not be coming to the production as a complete amateur. . . .*

They spent three days in rehearsal, going over and

over the play in a dusty warehouse located on Cortlandt Street off Broadway, with chalk lines marked on the floor to indicate the sets. The manager, Dustin Cerny, told them he could not afford even a day's rehearsal time in a theater.

Cerny, tall, thin, almost totally bald, sat straddling a wooden chair and shouting at them.

"Topsy, for God's sake, you're not from Brooklyn," he would shout menacingly at the young girl, Jennie Maud, who played the role of the young slave. "So change your accent, girl, and change it now—not that the hayseeds in Ohio will ever know the difference."

"Eliza!" he grated at Adrienne. "Have you never been on a stage before? Project your voice, dammit, project! I want every soul in the theater to be able to hear you, including those in the loge and balconies."

"Yes, sir."

"And get yourself a black wig for this part, do you hear me? Our dear Eliza may carry precious little black blood in her veins, but our audiences will certainly look askance if her hair is the color of wheat."

"Yes, sir."

"A curly black wig, my dear. And see that you have it by tomorrow."

The majority of the cast, she learned, had already been playing in *Uncle Tom's Cabin* for some months now, and thus were bored with the rehearsals and impatient with her when she missed a cue.

"Will I ever get it all?" she exploded in discouragement to Barrett on the second afternoon. "Cerny shouts orders at me until I want to shriek back at him. As for the rest of the cast, they keep looking at me as if they expect me to fail!"

"You won't fail," Barrett assured her sharply. "If you do, I'll ship you back to London on the first boat. I'll wager there are people there who would be overjoyed to find an escaped felon—and the Passion Star—back within their grasp."

It was true. Adrienne shuddered, biting at her lower lip until it stung. She made up her mind that she would work doubly hard. Let Barrett taunt her, let Cerny shout at her, let the cast of *Uncle Tom's Cabin* give her as many sidelong looks as they pleased. She, Adrienne, was going to be the best Eliza they had ever seen.

On the third day, Cerny informed the cast that they would do their first show across the river in Brooklyn. That evening, two trunks were delivered to their hotel room, black, shiny, square-cornered, each equipped with leather straps, two trays, hardwood slats and an iron bottom. Adrienne stared at them, feeling an almost irresistible uplift of excitement, so strong that she wanted to sing, to dance wildly about the room.

"Our trunks!" she cried in delight, remembering *Maman*'s stories.

"Yes." Barrett said it shortly. "And you had better see to it that yours is packed properly. You'll be opening and shutting that trunk hundreds of times in the next few months. Everything—including that new black wig of yours—must be at your fingertips, ready to grab at a moment's notice."

But Adrienne refused to allow his dour tone to spoil her pleasure. She was to have a genuine theater trunk—just like Adrienne La Rivière and all of the other actresses about whom *Maman* had told tales. She was to be a real actress! And some day, she assured herself, she would have not just one theater trunk but dozens of them, as did the famous actresses of the day.

"You're destined, Adrienne," Maman had said. *"I really believe that. Destined . . ."*

Thus began the most exhausting and hectic period of Adrienne's life, a year which was always to be associated in her mind with shabby theaters, dingy hotels and dressing rooms, and Barrett's voice lashing at her, sharp with sarcasm.

Uncle Tom's Cabin, the popular play itself, was like nothing Adrienne had ever imagined. It was full of sentimental lines, escaped slaves, Eliza floating across the Ohio River on a cake of ice, and mellow spiritual music. In some cities, the troupe also staged a "Tom parade," marching down dusty main streets in wagons rented for the occasion by a harried Dustin Cerny.

"Ah, a glorious spectacle of American life," Barrett would growl, drawing giggles from little Jennie Maud who, as Topsy, was one of the highlights of the parade with her mugging faces and "breakdown" dance. The finale of the parade, however, was Barrett as Uncle Tom. Splendid in blackface make-up and smiling benignly, he rode in a wagon with the twelve-year-old daughter of Dustin Cerny, who played the saintly Eva.

Much of it made Adrienne think of Xenos Shane. One day, in Ohio, she realized why. It was all flamboyance, all showmanship and tricks and illusion.

And yet—when they were finally in a theater or opera house and the gas footlights were hissing, and she came onstage in Act One, Scene One, to speak Eliza's first lines, the magic began.

Out beyond the footlights was the audience. At first they were merely cabbage faces, a noise of rustling, of feet shifting and coughs and programs rattling. Then it would begin, the feeling of something more, of a *presence*. And suddenly there would be a magnetic connection between herself and those people out there, so powerful that she could feel an almost physical wrench when the curtain came down and the play was over.

For a few hours, something magic had happened. Something not explainable in words, but nonetheless there. Even though she played a minor role, Adrienne had become something larger than herself. There was nothing like it, and there never would be.

She was an actress. The audience, by their applause, by their very presence, said so.

And some day, she vowed to herself, she would go far beyond *Uncle Tom's Cabin*. She would be a star on her own. She would make it happen.

Work. Disillusionment. Six one-nighters a week, with an occasional two-night stand. By their eighth week on the road, they had played in more than forty towns, places like Albany, Sodus, Clinton, Keyport, Jewett City, Putnam, Togus, Saco, Hope Valley, Bennington.

After a time, all of the cities blended together and all of the main streets came to look the same. Always there

149

were the dusty buildings, the livery stables, barber shops, dry-goods stores, waterworks and gasworks, the people gathered to watch the actors come into town, to gawk and to admire.

The trains, too, were the same: hot, dusty, smelly, undependable and inconvenient. Adrienne began to feel as if she had never lived any other way, as if she had spent her entire life jouncing on a wooden slat seat, struggling to do the voice exercises which Barrett continued relentlessly to set her.

It took long hours to get from town to town. The railroad cars, swaying and rattling on bumpy tracks, were filled with the stench of coal smoke, hair pomade, and human perspiration. Male passengers chewed tobacco and spat out the fluids, and usually the brown spittle landed on the floor instead of in the spittoons provided.

If they kept the windows closed, the car became stifling with heat and odor. But if they dared to open a window, in flew cinders and dust. Adrienne learned to blot cinders out of her eyes, to wear a long wrap to protect her gown, to wash her face whenever she was lucky enough to encounter a washstand with running water, and to look away from the tobacco juice on the floor.

It was the trains which set the pace for their entire lives. After going to bed at midnight or one A.M., they had to struggle groggily out of bed at dawn, because that was when the trains left. Most railroad lines were short, and there were many "broken night jumps," when Adrienne would be roused by Barrett at two in the morning to change trains, so sleepy that she was barely aware of what she did.

The trains were usually late and frequently broken down, which meant that the troupe had to spend hours sitting in drafty train stations, tensely worrying. Would they miss the connecting train—the only one which ran that day—and arrive too late for the night's show, thereby losing a day's pay?

It was the railroads, too, which determined their choice of hotel. Because it was so vital to make the trains—and not to oversleep—they settled for the hotel

150

nearest the station. This usually meant rooms which were sleazy and dirty.

Beds sagged, or were lumpy, or possessed unwashed sheets. Sometimes, to Adrienne's shrinking horror—*Maman* had always fought such dirtiness with a bitter vengeance—there were bedbugs.

In the halls, doors slammed and drunks sang. Sometimes they arrived at a room to discover a window broken or that there were no closets, or that the hotel possessed only public baths.

To Adrienne's amazement, these conditions were accepted stoically by the other members of the company. To her, they were a constant source of dismay. Had she come thousands of miles from Glasgow, so dank and burdened with human life, only to meet poverty again?

One day in the little town of Sodus, New York, she rebelled when she discovered that their room had no window shades or curtains and that she would have to undress in the dark if she did not wish the entire main street to gaze in upon her.

"Barrett, may I have no privacy? And will we never stay in a hotel which is clean?" Her voice rose. "I am so tired of dirty bedding! I can't stand to sleep in a bed which has been occupied by a stranger before me—"

"Don't be such a fool," Barrett said harshly. "These are part of the hazards of being an actress. Do you hear Jennie Maud complaining? Or even Dustin Cerny's daughter, young as she is? I must say *she* is a real trouper."

"I'm a trouper, too!" Adrienne shouted. "It's just that I don't like dirt and I can't stand being poor!"

She stopped, horrified at how close she had come to revealing her true background to Barrett. But he had not seemed to notice. Now he shrugged, taking off his coat to arrange it carefully over the room's one chair.

"My dear, you left a luxurious life in Scotland, did you not? More's the pity, I must say—any sensible girl would have stayed at home and learned to endure her lot somehow. But you chose to be an actress. And now you must accept the bad with the good."

"Oh, I know it!" she snapped.

She flung herself across the room, snatching up the worn pillow case from their bed. Angrily she draped it over the empty curtain rod at the bare window.

"There," she said. "Now no one will look in."

For a moment she stood holding the pillow case aside to stare down at the main street, where a middle-aged man stood watering two mares at a horse trough. His movements were weary, automatic. Adrienne caught her breath. Would that man be a part of tonight's audience? Would her performance somehow cause him to laugh, or feel excitement, change some aspect of his dull life?

She let the pillow case fall over the window again. She straightened her shoulders, lifting her chin with new determination.

"I do wish to be an actress," she told Barrett grimly. "I *will* be one. And I won't complain any more about our hotel rooms, I promise. And . . . and please give me some new voice exercises for tonight. I wish more work to do, harder work!"

Theaters. Even the smallest of towns had one, glorifying it with the grandiose name "opera house," although no opera had ever been seen there. Some were sumptuous marvels of painted plaster, gilt, cut-glass chandeliers, elaborate box seats and imported carpeting. Others were small, rickety wooden fire hazards. Sometimes the opera house was located on the second or third floor, over a store. Sometimes it was sandwiched between a feed store and a livery stable.

Adrienne and Barrett would arrive at the theater as early as they could, sharing a hack with other members of the company. First they would go to look at the list posted by Cerny on the callboard to see which dressing rooms they had been given.

Usually, Adrienne learned, the dressing rooms turned out to be in the basement or cellar. Often she found herself trying to struggle into her Eliza costume in a room situated next to the boiler, the air there so hot that her make-up would be running with perspiration before she could get her dress fastened.

152

Frequently there were exposed plumbing pipes in the ceiling, and stagehands tramping overhead would send bits of plaster and whitewash flaking down on her head.

Gas lighting provided uncertain illumination. The fixtures, installed with metal guardwork around the jet of flame to protect costumes and hair from catching fire, often seemed placed deliberately as far away from mirrors as possible. Clothes racks were rows of nails pounded into the wall, or consisted of a scaffolding made of leftover plumbing pipes. Often there was trash on the floor from previous companies.

But worst of all was the frequent lack of washing facilities.

"I hate it," she exploded to Barrett one night, breaking her resolve not to complain. "Why can't they at least provide washstands for us? Do they think we are animals?"

Barrett grimaced. "In England, actors were once classified with vagrants, beggars, and trollops. We're still considered of the lowest social order. I suppose it is assumed by the theater builders that we don't wash as often as church-going mortals."

"*I* want to wash! I was brought up to be clean!"

In Kalamazoo, Michigan, Adrienne finally rebelled. Before the night's show she rushed out to a department store and returned with a pair of Turkish wall hangings and a rug woven in bright shades of red and blue. She also bought a hammer and nails, and a metal box with a lid.

That night she nailed the hangings to the wall of the narrow, cluttered women's dressing room. On the floor she placed the colorful rug.

"What are those?" giggled little Jennie Maud, the girl who played Topsy. "Are you planning to set up housekeeping here?"

"No," Adrienne snapped, "I'm simply tired of looking at other people's dirt. I want to look at some beauty for a change." She brandished the metal box. "And I've bought something else. I've a damp rag in here so that I can wash my face when they don't provide us with any water. I'm never going home with my face covered with make-up again."

Jennie's eyes widened. Then she giggled again.

"Well, you're going to be mighty clean, I can see that. 'Course, it's going to be a lot of trouble to lug them rugs and stuff with you everywhere you go."

Adrienne lifted her chin. "I'll manage. If necessary, I'll buy another trunk. I just want something pretty to look at—and I don't see why I can't have it."

She was gratified when Jennie Maud gave her a look of respect. After that she was regularly visited by the other members of the company, who came to scoff and remained to finger the colorful wall hangings, or to ask to borrow the damp cloth she carried.

The company, Adrienne learned one day, had been in desperate straits before she and Barrett had joined it. The man who had played Uncle Tom had gone on a drinking bout and disappeared one night in New York. As for the woman who had played Eliza, Madeline Demoro, the wife of an actor in the company, she was expecting a baby and could no longer go on the stage.

Now Madeline served as wardrobe mistress and assistant stage manager, and rode the bumpy trains and endured the hotel rooms with stoic indifference.

It was from Madeline that Adrienne learned more of the difficulties of touring. According to Madeline, it was a life of crushing loneliness. You went from strange town to strange town. You walked into a store or hotel or restaurant, and were seen not as a person, but only as an actress.

"Oh, yes," Madeline remarked dryly. "They all love to look at your clothes, to admire you or compliment you. But then they're done with you, and you go back to your hotel room and you're alone again with your knitting—if you're lucky enough to know how to knit!"

Sometimes actors—especially the men—were not alone. Men, Madeline Demoro implied, had it much easier than the women. There were usually eager town girls, delighted to be in the company of a handsome actor. There were saloons and drinking places where a male actor could find, for a few hours, companionship and forgetfulness.

For the women, however, life was harder. Bars were

not open to them, and the townspeople looked on them with suspicion. Most of the actresses, according to Madeline, spent their nights alone, reading or writing letters, safely away from the eyes of their easily shocked public.

"Attachments? Love affairs?" Madeline shrugged bitterly. "How can an actress afford them? If she falls in love with an actor, he leaves her to go on tour with another company. If he's a townsman, she's the one who has to leave for the next city on the road. And if she gets pregnant"— Madeline glanced down at her own rounded belly—"why, there goes her career, smack into a pile of dirty diapers!"

Drinking, too, sometimes became a problem for the women.

"What else can we do?" Madeline demanded. "Sit alone in our rooms and ache for a man? Drinking is a real pitfall for an actress, God knows. It will ruin your looks eventually. Then where will you end up? Marrying some hayseed farmer?" Her face twisted. "Or going to work in a brothel? Oh, yes," she added, "there's always that for an actress. Half the townsfolk think that's our natural place anyway."

"Don't let your husband make you pregnant," she advised one morning as they sat in a train station in Bridgeport, Connecticut. On a bench near them, a mother and two daughters dozed. "A baby is death for an actress. Of course, you can always get an abortion—if you can find a doctor or nurse in one of these damned towns who'll do it for you. Best thing is to use a pessary, and God knows I wish I had."

Adrienne nodded, trying to seem worldly, although she had no idea what a pessary was.

"Those women"—Madeline made a contemptuous gesture which included the three sleeping women passengers and, indeed, the entire female population of Bridgeport—"don't know anything, anything at all, and nobody wants them to know. Why, there's a shield men can use, made of the dry gut of a sheep . . ."

She laughed bitterly. "But does any woman ever learn of such things? No. The churchmen think it's improper and ungodly even to mention such devices. Ha! They never lost a job because of something they carried in their belly."

Again Adrienne nodded. She thought of *Maman,* perpetually struggling to take care of her children. Anyway, she assured herself, she herself could not possibly be pregnant. Didn't she and Barrett manage to sleep each night without touching?

A week later, one night after a performance, she was horrified to discover Barrett looming over her bed.

She had gone to sleep early, exhausted by the full week of traveling, and by the demands of the show, which had been playing each night to a packed house. She had awakened with the uneasy feeling that something was wrong.

"Barrett!" She turned over in bed, opened her eyes, and gave a startled cry. "Barrett, oh, you frightened me. What are you doing? Have you been drinking? You smell of it."

"And what's wrong with taking a few drinks?" He came closer to her. She had never heard his voice so bitter. "I hate these damned towns! You're only real when you're onstage—the rest of the time they barely speak to you."

Madeline had said these same things, only in different words. Adrienne stirred uneasily, feeling the mattress move as her husband crawled in beside her. Then his hand touched her thigh. Instantly she froze.

"Adrienne." Was there appeal in his voice, or simply a demand?

"Your promise," she whispered in a choked voice. "You swore you wouldn't touch me."

There was a silence, and then her husband's voice changed to its customary harshness. The appeal in it—if there had been any—was quite gone.

"Damn you, girl. Damn you, I won't be held back from what's mine."

His fingers closed over her flesh, sliding up her leg and to the juncture of her thighs, pinching, squeezing, kneading her flesh. Adrienne stiffened, wild memories swirling through her mind. Xenos Shane's heavy body pounding over hers. The terrible moments aboard the *Thermopylae* when Barrett himself had taken her as if she were no more than a female animal. . . .

Desperately she fought him, with words and slaps.

"Barrett! Barrett . . . don't! Didn't I say I'd tell—I'll tell them all, they'll laugh at you!"

"Will they?" Now he had pinioned her to the mattress with his arms, while his mouth devoured her breasts, her nipples. "No, my dear, they won't laugh, because *you won't tell anyone*. You are a wife who shares a hotel room with her husband but won't consent to lie with him—oh, no, it's not me they'll laugh at. It's you. You are cold, icy, passionless. . . ."

Silently, locked in the sleazy hotel room with the sound of drunken laughter in the hall, they battled. Desperately Adrienne kicked out, hitting Barrett in his injured knee. He uttered a cry of pain. Then, in a quick movement he had thrust her legs apart and entered her. He shuddered in climax almost at once.

The bully, she thought in despair, has his own stubborn strength after all.

Chapter 11

Life went on. Sometimes, while sitting in a train station, Adrienne discovered a newspaper someone had left on a seat. In September, 1871, she read that Augustin Daly had opened another of his plays, *Divorce,* and it was having a successful run. *East Lynne,* a play adapted from a novel by Mrs. Henry Wood, was touring the country, wildly successful. The company began to whisper enviously of returning to New York, to talk of next season, next year.

In October came the Chicago fire. It seemed to Adrienne that it would be better to experience such a concentrated and colorful disaster than to endure her own existence: waking at dawn to struggle out of bed and rush to the train station; sitting in a jouncing car, grimly repeating the voice exercises which Barrett had set her; then arriving at the next town, which looked dismayingly like its predecessor, hurrying to the theater to look it over before the night's performance.

After the show, she would stumble back to whatever shabby hotel room they had taken. Then there was a new ritual—a swallow or two from Barrett's whisky flask.

She was not quite sure how the custom had begun. Perhaps it had started on one of the nights when Barrett had imposed his sexual will on her. Or after one of her nightmares of Glasgow, of Devin lying so still and cold, pennies laid over his eyes to hold them shut.

At any rate, the whisky, throbbing through her veins, seemed to drop a soft, gray veil between her and her longing for Kristian King, between her and her hatred for the man to whom she was married. With a swallow or two of the aromatic Scotch whisky, she could begin to relax the tense muscles of her body. Eventually she could sleep, and dream but little.

In December came a break from their routine. By a stroke of luck, Dustin Cerny had been able to book them for four nights at the Detroit Opera House.

The company was jubilant. Now, at last, there would be time to launder clothing and have it dry properly; time to sleep long, delicious hours, to play cards, to wander about the city, or shop. It was as close to a vacation as they would get.

Detroit, built on flat land beside the wide Detroit river, was a manufacturing town of nearly 80,000 people. It was a mixture of buildings—gracious stone churches, stolid red-brick factories, shabby frame buildings built next to the ostentatious new homes of the rich.

Woodward Avenue, lined with brick buildings fitted with awnings and adorned with signs proclaiming *Wholesale Grocers, Wholesale Millinery,* and *Carriage Furnishing Goods,* was the main thoroughfare. Shade trees, now in December skeletal and bare, dotted its expanse. Its surface was paved with a bumpy, dusty surface of decaying cedar blocks. Down its center ran horsecar tracks, each car pulled by a weary animal wearing a jingling bell on its collar to warn pedestrians and other vehicles out of the way. The horses' ironshod feet clattered over the cobbles which had been laid between the rails.

But Adrienne was in no mood to enjoy the street railway, or to go shopping when Jennie Maud begged her. She had something more pressing on her mind: the cessation of her monthly cycle.

It should have arrived as usual. But it had not.

She was familiar enough with *Maman*'s pregnancies to know exactly what this meant, and the thought filled her with a sick dread. No, she told herself desperately, there must be some mistake. She couldn't be expecting Barrett's baby! She wasn't!

But still she found no need for the clean rags all

women kept for this time of month. She was beginning to be plagued, too, by nausea in the mornings. Thus far she had been able to conceal her condition from Barrett—he seemed barely to look at her these days—but she knew it could not be much longer before even he would discover what was bothering her.

On the second day of their tour in Detroit, it began to sleet. Ice rattled dismally on the windows of their quarters at the Michigan Exchange Hotel. It was a room of better quality than most, for Adrienne, rebelling, had insisted that for once they deserved a few days of comparative luxury.

Although it was still only late afternoon, the sky had grown ominously dark. Barrett limped restlessly about the room, pacing back and forth. He stopped every few moments to stare out of the window at the street, where a brewer's big horses drew huge vehicles loaded with kegs of beer, and carts and buggies battled for road space.

In a moment, she felt sure, he would leave to seek what amusements he could find in the city. Drinking, card games, women—she was not sure what Barrett did in these restless moods. And she did not care.

Now her husband made an irritable noise. "God, you're quiet," he accused suddenly. "You give me the megrims, Adrienne. You're like a ghost these days! Don't you like Michigan?"

"It's very cold," she replied, saying the first thing that came into her head.

"Cold? Ah, but there are spirits to warm the body and chase away the December chills." As if making a decision, Barrett went to the room's closet and took out his coat.

"Where are you going?"

"Out—where else?" He laughed bitterly. "I'm tired of being cooped up with you. Your face is as pale these days as the white of an egg. And you do nothing but mope. One would think you were a lazy slut with nothing better to do than to lounge about all day dreaming of pretty clothes."

It was a bitter slap at her, for Barrett had never

allowed her to forget her shopping spree in New York—
she had refused to take back her purchases—and often
alluded to it contemptuously.

"I'm not lazy!" she snapped. "And my face is not
pale!"

"It had better not be. This tour still has some weeks
to go, and we've been promised a bonus if we complete it
well. I want to collect that bonus. It's costing me a good
deal to support a wife, and my check from London does
not take that into consideration."

"You don't support me—not now! I earn a full
salary!"

"So you do." Barrett gave her a strange little smile.
Then he jammed his hands into the pockets of his coat
and limped out of the hotel room, slamming its door
behind him.

For an instant Adrienne stood frozen, staring at the
closed door. Then she had to rush across the room to the
cabinet where the chamber pot was stored. For the third
time that day, she was thoroughly, helplessly sick.

At last she wiped her mouth and washed her face in
the basin provided by the hotel management. She finished
scrubbing and gave herself a sharp look in the mirror. A
despairing face looked back at her—oval, beautiful, but
with eyes heavily shadowed and somber, a look of desperation about the mouth.

Slowly she put away the linen cloth and sat down on
the edge of the bed. In spite of the chill of the hotel room,
clammy beads of perspiration had begun to gather on her
forehead.

How could her child, a product of hate, of virtual
rape, be blessed by God? Surely, she told herself, it would
bear the worst characteristics of both Barrett and herself.

What if—she caught her breath—it were born with
Barrett's bitter vindictiveness? The uncontrollable urges
which turned him periodically from an unpleasant man
into a frightening one?

Or, her thoughts hurried on, what if the child were
born with *her* worst traits? Her temper, which could

sometimes explode without thought. Her impulsiveness, her fears of enclosed places, of poverty, of the act performed in bed between men and women?

Slowly, barely realizing that she did so, Adrienne went to the trunk where she kept her clothing and opened its lid. In a pocket of the lining was the Passion Star, carefully wrapped in linen.

She peeled away the cloth until the sapphire gleamed in the palm of her hand, its blue as deep as a summer sky at twilight. The six-legged star in its center seemed almost to glimmer, like an omen. . . .

For long moments Adrienne sat staring at the star sapphire. Then, abruptly, she thrust it away from her. She sat very still. It was as if she could picture the child which she carried within her, could see its face.

It would be small, she thought wildly. Thin and wizened, with a face exactly like Barrett's.

And—she could feel something harden within her—there was her career to think of. *Don't let your husband make you pregnant,* Madeline Demoro had told her. *God knows a baby is death for an actress.*

Well, wasn't it? Adrienne thought of Madeline herself, riding the bumpy trains and enduring the travel. Now her infant, a small boy, was at the breast, and she struggled to care for him in shabby hotel rooms, constantly washing diapers and baby linens, her face tired and drawn.

Would that be her own fate? To continue to play the role of Eliza until the bulge of her belly could no longer be laced in by her corsets? Then to be relegated to backstage work, to bear her child at last in some boarding home or hotel, to be saddled with its care, as Madeline was?

Not that she didn't love babies, Adrienne reminded herself with a pang. She swallowed hard against the sudden lump which pushed at her throat. Hadn't she mothered little Devin almost from his birth? Changed his linens and bathed him and carted him about? So she knew what it was to care for an infant. They had a way of grabbing at your heart. . . .

Adrienne jumped to her feet and began to pace the room restlessly. *This* infant would not clutch at her emotions, she knew. Its father was a man she despised. And what of her career, her vow to become a famous actress?

A baby . . .

Oh, God, what did she want? What was she going to do?

Adrienne whirled in the direction of the room's closet. She reached inside to grab her heavy woolen mantle from where it hung on a hook. Then, only stopping to pull on a cashmere bonnet, she rushed from the room.

She must find Madeline Demoro. Somehow, Madeline would know what to do.

The boarding house room which Madeline shared with her actor husband, Art Demoro, reeked strongly of baby urine. Strung from the ceiling moldings were ropes hung with diapers and baby linens. Some of them, by the smell, had not been washed but were only being dried out.

In the midst of this, Madeline sat nursing her baby, a thin infant who suckled with gloomy concentration, his fingers curled into tiny, mottled fists.

"Are you sure, honey?" Madeline asked wearily. In her early thirties, she looked older. There were dark circles under her eyes. "I mean, you're so young, Adrienne, and if you're nervous about missing your monthlies—why, that in itself has been known to make a woman late. It happens."

"Yes, I'm sure." Adrienne sat in the room's only other chair and watched the baby suck. She wished that Madeline did not look quite so dispirited.

Madeline sighed and shifted the infant to the other breast. "Seems as if the role of Eliza brings bad luck, eh? First me, and now you. And you'll not be securing yourself another part for a while, not with a large belly."

"I know." Adrienne's teeth clamped down hard upon her lower lip. "Madeline . . . remember that day in the train station? When you were talking about—about pessaries, and shields men could use?"

Madeline gave her a sharp look. "Yes, I remember."

Adrienne flushed. "You also said that if a person could find a doctor or a nurse in the town . . ."

Madeline sat for a long time in silence, staring down at her baby. Sleet rattled desolately against the window panes.

"Adrienne, I know I said that. And perhaps there would be a way for me to find out what could be done for you. Detroit is a big town, and there's a large waterfront area—surely there would be someone . . . But are you sure you want to do it? Abortions are the way of the desperate. I had a friend who died from one. She was an actress, too, and the man wouldn't marry her."

Adrienne worried her lip between her teeth. Her hands were clenched in her lap. She thought again of Barrett, of the way the baby was bound to look, like him—a baby born of forcing and violation.

A shudder rippled through her. "Please, Madeline," she begged. "Help me!"

Twenty minutes later she was seated on a horsecar headed south on Woodward Avenue. The car was crowded, many passengers standing to clutch the leather straps which hung from the ceiling. Others, including Adrienne, were packed onto two long benches which ran along each side of the car. Particles of sleet rattled against the windows, and damp fingers of wind probed inside the car.

Two playbills, one for *Uncle Tom's Cabin,* the other for *East Lynne,* were posted near the front of the car. Evidently, Adrienne thought dully, *East Lynne* was also playing in the city. She sat fighting a surge of nausea and crumpling the piece of paper Madeline had given her. Madeline had a friend, another former actress, now married, who might know of someone who . . .

The car stopped. The passengers surged out, carrying her with them. It had begun to sleet harder now, and the air was bone-chillingly cold. With shaking hands, Adrienne adjusted the collar of her mantle.

Then she stared downward at the damp, slippery cedar-block pavement, coated now with sleet and horse droppings. She didn't want a baby—did she? And yet she

165

had adored Devin, her little brother, with a fierce love . . .

"Adrienne! My God, Adrienne Gill, is it really you?"

The voice startled her.

It had come from a small knot of people waiting to board the horse-car. Now a man separated himself from the waiting crowd and strode in her direction. He was clad in a black sealskin coat with a luxurious collar, and loped toward her with the same easy stride she had once thought she had seen upon a New York street. . . .

She stopped, her heart taking an enormous swoop within her. It was as if her chest housed some free-flying bird, struggling to be free.

"Kristian!" Her voice was a glad cry. "Kristian!"

"Adrienne, what are you doing here, in Detroit of all places! You're the very last person I expected to see!"

He held her back to examine her face, and she drank in the beloved familiarity of him—the well-sculpted, almost arrogant cast of his features, the somber blue eyes, the slash of dimple, the full mouth, smiling at her now.

"I'm in *Uncle Tom's Cabin*," she explained breathlessly. She could hardly contain her excitement. "I play Eliza. But what are you doing here?"

"I'm just back from the wigmaker's, having repairs done on this." With a flourish, Kristian waved a square box.

"A wig?" She stared at him.

He was grinning. "I'm in *East Lynne,* playing Sir Francis Levison—it's a foolish hotchpotch of a play if ever I saw one. It would take a doctor of philosophy to figure out all the convolutions of the plot. But the people seem to like it. They can't seem to get enough of us."

Adrienne thought of the two playbills she had seen in the horsecar.

"But—" she stammered. "You, here in Detroit—I didn't know you could act!"

Kristian grimaced. Taking her arm, he escorted her away from the street corner and into the shelter of a three-story brick building which, from its sign, appeared to house a printer. The rim of the soft hat he wore was coated with sleet.

"I didn't, either. I knew, though, that I wished to write plays. I decided after meeting you and your husband that perhaps a stint on the stage would be good for me. If you could learn acting, then so could I, and I would certainly gain more practical knowledge of the theater than in any other way."

"But I never thought of you as an actor!"

Again he grinned. "Actually, I'm good at it. Levison is rather an oily character, and every night I'm roundly hated for my villainy. It's quite exhilarating."

Casually Kristian set the wig box down on a stone carriage block.

"I'm writing a play now," he said. "I hope it will be better than trash like *East Lynne*. I have something worthwhile to say, I think, if only the American audiences will listen to me. I have been looking hard for a financial backer who will think so, too."

Adrienne let his voice go on, barely hearing a word he said. She stood huddled against the brick wall of the printer's shop, her heart slamming. To see Kristian again after all these months! She had not dreamed it possible. And to learn that he was, like herself, an actor!

But what would he say, she wondered feverishly, if he knew why she had been riding the horsecar today? If he knew that she was pregnant and seeking an abortion? She could feel a trembling take possession of her body.

"Adrienne!" His voice penetrated her thoughts at last. "My God, girl, I've been talking to you for at least ten minutes and you haven't heard a word I've said. I asked you what you were doing riding the street-trains alone at this hour? It's a devil of a storm and sure to get worse. Surely your husband doesn't permit you to wander about by yourself?"

"He doesn't know I'm here," she admitted. She pressed her arms close to her body, shivering under her mantle.

"And you're cold. My God, don't you own a wrap more substantial than that skimpy woolen thing? Here, take my coat."

Before she could protest, he had draped his sealskin coat about her shoulders, enveloping her in a warmth

167

partly composed of his body heat, trapped inside the fur. She could not help snuggling herself into it, savoring the second-hand nearness of him.

For a few moments they stood in silence, while the wind buffeted around the corner of the building, sleet stinging their faces.

"You still haven't told me," Kristian said at last. "What are you doing here? Surely you haven't been to the wig maker's, too?" He gave a short laugh. "It's sleeting, and soon the roads will be coated with ice. Sensible people are at home now in front of their fires. You have a performance to give in less than two hours. Surely you wouldn't be here now if you didn't have some purpose in mind. What is it?"

She whirled about to face the worn bricks. An advertisement for chewing tobacco was pasted there, peeling and tattered.

"It—it isn't your concern."

"Isn't it? Dammit, Adrienne, I suppose that according to the rules of polite society I have no business asking you anything. And yet you owe me something for slapping my face aboard the *Thermopylae*. And now I'm collecting on that debt. I want to know where you are going at this strange hour of the early evening in the midst of a sleet storm."

Tears sprang to her eyes. Angrily she blinked them back. "I don't want to tell you."

"Why not?"

"Because—because I don't wish to, that's all. It isn't your business!"

Kristian scowled. "Perhaps I can guess, then. Let's see . . . it must be something very important to bring you out on a freezing December night, when you risk being late for the show tonight. The shops are closed. And you can't be visiting friends—surely you have none here in Detroit."

He stopped frowning. "Then there must be something you want. Something you desire very badly." His voice went on musingly. "Or perhaps it is something you don't want. . . ."

A gust of snow-laden wind had whipped around the

corner of the building to slap at their faces. Kristian turned to stare at her, his eyes piercing her.

"Adrienne, I have the strangest idea that I know why you are here. And my God, I don't like it. . . ."

He held her to him, and their mouths met. They kissed, at first softly, then with the strength of held-back passion. Adrienne pressed her body into his. Wildly, forgetting the freezing sleet or the reason she had come here, she gave herself up to his embrace.

"Adrienne . . . oh, God, oh, my darling . . ."

He kissed her again, his mouth urgent, until she could feel the sweet, answering curl of desire deep within her own body. Her heart was slamming—or was it his? It didn't seem to matter. Never had her body been so hungry, arching itself into the hardness of a man, as if it demanded things of which until now she had not known or guessed. . . .

And then he pushed her away.

The face staring down at hers was stony.

"You're pregnant, aren't you, Adrienne Gill? By that old man you married."

"Yes . . ."

"And you've come to look for a way to get rid of it, haven't you? Of course! I should have guessed."

"I . . . I suppose I have. . . ."

"Damn. Oh, damn! I can't believe it of you, Adrienne. I can't believe it. Or perhaps it's just that I don't want to."

Kristian's eyes blazed a savage blue, and the muscles of his jaw were knotted. He began to pace back and forth in the narrow shelter provided by the overhang of the building roof. Adrienne could not help shivering. When Kristian was in this fierce mood she felt as if she did not know him.

"You needn't look at me like that!" she burst out. "Oh, you don't understand! I don't wish to do it. But it's his baby. *His!* I can't tell you what that means, but . . . oh, I hate him, I loathe him!"

Kristian's mouth was a grim line. There was an expression on his face which she could not understand.

"Well, girl, you must have an address in mind: some specific place you were going. Where is it?"

Adrienne fumbled in the pocket of her mantle for the scrap of paper Madeline had given her. Wordlessly she held it out.

He gazed down at it, his lips twisted. "So this is the address of the abortionist?"

"No. It's the woman who—who might know where I can find one. She is a friend of Madeline's, she has left the stage and is married now. . . ."

Adrienne's voice stopped. Shame flooded through her as she thought of Madeline's baby, of the trusting way its hands had curled into fists as it suckled. She thought, too, of Devin. She had loved her small brother more, perhaps, than any other human being save for *Maman*.

She heard the sounds of paper tearing. She looked up to see Kristian rip the address Madeline had given her into shreds. With a savage gesture he tossed the bits of paper into the sleet-laden wind. They mingled with the damp snow and were gone into the night as if they had never been.

An odd feeling of relief surged through her.

"A life . . ." Kristian muttered, almost inaudibly. "I must give the world back a life."

Had he really said such a thing? But before she could ponder it, he had raised his voice.

"There. So much for that, Adrienne. Why don't you go home now? Go back to your theater and your husband. Have your child as you should."

"But—"

"Go, girl, before I can't let you!" Kristian's voice was a shout. He grasped her shoulders and pulled her out of the shelter of the building and toward the street. "I'll find you a hack—if any are about at this hour of the night and in this miserable weather. You little fool, you'd better get back to the theater before you're missed."

Were there tears glittering on his cheeks? Or was it only the icy sleet, driving through the air to cling to every surface?

Kristian yanked her along the slippery walk so quickly that she stumbled. But he caught her arm and pulled her on.

"Please," she gasped, "I can't walk this fast."

He slowed his pace. "Very well. But you're going back to the theater, do you hear me? And you'll go onstage tonight, and you'll never think of an abortionist again. Never, ever again."

A hack had appeared around a corner. It skidded onto Woodward, the horse's hooves sliding against the ice which coated the avenue. The driver was hunched miserably under a carriage robe, his hat caked with ice.

Kristian waved the hack down.

"The Detroit Opera House." He thrust some coins into the man's hand. "And see that the lady gets there quickly. It's freezing and I don't wish her to catch pneumonia."

"But, Kristian—"

With a quick motion, he took his sealskin coat back from her, then lifted her into the hack. The touch of his hands was tender. He slammed the door shut behind her.

"Goodbye, Adrienne. Go back to your husband. Go and have your child and—and may God help us both."

"Kristian!" She screamed it. She clutched at the door of the cab. "Kristian, I didn't mean—Kristian, listen to me. I probably wouldn't have done it—I only intended to *ask!*"

But he had turned away. Snow and sleet drove in great gusts, silting the carriage windows with white. The last glimpse Adrienne had of Kristian, he was standing in the lee of the printer's building, his shoulders rigid.

Chapter 12

You're going back to the theater, do you hear me? And you'll go onstage tonight and you'll never think of an abortionist again. Never, ever again.

Kristian's words cut at her like shards of glass. The hack swayed on the slippery pavement, throwing Adrienne from side to side. She sat with her hands clenched, staring unseeingly out of the sleet-encrusted window. Had she ever really intended to go to the address which Madeline had scribbled on the sheet of paper? Was it relief which she had felt when Kristian had torn up the address and flung the scraps of paper to the wind?

She would never know now.

She closed her eyes, feeling a dull, painful throb in her head. *Damn. Oh, damn. I can't believe it of you, Adrienne. I can't believe it. . . .*

By the time she arrived at the theater, the driving sleet had turned to snow. Ice coated the pavements, and when the driver came to assist her out of the hack, she had to grab his arm to prevent herself from falling.

"Slippery," he grumbled. "Anyone out tonight in this weather is a fool. There'll be folks dying in the streets tonight, you can bet on that."

It was an ominous thought, and it was with relief that Adrienne pulled open the stage door and slipped inside.

The theater, like all theaters poorly heated at best, was tonight a mass of chilly air currents and cross-drafts. By the light of a hissing gas border light, two stagehands were making frantic repairs to a large papier-mâché rock which would appear in scene three. At the back of the stage, a scene painter clambered about on wooden scaffolding, a small gas stove burning nearby in order to heat the paint binder. The pungent smell of paint and animal glue rose in the air.

Adrienne drew a swift, appreciative breath. This was her world. She belonged here, didn't she? And nothing, not Kristian, not Barrett, not even the baby she carried within her, could change that.

She hurried toward the narrow stairs which gave access to the basement, where the greenroom and dressing rooms were located. She was late, she knew. Already the backstage held that indefinable air of tension which meant that the performance would soon start. Voices drifted up the stairwell, tense and sharp.

Adrienne paused. Were the voices perhaps too tense? But, she assured herself, that was surely because of the storm.

At the bottom of the stairs she met Jennie Maud. Jennie was already in blackface for her role as Topsy. The blackface make-up had never ceased to fascinate Adrienne. Jennie's face, neck, and hands had been coated with burnt cork, then her lips outlined and filled in with white. It gave her a ludicrously comic look.

Adrienne had often wondered what real black men would think of such make-up, and why real Negroes could not play their own parts. But when she had broached the question to Barrett, he had only scowled.

"Black people can't play blacks, any reviewer knows that," he had told her. "As for the audience, they like it this way. They expect to see blackface and we don't disappoint them. The theater certainly isn't realistic, Adrienne, so don't expect it to be."

Now, under the daubs of white paint, Jennie Maud's mouth trembled visibly. "Adrienne! Oh, Adrienne, you'd better come right away!"

"Why?"

"It's your husband—it's Barrett!" The girl seemed near hysteria. "They brought him here ten minutes ago in a hack—oh, it's terrible!"

"What's terrible? What's wrong with him?"

"No one knows! Dustin Cerny has to go on as his understudy and everyone is running around shouting at everyone else, and Dustin Cerny says Barrett may be out for the rest of the tour, and they're going to have to advertise in the papers for a new Uncle Tom—"

Adrienne did not stay to hear the rest. She lifted the hem of her dress and brushed down the stairs past Jennie.

The greenroom of the Detroit Opera House, a room set aside for the actors to rest, lounge or entertain their friends, was painted in the traditional drab green. It contained a long table, a number of battered wooden chairs, an upholstered chair with the stuffing coming out, and several spittoons. Stuck in the joints of the gas fixtures on the walls were yellowing cards from local businesses—wigmakers, milliners, tailors, and those who specialized in the padding of costumes.

Now the greenroom was a hubbub of noise, for most of the cast of *Uncle Tom's Cabin* was clustered at the far end of the room, where a row of doors gave onto the men's dressing rooms.

"The doctor, for God's sake! Where is that blasted man?" The voice of Dustin Cerny, irritable and harassed, rose above the general confusion.

"The storm, that's why he's late. They say horses are falling on the ice and no one will come to the show tonight—"

Excited voices rose.

Adrienne pushed her way to the front of the crowd. Barrett sat in one of the wooden chairs—or had been propped, was her instant thought. For his body was slumped to one side like a marionette whose strings have been cut. His face was a sick gray-white, and a stream of spittle drooled from one corner of his mouth, which hung open loosely. A light sheen of perspiration covered his face. Oddly, his eyes were open and seemed alert and malevolent, staring directly at Adrienne.

"There she is," someone shouted. "His wife is here!"

Faces turned to her.

Adrienne held herself rigidly, unable to take her eyes from the man propped in the chair. This was her husband, she told herself dully. The man with whom she had lived, who had been her teacher, who was the father of the child she now carried.

Why was it that as she looked at him she could feel nothing? Not concern, not fright or anger or even hatred. Just . . . nothing.

"Well, it took you long enough to get here." Dustin Cerny crouched near the sick man, slapping at his hands and face. "Where in the hell were you? If you'd been with your husband as a wife is supposed to be, none of this might have happened!"

Adrienne ignored this. She forced herself to kneel down beside Cerny, to take one of Barrett's flaccid hands in her own. The fingers, resting in her palm, moved feebly.

"Air . . ." she thought she heard him whisper.

"He needs fresh air to breathe," she said. "Please, would all of you stand back? He needs space."

Reluctantly, the cast moved back. Jennie Maud was sobbing.

"All right!" snapped Cerny. "Go and get in costume, all of you. And make it fast. Anyone who isn't in full costume in five minutes is going to be docked a night's pay. I'll play Uncle Tom tonight—not that it will matter anyway. With this storm, we'll be lucky to play to twenty people."

"And tomorrow?" said Jennie Maud, sobbing. "What about then?"

"Tomorrow is twenty-four hours away! Everyone, get moving, do you hear? Five minutes, no more! And quit that blubbering, Topsy, you're making white streaks in your blackface."

Somebody giggled nervously, and then the cast dispersed to the dressing rooms, leaving Adrienne and Dustin Cerny with the stricken man. Barrett's eyes, Adrienne noted, stared directly up at her, lucid with intelligence. Now his mouth twitched again, as if he were trying to say something. But the only sound which came from his mouth was a muffled, grunting cry.

"What do you think is wrong with him?" Adrienne whispered.

Dustin Cerny threw up his hands.

"God knows. Probably apoplexy, although I can't be sure. The doctor will tell us, if he can ever get here through this storm."

"But how did it happen?"

"At a saloon, where else? He'd had too much to drink and was showing off before the bar patrons. They all knew he was an actor; half had seen him as Uncle Tom. They were buying him another round of drinks when suddenly he fell down on the floor like this. The barkeep put him in a hack and sent him here. Wanted him off his hands, I guess—so now he's on ours. Or, rather, on yours."

"Mine?"

"You're his wife, aren't you?" A slamming of doors made Cerny turn. "Is it that damned doctor?" he shouted. "Send him down here, will you? And tell him he'd better be good. If he earns his pay, I'll give him more free passes to *Uncle Tom* than he ever dreamed of."

Resolutely Adrienne went through her part, trying to block out her own worry and to concentrate fully on the thoughts of the character, as Barrett had taught her.

Her role as Eliza was not large, and recently Cerny had also given her a second small part, that of Emmeline, a young slave girl who is taken as enforced mistress by the overseer, Simon Legree. For that role, she wore a simple blue gingham gown, different make-up, and a second black wig.

Now, at stage front, the footlights emitted a continuous hissing glare of flame. Beyond them the theater itself yawned black. How many people had braved the storm tonight to see the play? Not many. Yet it didn't seem to matter. As soon as Adrienne walked onstage, she *was* Eliza, she *was* Emmeline, and nothing else existed.

However, as soon as they had taken their curtain calls and the last curtain had rung down, Adrienne's mind again turned feverishly to Barrett. Had the doctor been able to do anything for him? Was his ailment curable? And what was she to do if it were not?

A sudden rush of nausea possessed her, so strong

that she had to cling to one of the painted wing sets for support. Grimly she drew deep breaths, waiting until the sickness subsided. Then she stumbled toward the stairs.

Downstairs, she found that Barrett had been moved to an empty dressing room, a cramped, windowless cubicle equipped with a long wooden bench which had been placed in front of the mirror. Barrett lay sprawled on this bench. His shirtsleeve had been rolled up, exposing pale, flabby flesh. He was snoring loudly.

Beside the patient, a plump, balding man was in the act of putting leeches into an earthenware jar with a pair of tongs. Adrienne gasped and averted her eyes from the sight of the worms, swollen and distended with blood.

"You must be the doctor," she said.

"Yes, ma'am, Dr. Aaron Porter, at your service." The man's eyes lingered on Adrienne with appreciation. "I saw you as Eliza, ma'am, and you were splendid, most splendid. You are a most lovely actress. Ah, yes, most lovely indeed."

"My husband," she interjected quickly. "Do you know what is wrong with him?"

"Why, yes, I do. Your husband has just suffered apoplexy—a stroke. He is a man of choleric disposition, your husband, that's obvious from his looks. These things must be expected now and again."

With a deft flick of the tongs, Dr. Porter deposited the last swollen leech in the jar and closed the lid.

"Well, at least I've bled him and gotten rid of most of the bad humors of the blood. He had too much blood and it was entirely too thick."

On the bench, Barrett still snored, his body looking smaller somehow, his bad knee twisted to one side. It was a position which Adrienne knew must be terribly painful for him. If, she thought dully, he could still feel pain.

"How bad is his condition?" she blurted.

"Oh, not bad, not too bad. He has a little paralysis on one side of the body. It will freeze up his tongue a bit; he certainly won't be able to go on the stage for awhile, perhaps not for the rest of his life. But he should be able to speak after a fashion, and if he's lucky, he'll improve with time."

"But—not to be able to speak . . . !" She stared at the doctor in horror.

"He'll get the use of his leg back first," Dr. Porter explained, avoiding her glance. "Then perhaps his face, tongue and arm. If he works at it, of course. You'll have to help him. Massage his muscles. Then later there will be exercises."

"Massage? Exercises?" Ugly, practical thoughts had begun to fill Adrienne's mind. Thoughts of train fare, hotel rooms, meals. Laundry and sickroom chores. All of the duties she had seen her mother perform for Devin.

"Of course," the doctor said.

"But—I'm an actress, not a nurse. We've been on the road constantly, we're in a new town almost every day. This tour in Detroit is the only time we've been in a city more than two days. How am I going to . . ."

The doctor tucked the leech jar into a black leather bag and carefully fastened its leather straps. His eyes flicked over her impersonally.

"How am I to know, ma'am? You're a woman, aren't you? You women usually manage such things."

"But I'm an actress! I can't—"

"As I said, women usually manage such things, and I am sure that you will, too. As for actressing—perhaps you should stop that and just settle down. Be a wife and care for your husband."

"Take care of him! With what, may I ask? Charity?"

Panic had begun to chill her, a quivering animal fear which had something to do with the Closes of Glasgow, the sound of an old man's accusing voice, the feeling of being hungry in London.

Dr. Porter started toward the door of the dressing room. "How should I know, ma'am? But I'm sure you'll manage. I have full confidence in you."

"Confidence!"

Adrienne felt like laughing, like weeping wildly, like rushing forward to smack this pompous man's face. How dare he be so smug?

But, of course, she reminded herself with a new twist of fear, he did not know that she was pregnant. Nor did he know what sort of husband Barrett had been to her.

"Have you no medicine for him? Nothing I can do for him?" she demanded.

"There are exercises suitable for a man in his condition. And you can give him laudanum as a sedative." Dr. Porter reopened his bag and fished in it for a small vial. He handed it to Adrienne. "A spoonful when he is feeling agitated should suffice. And give him regular cathartics. He is to keep his bowels moving regularly."

With that, Dr. Porter ducked his head, nodded, and was gone, leaving Adrienne to stare after him.

Kristian, was her first thick, unclear thought. *Oh, Kristian, you told me to go back to my husband.* Then she slumped down on the bench at Barrett's feet, and gave herself up to weeping.

It was half an hour later. The hooks on the dressing room wall were filled with the street clothes of the female members of the cast. The room reeked with their scents: perspiration, rose-petal sachet, hair preparations, stage make-up. Nearby, Jennie Maud struggled out of her Topsy costume, while Minnie Mayhew, who played Aunt Ophelia, yanked a brush through her frizzy brown hair.

The room was abuzz with talk of Barrett's stroke. Everyone, it seemed, had something to say on the subject. Shock, speculation. There was even, Adrienne suspected, an element of enjoyment.

She removed the black, curly wig which she wore for her Emmeline role, smoothed its curls, and placed it in the bottom of her theater trunk. Then, her hands trembling, she slipped out of her costume and stood before the cracked dressing room mirror.

In her corset cover and petticoats, her skin looked white, more lush than ever, the curves of her breasts fuller now since the beginning of her pregnancy. Her belly, however, was still flat enough, and desirable. But who, she wondered, was there now to desire her? Barrett had had an apoplexy, and Kristian had gone out of her life as abruptly as he had come into it again.

Go back to your theater and your husband. Have your child as you should. . . .

"You're shaking, Adrienne," whispered Madeline Demoro, coming up behind her. Adrienne turned to see the other carrying her baby slung over her shoulder in a piece of linen. The infant slept serenely, his eyelids fluttering.

Madeline's eyes looked a question at Adrienne.

Adrienne stared back in puzzlement. Then, abruptly, she knew. The abortion. Madeline wished to know if she had been able to obtain the name of an abortionist. Had all of that happened only this afternoon? Already it seemed as if it had occurred a long, long time ago.

"I . . . I didn't go," Adrienne whispered at last. "I couldn't."

"Good," Madeline whispered back at last. "I was hoping you wouldn't."

"Oh—"

There seemed nothing more to say. Around them the other women crowded, wiping off buttery make-up, putting on their street clothes. Several murmured sympathy to Adrienne.

"A darned shame, that's what it is," Minnie Mayhew said. "Your husband so sick and all. And what will you do with the poor man? Are you going to leave him here, darling? It's what's usually done when a show is on tour, you know."

"I don't know—"

"Well, you can't expect to drag him along to every hayseed town between here and the Indian Territory," Minnie went on relentlessly. "How'll he ride the trains?"

Adrienne sat rigidly in a wooden chair, her hand frozen on the damp rag which she always carried in her trunk. "I don't know," she whispered.

"Was it apoplexy he had, dearie?" quesioned Mary Hampton, who played Cassy. "My grandfather died from one. He lay there as though he was dead for four days. It was a mercy when God finally took him—"

Adrienne put her face in her hands. "Please," she begged. "No more! Oh, please, be quiet, all of you, and let me think!"

"Well, you can't be thinking too much, honey,"

Minnie said. "You've got to get that man back to your hotel tonight. The men will help to carry him out to the cab, I suppose, but . . ."

She shrugged, her meaning clear. Once Barrett was back at the hotel, he would be Adrienne's responsibility. And what was she going to do with him?

Feverishly, Adrienne wiped away every particle of make-up on her face, scrubbing at her skin with the damp rag. Her mind worked rapidly, and she barely noticed when the other women finished dressing and left. Even Madeline Demoro had gone, to find her husband.

How long, she wondered, before her pregnancy would begin to show? If Dustin Cerny learned of her condition, he would fire her, as he had done Madeline. And that must not happen—not yet. She needed money, all the money she could earn, in order to support Barrett and the coming baby.

She swallowed tightly against the great lump of fright which filled her throat.

If she were careful to lace her corset very tightly, and to wear concealing shawls and mantles whenever possible, perhaps she could hide her condition until the tour was over.

Meanwhile there was the problem of money. Somehow she must save as much of it as she could. Barrett owned two theater trunks, and in them were a number of valuable costumes from other productions in which he had played. She would sell these at once. There were some items of Chinese porcelain from his collection, a few articles of jewelry . . .

And the Passion Star, a small voice in her mind whispered. You could sell that, too.

No! No, I won't! I'll never sell that, not even if we starve. I'll work, I'll send to New York and find out about Barrett's remittance check, I'll play Eliza until I drop dead of exhaustion. But I'll manage somehow. I'll manage!

Outside the dressing room door she could hear a hubbub of voices as the cast milled about, discussing Barrett's condition, the storm, the possibility of getting a cab in such weather.

Soon, she knew, she would have to go out among them, to take charge of her husband and of the life which lay before her.

A life burdened down with an unwanted child, with a sick husband who hated her, and whom she loathed in return. A life whose only goal now must be to make of herself an actress, in spite of everything.

Two

Chapter 13

"Adrienne. Get me that book. That playbook, *As You Like* It. Damned bitch, I have work for you to do. Work, do you hear me!"

"No, Barrett, not just now. I'm busy."

Adrienne's needle flew in and out of the delicate lace fichu she was sewing for Mrs. Carstens, the dressmaker down the street. It was piecework, complicated and painstaking, and the pay was small. But it was work a woman could do in her home, and the few pennies it earned would buy food and milk. And, in a way, doing such work made her feel closer to *Maman*. It was *Maman* who, long ago in Glasgow, had taught her to sew. . . .

"Adrienne!" Barrett moved his tongue thickly over the syllables. "I said, get the playbook!"

"And much as I would like to, Barrett, I've told you I can't at the moment. I have five more collars to finish before Friday."

"Bedamn the damned collars! Bitch! I said I'd make you into a great actress, and I will. But you must work—work until you are ready to drop from exhaustion!"

A ghost of the old Barrett, with slurred, bitter voice.

"I am working, Barrett."

Adrienne gazed down at the half-finished collar, where a tiny red spot marked the place where she had pricked herself with her needle yesterday. She prayed that old Mrs. Carstens would not notice. If she did, she would only pay half-price for the collar and give Adrienne a scolding besides.

And they needed the money desperately. Even with Adrienne's small earnings, it seemed that she was always hungry. And she had lost weight, too, until the only plump thing about her now was her enormous belly. The rest of her was gaunt and hollow . . .

It was June, 1872, seven months after Barrett's stroke. They were back in New York, living in a small flat on Hudson Street, on the third floor in a building full of shops. *John Barker, Drug Broker,* occupied the first floor. *Leonard and Son, Carpenter's Shop,* filled the second. Adrienne and Barrett lived on the third, listening all day to the bang of hammers on wood, the scrape of saws and planes. In the hot June air, the smell of new wood drifted up to their windows, along with the stench of chemicals from the druggists'.

Now Adrienne sat in a battered chair near the window, where the light was better, trying to concentrate on the piecework she held in her lap. Somewhere down on the street, a man hawked hot pies in a loud, penetrating shout. She tried not to think about how good a cherry pie would taste.

Involuntarily, her mind drifted back to that night in December at the Detroit Opera House when Barrett had lain so sick. Outside, the sleet storm had continued, and several male members of the cast had ventured into the street in hopes of flagging down a cab to take them all back to their hotels.

Dustin Cerny, however, had seemed oddly slow to offer his help.

"Don't you owe my husband something?" Adrienne finally demanded of him on an empty stage, with only two stagehands remaining to strike what remained of the *Uncle Tom* sets.

"Owe him?"

"He was the best Uncle Tom you ever had—everyone said it! Any money this company made you owe to him! Now, just because he is sick, you want to turn your back on him!"

"What else do you expect me to do, girl? Support him in his old age?" Cerny's lips had pressed together in a thin line. "I can't afford it. I wish I could, but I can't. Any one of us could get sick, do you know that? *I* could get sick. Who would take care of me then, eh? Who?"

"I don't know!" she replied furiously.

"Well, then. We'll just have to do the best we can, eh?" Abruptly Cerny became businesslike. "We'll have to leave him here in Detroit, of course. Find some old lady willing to take care of him for a few dollars. When he's better he can join you."

"But . . . do you mean that he isn't to come with us?"

With a sinking heart, Adrienne remembered what Minnie Mayhew had said.

"Drag a man with apoplexy around the train stations? Try to make connecting trains with him? Are you insane, girl? No, this is the only thing to do."

She swallowed. "But just to leave him like this—"

"You're damned right we'll leave him. You, my dear, signed up for the duration of the tour, and I happen to need an Eliza and an Emmeline. You can't desert me now."

She nodded. "I'll finish the tour."

"That's settled, then. Well, Adrienne, I will do one thing for you. My cousin owns a drug shop in New York. They were living over the store, but his wife wanted a house and they moved out. The rooms are still vacant. I'll write to him. When the tour is over, you and Barrett can go there. They'll give you a good rate."

With the help of Bob Talmad, the man who played Simon Legree, they managed to get Barrett back to the hotel room, where Adrienne gave him a spoonful of the laudanum, and sank into bed herself, exhausted. The next morning she walked to a nearby church and was given the name of a widow in need of extra income.

Mrs. Pence was fifty years old and gaunt, with iron-gray hair pulled back from her face into a knot. She owned a small frame house kept immaculately clean. For a few dollars a month, she promised to care for Barrett, to exercise his arm and leg regularly, and to call in Dr. Porter for weekly consultations.

Adrienne paid her for a month in advance.

"You'll have to send me more when this is used up," the widow told her, sniffing. "Actors are flighty people, and I ain't got room in my house for no charity cases. If it hadn't been that I'm a good Christian . . ."

"I'll pay you regularly," Adrienne promised hastily. "You needn't worry about that."

Barrett had been installed in a narrow bed in the widow's spare bedroom, lying stiff and straight under a threadbare quilt. The room was chilly, its fire small, and Adrienne felt an instant's wash of pity for her husband. One moment he had been a free man, an actor applauded and admired. Now he was an invalid, a burden upon strangers. He had said nothing since he had collapsed. But his eyes continued to stare at her with the same burning hatred she had seen in them before.

Impulsively she knelt beside his bed.

"Oh, Barrett, are you going to be all right while I am gone? You know I don't wish to desert you like this."

His eyes were stony, accusing her.

She hesitated, bit her lip, and went on. "Can you nod your head, Barrett? Nod once for yes and twice for no."

He stared at her, holding his head rigid. His eyes, red-rimmed, seemed to scream hatred at her.

"Barrett, they told me it's customary . . . Cerny told me that when an actor is too sick to tour, he must be left behind. There's no other way . . . ." She caught her breath. "I must continue to work, surely you can see that. We need the money. As it is, I've had to sell almost everything we had. I sold everything in your trunks—"

He jerked in surprise and uttered a muffled noise.

"I'm sorry, but I had to do it. Mrs. Pence had to be paid in advance, otherwise she won't keep your you. And I must save enough for your train fare back to New York when the tour is over. It will only be for a month or two, Barrett."

His eyes flicked away from her.

She drew a deep breath. "There is something else I should tell you, Barrett. I am expecting a child."

Her husband's eyes swung back to her, widening. Under the quilt, one leg twitched.

"I must tell you, too, that I don't want your baby, Barrett. I loathe the thought of having it. The way it was conceived—"

Barrett made another grunting sound, as if he were trying to say something.

"Barrett?"

"B— Barr— ee—"

"I don't understand you."

"N-name."

"Name?" Adrienne stared at her husband. Then comprehension came to her. "Are you telling me that you wish to name the child Barrett? After yourself?"

A little flood of surprise and shock washed over her. She had not really thought of the baby as other than a vague entity. *Baby*. Now, abruptly, she wondered if it were to be a boy or a girl. Then she shivered. If it were to look like Barrett . . .

Her husband nodded once, vigorously.

"If it is a boy, you wish to name him Barrett?" she questioned.

He nodded.

"And if it is a girl?"

"Barr . . . Barr . . . ee . . ."

"If it's a girl, you want to call her Barrie?"

Barrett nodded once.

"Very well, then, Barrett, I'll follow your wishes."

Abruptly Adrienne felt very weary. The room at Mrs. Pence's was cold, grim, sparsely furnished, and already smelled of sickness and despair. She could hardly wait to leave it.

The next two months were difficult and tiring. The tour blended into a ceaseless round of cities: Ann Arbor, Romeo, Cadillac, Toledo, Piqua, Tippecanoe City, Bourbon, Lawrenceburg. Endlessly Adrienne sat in train stations, smoothed on her make-up, tried her best to keep her costumes and wigs spotless; the oriental hangings hung in a succession of bleak dressing rooms.

She saved every penny she could, going without meals, sharing quarters with Jennie Maud in the cheapest hotels they could find. She wrote letters to *Maman,* glossing over the seriousness of the tragedy, trying to find the light, happy incidents of the road so that *Maman* would not worry.

There were nights when she awoke screaming with nightmares, and had to be soothed by Jennie back to a restless sleep. In one of the dreams, an old man with filmy white eyes screamed curses at her. In other dreams, there was a prostitute in a bottle-green dress, a door which would not open, a stray dog rooting through food scraps while her belly ached with hunger. . . .

She received occasional letters from Mrs. Pence. These were penned by a professional secretary, for the woman could neither read nor write. In them, the widow noted Barrett's progress. He could now walk with the aid of two canes, and he could speak, although his voice was blurred and unclear. According to Dr. Porter, he would never go on the stage again.

Adrienne put aside these letters with a dulled mixture of pity and anger. She owed Barrett so much—he had taught her to act, had gotten her this job with *Uncle Tom's Cabin,* had introduced her to the world of the theater.

And yet . . .

If only she hadn't married him! If only she hadn't chained herself to a sick, helpless, hateful man. *But then you never would have become an actress,* a cold little voice whispered in her. *And you would never have met Kristian.*

As her belly grew with the advance of her pregnancy, a new fear came to haunt her. What if her condition were discovered and Dustin Cerny fired her as he had Madeline Demoro?

She kept her corsets laced as tightly as possible, and tried to avoid undressing in front of the other women of the cast. At night in the hotel rooms, she disrobed beneath her nightgown so that Jennie Maud would not see the new, swollen lines of her figure. As for Madeline Demoro, she had sworn her to secrecy.

Often Adrienne lay awake in bed at night, thinking

of Kristian King. Where was he now, and what was he doing? Had he returned to New York? Over and over, she reviewed in her mind the few moments she had spent with him. The stolen dawn hours on the *Thermopylae,* the kisses full of physical passion.

There were nights when she allowed her thoughts to wander even further. To imagine what it might have been like if it had been Kristian in her bed instead of Barrett, Kristian's body pressed against the length of her own, so that she could know the maleness of him, the strength. . . .

Dismayed, she would discover that her heart was pounding thickly, her body agonizing her with its insistence. Then, desperately, she would turn her mind to other thoughts.

Kristian, wherever he was, did not want her. Hadn't he made that fact very plain? For if he did want her, he would never have let her go on the night of the snow-storm in Detroit. He would never have told her to go back to her husband.

No, she must not allow herself to think of Kristian King, ever again. She must concentrate only on living one day at a time. She must endure somehow until her child was born. . . .

Now, pushing away thoughts of the past difficult months, Adrienne turned the fichu in her lap. How fragile it was! Crossing over the shoulders in wide lace straps and belted at the waist, the neck-shawl was decorated with rosettes and trimmed with yard after yard of hand-sewn, pleated lace. Some fine lady, she knew, would wear it to freshen the appearance of a daygown or an afternoon tea dress.

Adrienne sighed. Did any of the women who wore these lacy collars and neckpieces have the slightest idea of the long hours of labor required to pleat the lace and add the trimmings? Did they even care?

She picked up her needle and carefully gathered another pleat with her fingers, trying to ignore the twinging ache at the small of her back which would not seem to go away, no matter how she shifted about in her chair. She had been sewing too long, that was it. And worrying too much. . . .

"Adrienne, I said put down that damned thing and listen to me!"

Barrett spoke from the threadbare old couch where he spent his days, lying with his bad knee propped up, his two canes leaned against the couch arm, a half-empty flask of whisky on the table beside him. The rickety table was cluttered with the newspapers he insisted on buying even though they had barely enough money for food. He had to read the theatrical news, he insisted. Especially the columns and reviews.

In many ways, their month here in New York reminded her of the close confinement with Barrett aboard the *Thermopylae*. From the moment they had arrived here, Barrett limping heavily on two canes, his mouth slack with facial paralysis, her husband had been taken up with a fresh obsession for her career.

Was he trying to live his own life through her? To mold her as a substitute for what he would now never be able to accomplish himself? She didn't know. But whatever the reason, from the time she rose in the morning until she fell, exhausted, into her bed at night, Barrett drove her without mercy.

There were voice exercises. Exercises in timing, in rhythm and tempo and pace, constant repetition of scenes from a dozen playbooks. When she flagged, or pleaded that she had collars to sew, he whipped at her with sarcasm, with insults and jibes, all of it spoken in that slurred voice she had grown to hate.

There were moments when she lashed back. When she shouted at Barrett and then slammed out of the door, to walk the mean streets in anger and frustration. But always she came back. There were collars to finish. More than that, she needed Barrett. If she wished to be a great actress, then there was still so very much to learn. . . .

"Adrienne," Barrett said again, his tongue moving thickly over the words. "Put down that blasted collar, I said! I've sent out for a playbook of *East Lynne*. I want you to read the role of Lady Isabel. You aren't ready to play her, of course, but you need the experience of reading. You must learn to make even a mediocre part come alive."

"But—I promised Mrs. Carstens I would finish this fichu and the other five by tomorrow."

Adrienne shifted about on the hard wooden chair. Her backache had not gone away. Instead it had sharpened and intensified, spreading downward toward her pelvis. But grimly she anchored another pleat, using small, neat stitches as *Maman* had taught her. How carefully she had explained to Barrett that her upbringing as the daughter of a countess had also included fine sewing. . . .

"Why? Why must you finish it? Piecework! Something any ignorant wench can do!"

Angrily Barrett picked up one of the canes which leaned against the couch and threw it at the wall.

It landed with a dull clatter. Then it rolled onto the bare floor and was still. From downstairs came the staccato bang of a hammer on wood.

"Any ignorant wench, as you put it, is not expecting a baby," Adrienne snapped. She jabbed her needle fiercely through the cloth.

"Well, pregnancy is no excuse for laziness." Barrett's blurred tongue gave the words an odd emphasis. "Look at these rooms, will you? Cluttered! Dishes needing to be washed, bed linens which need changing, things which should be put away—"

Adrienne threw down the fichu. Anger poured through her, so strong that she could almost forget the pain which had begun to twist through her lower back.

"And when, Barrett," she demanded, "do you expect me to have time to cook and to clean? I was lucky to find this sewing to do, yet you barely allow me time to complete it. You have kept me busy with your playbooks until I am ready to weep with fatigue—"

"And it will pay off. Didn't I tell you long ago that you must be willing to work harder than you have ever worked in your life?"

"Yes. You did." She reached down with difficulty and picked up the collar from the floor. She stared at it, at the rust-colored fleck of blood on its reverse.

"Well, then? Get to work! Go and tell that mulish old woman of a dressmaker that you haven't time to do her foolish collars."

"You know I can't do that. Barrett, you haven't received a check from London in three months. I've been to the bank every week and they say there is nothing."

Barrett's slack mouth twisted. "Then I'll write them another letter! Write and tell them what has happened!"

Adrienne was silent. Although she herself had written immediately to Barrett's father in London with news of his son's stroke, she had received no reply. Nor had any check arrived. She was beginning to suspect that none would come. Perhaps Barrett's physician father was ill. Perhaps he had died, or had simply decided to write off his son permanently.

But whatever the reason, the results were the same. She and Barrett were penniless. Stuck here in two squalid rooms over a carpenter's shop with a baby on the way.

Grimly she sat sewing, barely listening to Barrett's acid complaints about the rooms in which they lived, his father, the theater people who had deserted him in his need. She began to twist in her chair; it was suddenly more difficult to concentrate on her needlework.

Didn't the pains in her back seem stronger now? They had begun to twist, knife-like, into her lower belly.

She caught her breath as a pang of fear stabbed through her. Surely she was not to have the baby so soon! She had not thought it due for a few more weeks. There was this batch of collars and fichus to finish, the pay for them still to be collected from Mrs. Carstens. And she had not yet arranged for a midwife. . . .

Again the cramps twisted through her.

She tried to breathe quickly and shallowly, to contain the pain and not to cry out. *Maman,* she thought feverishly. Her hands were perspiring on the fichu now, creasing it. *Maman* had always birthed her children quickly, the last three arriving even before the midwife could be summoned. Was she, Adrienne, to be the same?

The minutes ticked by. Barrett had stopped talking

and was now sunk into a sullen lethargy, his eyes focused dully on the cracked, stained plaster of the wall. Somewhere outside a church bell chimed the hour—four o'clock. The ring of hammer blows rose to a crescendo, and then stopped, followed by guffaws and laughter as the carpenters took a break in their work.

"Barrett," she whispered with effort. "You must go and get help for me. I think the baby is coming."

"Nonsense. You've just got indigestion. And even if the child is coming, these things take hours, especially for a first baby. I should know, my father spent enough time waiting for children to be birthed."

Adrienne's fingers dropped the needle. The fichu slid off her lap and fell to the floor as she arched her back in another spasm, stronger than the last. It ground and twisted at her insides.

"Barrett! Barrett, it—it isn't going to *take* hours," she gasped. "I'm going to be like *Maman,* it's going to come very quickly. You've got to get help for me now."

He stared at her. "So I'm finally good for something, eh? You don't want me as a husband, but I'm good enough to go and fetch a midwife for you!"

"Please!"

Again a contraction squeezed her in its powerful vise. It lasted for a long time, endless moments in which she clenched her hands into fists to keep from screaming. She couldn't show pain in front of Barrett; she would not give him that pleasure.

Then the pain slid away. Slowly, desperately, Adrienne slid down and out of her chair. She edged along the floorboards until she had reached the first of Barrett's two canes. Its wood felt cold and smooth in her hands.

She pushed the cane toward her husband.

"There, Barrett. There is your cane. And here is the other one. Take them and get help for me. Go downstairs to the carpenters. Tell them I need someone. Surely one of the men there will know of a woman who could come."

She lay helpless on the floor, listening to Barrett stump his way out of the flat. Another pain had come to seize her body in its monstrous fist.

197

The baby, she thought, letting herself weep at last. Even in being born it was exactly like its father.

Merciless . . .

"Take this, ma'am, it'll help you. God knows if there is one thing whisky is good for, it's making the pain go away."

Adrienne felt the mouth of a whisky bottle being thrust at her, and obediently she swallowed down the fiery liquid. She could feel the hot fire spread along her veins, mingling with the pain and somehow diluting it.

She was being split apart. Torn, torn . . .

A high, thin, mewling cry filled the room.

"Well, well, and it's a fine baby girl you have, ma'am. And healthy, too, I'll say that. Listen to her scream."

It was Leonard, the carpenter from downstairs, a fat, hearty man of forty-five with a fringe of thinning hair and shirt-sleeves rolled up to reveal enormous veined forearms. Five minutes ago he had come bursting into the flat to assure a panting, sobbing Adrienne that he was the father of eight, three of whom he had delivered himself and she was not to worry. If the midwife did not arrive in time, he himself could handle matters.

Gasping, biting at her lower lip until it bled, Adrienne could only nod. She was being crushed in the center of the most powerful physical pressure she had ever known. She did not care who delivered her baby, she was not even capable of thought. . . .

The midwife had not arrived in time. And now her child had been born, emitting high, squealing sounds like a rabbit.

"A girl?" she whispered.

"Yes, ma'am. I'd say she's about average in size, maybe even small, but healthy. A daughter to be proud of."

"Oh."

Adrienne sank weakly back onto the floor. She heard dragging sounds and knew that Barrett must be outside in the hall. She hoped he would not come in. She did not want to see him, not now, not yet.

"I want to see my baby," she heard herself say in a voice she did not recognize.

"Then look. Hold her if you want."

Gently the carpenter laid something on Adrienne's belly. She looked downward. Thin, scrawny, its skin red-purplish, the baby was covered with a cheesy white coating. Her black hair was ugly and matted down. She had small, rather flat lips, Adrienne saw with growing horror. The shape of her face was rectangular, as Barrett's was. Her eyes, too, were like his, small and narrow. . . .

Revulsion swept through her, in a wave so strong and physical that she could actually feel it push at the back of her throat.

It was as she had feared. Her child looked exactly like its father. The man who had raped her, forcing himself upon her body in hideous nightmare.

"Beautiful, isn't she?" asked the carpenter happily, as if he had not noticed her indrawn gasp of shock. "I'm sure her Papa will be mighty proud. Have you decided on a name for her?"

"Name?" Adrienne's throat seemed locked shut, her mouth dry. The tapping and scrape of Barrett's canes was louder in the corridor and now she could picture him as he lurched forward, his body tilted to one side as he struggled to walk.

"Her name is . . . is Barrie. Don't let *him* in yet, I don't want to see him."

The man nodded. "You don't want to see him until you're cleaned and fresh. Sure, honey, I know. Well, don't worry. The midwife should be here any minute, and she'll clean you up, that's women's work. Then you'll be ready to receive company."

The baby had begun to cry again. Her cry was high and piercing, as insistent as that of a street vendor.

Adrienne's eyes burned with tears.

"Please," she begged. "Please, oh, please, take her. Take her away. I don't want to hold her any more . . . not right now. . . ."

Chapter 14

It was mid-August of 1872, hot and sticky. The city air was full of thick summer smells: horse dung, rotting garbage, road dust.

Inside their two-room flat was the odor of drying baby linens and the faintly sour aroma of the infant herself, who spent most of her days asleep in a wicker basket near Barrett's couch.

Barrie was a quiet baby. She nursed efficiently, then fell asleep at the breast, her fingers still clutching at her mother's soft flesh. Her face had filled out so that she was no longer scrawny, and the matted black hair had been replaced by feather-fine wisps of light brown.

Yes, Barrie was a perfect baby. Even Leonard, the carpenter, who trudged upstairs weekly to visit her, informed them of that. And, grudgingly, Adrienne admitted that it was true. Barrie rarely cried, even when she was hungry, but waited patiently to be fed. She had begun to smile and would lie in her basket beside Barrett and gaze up at her father with eyes already showing signs of being the same color as his—a cool, transparent gray.

That, in fact, was the whole trouble. Barrie looked exactly like her father. The resemblance was growing more pronounced with each day. The set of her head, the shape of her skull, the firm, unbabylike mouth—each time Adrienne looked at her daughter, she felt repelled.

Barrie was a child born of ugliness and nightmare. The taint of her conception still clung to her.

Adrienne had had time to brood about this, to lie

awake at night on her narrow cot while the thoughts pricked at her brain like sharp knives. She had started a dozen letters to *Maman* and torn them all up. How could she possibly admit to her mother that she disliked her own baby?

Now that the baby had arrived their situation was even worse than it had been. Adrienne had begun to suspect that Barrett had suffered another, smaller stroke. Probably it had occurred on the night Barrie was born. Since that day, his voice had become more slurred than before, and there were times when even she could not understand what he said.

His mouth hung slack, and one side of his face was stiff and expressionless. When he tried to get about with the aid of the two canes, he lurched as if drunk. He could not work, would obviously never act again, and spent his days sprawled on the couch with his whisky flask beside him. Sometimes he would hold Barrie, rocking her and talking to her in a garbled voice.

Sometimes, however, seizures of despair would come upon him. Caught in one of these moods, he would shout at Adrienne, or hurl both canes at the wall, throwing newspapers and playbooks after them, until Barrie would begin to cry in fright.

Only then would Barrett stop, to gulp down a spoonful of the laudanum which Adrienne kept ready for him, then to sleep for hours on end. It was, she thought in desperation, as if he blamed the entire world for what had happened to him. But most especially did he blame her.

The day after Barrie's birth, she had dragged herself out of her bed to walk down the street to the dressmaker's to deliver the collars and fichus, collect her pay, and get more piecework. Now she spent seven hours a day hunched over her sewing, pleating lace with small stitches as fine as any *Maman* had ever made.

Now, on a humid Tuesday morning in mid-August, she laid down the Swiss muslin collar on which she had been working, and walked to the shelf where she kept a small hand mirror. Barrie, cooing in her wicker basket, turned her head as she walked by, her eyes following her mother as they always did.

Adrienne glanced at her child, frowned, and then stared hard at her own reflection. She had lost weight; it showed in the new boldness of her cheekbones, the sculptured lines of her face. But her pale hair glistened with its old, shining luster, and the color in her cheeks was high. If one did not know, she assured herself, one would never suspect that she was the mother of a three-month-old baby.

"Well? And what are you staring at? The Great Lady of the American Theater?"

Barrett's words, muffled as they were, were still clear enough for Adrienne to understand. She froze, feeling her cheeks sting under the sarcasm. Great lady of the theater? She was no such thing, and she knew it. There were days when she felt as if her dream were no more substantial than a wisp of French lace. And Barrett knew this. Unerringly, he had hit upon the one way in which to really hurt her.

"Your face is too thin," she heard him add. "Fullness and voluptuousness is what theater patrons want these days, my girl. Round figures, like those of Alice Atherton and Fanny Davenport!"

Adrienne flushed. "Perhaps," she admitted. "But I need food if I'm to grow plumper—cream and butter and eggs."

"You'll have it when my remittance check comes."

"But it isn't *going* to come, Barrett, that's been made very plain by now." She surprised herself by the sharpness of her voice. "And I'm tired of being imprisoned here in the flat with you. The baby is old enough to be left, and I've been thinking. I'm going to go out and audition for a part."

The slack mouth twisted. "You're not ready yet. Not for a starring role, which is the purpose for which I've been grooming you."

"But—"

"Oh, certainly, you can go to Union Square and promenade with the others, just as you wish! But I want you to break upon the theater scene like a meteor. Burning, incandescent! I want you to be unforgettable. And you can't possibly achieve that just yet."

"I can! I will!"

"Oh? I saw you play Eliza. You're good, yes. More than good. But you haven't the inner strength yet, the magnetism, the confidence with which to enthrall an audience—"

"I do have it, I do!" Angrily Adrienne flung the hand mirror back onto its shelf, hearing the splinter of glass. "Barrett, you've been my taskmaster for months, you've forced me to work until I wished to weep from fatigue. Now I'm ready. It's time, I tell you!"

Barrett scowled. "What's your hurry? There is always that precious star sapphire of yours, you know. If you would only consent to let it out of your hands—"

"I won't sell the Passion Star!"

"Why not? Good God, girl, you act as if that sapphire were magic. Well, it isn't." Barrett's partly paralyzed face was twisted, his mouth slack and ugly. "Get some sense into your head, Adrienne. It's merely a stone, after all, a saleable jewel. Somewhere in this vast and dirty city of New York there is someone willing to pay for it. If you were not so stubborn—"

"I don't care. I won't sell it. I can't. It . . . it means something to me."

She pressed her lips together, thinking of the deep blue beauty of the stone. Often, when she felt most discouraged, she would take the Passion Star out of its hiding place to gaze deep into its depths. Sometimes she felt as if she could almost see the girl who had worn it to her death. That girl's heart was locked somehow inside the gem. No, she could never sell it, not while she was able to work at all.

"You are a fool then," her husband's voice taunted her.

"Perhaps!"

She turned and flew into the second small room of the flat which contained her cot, three theater trunks, a bureau and a chair. A row of hooks on the wall held their clothes—the few she had not sold. Now she reached for her last presentable dress—a green foulard, well worn now, its hem frayed from sweeping countless pavements and floors. But its deep color would set off the glow of her hair, and the gown, she was sure, would look well enough if one did not stare at it too closely.

Swiftly she stripped off the old dress she was wearing. At last she stood naked. Gazing downward at herself, she saw that her breasts were full and firm, her belly unmarred by stretch marks, her thighs slim. Perhaps her body was not robust, as was that of Fanny Davenport, but surely she was desirable. Surely there would be men who would view her onstage and find her pleasing. As Kristian had. . . .

She reached for a cloth and the ewer of tepid water which waited on the bureau. Slowly, volumptuously, she began to wash herself, running the cloth over the swell of nipples, the curve of hip and belly and inner thigh. An odd, insistent urgency was growing in her.

Kristian, she thought slowly. *Oh, God, Kristian, I need you.*

She finished washing and pulled on a clean corset and fresh petticoats, laundered and pressed with flatirons as *Maman* had taught her.

"What are you doing, Adrienne?" Barrett's voice demanded from the other room.

"I've told you, I'm going out!"

"Out?"

"I'm going to Union Square to look for a part."

"And the baby? Myself? What do you intend to do about us?"

"I intend to feed you!" she snapped. "Perhaps, as you said, I can't get a starring role—but I don't care. I want a job, any job. And you, Barrett, will have to care for the baby while I am gone."

There was abrupt silence in the other room, followed by the sudden smash of a cane hitting the wall.

"How? Damn you, bitch, she is still an infant at the breast!"

Adrienne's fingers flew over the green foulard as she fastened its side buttons and adjusted its long flounces. A feeling of wild, reckless elation pushed through her.

"Then I'll have to wean her, or we'll get a wet-nurse. But you'll have to manage for now. I'll feed her before I leave, and then it will be four or five hours before she must nurse again. I'm going out, I tell you; I'm going to get a job as an actress!"

She felt as if she had been released from prison, as if this were the most wonderful day of her life. After all these long months, at last she was free! Well, almost free. For a few hours, she did not have to think about Barrett and the baby, about the bleak little flat which smelled of diapers and despair.

Overhead the sky was flat white, and the air shimmered with moist August heat. Adrienne hurried down Hudson Street, savoring everything: the three-story brick buildings emblazoned with painted business signs, the wooden sidewalks piled with goods for sale, the pedestrians intent on business.

On the corner a girl was selling fresh doughnuts, their smell so yeasty that Adrienne's belly gave a demanding growl.

"I'll take two," she said recklessly, fishing a precious coin out of the small change purse she carried.

The vendor smiled. "They're fresh, and they're good. I should know, my Ma just fried 'em not an hour ago."

"Oh, they smell delicious! And isn't it a lovely day!"

Adrienne took her purchases, wrapped in brown paper, and, like a child, ate them as she walked, savoring each crusty, sugary bite.

On the corner of Hudson and Chambers she spotted a cab and waved it down. Then, ignoring the stare of a lady passerby, who was not accustomed to seeing a woman manage for herself so boldly, she climbed in and told the driver to take her to Union Square.

Union Square, Barrett had told her, was a great theatrical center where out-of-work actors and actresses congregated. True, the section of Broadway from Madison Square to 42nd Street, known as the "Rialto," was popular also. But still the theater people came to Union Square to look for jobs, hanging around the stretch of sidewalk along 14th street in front of the Morton House and the Union Square Theater known as the "slave market." It was said that on certain days of summer, a pro-

206

ducer or theatrical manager had merely to look out of his office window to cast a play.

Now, as Adrienne paid the cab driver, she tried not to wince as the money slipped from her hand to his. Today was not a day for counting pennies, she told herself, or for worrying, either.

She jumped down from the cab and looked about her with mounting excitement. The Square was a hive of activity. Around its central area, and the statue of a mounted horseman, the ceaseless traffic flowed. Horsecars jostled buggies and carts. Two-wheeled cabs darted in and out. Pedestrians crossed recklessly between the carriages, wherever they could find the room and courage.

Signs caught her eye: *Union Square Hotel, Steinway, New York Mirror, Hotel Hungaria Table D'Hote Restaurant; A. A. Fleming and Co., Plumbers and Gas Fitters, Tiffany's.* There were restaurants, cafés, shops, a man hawking roasted chestnuts, a drayhorse wearing a straw bonnet—like a kaleidoscope, all of it vied for her attention.

She passed the German Savings Bank with its impressive cupola, its flag hanging limp in the humid air. Ahead were the Morton House and sidewalk posters advertising the current offering of the Union Square Theater. And on the walks crowded men and women with a brash, flamboyant air.

The men, well-built, had handsome faces and walked with swagger. The women, too, had a look of pride to them. They were fashionably dressed, with tightly corseted waists and hair done in the latest styles. They promenaded with the confidence of women who were not helpless society belles, but accustomed to hailing their own cabs, carrying their own luggage, and even smoking cigarettes in privacy when they pleased. And both men and women chattered to each other with animation, a vivacity exaggerated larger than life.

Theatrical people, she had concluded after traveling with the cast of *Uncle Tom's Cabin,* were a special breed, recognizable anywhere.

Now a trio of young women approached her, walking arm in arm and laughing among themselves. Adrienne could not help staring at them. She was sure that they were actresses. With their air of fashion, their high spirits and confidence, they could be nothing else.

As the three drew closer, their long skirts sweeping the sidewalk, Adrienne started. One of them, with chestnut hair and a merry face, looked older than the others and somehow familiar. Hadn't she seen her somewhere before?

Then she remembered. In Bedesco's, the department store she had visited when she had first arrived in New York, she had met a young sales clerk who had also been a stage dancer. Miss Fanny Pepper—that had been her name.

Without stopping to think further, Adrienne ran forward and tugged at the sleeve of the brown-haired woman.

"Miss Pepper—oh, Miss Pepper—do you remember me?"

"Did you say that you know me?"

Fanny Pepper pulled away from her companions to stare at Adrienne in puzzlement. It was obvious that she did not recognize her, and now Adrienne could feel herself flush scarlet. It had been a chance encounter in a department store more than a year ago—a few moments of conversation, that was all. There was no reason why the other should be expected to know her now.

She moistened her lips. Behind them, a boy hawked the *New York Mirror*, the theatrical and entertainment newspaper, in a piercing soprano voice. The street life swirled.

"I'm sorry," she stammered. "I bought some things from you at Bedesco's Department Store. You told me you had been a dancer in the *Black Crook,* you said you danced only the last two weeks—"

Fanny Pepper grinned. In her mid-thirties, she was plump and rounded in the current fashion, with a curved bustline and a narrow waist. She would never be called beautiful, yet she had a look of russet good health.

"Ah, I told so many folks about that. And what did

you say your name was?" With a quick gesture, Fanny waved her companions on.

"I'm Adrienne Gill. At any rate, that's my stage name. I was in a road tour of *Uncle Tom's Cabin.* My husband is Barrett Kendall. Do you recall that I bought some things and had them delivered to our hotel—"

Fanny Pepper's smile faded. "So it's you, is it? I had to pay for your purchases that day out of my own pocket. And got fired into the bargain."

"Fired!"

"It seems that you and your husband left without paying your bills," the other explained dryly.

"Oh . . ."

Adrienne could feel the blood pound to her face. Of course; now she recalled Barrett's sarcastic talk that day of slipping out of the room in the middle of the night like thieves and felons. And she had refused to take back the collars and other things she had bought, thinking to force Barrett into paying for them.

Now, it seemed that he had not.

"I thought we paid," she began. "I'm dreadfully sorry—"

The smile which creased Fanny Pepper's face was sudden and transforming. "Ah, well, it doesn't matter. I didn't like the job anyway. That old Mrs. Carlson was always cross, and I got tired of stacking everything in pyramids. I kept wanting to snatch a tin of canned meat from the bottom of the stack and watch it all fall."

"But, Miss Pepper, they docked your pay for what we did. And you lost your job—"

"So I did. But now you're here and perhaps you can pay me back. To tell you the truth," Fanny moved confidentially toward Adrienne. "There are a few times when I've skipped town without paying, myself."

She took Adrienne's arm in a friendly manner. "Let's walk together, eh? I know a good café where women can go, and they sell the best chops. I'm hungry, aren't you?"

Adrienne fell into step beside her companion.

"I haven't much money," she said slowly. Her elated

mood had begun to slip away. Now the promenading actors and actresses looked merely tawdry, over-bold. Some of them, she saw, wore shabby clothes and expressions of despair. Walking among them, too, were women with the provocative mannerisms of the prostitute.

"I'll buy your chops, then," the other said. "God knows why—when it's you owes me money and not the reverse. Ah, are you a bit down on your luck, honey? That dress of yours has seen better days, hasn't it?"

Adrienne glanced downward at the worn hem of the green foulard.

"Yes."

"Managers notice things like that right away. And it's proper they should, since you've got to provide your own costumes if you are hired."

"Oh—"

"By the way," Fanny chattered on. "You can call me Fanny. Seems like Miss Pepper is just too formal, and besides, it isn't really my own name anyway. I made it up when I came to New York ten years ago—I thought it sounded more elegant. My real name is Fanny Flesch. Ugh, can you imagine *that* on a billboard?" Her laugh was infectious.

Adrienne could not help smiling back.

Fanny nudged her. "See those two men? See the handsome one with the black, curling hair and the mustache?"

"Yes—"

"That's Lester Wallack. He's playing right now in *The Veteran*. Isn't he good-looking? He manages one of the greatest stock companies in the city, and any girl would be lucky to be sponsored by him—he's made more than one famous!"

As they strolled, Fanny talked happily of the theater. She mentioned names of actors and actresses—Edwin Booth, Rose Coghlan, Maurice Barrymore, Fanny Davenport, Charlotte Thompson. One, a boyish-looking girl named Bijou Heron, they actually saw on the street talking animatedly with another actress.

But Adrienne barely heard the theater gossip. As

they walked, she grew more miserable by the moment. Everyone here on Union Square seemed to belong, save herself. And, worse, she owed Fanny Pepper money—and a job. How was she to pay her back? She had no funds but some coins in her change purse and a few dollars to pay the following week's rent.

The café was small and evidently patronized by theater people, for it was full of the same sort of men and women Adrienne had seen on the sidewalk outside. It smelled of a rich mixture of frying chops and kidneys, beer, whiskey, hair pomade, and perfume. There was an elaborate wooden bar with inset mirrors, metal rails, and a carved lion's head. A number of men were crowded at the bar and gave the two women an appraising look as they entered.

But Fanny led her to one of the scattered tables, each set with six dark bentwood chairs and covered with a starched white tablecloth. Here more patrons were seated, including several women, one of whom, to Adrienne's amazement, was smoking a cigarette.

"I haven't any money to pay you back right now," she told Fanny Pepper when they were seated. "At the time I bought the things, I didn't know my husband wouldn't pay for them," she explained uncomfortably. "We—we had a quarrel and I refused to take my purchases back. This was just before we left to join a road company of *Uncle Tom's Cabin.*" Now her words poured out. "Barrett played Uncle Tom. Everyone said he was the best Tom they'd ever seen. And he was, until he was taken ill with apoplexy. Now he is paralyzed, and can't work, and the baby finally came, and I had to do piecework for a while. Now I'm here today to look for a part, any part—"

Fanny frowned. "Any part, Adrienne, is probably what you'll get. Jobs are scarce this year, the good ones, anyway. I should know, I've been looking for three months now. I want something more than a walk-on, I want a role with some meat."

"Oh."

"You say you had a baby?" For an instant a look of

yearning crossed Fanny's face. "Who's taking care of it for you?"

"My husband."

"But you said he'd been ill."

"He is ill. He can barely speak, and must walk with two canes." Adrienne's voice had filled with despair. "But he is well enough to watch the baby, and he must try, otherwise what will I do?"

A waiter had brought them each a foaming glass of brown beer, and Adrienne lifted her glass and downed hers with a long gulp. The afternoon was hot, and she swallowed thirstily, savoring the wet, dark flavor. The room, with its white, pressed-tin ceiling, its gas chandeliers hanging on wires, seemed to tilt slightly about her.

The waiter returned and Fanny ordered lamb chops, boiled potatoes, fried oysters, and lemon pie for each of them.

When he had left, she said, "Then we must find you a job, eh? Then you can pay me back and also you can find a woman to care for that baby of yours. Do you think it will do to leave a small baby with an invalid for very long? Infants have a way of learning to walk, and then to run."

Fanny toyed with her glass of beer. "I had a baby once," she explained in a low voice. "I left him in Grand Rapids with my mother. She said she'd care for him while I was touring. What else could I do? He had no father, and certainly I couldn't take him with me, could I?" Fanny's mouth was bleak. "Diphtheria took him when he was only three years old."

"I'm sorry." Adrienne, thinking of Devin, felt a pang of sympathy.

"Don't be. It happened six years ago." Fanny lifted her glass and took a swallow of her beer. Abruptly the grin transformed her face again. "And what sort of job shall we get for you, Adrienne Gill? It will probably be a walk-on, but I hear that Wallack is casting, and Augustin Daly. There is also a Mr. King who is casting a new play—a very shocking one, they say. Very, very modern!"

"A Mr. King?" Adrienne's heart begun to thump.

"Yes, he is a new playwright who has gotten himself the backing of a rich manufacturer of shirt collars!" Fanny made a face. "At any rate, his backer, Phineas Magruder, lives on West Thirty-fourth Street and has money—and it takes plenty of money to frame a play. Some say he took up with an unknown playwright because his daughter has fallen in love with him—the playwright, I mean. It's all the gossip."

Adrienne took a long swallow of the cool beer. "Is Kristian King the playwright of whom you speak?" she managed to inquire.

"Why, yes, do you know him?"

Adrienne stared at the russet-haired actress. She felt as if her head were whirling. What coincidence that she should meet Fanny Pepper and hear of Kristian, all in the same day! Yet wasn't the theatrical world really a very small one? Everyone knew everyone, and gathered in the same places.

"Yes," she whispered. "I know him."

"Well, then. Put in a good word for me, will you, Adrienne? God knows I need it. I've danced a bit, and played maid parts, and it's been a long, dry spell for me. The ten dollars you owe me would come in dreadfully handy right now, I'll admit."

An hour later, saturated with theater gossip—it seemed that Fanny Pepper came to Union Square every day to lounge about with the other out-of-work actors— Adrienne left the café to join the throngs on the sidewalk again.

Kristian, Kristian! her mind kept repeating feverishly. The *Mirror* newsboy approached her, laden with his canvas sack of papers. Adrienne rushed up to him and bought a copy. Quickly she thumbed through its pages, looking for mention of Kristian and his new play.

At last, on a back page, she found it. A threatrical column written by a man named William Stauffer mentioned a new play, *Melissa Charles*, the story of a newly divorced woman and her affairs with two men.

"Most shocking and controversial, this play will put

213

the fashionable folk of Fifth Avenue a-twitter," Stauffer had written archly. "Handsome playwright Kristian King, currently in residence at the Astor House, is going to set New York on its ear—if they don't set him first out of town. The play will open in October at the Olympic Theater."

Adrienne folded up the newspaper and hurried on, her heart slamming. No longer was she aware of the street with its throngs of promenading actors, its swarms of carriages and drays, the pair of sandwich men who paraded up and down in front of the Union Square Theater —boards on their backs advertising the latest play.

Her thoughts were feverish. Kristian was not only here in New York, but he had also written a play which was the topic of gossip and conjecture. Barrett, with his newspapers, must have known, and deliberately kept quiet.

Her breath quickened. What if—

Yes, her thoughts tumbled on, why not? She must go to Kristian and ask him for the starring role, that of the divorcée.

Surely he would not refuse her. *Go, girl, before I can't let you!* He had said that in Detroit, had kissed her with passion, had been enthralled by her.

Yes, she assured herself, no matter what Barrett said, she *was* ready for a starring role. And she did not want to be like Fanny Pepper, hanging about Union Square day after day, gossiping with other actors and hoping for the big part which never came.

She glanced down at the green foulard gown she wore. With fresh dismay she noted its frayed hem. Even Fanny had commented upon the shabbiness of the dress.

She couldn't go to see Kristian in a threadbare gown. She must look splendid and fashionable. She must look the part of Melissa Charles.

She had been away from the flat for three hours, and already her breasts were beginning to swell and grow painful with the pressure of the incoming milk. Soon, she knew, she must go home and nurse her baby.

Meanwhile, there was much to do. She still had a

few coins, left in her purse, and next week's rent money. She must go to Mrs. Carstens, the dressmaker on Morton Street, and beg her to sew her a new gown. Perhaps she would be willing to take a very small down payment. . . .

Chapter 15

It was three days later. Her stomach a boiling knot of tension, Adrienne stared nervously out of the window of the public hack which battled its way through city traffic. Park Row, at Broadway, was a terminal for horse-car lines, the cobbled road a maze of metal tracks. To her right loomed the six-story granite Astor House, its windows shielded from the scorching summer sun by striped awnings. Its shops, at ground level, were scalloped by a long, irregular row of awnings extended over the walk.

Inside the hotel, she knew, was Kristian. In only a few moments she would see him, talk with him.

The hack slowed up, its driver swerving to avoid a sleek brougham carriage. Swallowing hard, Adrienne glanced down at her new gown. She had bought it from Mrs. Carstens at a reduced price because the woman for whom it had originally been sewn had canceled the order before all of the fittings had been completed.

Nevertheless, it was a magnificent gown, made of dusty rose faille with an elaborate overskirt, a looped-hip-sash of matching faille ribbon, and a bodice with a decolleté neckline. It had taken all of the money she possessed to pay for it—together with a reckless promise to complete a new batch of collars within the week.

But blithely Adrienne had promised. She would have sworn anything in order to get the dress. Perhaps she had been extravagant—*Maman* would certainly have said so. Yet even *Maman* would agree that it was vital she look her best. She had to get this part, she had to!

It had taken her nearly two hours to dress and to loop and braid her hair into the fashionable coiffure she had seen in a copy of *Godey's Ladies Book*. At the last moment, she had opened her theater trunk and slipped on the Passion Star, noting with a thrill of pleasure the opulent way it gleamed at her throat, as lovely as a fragment of twilight sky.

She had regarded her reflection in the mirror critically. It was strange what a feeling of confidence the Passion Star gave her. Wearing it, she felt strong and beautiful, as if she could do anything, accomplish anything. Was it, she wondered feverishly, due to the spirit of the girl who had once worn it? Had that girl's soul remained to haunt the sapphire?

Of course not! she chided herself. It was a foolish, silly fantasy. Jewels did not really have spirits in them. . . .

Now, she sat rigid as the hackman parked his vehicle in front of the hotel near a carriage block. A uniformed doorman hurried forward to help her down. She paid the hack driver, trying not to wince as the coin—one of her last—left her hand.

Then, lifting her skirts above the dirt of the pavement as Countess Aurelia Prendergast might have done, she swept toward the hotel entrance.

The lobby of the Astor House was an elegant mixture of molded plaster, gilt, balconies, oriental rugs and potted plants. A few people sat in chairs, the ladies fashionably dressed, corseted and bustled. Several looked up as Adrienne entered the lobby. One, a plump woman clad in gray silk, gave her a sharp stare.

Adrienne hesitated, feeling the color flow to her cheeks. During her tour with *Uncle Tom's Cabin,* she had often encountered that sort of look. She was unescorted, of course; that was why the woman had glared at her. Why, she wondered, did a woman always have to be accompanied by a man before she was considered socially acceptable? It wasn't fair!

But she pushed back her dismay and took a few more steps into the room. She tried to move confidently, like the countess she pretended to be, as if she belonged here among all this discreet elegance.

The woman in gray leaned forward to whisper something to a female companion. The two of them giggled.

Adrienne stiffened. How was she to talk to Kristian in such an atmosphere? Her mind shrank from the idea of asking him for the part in this ornate lounge, populated by well-dressed ladies and gentlemen. What if she had to read from the playbook? What would these stuffy people think of that?

A hotel employee approached her. He wore a black suit as sober and correct as his bearing, and a high, stiff collar.

"You are waiting for someone, ma'am?"

Carefully his eyes slid over her, noting the expensive gown, the sapphire gleaming at her throat. She saw that his eyes were puzzled. Did he, too, wonder why she was unescorted?

She lifted her chin and threw back her shoulders, assuming the imperious look of a dowager who is accustomed to have all servants obey her orders Commandingly, she lifted her left hand, upon which the wedding ring Barrett had given her was visible.

"I am Mrs. Kristian King," she informed him grandly. "I have come here from Boston in order to join my husband for a month in New York. Please show me to his rooms at once."

Immediately after she had said it, she wanted to bite out her tongue at its root. Whatever had possessed her to say such a preposterous thing? Yet the lie had been told. There was no way she could take it back now.

She stood trembling, feeling sick.

"Ah." For an instant the hotel man hesitated. Then, seemingly reassured by the look of the expensive gown and the star sapphire, he bowed deferentially. "Yes, ma'am, of course. I believe Mr. King is out at the moment. However, I will show you to his rooms and you can wait for him there." A discreet pause. "I believe that your luggage is being brought?"

Luggage! For an instant panic leaped through her. Of course she would be expected to have trunks and bags, especially if she had just arrived, as she had stated, for a month's visit.

"The baggage is being delivered," she lied quickly. "You may expect it within the hour. Meanwhile, I am tired and wish to order a meal while I wait for my husband. Would you see to it, please?"

The dinner consisted of roast lamb with mint sauce, cold ham, stewed tomatoes, rice, tapioca pudding with apples and hard sauce, and fruit and cheese.

But, although she was hungry, Adrienne could not touch the food. All she could think was that she was here in Kristian's rooms under false pretenses and without his knowledge. Any minute he would be back. He would be furious with her.

She pushed away the meal tray and sat twisting the elaborately folded napkin into small triangles. In the hack, rattling through the streets of New York, she had been filled with near-confidence. But now, here in this hotel room with its heavy furnishings, she could feel only dread. What would Kristian say when he found her here? What would he think?

She had almost decided to flee the room—let Kristian wonder later who the strange woman in it had been —when she heard the sound of steps in the corridor, and then the turn of a key in the lock.

"My God, it can't be! Adrienne, is it really you again?"

"Hello, Kristian."

Her mouth went dry as she stared at him. He had not changed. His eyes were still a somber blue, his face arrogantly carved, his crisp, curling hair giving him the look of a Roman warrior.

But Kristian was scowling now. "How on earth did you get into my rooms? This is a very proper hotel, you little fool, and they definitely do not allow unescorted women into men's rooms."

Adrienne rubbed damp fingers up and down the looped hip-sash of her new gown.

"I told them I was your wife," she managed to say.

"You what!"

"Yes, I had to speak with you in private, Kristian, and I didn't know any other way to do it. I certainly couldn't talk to you downstairs in that lobby with all of those people there—" She stopped, swallowing. "And that hotel man, if I hadn't been wearing a fine dress he would have . . ."

Again she stopped. "I told a lie, I know I did, but surely you can put it right somehow, can't you?"

Red spots of color had risen to Kristian's cheeks. He had been carrying a parcel, and now he slammed it down on the top of a mahogany bureau.

"So you have tarnished my reputation, Adrienne, merely to get yourself into my rooms! If you had wished a private interview, surely you could have left a note at the desk requesting it. I would have obliged. Instead, you chose to pose as my wife—"

Kristian's mouth was twisted with anger. "Don't you realize, girl, just what a very old trick that is? Why, half the floozies in New York use that ruse to get into a man's quarters."

Fury pounded through her.

"I'm not a floozie! How dare you—"

"Then don't act like one." His voice had turned cold, colder than she had ever heard it. "All right, Adrienne. Now you're here, you got in somehow, evidently by using your considerable powers as an actress. It will cost me a pretty bit of talking to undo what you've done. So go ahead, tell me. What is it that you want of me?"

Her anger seeped out of her so rapidly that she felt drained and ill. She walked shakily to the window to stare downward at the street. How many times in the past hour had she gazed out at the same horsecar stored on a side track, the same resigned horses waiting to be hitched to their burdens? In spite of the heat of the afternoon, she could feel cold perspiration chill her skin.

"I read about you in the paper," she said at last.

"Oh?"

"Yes, I read about your play, *Melissa Charles*." She caught her breath, then forced herself to go on. "It's quite controversial, according to that columnist, Mr. Stauffer."

Kristian made a face. "Yes, Mr. Stauffer is fond of stirring up talk, I'll say that for him. And the notorious Melissa Charles, gay and free divorcée, is also attracting her share of gossip, not to mention all of the actresses who wish to play her part. The lovely Clara Morris, and even the great Fanny Davenport wish to play my Melissa. Sad to say, none of them are right for the part. Miss Davenport certainly is not. She is far too plump for the character I had in mind."

Adrienne felt her heart give a small, insistent thump. She stepped toward Kristian, half-aware that her knees were shaking.

"*I* am right for that part, Kristian. I know I am. I could play Melissa Charles beautifully, it's the part for which Barrett has groomed me."

"You?" Kristian threw back his head and laughed. He let himself fall into a straight-backed chair, his body shaking with mirth. "My God, Adrienne, what are you talking of? My backer, Phineas Magruder, has made it very plain that he wishes the female lead to be played by a well-known actress, someone capable of drawing crowds."

Adrienne's heart sank. But she lifted her chin challengingly. "Kristian, I could play Melissa, I know I could! And I'd be better than Fanny Davenport or Clara Morris or any of them!"

Kristian quirked an eyebrow.

"Would you?" He uncurled himself from the chair and strode toward the untouched dinner tray which Adrienne had left upon a small, low table. "Ah, peaches! And plums!"

He selected a plum and began to eat it.

"Kristian! Listen to me! I would be good in the role!"

"I doubt it. Pretty as you are, you are not yet a seasoned actress."

"But I toured in *Uncle Tom's Cabin!* I've been doing little but work, practice, rehearsing with Barrett to help me."

Never, she thought, had she wanted anything so

desperately. She clenched her fists at her sides, her nails cutting into her flesh, willing a pretty smile to appear on her face. She mustn't look too intense, she must not reveal how hungrily she longed for this role!

"One small part, Adrienne," Kristian said. "Eliza, in *Uncle Tom's Cabin*. That's all you've ever done. No one in New York has heard of you. I'm afraid that Magruder—"

Forgetting her resolve, she glared at him. "I played two roles, Emmeline as well as Eliza. As for your Mr. Magruder, is he the shirt-collar manufacturer? The one who is paying for the luxury of this fine room here at the Astor?"

"Yes, he is my sponsor," Kristian said quietly. "I met him and his family one day by accident in Central Park. It took me months of hard work to build my friendship with Magruder, and now I'm lucky I've got him. He has faith in the play, Adrienne, and he's convinced that it's going to make us a lot of money."

Kristian had finished eating the plum and now he put the pit back on the tray and wiped his mouth.

"Please give me the part," Adrienne begged. "I can do it, I know I can, if you'll just give me the chance to try. Let me read one scene, that's all I ask."

She was pleading, and she hadn't wanted to do that. Yet she could not seem to stop herself.

"Adrienne, I've told you. Magruder has made it plain what sort of actress he wants."

Yet Kristian's mouth, she noted, had softened. With a start, she realized that the old, electrical charge between them was as strong as ever. They were, she thought shakily, like two candle flames arching toward each other. If they were ever to touch, their fires would ignite into one gigantic, incandescent explosion. . . .

"Adrienne," Kristian said softly. "I'm sorry I had to say that. I don't wish to hurt you, and I am glad to see you again, truly I am. I've often thought about you in the past year and wondered what happened to you."

She turned. There was an ugly little lump choking her throat and she did not know how it had gotten there.

"Tell me what you've been doing," he said.

"I finished my tour with *Uncle Tom's Cabin*. My husband had a stroke of apoplexy and now he is partly paralyzed and an invalid. My—my baby was born in June. She is named Barrie, after her father."

Kristian's face had gone gentle. "I am sorry to hear about your husband. But to have a little girl . . . Barrie—such a pretty and unusual name. I like it. If there is any part of her mother in her, then your daughter must be very beautiful, Adrienne."

"Well, she isn't." Adrienne's voice was low. "She is nothing but a baby—that's all. And there is no way she can be pretty if she resembles her father, which she does. Her eyes, her nose, even the shape of her skull—ugh! That anyone should wish to look like Barrett!"

Kristian frowned. "I like children, did you know that, Adrienne? Even little girls who resemble to an uncomfortable degree the fathers whom their mothers don't happen to love."

His words had a sharp edge to them, and Adrienne could not help flushing.

"I didn't mean that to sound as it did," she began quickly.

"Didn't you? That child, my dear, is the baby which you were so determined to get rid of the last time I saw you."

"But I didn't get rid of her. I took your advice, Kristian, and went back to the theater and my husband." Tears stung her eyes and furiously she dashed them away. "And now I'm stuck with an invalid husband and a baby to support. I need this role, Kristian, I need it very badly."

Kristian narrowed his eyes. "I see that you are wearing a lovely pendant, Adrienne. It must be very valuable."

"Yes." Her fingers flew to the Passion Star, gleaming at her throat. "It is a star sapphire, weighing more than three hundred and fifty carats."

"I'm sure that it would fetch a large sum of money if you were to sell it. You and your husband and baby could live for a very long time on that."

224

Again that hurtful lump pushed at her throat. Kristian had moved closer to her and was now so near that she was acutely aware of the maleness of him, the clean odor of shirt starch and soap.

"Kristian," she whispered. "Let's not talk about the Passion Star . . ."

Kristian's breathing had quickened. She knew that her own breath was coming irregularly, too. And the bond between them, the magnetism or incandescence, whatever it was, had grown stronger.

It seemed to stretch taut across the space which separated them.

Slowly Adrienne took a step forward. She heard the faint rustle as the hem of her new gown scraped the Turkish rug which covered the floor.

"Kristian," she whispered huskily. "Hold me. Please, please, just hold me."

"Adrienne," Kristian murmured. "Oh, God, my wild, sweet Adrienne. Do you know how long I've waited for this?"

They were locked in an embrace. Kristian's lips rained soft kisses on her cheeks and ears and neck. She could feel the length of his body along hers, his hard, insistent masculinity.

She clung to him. Her knees felt weak, and a warm melting had begun to spread like butter through her belly and thighs. Never with any man had she felt like this. It was as if she could give up her entire self to him, let him do with her whatever he wished. . . .

Now Kristian kissed her harder, and Adrienne found that her eyes were closed and her lips parted to admit the soft probing of Kristian's tongue. Feverishly she strained her body against his.

"Darling . . ."

"Oh, Kristian—"

He groaned. "You shouldn't have come here, Adrienne. From the first moment I walked into this room and saw you here, I knew this was going to happen, it had to."

"And what's wrong with it happening?" she was amazed to hear herself blurt boldly.

"God help us both, you're married to someone else. You have a child, responsibilities—"

"I don't care! I love you, Kristian. Please . . . kiss me again!"

But he drew away, although his hands did not release her shoulders.

"Adrienne, this is insane. I'm drawn to you; I can't seem to help myself, nor do I want to." He shook his head angrily. "For a whole year, Adrienne, I thought about you. About the way you looked in Detroit in the midst of that sleet storm, your face so frightened and determined and wilful. Yes, wilful! Girl, you are so headstrong and ambitious. Yet there is something weak inside you, too. Something vulnerable, something which makes me fear for you."

"Fear? For me?" Frightened, she pulled away. "What do you mean?"

Kristian was scowling. "I don't know. It's something I sense in you, that's all I can say. You have needs, Adrienne, so strong that they can suck away at a man as a spring flood rips away a tree trunk."

"That's silly!" She was angry. "I've never heard of such a thing!"

"Nonetheless, it's true. But God help me, at this moment I don't even seem to care." Kristian seemed to hesitate. "I'm a playwright, Adrienne, and perhaps I have instincts keener than other men's. But I know it's true. Disaster lies ahead somehow, I'm sure of it."

"Disaster! What nonsense you talk!"

Yet she could feel her whole body shiver convulsively. She threw herself toward him, flinging her arms around him. "Oh, I don't want to hear such things, I hate to hear them! All I know is that I want you to hold me—"

"I'll hold you, darling. Yes. . . ."

He half-carried her toward the bed, with its neat coverlet of white, its dark, carved headboard. For a moment, like a bad dream, a picture flashed into her mind. Xenos Shane crouched over her body, choking out curses and blasphemies as he raped her. And Barrett, forcing her deeper and deeper into sexual nightmare . . .

"Don't be afraid," Kristian whispered, as if he had read her mind. "Don't be. I'll never hurt you. I want only to hold you, to please you."

It was as if it all passed in a hazy, wonderful dream which had no beginning and no end, but only *was*. The hotel room was dim with approaching dusk, its air moist with the steamy heat of August. Yet the awnings on the windows shielded them from the setting sun, and after a while a breeze rose from the East River.

Slowly, luxuriously, Kristian stripped the clothes from her body, until the rose faille gown lay crumpled on the floor and she was stretched naked on the bed, her body bared to his gaze. Only the Passion Star remained, glowing barbarically at her throat, for she would not let him remove that. It was a part of her, especially tonight, and she could not let it go.

"Beautiful," he whispered. "You are lovelier than I had dreamed. And your hair—no other woman in the world has hair like yours, like a fall of molten sunlight."

His fingers touched her hair, then slid down to cup her breasts, to caress them.

When Kristian paused to pull off his own clothing, it was to reveal a body so different from that of Barrett that it was as if he did not even belong to the same species. There was not an ounce of fat to spoil the lean, taut lines of chest, hip, thigh. Broad shoulders tapered to a narrow waist and downward to firm, muscular thighs. And between his loins was the erect insistence of his masculinity. . . .

They made love. Slowly at first, almost tentatively, for Adrienne was still new to this act, so private, so achingly intimate. Twice Kristian had to whisper reassurance, to hold her and pet her and caress her as if she had been a child.

But at last their embrace grew more passionate, their bodies straining into each other until it seemed as if there was no separation between them, as if they were both a part of the same force.

Then slowly, slowly, the warm flame of feeling which had begun in Adrienne's groin began to grow. It flickered and ebbed, hung achingly on the edge of unknown sensation.

Suddenly, almost without warning, it blossomed into white-hot fire. It was as if the two candle flames which were herself and this man had suddenly touched and exploded.

Time seemed to hang still, to have no meaning.

"The Passion Star," Kristian whispered. His finger touched the opulent jewel, caressing it as he had, earlier, her skin itself. "It is a lovely thing, Adrienne, and it seems almost in some strange way to be a part of you. To draw some of its beauty from you."

"No, you're wrong, Kristian. It is *she* whose spirit is a part of the Passion Star. I feel that, anyway. Sometimes I sense it very strongly."

"She?"

"Yes. She was a king's wife. She was very young and very beautiful, but he was old and hardened and bitter—at least, I think that he must have been. One day she met a man who was all the things to her that the king could not be. He became her lover. The king found out. He—he had her punished according to the law of the land—she was executed by beheading."

Adrienne's voice had sunk to a barely audible whisper. "It was only later, after she was dead, that the king was consumed by regret. But there was nothing he could do to bring her back. He could not bear to have the Passion Star around to remind him, and sold it in the marketplace. That—" She hesitated, thinking of Xenos Shane. "That is how it eventually came to me."

Kristian looked thoughtful. "Do you mean that she actually wore it to her death?"

"Yes." Adrienne swallowed. "I cannot get it out of my mind. It's almost as if—oh, I'm sure you'll think I'm silly—as if her spirit somehow fled into this sapphire. It is as if it is her soul which resides in the stone, lending it its beauty."

Kristian's face was a mask. "Yes, you are being silly. That sapphire is merely a stone—a piece of rock dug out of the earth by men, cut and polished. No more than that. As for the story of the young queen and her lover, I see that entirely differently. What I see is the story of people caught up in the ironbound traditions of the society in which they live. A girl is forced into marriage with a man whom she does not love, because that is the way things are done. She tries to break away from the iron manacles of her surroundings and fails. Her husband, the king, is also bound by society. He does what he must—and only when it is too late discovers that he, too, could have broken away, could have found a freedom of sorts. . . ."

Kristian had totally forgotten her. He sat up in bed, his naked body a study of smooth, well-toned muscles. His eyes were dreamily distant.

"Adrienne, this Passion Star of yours—it is only a stone, after all, no more than that. And yet . . ."

"Yes?"

"Where is a piece of paper?" Kristian asked suddenly. He thrust aside the linen sheet and jumped out of bed. "And a pencil! I must write something down immediately, before I forget it—"

"Adrienne?" Still caught in that timeless dreamy spell, they had made love again. Now they were lying in bed, naked, warm and perspiring. The Passion Star was still at her throat, cool against the love-moist sheen of her skin. Adrienne felt pleasantly relaxed, as if she could float forever on a warm sea.

"Was it good for you?" Kristian asked it lazily. "Sometimes a first time for a man and a woman isn't perfect, you know. It takes two people time to get used to each other's bodies, to learn to experience each other."

How did Kristian know of such things? Adrienne stifled a quick flash of jealousy.

"Yes," she whispered. "It was good."

Possessively she reached out to touch Kristian's belly. It was flat, hard with muscle, and spired with crisp, honey-colored hair.

"I'm glad," he said. "I wanted it to be good. Adrienne, you don't know how often I've thought of you. And wondered how it would be with us. When I knew all the while, of course, that none of it should be, that for us it would be disaster . . ."

Disaster. It was the second time he had said it. Adrienne stiffened. Darkness had sunk upon the room now, creeping outward from the corners. Abruptly her euphoric mood was gone, as if it had never been. And a squeaking rattle from the corridor outside the room brought her back to full reality.

She had come here in order to secure for herself a starring role in Kristian's play. . . .

Purpose flowed into her.

"Kristian." She moved her body seductively, reached out to caress him. "Kristian, about that role, the part of Melissa Charles. I know I've no right to ask for it. I haven't a name, I've nothing to offer you other than my talent. But I do have talent. I know I do! And I'll work hard!"

"Darling, you know that I—"

"Oh, I know I can handle it," she pressed on. "I'm so sure! If only I could have a chance to try. I promise you, Kristian, I could get myself talked about if that is what your Mr. Magruder wishes."

"How?" He sat up in bed, his body long and lean, shadowed now in the dusky light.

"Why, by being written up in the papers," she told him recklessly, remembering the gossipy column she had read in the *New York Mirror*. "You can announce that I am the daughter of a countess about to make my debut on the New York stage—my triumphant debut!" she added. "How will anyone know what roles I have played in Scotland?"

Even in the darkness, she knew that Kristian was staring at her intently. "You are a devious one, aren't you, my Adrienne?"

His voice did not hold admiration.

Adrienne caught her breath. Kristian didn't understand. All of her life she had listened to *Maman*'s stories and dreamed *Maman*'s dreams. Now those dreams were her own. And she had to make them come true for herself. There was no one else who would help her.

She heard her voice pour out passionate persuasions. "Kristian, you've already told me that my hair is like sunlight, that no other woman in the world has hair like it. Well, if that's true then no other New York actress can look like me either. Your Melissa Charles, if I play her, will be quite unusual!"

There was reluctance in Kristian's tone. "I hadn't visualized Melissa as looking like you, Adrienne. But I suppose it could be done. And certainly Fanny Davenport is too plump for the role. She may be fashionable, but she reminds me of a stuffed pigeon."

Adrienne clapped her hands in delight. "Oh, Kris, do you mean it?"

"Don't call me Kris!" Kristian's mouth had twisted savagely. "Never call me that again."

"But I only called you K—"

"I said never use that name again, ever!" Then, abruptly, Kristian's voice softened, took on the familiar timber she knew. "Well, Adrienne, maybe you are right after all. New York has certainly never seen anything like your beautiful hair."

"New York has never seen anything like me."

Adrienne was smiling as Kristian again took her in his arms.

Chapter 16

The next day, Kristian took Adrienne to meet his sponsor, Phineas Magruder. As they rode in the cab, Adrienne could feel herself shiver from excitement and apprehension.

"Now, remember," Kristian warned. "You don't have the part until Magruder approves you."

"I—I know."

"I still wonder if you're right for the role," he went on. "The character, Melissa, is a very unusual woman for her time. She is a modern woman, a free person not bound by ordinary conventions. She has tremendous warmth and gallantry of spirit, and is able to rise above her background and the times which stifle her. It's a very difficult part to play, and will demand much skill."

"I *know* I can do it, Kristian," she pleaded. "If only I am given the chance—"

"Well," Kristian sighed, "that will be up to Magruder. I spent six months getting him to sponsor my play, and I can't let anyone—not even you, my beautiful, wilful Adrienne—stand in my way now."

The Magruder home was a handsome, four-story brick mansion guarded by an ornate wrought-iron fence, located on Fifth Avenue near East 10th Street.

Inside, it was sumptuously furnished with Turkish rugs and an Aubusson carpet woven in cream and deep red. There were velvet draperies, crystal chandeliers, and cream-painted paneling. And everywhere, on mantlepieces and tables, were cut flowers, so plentiful that Adrienne exclaimed with delight.

A maidservant ushered them into a large library. The room was lined with leather-bound volumes all the way up to its high ceiling, with ladders provided on which to climb to reach the books. Everywhere were small objects: decorated Chinese boxes, glass paperweights, collections of stones and feathers, even a woven basket which, Kristian whispered, had come from the Indian Territories of the Far West.

They waited ten minutes for Magruder to arrive, and Adrienne could feel her belly muscles begin to tense with nervousness. This easy luxury—so far removed from the poverty of Glasgow or the flat on Morton Street—was almost overwhelming. And there was a feeling of power here, too. As if the owner of this house could buy and sell a hundred actresses, or finance a dozen plays if he wished.

Phineas Magruder did not bother with introductions. He merely strode into the room and began speaking.

"Well? So this is the girl, then." The eyes which inspected Adrienne were sharp, and traveled over her body without missing any details, exactly as if he had been a drayman inspecting a street woman.

"H-hello, Mr. Magruder." Adrienne rose and stood trembling as the industrialist finished his inspection. Why, she thought with growing anger, it was as if she were no more than a piece of meat!

Yet there was nothing to do but submit—if she wanted the part of Melissa.

"Your home is beautiful, Mr. Magruder," she blurted to cover her awkwardness. "I love everything in it. And that Indian basket is quite fascinating."

"It is a Sioux basket. Notice the snake perpetually ready to eat the frog it is chasing. Or is it the frog which is chasing the snake? To me, the basket is an enigma." A pause. "So you like my house, eh? My wife furnished it for me. She is old New York money, and I am new."

She found it almost chilling that Magruder could say such a thing about himself with such easy, offhand confidence.

"Gloriane and my three daughters are in Spain just now, making the Grand Tour," Magruder went on casually. "My wife says such an expense is most essential for their education. Not that I would know. I'm a common man, really. All I know is money and manufacturing. But I know them very well indeed."

Adrienne was sure that he did. Again she had the impression of power crackling from this man. Magruder was unprepossessing in looks: short, squat, muscular, with a thick neck and a balding fringe of hair. Yet behind those piggy eyes were intimidating force and intelligence.

Phineas Magruder, she knew instinctively, was a man who got what he wanted.

A maid brought in a tray of hot, strong coffee, and French *petits fours*. While Kristian and Magruder talked, Adrienne sat nervously, toying with her cake. She had dressed carefully for today, wearing the same rose-colored faille she had worn yesterday to visit Kristian. The color was becoming to her, bringing out the creamy paleness of her skin, the shining blondness of her hair.

Still, sipping coffee while Kristian and Magruder discussed details of script and rehearsals—Kristian, it seemed, was being given a free rein with the play and would both direct it and play the leading man—Adrienne found it difficult to keep a look of ease. Did Magruder like her? It was impossible to tell.

Restlessly her eyes traveled over the library, coming to rest at last on a portrait hung over the fireplace. It showed a lovely, dark-haired woman holding a cocker spaniel on her lap and surrounded by three pretty little girls of about five, seven and nine. One, the middle one, seemed especially charming, with wild, shy, dark eyes. There were the three Magruder daughters, Adrienne surmised, but now they were grown enough to be touring Europe.

"Well, Miss Gill?" Magruder's flat voice cut through her revery. "I suggest that you read the part for me now. I'd like to see how you do. Not that I don't respect Mr. King's judgment. Still . . ."

Gone were the tones of jovial affability. Now Ma-

235

gruder was all business, and Adrienne found herself beginning to shake.

Kristian glanced at her, and their eyes met. Adrienne knew that he, too, was hoping that she would do well. If she did not . . .

"Very well." She tried to conceal the quaver in her voice. "I'll be happy to read. Is there a playscript?"

"I brought it with me." Kristian handed it to her, and Adrienne leafed through its pages, trying to stall for time. Surely the moment she opened her mouth to speak there would be a frog in her throat. . . .

She fought down panic. Stage fright, Barrett had told her, was the most dangerous malady that could strike a novice. Perilous, insidious, it could ruin a play, even a career.

She swallowed hard, putting her hands behind her back and digging her fingernails into her flesh until she wanted to cry out with pain. She wished she could have a sip—just one sip—of Barrett's whisky to steady her.

"Well, go on, Adrienne," Kristian said impatiently. "What are you waiting for? Don't keep Mr. Magruder waiting. Start with Act I, Scene I, and do your best."

A nightmare twenty minutes later, she had finished the reading and closed the playbook. She was not aware of anything she had said or done, she only knew that she had finished, that both Magruder and Kristian were staring at her.

Were they pleased? Or had she failed?

"Well." Magruder spoke to Kristian, not to her. "She is certainly a lovely little piece of womanflesh, no doubt about it. And she reads the part superbly. Still—"

Tensely Adrienne waited.

"She is the actress I want," Kristian said firmly. "I won't accept any other."

The two men faced each other. A silence seemed to settle like dust in the library. Magruder's small, piggy eyes had narrowed. "But she has no name. No one has ever heard of her."

"She is the daughter of a countess and has played many leading roles in Scotland and in England. And they *will* hear of her here in New York, I can assure you of that. She is going to be memorable indeed."

"Memorable. Yes. . . ."

Magruder was thoughtful, his glance sharp on her. Adrienne was perspiring. It was as if he could see directly into her head, see that her background was a lie. But of course, that was nonsense, she assured herself quickly. Hadn't she practiced her accent, had she not worked on moving and talking like a lady of quality?

No one, no one at all, knew of her real background now or ever would.

Phineas Magruder moistened his lips. "Very well, Kristian. She will do, I guess. Give her an advance on her pay, a generous one. I want her to work hard for us—very hard. We are taking a risk on you, young lady," he added, turning to Adrienne. "I hope you prove yourself worthy of that risk. Because if you don't—"

He made a coarse, chopping motion with his right hand.

"Yes, Mr. Magruder," she said hastily. "Thank you, Mr. Magruder. I'm so very grateful!"

The small eyes were stony. "It isn't gratefulness I wish from you, Miss Gill. It's star quality. Do you think you have it? I hope to God you do."

Ten minutes later, in the hack Kristian had hired, Adrienne leaned back, almost giddy with her relief. Already she had pushed Magruder's ominous last words out of her mind. She did have star quality, of course she did! Hadn't *Maman* told her so, over and over?

"He liked me, Kristian," she bubbled happily. "Oh, I know he really did!" She felt like singing, like running and skipping with joy.

Kristian scowled. "You saw him for yourself. Phineas Magruder doesn't *like* anyone, Adrienne, including me. He merely uses people, that's all. Get that through your head, will you? To him, the theater is a business, the same as any other."

Her mood began to wilt.

"But I did get the part. I'm going to be Melissa Charles! And I'll be good, Kristian, I swear I will."

"I hope so." Kristian stared out of the window of the cab, his eyes somber.

That day, on the strength of her advance in pay, Adrienne found and rented a brownstone house to which to move Barrett and the baby. It was located on a street lined with identical dwellings, each one attached to the next. Dozens of railings and balustrades led up to identical high stoops. Above each stoop were two higher stories, equipped with tall, narrow windows. The total effect, Adrienne decided, was strange. Long rows of stoops, rows of railings, rows of doors, of tall, narrow windows . . .

Inside the brownstone was a narrow parlor. The dining room was located at the back of the house on the second floor, and food was hauled up to it in a dumbwaiter. On the top floor, two bedrooms were connected to each other by dressing rooms equipped with washbasins and clothes closets. The furniture, supplied by their landlady, was solid and heavy.

It was certainly nothing like the Magruder home. Yet, after the two rooms over the carpenters' shop, the house seemed the utmost in luxury to Adrienne. It was clean and relatively roomy, on a respectable street. And now, with her salary, she could hire a girl to come in to cook for them and to care for the baby.

Jubilantly, she went back to the flat to give Barrett her double news.

"And so, instead of playing Juliet or Lady Macbeth, you are to play a divorcée, a modern-day kept woman."

The right corner of her husband's mouth drooped as always, and a little runnel of saliva streamed down his chin. His face was the pasty color of one who never goes outdoors. The bottle of whisky was at its usual place by his bedside, and the entire room reeked of its contents.

Impatiently Adrienne took three-month-old Barrie out of her basket, found a clean diaper, and began to change her. She did it efficiently, glancing down at the small infant face with distaste. How like Barrett the child looked! Her very facial structure, the color of her hair, the cool gray eyes! And did Barrie possess her father's other characteristics, too? The hateful desire to hurt, the drive for power over others?

She finished changing the baby and set her back in her basket.

"Oh, what does it matter what role I play?" she asked Barrett. "The fact is that I did get the part, and we need the money right now."

"And how did you get the role? By sleeping with the playwright?"

Adrienne gasped.

"Ah, yes, I buy the *Mirror,* you know, and I can also read between the lines. Kristian King is your old shipboard romance, is he not? And how else could you have possibly gotten the part? There are dozens of other actresses far more qualified than you to take that role."

Adrienne faced her husband angrily. "Perhaps. But *I* got it. I'm the one who will play Melissa, not any other actress!"

"Yes. But what you will do with the role is something I am most interested to see. I've told you that you are not yet ready for stardom, and I'll wager I'm right. Stardom is a state of mind, Adrienne, a way of thinking you do not yet possess."

"I do possess it, I do! Oh, Barrett, what utter nonsense you talk!" Adrienne threw off her mantle and marched toward the table where Barrett kept his flask. She found a glass and poured into it several inches of the golden liquid.

As she hesitated, staring into the depths of the glass, fright began to pound through her. At Magruder's, and in the cab with Kristian, she had been filled with a heady triumph, so giddy that she felt she must sing, or dance.

Now all that golden mood was gone.

Was she ready, or was Barrett, damn him, right?

Chapter 17

Indian summer had cast its spell upon the city, touching the trees which lined the streets with gold, and filling the air with a smoky blue haze. Outside the window of the brownstone, an old woman sold fresh apples from a cart to housewives who flocked around to buy.

"Tell me, Miss Gill," the columnist said, leaning forward in the upholstered parlor chair. "Tell me, what would bring a girl like you—purported to be the daughter of a countess—" He inclined his head in disbelief. "What would bring you here to become an actress?"

Adrienne caught her breath, staring at the man from the *Mirror*. William Stauffer was short and dark-mustached, with the black, eager eyes of a ferret. His right hand toyed with a pencil, a faint smile on his lips.

Her voice tumbled on. "I suppose my background may seem strange to you, Mr. Stauffer, but I assure you I have wanted to be an actress ever since I was a child."

That, at least, was true enough.

She hesitated, lowering her eyes. The lies flowed easily. "The truth is, Mr. Stauffer, that I *am* the daughter of a countess. Although you can't print this, I had to run away from home after my stepfather . . . made improper advances to me. Friends helped me to find shelter, and eventually I ended up on the stage in Glasgow, Edinburgh and London. From there I came to New York."

"Ah." Stauffer's eyes gleamed, and she noted that they roved appreciatively over her fashionably cut gown, another dress purchased from Mrs. Carstens on the promises of salary yet to come. Her pale hair had been carefully dressed and adorned with a bonnet sewn with ostrich feathers and small satin ribbons, another extravagance she had not been able to resist.

And, on the advice of Fanny Pepper, Adrienne had reddened her lips slightly with carmine in order to bring out their delicate color. In repayment of her debt, Adrienne had secured for Fanny a supporting role in *Melissa Charles*, the female lead second only to Melissa.

"Ah, Miss Gill," the columnist went on inexorably. "Tell me, how does it feel to be the subject of more gossip than any other woman in New York?"

"I didn't know that I was, Mr. Stauffer. *Is* the city talking about me? I'm sure I don't know why they would wish to. Opening night is not for another week."

The newsman scribbled on a pad of paper. "Then, Miss Gill, do you mean to tell me that you have no idea what controversy this play of Kristian King's is causing?"

"Controversy?"

"Why, yes. Every woman in New York is chattering about this new, modern play which dares to depict life in all its rawness. A divorced woman, having affairs! And what's more, enjoying them!"

Stauffer had moistened his lips.

"I am only an actress, Mr. Stauffer. I merely speak the lines as they were written by the playwright and try to interpret them as best I can."

Abruptly, Stauffer changed tack. "And how do you feel, Miss Gill, about being introduced into a starring role so quickly? Don't you think it a bit—ah, unusual?"

"Unusual?"

Adrienne had stiffened slightly. Outside the brownstone, the apple woman had moved on, her cries fainter now.

"Yes, my dear. The gossip on Broadway and Union Square was that a more established American actress would get the role. Perhaps Fanny Davenport, or Kate Claxton, or even Kitty Blanchard."

These were names of popular actresses—women well known in the New York theater. Adrienne narrowed

242

her eyes at the columnist, the lies she had told him quite forgotten.

"What do you mean, Mr. Stauffer? What are you trying to say?"

"Why—why, nothing, of course. Just that you and Mr. King—well, rumor has it that you are more than just actress and playwright. That you are perhaps closer friends than that."

Closer friends than that. *Spawn of the devil.* The voice of the old man in Glasgow, harsh as lye soap, seemed to burn in her mind. Adrienne found that her fists were clenched in her lap.

"Those are strong accusations!" she snapped. "This is 1872, Mr. Stauffer, an age of propriety. I am certain that your paper would never allow you to print such wild speculations!"

"You are right, Miss Gill. Our paper is respectable." The ferret eyes gleamed at her. "Still, a certain amount of reader curiosity has been aroused, and I am sure it will have to be satisfied somehow."

"With dirty gossip?"

Stauffer licked his lips. "My readers want to know if you, Miss Gill, live the same sort of personal life which the character Melissa Charles lives onstage. Did you get the role by sleeping with the playwright? Rumor has it that you did. And, if so—"

But Adrienne had heard enough. She leaped out of her chair and sprang forward. The smack of her open palm against the columnist's cheek was loud in the room.

For an instant they stared at each other. The man's hand was pressed to the red spot on his cheek, and Adrienne's mouth was open in shock at what she had done.

Then the writer grinned in triumph.

"Well! So the lovely Miss Adrienne Gill has slapped a columnist across the face! What wonderful gossip that will make! And perhaps I will be able to think of a way to put it in my column. I will certainly try."

Adrienne could feel herself breathe in raw, shaking gasps.

"Do that, Mr. Stauffer!" Her voice rang out, full and

rich. "I did slap your face, and I'm glad of it! I'll do it again if you don't leave my home at once. And you may write about me in your column as you wish. I really don't care!"

Adrienne climbed out of the cab, paid the driver, and started to walk the few hundred yards to the entrance of the alley which led to the stage door of the Olympic Theater. It was three days later, but the incident with the columnist still preyed on her mind.

Do you, Miss Gill, live the same sort of personal life which the character Melissa Charles lives onstage? Why had William Stauffer said such a thing to her? Was it jealousy, an unwillingness to see an unknown girl catapulted into the public eye? And how dare he take pleasure in goading her, as if she were not a person with feelings, but merely a creature to be used to gain readers for his paper?

Two girls of fifteen or sixteen were loitering outside the theater, gawking at the playbills nailed on frames to the three gaslights in front. Adrienne brushed past them, her mind still on William Stauffer. She did care, of course, what he wrote—and she was sorry now that she had lost her temper.

To have slapped an important theatrical columnist —what had possessed her to do such a foolish thing? Yet she had done it, and she must now take the consequences, whatever they might be.

"Is that Adrienne Gill?" one of the girls asked the other as she passed them.

Adrienne, crossing now by the gaslights, stopped in her tracks. But the girls were not looking at her. Instead, they were gazing at the lithographed playbill which advertised *Melissa Charles.* The playbill, printed in full color, showed a fashionable woman in long, flowing skirts and elegant bonnet, holding a frilly parasol.

"Gosh, but she's pretty!" the first girl breathed. "And her hair, it's just like they say. Like spun sugar!"

"Oh, but that's only a picture." The second girl, short and plump, was superior. "She is notorious, Edith.

244

My Mama has said so. Why, she leads a life every bit as wicked as that Melissa Charles in the play."

Adrienne, pausing to listen, did not know whether to smile or to weep with frustration.

"How do you know that, Nelly?"

"Why, Mama says so! And everyone knows she slapped a newspaperman across the face. It was in the *Mirror* yesterday. Who but a common woman would do that? And Mama says—"

"Oh, what does your Mama know?" The first girl's voice was indignant. "Nelly! Just imagine what it must be like to be an actress. A countess, Nelly—that's what the paper said she is. And to think that tomorrow is opening night. All the society women in the city will be here." She giggled. "The ones whose husbands will let 'em, that is."

"My Mama would beat me with a strap if she knew I was here," the second girl confided. Then she giggled and thrust something into her friend's hand. "But I did get tickets! I sent my brother to fetch them. We're going to see Adrienne Gill in *Melissa Charles,* what do you think of that? We're going to see everything!"

The girls moved on, and Adrienne crossed thoughtfully toward the stage door. Opening night. William Stauffer's malicious face, the new clothes, the frenzied rehearsals, the frantic schedule of her days . . . was any of it real? Or was it all just some fantastic dream, conjured up by *Maman* as she sat over her sewing?

She turned to give a last glance at the front of the theater. Dusk was falling and the gaslights were aglow, lighting up the three playbills.

Behind the playbills was the Olympic itself, sandwiched between a publishing company and a store selling straw goods. But the theater was jaunty in appearance, its rows of windows on the upper three stories fitted with striped, scalloped awnings. At street level, five pillars were topped by a white-railed balcony set with a row of cheerfully waving American flags. Emblazoned across the front of the building was raised gilt lettering: *Olympic Theater.*

245

To Adrienne, those two words gleaming in the gaslight were magic.

Earlier today she had written *Maman* a long letter about the theater and about *Melissa Charles,* copying it over three times until she had captured just the right confident mood. There was so much now that she could not tell *Maman.* Her mistake in slapping Stauffer, her doubts, her fears, her nervousness over opening night, her relationship with Kristian . . .

For, she supposed, Stauffer had been right. She and Kristian were certainly more than just "friends." After that night at the Astor House, they had continued to see each other. It was as if they were driven, as if they could not help themselves. There were moments stolen after rehearsals, the two of them devouring chops and wine in a small café near the Olympic patronized by tradesmen, where theater people did not go. There were sweet, forbidden hours spent in Kristian's rooms in the new, small boarding house where he had taken lodgings.

"Darling," he had whispered to her as they lay locked together on his narrow bed. "What is happening to us? My God, you're married, with an invalid husband and a child. This is wrong, it can only lead to disaster for both of us. I feel it, Adrienne, deep in my bones, or my instincts, or wherever such feelings lie."

"No, no," she had whispered back, putting a hand to his lips to close them. "Don't say such things."

"Not saying them doesn't make them not true."

But Adrienne had pulled him to her violently, burying herself in the physical warmth of him until the words were lost, and she did not have to hear them or remember them.

She didn't want to think about disaster, or Barrett, or a love which was wrong and could not work. There was only Kristian, so real that when she was in his arms there was nothing else for her.

Each time their bodies came together, it was with a wild ecstasy almost painful in its sweetness. She could not seem to get enough of him. It was as if he were a drug which her body must have for its survival. He was a considerate, untiring lover. His kisses could be soft, or demanding, or rough with passion. There were times when he kissed the small of her back, the arches of her feet, the creases of her neck and breasts. Times, too, when he kissed other parts of her body, bringing her to a fiery joy she had never known before.

Later, when the lovemaking was over and she was in a hack on her way back to the brownstone, she would sink into a strange mood of depression. Ugly thoughts would whirl in her mind, as ephemeral as cigar smoke. *Miss Gill, how does it feel to be the subject of more gossip than any other woman in New York? Did you get the role by sleeping with the playwright? Rumor says you did. . . .*

The dress rehearsal did not go well. There were problems with the gas table, and a repairman had to be called. Bettina Smithe's costume, Kristian suddenly decided, needed extensive alterations, though her role was only the minor one of Melissa's maid. The first-act curtain was far too slow. And the entire production, Kristian decreed, needed speeding up, or the play was going to drag.

He objected, too, to the way Adrienne portrayed Melissa.

"Dammit, Adrienne!" he shouted after they had run through the first two acts. Several cast members tittered. "Dammit, girl, do you think that Melissa Charles is a floozy out strolling the streets and looking for customers? No matter what the newspapers say, Melissa is a woman of dignity and honor! Please play her as such!"

Adrienne stared at him. Why hadn't he told her these things before? Why was he waiting until now—almost the last minute—to speak to her so?

"But I am," she protested. "That's why I've walked downstage like this, and why I—"

"You haven't walked as I've told you at all," Kristian snapped. "How many times must I tell you what I have in mind for this play? You're playing Melissa in the old-fashioned manner—in the mode of the 1860's. You sweep downstage with exaggerated motions. You declaim. You stop in the midst of a speech to look at the audience and gauge their reaction."

"But," she sputtered, "Barrett said—"

"Never mind what Barrett Kendall said! Just listen to me, Adrienne. Not only did I write this play, but I am also directing it, or had you forgotten that?"

They faced each other angrily. Again someone giggled, and harshly Kristian told the rest of the cast to take a break. He pulled her aside to the wings, where two stagehands were lowering flats from the cavernous area overhead known as the "flies."

"Your husband is nearly fifty, Adrienne—an aging man. He has taught you the theatrical techniques of a past generation. My play is modern! And it isn't a fairy tale like *East Lynne* or even *Uncle Tom's Cabin*. It's real—as real as I can make it. Melissa Charles is real."

"But, Kristian—"

"No, listen to me. I suppose that some of the fat belles of Fifth Avenue are going to find my play shocking. But I really don't care, just as long as they'll buy seats. I feel sure that the theater is going to change, Adrienne, within the next decade. I wish to be part of that change —I am going to be."

"Very well!" She had barely listened to Kristian's words, so angry was she at the way he had humiliated her in front of the entire cast. Now she tossed her head furiously. "Very well, then. It *is* your play, isn't it? You are the playwright and the director. You've made that fact very clear to me, Kris."

Deliberately she had used the hated nickname.

The color drained from Kristian's face, leaving only two spots of red.

"Didn't I tell you not to use that name?" His hands gripped her shoulders, cutting into her flesh with fierce strength.

"Let go of me, Kristian! You're hurting me—"

"Not until you promise you'll never call me Kris again."

"But why? What difference does it make? A silly old nickname! Why, in Glasgow—"

She stopped, nearly biting her tongue. *In Glasgow,* she had been going to say, *everyone called me Addie—*

Kristian's jaw had squared. Knots of muscle roped along his jawline. His eyes narrowed at her, their depths filled with ice.

"Someone called me by that name once. I don't wish it ever to be used to me again."

She stared at him. *Someone called me that name once.* Who? Why would a mere nickname throw Kristian into such savage anger? Was he afraid of something? Some secret from his past?

She drew a deep breath. She, too, could be angry. She needn't put up with public humiliation from anyone.

"I have a splitting headache," she told him spitefully. "I'm going to my dressing room to lie down for a few minutes. Let the rehearsal wait—let the entire cast wait. I just don't care!"

She picked up the hem of her gown, and with all the dignity she could muster, swept to stage right and the narrow little stairway which led downstairs to the dressing rooms and greenroom. She did not look back at Kristian.

"How dare he do that to me in front of the whole company! I'm so angry at him, Fanny, that I could kill him. I could! If you could have heard that dumpy little Bettina Smithe laugh at me—"

"She's so empty-headed, she would laugh at anyone," Fanny Pepper consoled. "And she's jealous of you as well. You're everything she can never be, Adrienne, and she knows it."

It was two hours later. The rehearsal, every long, agonizing moment of it, was finally over. Adrienne felt drained with exhaustion and discouragement. Now she and Fanny Pepper sat alone in one of the dressing rooms, a dingy cell painted leaden green. It was fitted with a wooden shelf, a mirror, a crude wooden bench and the usual gas fixture on the wall, its jet of flame guarded against possible accident by metal grillwork.

Adrienne, in a burst of optimism, had already hung her two wall hangings and laid down her Turkish rug. But nothing could make the dressing room other than what it was, bleak and shabby.

"But," Adrienne went on hotly, "to laugh at me because Kristian had the bad manners to speak to me in front of the cast—"

"Don't let it upset you. Kristian, too, has much to learn about the theater."

Fanny, seated on the long bench, was pulling the pins out of her hair and unbraiding the elaborate coiffure which Kristian had decreed necessary for her role as Betty, Melissa's best friend.

"But it does upset me!" Adrienne paced back and forth, still wearing her Melissa costume, a dark green watered silk whose fabric caught the light sumptuously.

"I'm a good actress, Fanny, I know I am. I can feel it, here inside me." She touched her breast. "But Kristian acts as if I don't know anything at all. Do this, do that! Don't declaim, don't go out of character and play to the audience—"

"Perhaps he's right."

"But I'm the star of this play! I'm Melissa Charles, I'm the one who will be making her debut tomorrow!"

"And so you are." Fanny turned from the mirror. "But did it ever occur to you that Kristian's making his debut too? His debut as a playwright? His entire career hangs on this play, Adrienne."

"I . . . I suppose you are right." Adrienne bit down hard on her lower lip, stifling shame. "Oh, Fanny! I—I'm just so frightened about opening night! What if I should make a terrible mistake? Forget my lines? Or—or worse?"

Fanny grinned. "What can happen that would be worse than that? But don't worry, it won't happen to you, why should it? You've worked hard, even Kristian King must admit that. You've put in long hours after everyone has gone home in order to get the characterization just right. Why shouldn't you be a success?"

Adrienne gazed at the older actress. Happily, Fanny had accepted the secondary role as Melissa's best friend. She had befriended Adrienne, given her advice, shown her how to do her hair and make-up. Now, thanks to

Fanny's warmth, the gnawing rat of apprehension in Adrienne's belly had begun to abate a little.

"Yes," she admitted. "I have worked hard."

"Well, then! Why are you fretting? Worrying, my dear, is what causes stage fright. Relax! Let's you and I go out tonight to that little café near Union Square—we'll have a few drinks and some fun. What do you say?"

Adrienne hesitated, thinking of Barrett waiting at home in the brownstone with little Barrie, waiting to hear how the rehearsal had gone. Even the new maid, Annie Smith, frizzy-haired and eighteen, would be wanting to know, keeping a supper warm on the stove for her. . . .

"All right," she replied. "I suppose just for an hour or so I could go. And I am hungry—"

But as she and Fanny hurried out of the theater, an ugly little knot seemed to swell up inside Adrienne's throat, so thick that she could not swallow it down.

Opening night was tomorrow. That would be the test of all she had learned, the test of Adrienne herself, the culmination of all *Maman*'s dreams. *Was* she star material, as the billboards had proclaimed in huge block letters? Or, as Barrett had predicted, was she just not yet ready?

Tomorrow she would know. The whole of New York would know.

She was consumed with terror.

It was raining. The air was full of a fine, cold spray which coated the pavements with moisture and made them slippery. Horse droppings added to the hazards, and, on the way to the theater, they had already passed one carriage accident.

But Adrienne, although she felt sorry for the people involved in such mishaps, could think of little else save *Melissa Charles*. Tonight was opening night.

"Damned rain," Barrett muttered beside her in his slurred voice. "It will affect attendance."

"Will it?"

Inanely, their conversation went on. Adrienne responded automatically, without the slightest awareness of what she said. In only a few hours, she would be onstage, the target of hundreds of eyes. Curious eyes, condemning eyes. An audience, having paid good money to see her, would have to decide whether it liked what it saw. . . .

"You are sitting very stiffly, *dear* wife." Barrett's voice, thick with sarcasm, caught her unprepared. "Are you quite sure you're prepared for this premature debut you are about to make against my advice?"

"Yes, of course I am." Her mouth felt cottony, and her tongue was as dry as a linen towel. And she had to use the commode. Desperately, she had to relieve herself. Yet she had gone just before they had left the brownstone.

Fleetingly she thought of little Barrie, now safely at home with the new maid, Annie. Barrie was too little to know that her mother was about to make her debut in a starring role. Only Annie, with her watery blue eyes and sturdy peasant figure, knew that. When she had left, the maid's eyes had swept over her mistress with ill-concealed envy.

"Everyone's talking about you, ma'am. Everyone wants to know how you'll do."

Now the hack swayed through the streets, the city passing before her: rain-wet stone buildings, pedestrians huddled under awnings or stone fronts. She saw all of it, yet she saw none of it. Tonight all of New York was a blur. In only a few hours, she would be onstage as Melissa Charles. . . .

"Here," Barrett said. "Have some of this. It will loosen you up. God knows you need it."

With his good hand he fished in his greatcoat. He produced the flask which he always carried with him. The amber glass, embossed with the elaborate emblem of its maker, gleamed in the glow of a gaslight. With difficulty Barrett extracted the cork.

"Swallow it down, wife. Go on. Haven't I used it often enough? And hasn't it always helped?"

Wordlessly, Adrienne took the flask from him. Too much drink, of course, would be a mistake, she knew. It might cause her to slur her speech, to stumble or miss her lines. Yet one or two swallows would not hurt. And she needed to ease her frantic tension.

If she did not have something to calm her, surely she would collapse from fright.

"Well, what are you waiting for?" Barrett demanded.

Adrienne grasped the handles of the flask.

She tilted it upward and took a long gulp of the fiery liquid. It burned down, choking, aromatic.

She gasped and swallowed. Then she leaned back against the cracked leather seat of the hack, letting her body sway with the jogging motion of the carriage. A languorous glow was already spreading down her arms and legs, lending softness to the night.

Backstage, the tension was thick. The gas wing and border lights had been lit, sending wavering shadows up the brick walls into the flies. Two stagehands frantically filed away at a sharp corner of one section of *Melissa*'s box set, in order to remove a "curse of a board," a rough edge which might injure someone.

Voices echoed, and somewhere a man and a woman were bickering. William Mancin, the tall, thin, dark-haired stage manager, paced about the interior of the set, kicking at a wrinkle in the floorcloth, which had been painted to resemble wooden parquetry.

Bettina Smithe, the plump blonde who played Melissa's maid, hurried past, teeth clamped down on her lower lip.

One of the stagehands looked up from his work as Adrienne passed. His name was Quince, she knew. In his fifties, he had a chin stubbled with gray bristles and eyes of a faded blue.

Warmly, he wished her luck.

"I've been watching you, Miss Gill, and I think you have good stuff in you, the best."

"Oh, do you think so?"

"I've been in the theater for twenty years and I've seen hundreds of actresses in my time. None of 'em, I might add, were as pretty as you."

"Oh—why, thank you!"

She hurried toward the back staircase, feeling curiously warmed. Seldom did flymen or stagehands speak to the actors in such a way. Surely the fact that one had done so was a sign of good luck. And she needed all the luck she could muster.

In the women's dressing room, all was pandemonium. Bettina Smithe now sat cross-legged on a bench, nearly in tears as a wardrobe mistress squatted beside her, frantically mending a rent in the flounce of her skirt. Gertrude Wing, an older character actress, leaned tensely toward the mirror, smoothing on her make-up with hands that shook visibly.

Only Fanny Pepper seemed calm. Seated on the bench, already made up and in costume, she was knitting a pair of black wool socks.

"For my nephew in Grand Rapids," she explained, waving them in the air. "I always knit on opening night. It relieves tension."

Adrienne stared at her friend. "But how can you be so calm? My heart is thumping so badly I'm afraid everyone can see it!"

Stage fright, she thought in growing alarm. Was this how it began, with this sour turmoil in the belly, the uncontrollable urge to urinate, the dread that you might become sick at any moment?

Fanny smiled. Her needles clicked comfortably.

"I'm not calm at all, Adrienne. I'm just pretending that I am. And most of the time it seems to work. And at least I get plenty of knitting done. I promised my sister that I would try to keep her boy in socks—a job that might take me the rest of my life!"

"Half an hour, ladies," came the voice of the callboy from outside the room. "Mr. King says for all of you to hurry; he wants to inspect you before the curtain goes up. He wants everything to be perfect tonight!"

Adrienne, in the act of pulling her make-up box out of her trunk, froze. She put the box down and extended her right hand, staring at it dully.

Was her hand trembling? In fact, was her entire body trembling?

Yes, she admitted to herself. It was.

Chapter 18

She was ready. She leaned forward to inspect herself in the wavery mirror, the gas flame in its protective grillwork casting leaping shadows on her face.

Her make-up box, with Fanny's assistance, was now well stocked with supplies. It contained such items as pearl and violet powder, fuller's earth, rouge, carmine, *crayon d'Italie*, powdered antimony, burnt cork, spirit gum, burnt umber, Indian ink and eye lining brush, plus the soap, sponge, and towels which Fanny recommended for removing make-up.

"Lard or butter as a make-up base is so greasy and old-fashioned," Fanny had insisted. "If you want to look really lovely, Adrienne, you should forget all that and wash your face as soon as you get to the theater. Then just pass a powder puff over your skin. The rouge will adhere so much better."

So Adrienne had followed the older actress's instructions. She had scrubbed her face clean. From her make-up box, she had taken the little bottle of pearl powder and dusted it carefully over her skin. Then came the rouge for her cheekbones, lips and chin. Lastly, with a fine camel's-hair brush, she had penciled a thin umber line above and below her lashes.

Now she gazed at herself in the mirror, almost shocked at what she saw.

The girl who stared back at her out of the glass was exotically lovely. She had bold cheekbones heightened by carmine, and eyes emphasized by underlining. Her chin was firm, her mouth full, yet delicately curved. Her hair, gold-white and shining as a Roman coin, was swept up from her face and fastened in a high crown at the back of her head. Two long, coiled ringlets fell luxuriously at her back.

She looked—Adrienne caught her breath—exactly like a woman bold and independent, a woman who might smoke a cigarette, order her own carriage, tote her own luggage and take a lover if she desired. In short, she looked like Melissa Charles.

"Oh, Adrienne! You're beautiful!" breathed Fanny, who had been hovering about supervising the application of the make-up. "You *are* Melissa, the very image. I'm sure Mr. King will think so, too, when he sees you."

Adrienne tried to smile. Her right hand stole to the bodice of her gown where, strung on its chain underneath her dress where it would not show, was the Passion Star. She had worn it for good luck.

"I hope so."

As soon as Fanny had left, Adrienne felt another wash of terror so strong that she sank back onto the hard wood of the make-up bench. This was her debut. What if she failed? What if *Maman*'s dreams were all to crumble like stale cheese, worthless?

A fragrant bouquet of pink hothouse roses and a tissue-wrapped bottle of champagne had been sent to the dressing room—a gift from Kristian. Now, blindly, Adrienne fumbled at the wrapping around the champagne bottle, then twisted the mushroom-shaped cork, working it loose. The cork finally popped, making a shockingly loud noise. Liquid gushed onto the floor.

Adrienne froze. Had anyone heard?

But the corridor outside the dressing room continued to echo with the ordinary backstage noises, and, after a hesitation, Adrienne reached into her make-up box for the small metal water cup she kept there. She poured herself some champagne.

Again she hesitated, staring deep within the depths of the cup at the pale wine, effervescent and bubbly. But champagne was only a wine, she assured herself. It was not like whisky, and, anyway, she would only have one cupful. It would relax her and assuage the terror which consumed her.

Five minutes later, Kristian was waiting for her in the narrow passage outside the dressing room, dressed in the tweed suit which was his costume for the role he played as George, Melissa's lover. His make-up was already on, its application emphasizing the bold sweep of his cheekbones, the faint bump of his nose where it had once been broken. In the dim, gaslit corridor, his eyes looked somber. His dimple was barely visibly save as a line slashed in his cheeks.

"Well, Kristian?" The champagne seemed to spin in her brain, softening her thoughts. "Last night was only the dress rehearsal, but tonight is the real thing. How do I look?"

He regarded her. "Who did your make-up?"

"Why, Fanny Pepper helped me."

"She did a good job, then. She is adept at matters of the theater, isn't she?"

A compliment for Fanny instead of for herself. Adrienne pressed her lips together. The sour churning in her belly had begun again, abated somewhat by the wine. However, Kristian seemed deadly calm.

"And how do you feel tonight, Adrienne? According to the *Mirror,* tonight is the debut of New York's most talked-about new actress, a woman with a temper as fiery as her hair is golden."

Adrienne forced a laugh. "That columnist I smacked has never forgotten, has he?"

"Would you?" Kristian's mouth was grim. "It was not a good idea to slap him, Adrienne. In fact, it was a damned poor one. You've alienated a powerful newspaper man, and Magruder was not at all happy with you."

"Oh." She pressed her hands together. "I . . . I'm sorry."

"Very well. You have a hot temper. God knows I should know that by now. I suppose we must accept it."

Looking at Kristian now, glittering and tense, it seemed impossible for her to believe that she had actually lain in this man's arms, had trembled under his touch.

Yet it had happened. And even now, something in her wished to reach out, to touch him. To finger his hair with its crisp curls, to run her hand along the powerful thrust of his jaw.

Suddenly he leaned forward and kissed her on the lips. It was a swift kiss, yet soft and tender, and it sent a little thrill through her.

"Well, darling, I must admit that you do make a beautiful Melissa. I should have told you that last night. That hair of yours is like spun sunlight. And your eyes are cornflowers."

"Oh, Kristian!" She could not help sliding her arms about him. "Do you really think I am beautiful? Oh, I want to be! I want them all to look at me, and to love me!"

The sick fear was leaving her. Now joy swept through her veins like spring floodwater. She would be good tonight, of course she would be. Hadn't *Maman* always maintained faith in her, didn't *Maman* say that she was destined?

Maman. If only her mother could be here tonight to see her dreams come true. She felt a twinge of sadness. And Devin. If only Devin had lived, to know that his big sister might one day be famous . . .

"Yes, darling," Kristian was saying. He tilted up her chin. Carefully, so as not to smear the make-up both wore, he again touched her lips with his own. "You are lovely. Beautiful to me always, God help me."

"Curtain going up! Curtain going up!"

The callboy's cry echoed down the corridor, causing Adrienne's heart to leap inside her chest like a frightened sparrow.

Kristian, too, had frozen.

"There it is," he whispered. His hand found hers and squeezed it. "The call. Soon, darling, soon—"

Adrienne stood in the wings waiting for the rustling whirr of the curtain's rise and tried to concentrate. *You must have in your head the thoughts of the character you play rather than your own,* Barrett had insisted over and over. *When you go onstage you must move and act as if you are that person merely continuing with what has gone before in his life. . . .*

She was Melissa Charles.

Grimly she shut her eyes and tried to close out the backstage noises: a rustle of pages as William Mancin, the stage manager, leafed for one last time through his promptbook. A rattle as the boy stood at the gas table with its rows of cocks and handles. The hiss of the wing lights and footlights.

And, lastly, the expectant stirring and coughs of the audience which sat like some huge, composite beast beyond the curtain.

The audience. Barrett, seated with his two canes, waiting out there for her to fail. The two little girls she had seen the other day at the box office, come to gawk. Critics, ready with paper and pencil to mock or praise.

She tried to swallow. Even Mr. Stauffer, the columnist whose face she had slapped; he, too, would be among those endless rows of faces, waiting for her to make a mistake. . . .

Adrienne's throat gave another convulsive swallow, totally beyond her power to stop it. Her tongue was dry, almost barren of saliva. And, for the dozenth time, she had to use the bathroom.

What if she forgot her lines? What if the other actors had to improvise for her, making up lines to cover her mistakes? What if—horrible thought—she tripped and tumbled flat in front of everybody? What if—

The sound of the expectant audience had changed slightly. Its murmurs had blended together like a hum of bees. Adrienne knew what that sound meant. The house lights were going down.

Slowly, majestically, with a rattle of pulleys and a sweep of heavy velvet fabric, the curtain rose. Adrienne drew a short, sharp, panicky breath, then another. She felt as if she could not draw in enough air. As if she would strangle . . .

She found that she had stumbled onstage, that her mouth was speaking lines. Words, sentences. Words which Kristian had written and which now seemed totally devoid of meaning.

259

The footlights glared in her eyes, their flames so bright that the people seated beyond them seemed to occupy a dark cavern. Their faces floated in long rows. Row after row of cabbages.

Scene One. Scene Two.

The scenes passed, one after another. Words issued from her mouth as if spoken by someone else. Her body seemed to move as automatically as one of the cast-iron automata which children used for money banks.

As she worked her way through Melissa's lines, the other actors' faces moved before her, shining with perspiration, for the footlights were hot. There was the peculiar, oily smell of the gas, and the odor of scene paint, of lumber and hempen rope and human sweat and costumes kept too long in theater trunks.

There were sounds, too; the scrape of a chair leg against the painted floor-cloth, the coughs, rustles, sneezes, and seat-stirrings which bespoke the presence of hundreds of people beyond the footlights.

There were too many "barkers" in the audience, she had time to note with tight-drawn fear. Barkers, those who coughed, meant that the audience was growing bored. . . .

The second act came. Kristian, in his role as Melissa's lover, was charming and handsome. In the second scene, however, he stumbled over the wrinkle in the floor-cloth. Adrienne, seeing this, gasped and caught her breath, losing the rhythm of the lines.

For an instant she swam in panic.

It was as if the character of Melissa Charles had dropped away, and she was Adrienne again. Or, worse, she was little Addie from Glasgow, standing on the stage of the Brittania with Xenos Shane, frightened and hungry and alone. . . .

With an effort, she forced herself back into the part. Said the lines, spoke the words which Kristian had written. The words which, in reading over the playscript, she had thought beautiful and poetic . . .

During the intermission, the actors gathered glumly in the greenroom, speaking little to each other.

No one spoke to Adrienne.

George Rignold muttered, "They're coughing too much out there. Barking, damn 'em. I can hear 'em squirming in their seats and wishing they were back home in front of the fireplace."

"Yes, and that's where I wish I was, too," someone else said bitterly.

Kristian said nothing. His face was grim, and he sat alone at one end of the battered long table, puffing on a cigar. Blue smoke rose in clouds about him.

Adrienne sat down beside him. "Kristian," she began.

"Don't talk to me now, Adrienne." Abruptly Kristian got to his feet, tossed the cigar into a cuspidor, and stalked away.

Bewildered, Adrienne could only sit rigid, staring after him, until at last he disappeared into the men's dressing room, slamming its door behind him.

"Never mind," Fanny Pepper said. She had found her knitting again and now her needles clicked and flashed. "We're all tense. It's opening night, remember?"

They were silent again, the others staring downward into half-empty coffee cups, or simply sitting. Bettina Smithe toyed with her maid's cap, pleating its lace over and over between her fingers. Her eyes, when they met Adrienne's, were resentful.

At last Adrienne could stand it no more. She jumped up and fled into the dressing room, closing its door behind her and leaning against it until her body had finished shaking. How was the play going? Surely all was not as bad as she feared. Yet everyone had been silent around her. Bettina Smithe had glared at her as if all the "barkers" in the audience were her fault.

Barely realizing that she did so, Adrienne reached into the depths of her trunk and pulled out the bottle of champagne. She poured herself two quick cupfuls, gulping down the wine without tasting it. There wasn't much time, and she needed the relief the champagne could bring, the blurred, fuzzy softness which would dull her distress and get her through the rest of the play. . . .

The third act seemed interminable. The lines which once had appeared so brilliant and witty now seemed

261

dull, without life. Or was it only her own interpretation of them?

She felt self-conscious. As if her arms and legs were too clumsy, her hands too big. Her dress felt wrong, its folds too heavy and not flowing gracefully enough when she walked. In the second scene of the last act, when Melissa was supposed to pour herself a glass of sherry— consisting for theater purposes of weakened tea—the decanter had been placed in the wrong spot. Adrienne could hear the crystal clatter as she poured. Her hands were shaking.

Desperately she recalled the feeling she had had so often while on tour with *Uncle Tom's Cabin*—the feeling of kinship with the audience, the almost physical bond which had flowed from them to her and back again. The giving and the taking, the knowledge that for these few hours she owned these people, could do with them almost as she wished.

None of that was present tonight. She felt nothing. There was only the scrape of feet, the interminable coughs which never stopped.

God, oh, God, she found herself praying. *Let this be over with, let it be done. And please, please, let it not be as bad as I fear it is. . . .*

It was over.

Adrienne stood with the other members of the cast, taking the obligatory curtain calls.

One. Two. The footlights, with their continuous row of gas flames, seemed unnaturally bright, making her eyes water. She stood blinking her eyes and trying to smile. Dimly, she heard applause. Was it loud or weak? Adrienne could not tell.

A bouquet of roses came skidding onstage and landed at Kristian's feet. It was followed by a boutonniere. The clapping of the audience swelled and receded.

Kristian came forward to take his bow as playwright. He stood rigid, unsmiling, his head inclined only slightly. At the back of the theater someone whistled. Then a young girl dressed in white came running onstage to throw her arms around Kristian and kiss him.

Young, extravagantly pretty, her body strained toward his, her dark hair flowing down her back.

For an instant, Kristian seemed stunned. Then his mouth curved in a smile. He bent over and plucked a rose from a bouquet which had landed at his feet, and, with a flourish, handed it to the girl.

Then he stood with her facing the audience.

Who had the girl been? And why had Kristian given her a rose? Adrienne, fleeing once more to the women's bathroom, could only huddle in the room's one stall, wiping helplessly at the tears which streamed down her cheeks. The play had been a failure. All of it, all of *Maman*'s dreams, had been for nothing.

The door of the bathroom banged, and she could hear impatient voices.

"Well, now all we must do is to wait for the reviews, it appears." That was Bettina Smithe's tart voice. "That snobby little bitch Adrienne Gill really is the limit, isn't she? Just because she has a drop or two of noble blood —I *knew* we should have got Fanny Davenport. *She* could have carried off the play—"

Another voice, belonging to Gertrude Wing. "Our bad luck, that's true. Did you know that Phineas Magruder is here, backstage? And he has brought his daughter. They say that she is stage-struck, the foolish little thing—" A burst of malicious laughter.

Adrienne pushed her way out of the booth and marched past Bettina and Gertrude without speaking to them. In the greenroom, a crowd was gathered: members of the cast, newspaper reporters, friends and well-wishers. Phineas Magruder, bulky in a well-tailored black broadcloth suit, puffed on a large cigar. The columnist William Stauffer shot Adrienne a resentful look as she entered the room. He leaned forward to whisper something to the sketch artist who squatted in one corner, making quick drawings.

Adrienne was beginning to perspire. She lifted her chin and pushed past them all. At a small table in the far corner of the room, Barrett sat waiting for her. He beckoned to her.

Reluctantly, she went to him.

"Well, wife, I was right, wasn't I? You weren't ready." His blurred voice prodded at her. "And now I think you've proved it."

The good side of Barrett's mouth twisted. Shadows, cast by the pair of gas fixtures near the door of the greenroom, danced up and down his features.

"The gloom in this room is thick enough to cut, Adrienne! Or hadn't you noticed?"

Adrienne was silent. Barrett was right, of course. The gathering was glum, voices low. Even Fanny Pepper, talking in a corner with William Mancin, looked drained and tired. And across the greenroom, people were clustered about Kristian. Were they commiserating with him, she wondered with a sick feeling, because his leading lady had played Melissa less than perfectly?

She looked at the man whom—it seemed a thousand years ago—she had married.

"You wanted me to fail, didn't you, Barrett?"

Barrett's good hand came up to wipe saliva from his mouth. With a secretive motion, he extracted the amber whisky flask from his greatcoat and put it to his mouth, taking a long pull.

"Yes, I suppose I did wish to see you fail. And your lover as well. That gave me exquisite pleasure."

She could only stare at him.

"Oh, yes, dear Adrienne! Don't think I didn't know what you've been up to these weeks! You would come home glowing like a candle flame after being in bed with him. You are a whore, dear girl. A harlot selling your body to get what you wish."

Adrienne could feel the blood leave her face. "How dare you say such things to me?"

"I dare because it's true. You'll use anyone, won't you, Adrienne? Any man who can further your career. Well, this time you've failed to get what you want. You chose the wrong man—because Kristian King isn't going anywhere at all. His play stinks. Stinks, did you hear me?"

"No!"

"Oh, yes. Just wait until tomorrow when the first of

the reviews appear. You'll see. They'll tell the truth—and they won't bother to varnish it with pretty words."

She felt sick. She thought of Kristian's taut nervousness before the performance, the way he had stalked out of the greenroom without speaking to her. Unconsciously her hand stole to the sapphire which she wore under her dress for good luck, and touched its hardness, as if seeking comfort.

"You're wrong, Barrett." The words seemed to clog in her throat. "The truth is, it isn't Kristian's play which has failed, it's me."

Barrett nodded. "Truth? We'll see. Meanwhile, here is another truth, unpleasant though it may be. Your lover, it seems, has someone else."

"What?"

"Well, girl, are you blind? Just look for yourself."

Adrienne's eyes swept the greenroom. Kristian stood near the door of one of the dressing rooms, talking to a young girl, the one who had run onstage to throw her arms about him. Delicately pretty, she had an oval face and shy, dark eyes. Her gown, expensive and trimmed with French lace, accented the sweet curves of her body.

She looked, Adrienne thought, swallowing hard, as delectable as a ribbon-trimmed bonnet.

Kristian's arm lightly touched the girl's waist. His eyes looked into hers.

Ice chilled Adrienne's heart. She felt a surge of nausea, and moisture began to crawl down her sides beneath the heavy costume she wore. Feeling as if she were moving in a dream, she jumped up from the table where Barrett sat and swept across the greenroom.

Kristian gave her a curt bow. Never, she thought dully, had he looked more handsome than he did tonight, or more somber. His eyes were cold, his face carved from granite.

"Adrienne, I want you to meet Primrose Magruder. She is Phineas Magruder's middle daughter, just back from Spain in time to attend my opening, it seems."

The young girl smiled up at Kristian happily. Of course, Adrienne thought with a stab of jealousy—the portrait she had seen in the Magruder home, the one child prettier than the others. She felt something pierce within her, like a dagger of glass.

"Primrose," she heard herself say in a high, sharp voice totally beyond her power to alter. "What an unusual name."

It was as if the anger and fear she had felt all evening had funneled down at last to this beautiful young girl in white.

"Yes," Primrose agreed. She seemed unaware of any tension. Even her smile was lovely, showing small, white teeth and a slight dimple at the corner of her mouth. "It was my father's choice. He has always been fond of primroses."

Adrienne tried to imagine Phineas Magruder being fond of anything as ephemeral as a flower.

"Indeed," she replied coldly.

"Yes, oh, I loved you in the play, Miss Gill. You were so wonderful—how I'd love to be an actress myself, just like you!"

Kristian's lips were pressed into a hard line. "Primrose is a very inexperienced theatergoer, Adrienne. She is not very discerning in what she likes, I fear."

Each word fell like a slap, the meaning clear. The play was a failure, and Kristian blamed her. As, she thought with despair, he had every right to do.

"But, Kristian—" she began.

Primrose had begun to giggle. "Oh, Miss Gill! I do believe that artist from the newspaper is sketching you! Won't it be fun? I think you're going to appear in the paper!"

Neither of them heard her. Kristian's eyes had locked with her own, a dark, cold anger leaping between them.

"That will be very nice," Kristian muttered at last. "A portrait of a failed actress. Perhaps you will wish to clip the sketch for your scrapbook? Along with the ruinous reviews?"

"Oh!" Primrose gulped.

Adrienne could not help herself, nor, at this point, did she wish to. The evening had been a nightmare, the disappointment of its failure so crushing that she felt numbed beyond pain. And the last straw of all had been the sight of Kristian with this girl, this stupid Primrose who could not even sense the aura of gloom in the greenroom.

Suddenly, driven by an instinct she could not name, Adrienne's hand shot out.

For the second time in three weeks, she slapped a man. The crack of her palm on Kristian's cheek was loud in the room.

Chapter 19

"That's the second time you have done that to me, Adrienne. It's getting to be an ugly habit of yours. You are very lucky that I don't believe in hitting women back."

Adrienne gasped, choking back a sob. Then, lifting her skirts, she turned and fled toward the door, its twin gas fixtures, their flames orange-red, mocking her.

Perhaps you will wish to clip the sketch for your scrapbook? Along with the ruinous reviews?

Deadly words, cutting, killing.

She felt sick now, the nausea a boiling knot in her belly. Perspiration stood on her forehead, clung clammily to the skin of her chest and neck. She wanted only to get away, to reach the solace of the dressing room where she could cry in semi-privacy.

People looked up as she passed, their faces shocked or curious or amused. Voices whispered, and Adrienne caught fragments of what they said. *She's done it again . . . slapped a man . . . tempermental creature . . . they say she's in love with him . . . tied to a crippled husband . . .*

The greenroom was crowded, and a large group of people had chosen that moment to leave. They were clustered by the door, near the two gas fixtures which flared and smoked in their sockets. Adrienne glimpsed Fanny Pepper standing among them, her eyes wide and shocked. Evidently she had seen everything.

"Excuse me." Adrienne reached those jammed about the door. "Please, let me pass."

269

"Miss Gill!" A man pushed his way through the crowd to her. She turned to see the columnist whom—was it a lifetime ago?—she had also slapped.

"Miss Gill, I saw you smack Kristian King's face. It seems that I travel in exalted company." Will Stauffer's mouth, under the tight little mustache, smirked at her. Evidently he was enjoying this.

Someone tittered.

"No—yes—oh, please, just let me by. I must go home. I . . . I have a headache. . . "

"A headache, is it? Oh, yes, I would imagine that you have a giant one. How do you feel about the play *Melissa Charles* now, Miss Gill? Tell me—"

"No! I won't talk to you! I won't!"

Blindly she elbowed someone, desperate to get away from the voice that harried her. A woman in a full-skirted dress with an enormous bustle was blocking her exit.

Stauffer pursued her. "But, Miss Gill, tell me, is it true that you slapped Mr. King because he told you that your acting ruined his play?"

"No! No! No!" Her voice was hoarse. "Please, just let me through, I want to leave!"

Now Bettina Smithe stood before her, arms akimbo, the black skirts of her maid costume filling the floor space. "What's the matter, Miss Gill?" the blonde actress taunted. "Don't you like it here with us? Do you want to go home and crawl into a hole and wait for the reviews to come in?"

"No! I—"

"Oh, you act so high and mighty, walking past everyone with your nose in the air as if you were royalty or something! Well, I know better. No, all your high-born blood can't give you good reviews this time!"

Ugly, triumphant words. Feeling sick, Adrienne could only stare at the blowsy, blonde actress. Why did Bettina dislike her so?

"No," Bettina repeated. "All your fine blood can't make you a real actress. By tomorrow morning, you're going to be the laughing-stock of New York!"

Adrienne swallowed hard. It was as if some taut-drawn thread, yanked tight within her, had finally snapped. The room was stuffy and packed with people. And she had to get away—from Bettina, from Stauffer, from all the unfriendly eyes staring at her now. She had to be alone, to suffer in privacy. No one must see her anguish.

"Please," she whispered. "Please, Bettina, enough. If you would just let me by—"

She started toward Bettina, and the dressing room door beyond.

Then it happened.

The blond actress, full of vicious spite, gave Adrienne a little push on the shoulder. It was only a small push, a show of temper. But Adrienne, weakened by nausea, by her despair and by the effects of the champagne she had drunk earlier, stumbled forward, crashing into Bettina.

Bettina, caught off balance, reeled backwards, clutching at those behind her for support. A man shouted. Bettina's hands grabbed air, and someone else cried out and stumbled.

There was a flare of light from the gas fixture to the right of the greenroom door. Then someone began to scream—

—to shriek in a high, frightened, terrible voice that went on and on and on. . . .

For a second the scream hung in the air of the greenroom, as ugly as a gashing open wound. A woman sobbed, then someone else began to scream, too. The crowd shifted, the women's full hoopskirts rustling, and then Adrienne was able to glimpse what had happened.

It was Fanny Pepper who was on fire.

It had been like tumbling dominos. When Adrienne had stumbled into her, Bettina Smithe had fallen into someone else. Several people had fallen, and Fanny, nearest the door, had been pushed directly against the metal grillwork of the gas fixture. The flames, greedy, always dangerous, had licked through their protective cage and tongued the lace of Fanny's costume. Now Fanny, her eyes bulging with terror, slapped at her dress, at the red and orange which flowered there like some grisly blossom.

Again Fanny screamed.

The flames bloomed up her bodice, burst open on her hands.

Fanny, Adrienne thought with a sick gasp. Fanny, who had been kind to her, who had given her advice and encouragement, who had bought her beer and chops, and waited patiently for her money to be repaid. . . .

Adrienne plunged forward, her body moving without thought. This time people fell back from her, letting her pass.

She snatched up the front of her own gown, with its voluminous yards of flowing silk, and wadded it into a mass. Quickly she thrust it at the burning woman and began to beat at the flames.

Fanny screamed and struggled. With a strength she had not known she possessed, Adrienne shoved her against the green-painted wall of the greenroom, pinning her there. With the wadded cloth, she pounded at the fire. Beat it, crushed at Fanny's breast and neck and chin and hands until the flames were gone.

"Adrienne. Oh, God, Adrienne . . ."

Fanny's eyes were wide and imploring. Then her knees buckled and she slid to the floor in a faint.

"Get a doctor!" Kristian called. "Hurry, she's badly burned!"

Kristian and William Mancin lifted the unconscious Fanny and carried her into the nearest dressing room, to lay her upon the long bench there. Fanny had begun to emerge from her faint, to moan and cry, and Adrienne saw with horror that her hands were already dark and blistered. The front of Fanny's dress was charred, with burns extending up to her chin.

People crowded about, pushing to get a better view. Among them was William Stauffer.

"Get back, you fools!" Kristian snapped. "Give her some space to breathe!"

"But—" the columnist began.

"I said get back, and now!"

The ring of people around the bench receded a few feet, while voices rose in excited speculation. What had happened? No one seemed sure. A woman was sobbing.

"Adrienne . . ." Fanny writhed and moaned, her burned hands flailing the air.

Adrienne knelt beside her. "Yes, Fanny, I'm here."

"Adrienne, I'm burned. God, I'm burned. It hurts—"

"I know it does. But Kristian has called a doctor. He'll be here soon. Oh . . . Fanny, I'm so sorry."

Adrienne did not know how long she crouched by Fanny, holding on to the other's upper arm, for Fanny's hands were too severely injured to touch. She was only half aware of the people who milled about, or of the blisters on her own hands now beginning to smart with pain.

Voices chattered above her head.

"This was *her* fault—I saw it all, I saw her fall into Bettina. . . ."

"She'd been drinking, that's obvious. I smelled it on her breath."

"Wait till the papers get hold of this, they'll make a pudding out of Miss Adrienne Gill."

Numbly Adrienne stared down at Fanny, who was moaning and tossing her head from side to side. *Was* this her fault? Oh, surely it wasn't, not entirely. Bettina had pushed her. She could not help stumbling—anyone might have done so.

She had looked up and was about to protest, to defend herself, when Kristian spoke. "Adrienne, the doctor is here. You must move and give him room to work."

A short, dark man with a long nose bent over Fanny, taking something from a leather bag.

"All right."

Blindly she got to her feet, stumbled, swayed. She could feel Kristian's arms, supporting her out to the greenroom.

"Come, Adrienne. I'll find a hack to take you and your husband home."

Her husband. Barrett. Adrienne had forgotten him entirely. Now she saw that he still sat at the far end of the greenroom, where she had left him, his head down on the table. He was either asleep or had passed out from the whisky he had been drinking.

She whispered, "Will Fanny be all right?"

"I don't know. The doctor will do what he can. Her burns are pretty severe, though, and I'm afraid there is going to be scarring—a lot of it. Damn, I still don't know how it happened! Those gas fixtures are so damned dangerous. We are just lucky that the whole theater didn't go up in flames. It happens often enough."

So Kristian hadn't seen, didn't know. At least not yet. Miserably Adrienne let herself be led out into the corridor and upstairs to the stage door.

"Sit here," Kristian ordered. He motioned to an old wooden chair upon which sat a "thundermug" full of dried paint. He moved the paint so she could sit down. "I'll go back downstairs and fetch your husband. The doctor is with Fanny now, and she'll be taken care of. You needn't worry about her."

"Kristian." She held out both hands to him, tears streaming down her cheeks. "Kristian, I'm sorry, so sorry—"

His eyes looked away from her. "Of course you are. Fanny was your friend. As for the play—" He stopped. "Well, it doesn't matter. Perhaps I was too harsh. The reviews have not yet come in, and perhaps all is not as bad as I fear."

His hand brushed hers. "I'll see you tomorrow night, Adrienne. Reviews or not, accidents or not, we still have a play to put on. Until they close us, that is."

At home at last in the brownstone, and Barrett in bed and the baby fed, Adrienne sat alone in the front parlor.

"Ma'am?" It was the little maid, Annie, her eyes sleepy, her frizzy red-gold hair seeming to stand straight on end. "Is there anything you want before I go to bed?"

"No, Annie," Adrienne said dully, "there's nothing. My gown, my Melissa costume, you can give that to the rag man when he comes by. It is charred and ruined."

"Yes, ma'am. Good night, ma'am."

It was very late, and the gas fixtures sputtered and flickered, sending dark shadows to leap up the walls of the parlor. They cast odd patterns upon the pair of heavy couches, the walnut table with its French antique side

274

chairs, the Brussels carpet. Outside in the street, a lone carriage rattled by, horses' hooves making loud, clopping noises.

On the table beside her (had it been left there earlier in the day by Barrett?) was a new bottle of whisky. Beside it was a tumbler. Slowly, deliberately, Adrienne untwisted the wire which protected the cork. She pried out the cork. Then she poured an inch of the golden whisky into the tumbler.

She stared at the glass.

Scars, she thought, feeling sick. Fanny would have scars on that smoothly plump and fashionable body which once had danced, for two weeks, in the *Black Crook*.

She lifted the glass and took a long, desperate swallow. The whisky burned its way down her throat like a punishment.

Perhaps you will wish to clip the sketch for your scrapbook? Along with the ruinous reviews?

This was her fault. I saw it all . . .

It hurts, it hurts. . . .

You weren't ready and now I think you've proved it. . . .

Weren't ready . . .

She took another swallow, and another. Wth a trembling hand she set the tumbler back on the walnut table. Then she waited for the alcohol to take its effect, to relax her, to numb her fear and despair.

She didn't know when it was that she awoke. Morning? Or already afternoon? All she knew was that it was now light, and that outside in the street, children shouted at their play and horse traffic clopped along the paving-bricks. It was another day. The street life of New York went on just as usual, as if an actress had not failed in her debut, as if a woman had not been burned and scarred.

Adrienne stirred. She closed her eyes, then opened them again. The ceiling above her head was marred with a crack, a hairline meandering along the plaster in a halfmoon shape. The parlor, she thought dully. She had slept all night in the parlor. Her mouth tasted sour and metallic. Her head ached. And her hands hurt where she had blistered them.

What time was it?

She struggled off the couch, noting with dim surprise that somehow the whisky bottle had fallen on its side. Whisky had pooled across the walnut surface of the table, damaging the finish.

An ornate wall mirror hung near the door, its carved borders painted in gilt, and Adrienne went to it, to stare at herself in the glass. She drew in her breath in a gasp. Her hair, last night elaborately brushed and braided and teased for her role as Melissa, was now a disheveled mess. Tufts of blond hair stood up at angles, or fuzzed unbecomingly at her cheeks. Her ringlets now simply streamed in a tangle down her back. Her eyes looked wild and heavily shadowed, and her skin was pale, as if she had been ill.

My God, she thought, *look at me!*

Abruptly she whirled away from the mirror. She would go upstairs at once and scrub her face, she decided; rub some carmine into her cheeks. Comb and braid and loop her hair into a proper coiffure. Then she would get dressed. After that, she would—

On the stairs, she encountered the little maid, Annie. The servant's eyes were accusing.

"Ma'am, I looked for you this morning in your room to take your breakfast to you and couldn't find you. Did you sleep all night in the parlor?"

Her eyes flicked curiously over Adrienne, and Adrienne knew that the girl had missed no detail of her appearance.

"Yes," she told Annie defiantly. "I fell asleep there. It was late, and I—I was tired. Would you please go out and buy me the morning papers? I'd like you to pick up all the ones you can find. Bring them back here at once."

"Yes, ma'am."

"After that, I'll give Barrie her bottle. So you may come back and heat it up."

"Yes, ma'am."

A second accusing look from Annie told Adrienne that here, too, the maid held her own opinions of her mistress. She had not been giving Barrie enough attention lately, that look said. She had not asked enough questions about her daughter's welfare, or in any way shown a mother's proper concern.

"Oh, go on, Annie," Adrienne snapped crossly. "What are you waiting for? Go out at once and get the newspapers. Do as you are told!"

A chill afternoon sun streamed in the tall, narrow window of the back bedroom where Adrienne had just finished feeding Barrie. It patterned the Turkish carpet with squares of pale light, and fell over the basket where the baby now lay, playing with her feet and babbling to herself.

Dutifully Adrienne leaned over the bassinet and crooned to the infant as she had seen *Maman* sing to her own babies. Was that not the proper behavior of a mother toward her child?

Drawing a deep breath, she moved the basket so that the sun would not shine directly into Barrie's eyes. She sang another lullaby, forcing her voice into sweetness and purity. Then, this chore accomplished, she picked up the stack of newspapers which Annie had bought her.

The *New York Sun,* the *Mirror,* the *Morning Herald,* the *New York Herald*—their close-spaced print seemed to stare up at her accusingly.

She reached for one paper at random, and leafed feverishly through its pages. At last she found the theatrical section and, her heart pounding, began to read.

The play Melissa Charles, *authored by Kristian King, newcomer to the world of the theater . . .*

Print seemed to dance in front of her eyes. Isolated phrases jumped up at her. *Brilliantly conceived and written in every respect . . . However, the star, Adrienne Gill, whose debut in New York was much touted by the press beforehand, failed to live up to her billing. . . .*

Adrienne froze. She was utterly unconscious of the small infant noises Barrie made, of the clatter of another carriage in the street outside. Perspiration had begun to dot her forehead, to run in streams down her sides beneath the dress she wore.

The review was bad.

Her fingers squeezed convulsively on the newsprint, crumpling it. Then she threw the paper aside and reached for another one.

Mr. King's is a voice which will surely be heard often in the theater world, for the play Melissa Charles, *although its realism will be shocking to many, is bound to become a classic. Would that the same could be said for its leading lady, Miss Adrienne Gill, who could not carry off her role. . . .*

Another!

And, placed next to the review where the eye could easily spot it, was a short article. Its headline, set in small type, was nonetheless startling.

Actress Stumbles, Causes Fire Injury. Following was a story of Fanny's accident, with emphasis on the "domino" effect which had caused the fire. Although Adrienne was not totally blamed for the incident, the implication was clear enough.

Adrienne swallowed hard, her mouth gone suddenly cotton-dry. Her head had begun to pound, her blood to drum against her temples. She picked up the offending newspaper—was it the *Sun?*—and flung it to the floor. It landed with a thud against the floor molding.

The third paper was the *Mirror,* and when she opened it, the pages seemed to fall open naturally to three artists' sketches.

At first her eyes focused on the drawings without full understanding. Each of the three panels depicted a lush young woman. She wore an elaborate wasp-waist costume, the lines of her body caricatured so that her waist seemed abnormally small, her bust swelling and voluptuous. Her facial features had been exaggerated to include small eyes, a mouth petulant and sly.

It was herself, drawn in broad, cruel lines that made her look flamboyant, almost a woman of the streets.

Which, of course, had been the intention.

Adrienne examined the three cartoons angrily. In the

first she stood onstage holding a wilted bouquet of roses. The meaning of that one, she thought with growing despair, was clear enough. In the second, she was shown slapping a man—Kristian, she assumed—across the face. And in the third she was shown blotting out flames on the bodice of Fanny Pepper.

The newspaper artist, she thought dully. He had been busy last night with his sketchpad, and these drawings were the result.

Her eyes skimmed the accompanying column, written by William Stauffer himself. *Adrienne Gill . . . backstage . . . seemed to be in disagreement with her husband . . . slapped . . . playwright Kristian King across the face . . .*

There was much more, but she couldn't read it. She let the paper drop to the floor. Then she sank back into her chair, not hearing the cooing sounds Barrie made in her basket or the banging noises which came from downstairs as Annie moved furniture to dust it.

A feeling of nausea welled up in her throat. Kristian's play had received good mention, even encouragement. It was only she who had had the bad reviews.

Barrett had been right. Her debut had been a failure.

Adrienne pulled on a fresh gown—any dress, what did it matter today?—and threw a brown woolen mantle over her shoulders. It was ten minutes later, and she was on her way out.

Just as she reached the door of her bedroom, Barrett came lurching into the narrow upstairs hallway. He walked with difficulty, thrusting the two canes ahead of him for support.

"Well?" His voice was slurred, loose. "I see that the great actress Adrienne Gill is going out. To drown your sorrows as you did last night, in whisky?"

How had he known that?

"No," she said dully. "I'm going to see Fanny Pepper. She was badly burned last night—if you yourself were sober enough to notice."

"*Touché.*" Barrett gave a little bob of the head.

279

"Fanny is finished as an actress," he announced. "My father had many burn patients. Most died of infection, and those who did live were often cripples."

Adrienne's heart seemed to stop still. "No! Fanny won't die! She can't!"

"You should have thought of that last night, dear wife." Did Barrett's eyes seem to gleam at her knowingly?

Again Adrienne felt the surge of nausea, the headache gonging in her skull. "It—wasn't my fault," she whispered. "Tell Annie not to wait supper for me," she added quickly. "I don't know how long I'll be."

"And the play?" His eyes burned into hers. "What of that?"

"What of it? My debut was a failure, as you were so pleased to point out to me. The reviews were poor. Surely it will close soon."

"No, it won't," Barrett said surprisingly, *"Melissa Charles* will have a decent run, thanks to you."

She stared at him. "What do you mean?"

"Why, didn't you know, girl? Annie brought me some papers, too. You are now the most notorious woman in the city. Every woman in town will fall out of her petticoats to get to the Olympic to see you in *Melissa Charles.* It doesn't matter that you were weak in your portrayal, or that you fluffed lines and misjudged your timing. The play is going to be a rousing success anyway."

"But—" She could feel the color drain from her face as, slowly, her mind grasped the meaning of what he had said. "Barrett," she whispered, "you can't mean . . ."

"Yes, I do mean it!" Her husband gave a little shrug, and banged the head of one cane onto the floor. "Your newspaper publicity was splendid, Adrienne. People are going to pay a good deal of money to come and see . . . the most infamous woman in New York!"

The most infamous woman in New York. Adrienne leaned back in the cab, her eyes seeing nothing of the streets.

Every society woman will fall out of her petticoats to see you in Melissa Charles.

This was her fault . . . she'd been drinking, that's obvious. I smelled it on her breath. . . .

Adrienne bit down hard on her lower lip. She could not help thinking of her father, of the way liquor had changed him, of the desperation she had once seen in his eyes as he stared downward at the bottle in his hands as if it held both his doom and his salvation.

Then, with revulsion, she pushed the thought away. She had drunk some champagne, yes, during the intermission of *Melissa Charles*. But it had only been a cup or two, no more, and it had not affected her, she was sure of that.

She shivered convulsively. Still, if it had been the wine which had started the ugly cycle of events which had led to Fanny's accident, then she would simply eliminate it from her life. She wouldn't drink again. She didn't need it, surely not. It had only been a way of quelling the terror in herself, of smoothing down the panic in her mind.

As the cab rounded a corner, a woman about to cross the street gave Adrienne a curious stare. Defiantly, she lifted her chin and stared back. She would let no one see her shame and despair—no one!

Fanny Pepper lived in a small brick boarding house on Great Jones Street, an establishment which catered exclusively to female theatrical performers. Twice Adrienne had visited Fanny here, and each time Mrs. Muldooney's untidy house had shaken with the sounds of acrobats doing flip-flops and dancers limbering up in the hallways. Singers practiced scales, and actresses rehearsed, or sat in the downstairs parlor memorizing their lines. And sometimes the parlor was blue with cigarette smoke, for Mrs. Muldooney, herself an ex-vaudevillian, was an ardent smoker.

But today the boarding house held a hushed quiet. Even the piano in the parlor was still; and if anyone practiced her lines, she did it under her breath. Mrs. Muldooney, fat, black-haired, and perspiring, met Adrienne at the door.

"Well, Miss Gill! Is it Fanny Pepper you're here to see today, me girl?"

"Yes."

"Well, the doctor's just been, and given her a good dose of laudanum so she can sleep, poor thing. We're all so upset we hardly know what to do. All the girls have been crying about it. And who's going to pay for her room now she can't work, I don't know."

Black eyes regarded her expectantly.

Adrienne fumbled in the small chatelaine purse she carried. "Here," she said harshly. "Take this—it should pay for another week's rent."

She thrust a bill into the woman's hand.

Mrs. Muldooney fingered the bill. "Aw, well, now, I didn't mean—you understand, don't you, that a person has got to make a living somehow? I haven't been on the boards in ten years, God knows, and—"

Adrienne fled upstairs. Fanny's room was on the third floor, the last one toward the back. She knocked once, then pushed open the battered door.

Fanny lay flat in a narrow bed, her hands, breast and neck wrapped in what appeared to be oiled silk. The room was strewn with the paraphernalia of sickness—a tray, a pitcher of water, a pile of damp rags, a metal bath basin.

"Fanny?"

The actress's eyes were open, fixed on the ceiling. Her cheeks were flushed.

"Fanny, are you awake?"

"Yes." Fanny's voice came slowly. "Adrienne, is it you? I can't turn my head because of the bandages. It hurts too much."

"It's me—oh, Fanny!" Adrienne rushed to the bed and knelt down beside her friend, for there was no chair. "Oh, God, Fanny, are you all right? Does it hurt very much?"

Fanny sighed. "It isn't the pain, Adrienne. It's knowing what's coming next for me."

"Coming next?"

"Yes. Dr. Bedford was a kind man and didn't want

282

to alarm me, but I made him tell me the truth anyway. I'm going to have a lot of scarring, especially on my hands and face and neck."

"Oh—"

"My hands," she went on, "are going to be crippled, bound into claws by scar tissue. If I am lucky, it will only be the ring and little fingers. If I am not—" Somehow Fanny's shrug was terrible. "As for my face, there is nothing that can be done about that. I'm ruined forever for the stage."

"No . . . oh, no . . ."

"I am afraid it's true. When I am well, I will have to look for some other work. Perhaps I'll go back to Bedesco's Department Store and old Mrs. Carlson." Fanny's mouth curved in a faint, ironic smile.

Cross Mrs. Carlson, who docked the girls' pay when they did not arrange the stock in symmetrical pyramids. Adrienne pressed her lips together. She remembered what Barrett had said about burn infections, and felt a stab of fear.

"Fanny." She reached out to the injured woman, started to take her hand, remembered the bandages, and stopped. "Fanny . . . there is something I must tell you."

"And what is that, Adrienne?"

Fanny's eyelids had begun to droop, her voice to slur. The laudanum was at last taking its effect.

"It—it was my fault in a way . . . and yet it wasn't!" The words poured out of Adrienne in a rush. "I was angry and upset and all I wanted to do was to get out of that room. That awful William Stauffer kept pursuing me, and—and Bettina Smithe was laughing at me. I—I'm still not sure how it happened. Bettina pushed me, and then I fell against her . . ."

Adrienne's voice stopped.

Fanny had fallen asleep, her breath shallow and jerky. Her cheeks were flushed, as if she were suddenly feverish.

Adrienne sat by Fanny's bed until it was time to leave for the theater. She had eaten nothing all day—and

283

did not care if she ever ate again. Fanny's predicament was due partly to her. Fanny would surely be crippled and might even die.

She wished that she could die, too.

When she arrived at the theater, she discovered a crowd milling about in front, many of them standing in line at the box office to get tickets. When her hack slowed down, a middle-aged man stared in her direction, then raised his voice in a shout.

"There she is, folks. That's her, that's her!"

"That's who?"

"Why, *her*. Adrienne Gill, the actress. You know, the one who—"

People began to surge forward to the curb; women in house dresses, men in work clothes and well-cut suits. A little girl giggled. A woman stared at Adrienne fixedly, her mouth hanging open as if she were not very bright.

"That's her!"

"Yes, she's the one who got that actress burned, they say she pushed her right over, oh, it was shocking. . . ."

Voices rose in excitement and speculation. Adrienne's heart had begun to pump strangely. She leaned forward and rapped on the window of the carriage, ordering the driver to go around to the stage door.

"Yes, *ma'am*."

When the driver stopped the vehicle to help her out, she saw that he was grinning. His eyes traveled over her body with insolence.

So even he knows, she thought in desperation. She thrust a coin into his hand and ran into the theater.

Kristian met her near the stage door. Already in costume and make-up, he looked fully the part of Melissa's lover, his good looks arrogant and charming. Yet beneath the make-up she could see that his face was weary. His eyes were heavily shadowed as if he had slept poorly. Did he know? Did he blame her?

"Well, Adrienne? You're late. You should have been here twenty minutes ago. You'll barely have time to get into costume."

"I've been to see Fanny Pepper at her boarding house."

"And how is she?" he added.

Adrienne thought of Fanny as she had last seen her, asleep in her bed at Mrs. Muldooney's, small and flushed.

"She is doing poorly," she managed to say. "She has little money and Mrs. Muldooney says the women at the boarding house are taking up a collection for her."

Kristian nodded. "We'll do the same. And we'll give her a benefit performance. That should help her out."

"Oh, Kristian, could we?"

He nodded grimly. "We owe it to Fanny. And thanks to you, *Melissa Charles* is going to have a long run."

She remembered what Barrett had said, and again felt her cheeks begin to flame. "Kristian, I—I'm sorry. I'm sorry for everything. I didn't know—"

His eyes met hers bleakly. "It doesn't matter, Adrienne. I realize Fanny's injury was an accident. As for the part, you were a failure. I know that and you know it; the critics realize it, too. But evidently the general public does not. They wish to see more of you. To come here and stare at you as if you were one of Mr. Barnum's famous exhibits. My play was good. More than good, it was brilliant. But they don't care about that. It's excitement they crave, damn their small souls. Excitement and notoriety!"

She could feel her heart twist with pain for him. She wished to reach out to him, to hold him. But something stopped her.

"Kristian, what can I say? The crowd out there, all of them looking and staring and pointing. Those newspaper sketches. I—I thought the play would be closed by now."

He grimaced. "It will only be finished when the public tires of you, my beautiful Adrienne. So you might as well relax and enjoy your fame."

Kristian nodded toward the stage door behind them, which had just burst open to admit a trio of men in rumpled suits, carrying pencils and paper. "There are our reporter friends, my dear, come to interview you in greater depth than they were able to manage last night. Do you wish to go and speak with them?"

Adrienne stared at the three reporters. She could feel her mouth go dry, her hands dampen with moisture. She clutched at Kristian's arm in panic.

"Must I?"

"Of course you must! My play has to be a success, does it not?"

She felt sick. "But, Kristian—"

"Go. Talk to them, Adrienne. Say whatever comes into your head. I'm sure they will love it. And then go and get into your costume. Tonight after the performance you and I will begin working on the Melissa role again. Maybe we can inject some life into it."

The words hurt. Adrienne turned widly, to see the reporters heading in her direction, their eyes sharp with the prospect of a good story.

"But, Kristian," she implored. "I don't want to talk to them—"

"Girl, don't you understand?" he said savagely. "You are to be a star after all! A star! Isn't that what you wanted all along?"

Kristian turned on his heel and strode away from her.

Chapter 20

Fanny Pepper lay in her bed, tossing and turning with fever. Her hands, Dr. Bedford had told them, had become infected. Now red streaks had begun to extend from her hands to the inner surface of her upper arm, and from there to the glands in her armpit. Adrienne knew this because she had assisted Mrs. Muldooney in rubbing Fanny's body with alcohol in an attempt to bring the fever down.

"No, no!" the actress kept moaning at the height of her delirium. "No—oh, Jimmie, Jimmie . . . don't die. . . . God, God, don't die!"

With pity Adrienne knew that Fanny was reliving the death of her child. She sat by the sick woman for long hours—every hour that she was not actually at the theater—holding her hands, sponging her face, or simply praying.

This was her fault, she knew, and the thought preyed on her. She, Adrienne, through her carelessness, had caused this suffering.

Again, in one of Fanny's more lucid moments, she had tried to tell her so.

Fanny had given her a long look, then closed her eyes wearily. "It doesn't matter, Adrienne. It happened. Nothing can change that now. And no matter how the accident happened, I'm sure you didn't mean to hurt me deliberately. You never would do that, I know."

A bandaged hand reached out to touch her own.

Adrienne was crying. "But, Fanny! For God's sake,

Fanny, I fell! That's what caused it all, made you fall into the gas fixture—"

"Hush. Don't think of it again. What good will it do now?"

That night the fever raged higher, and when Adrienne stopped by the boarding house after the performance, she learned that Mrs. Muldooney had tied Fanny to her bed with torn-up strips of linen.

"Just about goin' wild she was, poor thing," the landlady informed her. "Tossing and turning and calling out for that little boy of hers—land! I tell you, Miss Gill, I'm not going to be able to stand much more of this, I'm not. Puttin' all this burden on me when I've a full house to run here and meals to get for twenty girls."

Adrienne narrowed her eyes in fury. "Is it more money you want, Mrs. Muldooney?"

"Well—"

"Take this, then—and see that you treat Fanny properly!" Adrienne glared at the landlady. "If Fanny gets well, there will be more for you. If she does not—"

Hastily Mrs. Muldooney pocketed the bill. "Oh, she'll get on all right. She's a tough one, God knows. And I'll make her plenty of beef soup—it's the best thing for a fever."

"Good," Adrienne said tightly. "Just keep Fanny well—or you'll have to answer to me."

In the room, Fanny tugged and tore at the linen bands which bound her. Her bandaged hands flailed the air. Her hair was lank upon the pillow, her face flushed a hectic red.

"No—no—" Her voice was hoarse. "For God's sake —Jimmie . . . Jimmie . . ."

Half an hour later, the doctor arrived for his daily visit, bringing with him a container of leeches and a supply of oil-soaked silk, salves, ointments, and infusions. He wished to change the bandages; and so, chafing, Adrienne was forced to wait outside in the corridor.

The hall echoed now with the nighttime sounds of the boarding house: coughs, low voices, the sound of bedroom slippers slapping on wood floors. Somewhere a girl giggled.

Adrienne leaned against the dingy wall. She had worn the Passion Star inside her gown, as always, for good luck. Now her fingers sought the cool, smooth comfort of the sapphire. She thought of the girl who had worn it so bravely.

"Please," she implored, although she could not have said to whom. "Please, help Fanny and make her well. And . . . and please, help me, too. . . ."

But what exactly she had meant by the last part of this plea, she could not have told.

By dawn Fanny's fever had gone down. Dr. Bedford emerged from the sickroom to inform Adrienne that the patient had passed the crisis of her illness and would now make a slow recovery.

"Of course, she will have scars from the glands in her armpits, and from the burns, but at least she is alive. If she is given a hearty diet with plenty of animal foods and good red wine, she should be fine in a month or so."

"But her hands?" Adrienne whispered. "Her face? The scarring?"

The doctor shrugged. "What of it? There is little that can be done. If she is fortunate, she will lose only the use of her ring finger and little finger of her right hand. If she is not—ah, well, let us hope that that is not the case."

"Oh—"

Somehow Adrienne managed to stumble out to the street. She took a horsecar home. There she found Barrett asleep, a half-full flask of whisky on the table by his bedside.

Her husband snored softly.

For a long moment, Adrienne stood staring down at the flask. In it was whisky, the soft curtain which could blur the jagged edges of her nerves, making everything seem safe and right. And her nerves *were* jagged. Her failed debut, Fanny's scarring, her uncertain future—

Somehow, without her knowing quite how it happened, she found that her hand was reaching for the bottle. Quickly she poured herself a drink. A shudder racked through her as the liquid burned its way down.

And then, like a familiar miracle, it came. The luxurious, warm ease as the whisky flowed through her body . . .

That day, she slept restlessly. Her dreams were haunted by disturbing voices. Xenos Shane: *Everything in life has its devices, its secrecies. Surely you know that, Miss Gill?* The doctor's voice, irritable from lack of sleep: *There is little that can be done. . . .*

She awoke moaning. She lay for a moment in the bed, a sour taste filling her mouth. Why had she taken that drink? Hadn't she vowed not to? Despair filled her. Somewhere in the house, pots banged as Annie prepared a meal.

Adrienne struggled out of bed, bathed and dressed, and dutifully went to the small nursery to play for a few moments with Barrie. As usual, the child's eyes followed her about the room, and when she tickled the baby's belly, Barrie uttered a little chortling peal of laughter. Why, Adrienne wondered dully, couldn't she love this baby as much as *Maman* had loved all of her children? Why did Barrie have to look so much like her father?

At the theater, she discovered another line at the box office, and more crowds of people clustered about the three playbills which advertised *Melissa*.

"Miss Gill—Miss Gill—"

Voices cried out to her. Faces craned to see her, and this time Adrienne managed a small smile and a wave of her hand. A bouquet of flowers flew toward her, sailing into the gutter to be squashed beneath the wheels of a passing carriage.

Her eyes followed it, lingering on the wrecked roses. The roses had been smashed, as her dreams had been. And yet—wasn't she still a star, in spite of everything? Weren't people gathered here at the theater to see *her*?

She pulled open the stage door, feeling confused.

"And how is Miss Fanny?" a voice asked her at once. It was the stagehand, Quince.

"Fanny is fine, her fever is down. The doctor says there'll be scarring, of course—"

The man nodded. "Miss Fanny is a real trouper. I have every faith that she'll manage."

"I hope so." Quince's smile had been kind, and unaccountably Adrienne's eyes filled with tears. "Oh, Quince! The accident was my fault. I didn't mean to stumble, it was an accident."

"All things happen in God's own way, Miss Gill." The stagehand picked up his hammer and began to repair the "practical" door through which Melissa would slam in Act I, Scene I. "Rest easy, Miss Gill. I didn't see what you did, but I am sure you would never hurt anyone deliberately. You don't have such malice in you."

Her eyes stung. "Thank you, Quince."

He nodded. "Well, I hope your performance tonight is the best ever. I've been watching you, Miss Gill, and believe it or not, I think you're growing in the part. You're already better than those reviews said. If it was opening night tonight, I'm sure it'd be quite another story."

"Do you think so? Oh, Quince!"

Impulsively, she threw her arms about the stagehand. "Oh, I adore you for saying things like that!"

It was, she knew, because of Kristian's work with her that her performance had improved. Each night after the curtain went down, he insisted on taking her through her lines, going over and over them with her.

"Life, Adrienne, life! That is what you must give to Melissa. She isn't just words on paper, she's a real woman, made of flesh and blood and bone. You must play her as such. Make her real, Adrienne. Make her breathe!"

So, grimly, she tried. At Kristian's suggestion, she spent time alone in the property room, her head cradled in her hands, trying to imagine what it would be like to be Melissa Charles, divorcée. She began to try to think as Melissa would, to speak as she might do. Sometimes, late at night, she had the eerie feeling that she *was* Melissa —that the girl named Adrienne Gill was only a far-off image in the mind of someone else. . . .

There were times, now, onstage, when she could sense a change in the audience beyond the footlights. It was a breathless, suspenseful hush that began when she entered and lasted until she took her final bow. It was—

yes, it was that same magic, that communication which had taken place when she had toured with *Uncle Tom's Cabin*.

Kristian verified her feelings.

"There's something happening," he told her one night after they had taken six enthusiastic curtain calls. "I'm not sure what it is, but I like it. It's what I was thinking of when I created the role of Melissa."

"Oh—"

"But of course there's still much work to do," Kristian added. "And then I must begin work on another play."

"Another play?" she asked eagerly.

"Yes, I'm doing the synopsis for it now. It's to be called—" He hesitated.

"Yes? Yes?"

His eyes were fixed on hers. "I keep thinking of that sapphire of yours, the stone with the marvelous story. I've thought of writing a play about it."

"A play about the Passion Star?" Her heart had begun to pound. If Kristian were to write a play about the Passion Star, then the leading role could be hers. Perhaps . . .

But before she could pounce on him with more questions, Kristian shrugged. "Well, that's in the future. First we must take *Melissa* on the road. Magruder has made plans for a tour. And this summer he has offered me a cottage at Saratoga. I'll go there to work on my play."

"Saratoga!" It was an exclusive New York resort, where the rich went to gamble and play and enjoy the sun, as well as to take the medicinal waters.

"Yes, Magruder owns several cottages there and has placed one of them at my disposal." Kristian's eyes were unreadable. "After all, he is my sponsor, and if *Melissa* does well on tour, I will add a good deal to his coffers. He is hoping that we can have equal success with a second play."

Adrienne frowned. Would Primrose Magruder, with her wild, shy beauty, be at Saratoga, too? She wouldn't be surprised. But she forced herself to push away the thought. Primrose might be lovely, but she was also naive and empty-headed, surely not the sort of woman who could attract Kristian for long.

She, Adrienne, was the one who loved him.

That night, when they had finished their work on *Melissa*, Kristian took her to the rooms he had rented, and they climbed the outside staircase to his quarters on the third floor. There Kristian stripped off her garments so fiercely that a flounce ripped, and then, with heart-stopping ardor, he made love to her. Kissed her on her mouth, on her breasts and arms and belly and thighs, until she uttered little abandoned moans of pleasure and clung to him, arching her body against his need.

Her climax when it came was long and slow and full of an unutterable sweetness, so intense that she cried out, sobbing.

"Kristian—Kris—Oh, God, Kris—"

But if he heard her use the forbidden nickname, he said nothing, only held her close to him; and then they sank down together into the after-love sleep. Their arms were around each other, her head resting in the hollow of his shoulder.

Two days later, William Stauffer came to Adrienne's dressing room after the afternoon show to interview her again. It had been a benefit, the proceeds to go to Fanny Pepper; and now that the high tension of the performance was over, Adrienne felt tired and irritable. She sat alone in front of the wavy mirror, scrubbing off her make-up as Fanny had taught her, and wondering, for the hundredth time, what Fanny was going to do once she had recovered from the shock of her burns.

"Yes?" She turned impatiently at the knock on the door, thinking it was the callboy with a message, or perhaps William Mancin, the stage manager, come to discuss some technical detail.

"May I come in, Miss Gill?"

"Who is it?"

"Why, it's William Stauffer, from the *Mirror*. Surely you have a few moments to spare for me—a star such as yourself—" Even through the closed door she could sense the sarcasm in his words.

Her hand, holding the water-soaked sponge to her temples, paused. She thought of the cruel drawings which had appeared in the *Mirror* and felt suddenly cold.

"No," she snapped. "I don't have a few moments. I am removing my make-up, and then I must go to visit a sick friend."

"If I remain here outside this door, you really have no choice but to see me, Miss Gill. I'll wait here until you come out."

She flung down the sponge. "Oh, very well! I'll be out in a moment!"

Thirty minutes later (she took her time, delighting in the thought of making him wait) she swept out of the dressing room. She wore a new gown, made to order by Mrs. Carstens only last week, made of blue silk and richly trimmed with matching velvet and fringe. It had been an extravagance—her bill at the dressmaker's was slowly mounting—but Adrienne had felt the expenditure well worth while. If she was to be a star, then she must look the part. Her wardrobe, her gowns and bonnets and slippers and accessories—all must be in the latest fashion, all must fascinate.

"Miss Gill!" He rushed after her. "Miss Gill, I have a question for you. Is it true that you were the one who caused Miss Fanny Pepper's fire injuries? That she'll be scarred for life, that she'll never work in the theater again and blames you for that?"

Adrienne turned, feeling her face flush a deep red. She thought of Bettina Smithe, of the malice in the blond actress, the push which she had given her. But theater folk stuck together. She could not betray even Bettina to this ferret-like newsman.

"Miss Pepper's injuries were a terrible accident and nothing more," she told the columnist coldly. "She herself blames no one."

The man nodded quizzically, as if he did not quite believe her explanation. His second question, when it came, was so sudden and so startling that she drew in her breath in a gasp.

"Miss Gill, is it true that your husband, Barrett Kendall, is a cocaine addict?"

"A what?" The question was so sudden and so startling that she stopped dead in her tracks. "What did you say?" she repeated.

Stauffer shrugged. His small eyes were sharp on her. "It is common knowledge in Union Square that your husband is unable to speak or to walk properly, that he is a drunkard and worse."

"My husband had a stroke of apoplexy, Mr. Stauffer. That is why he must walk with such difficulty—and for no other reason! He suffered the stroke a few months ago, and now I am his sole support. If that would interest your readers, you may feel free to print the *facts*."

He bowed sardonically. "There are many facts, Miss Gill, are there not? And here is another one in which you may be interested. Your friend Kristian King and Miss Primrose Magruder were seen dining together very intimately at a chop-house on Broadway. What do you think of that?"

The columnist's expression was triumphant.

Adrienne could feel blood, thick and ugly, rush to her temples. Desperately she tried to keep her voice calm.

"Very well, Mr. Stauffer. This interview is finished. Please leave the theater at once, or I will call the stage manager and have you thrown out."

"As you might toss out a stray cur?" The columnist's lips, beneath the bristly mustache, had tightened. "I'm not that easy to get rid of, my dear." His eyes raked her. "And there will be news of you as long as I am here to write it. I am going to watch you, Miss Gill. Sooner or later I'm going to make you the most scandalous woman in New York!"

Adrienne arrived at Mrs. Muldooney's boarding house feeling shaken and miserable. She did not know which disturbed her more: the news that Kristian had been seen dining with Primrose, or the fact that William Stauffer had brought his hatred for her so obviously into the open.

I'm going to make you the most scandalous woman in New York. That had been Stauffer's threat, and she was sure he could make it happen. Newspapers were circumspect in what they printed, but there were still ways a clever writer could imply more than he actually said. There was, too, the potent weapon of gossip. Stauffer was a real part of the theater world. He could, if he chose, spread vicious lies about her. . . .

She found Fanny sitting up in her bed, newspapers strewn about her on the coverlet. The fever had left Fanny's complexion waxy, and there were dark circles under the actress's eyes. But her russet hair had been washed and now streamed about her shoulders, partly hiding the bandages which covered her neck and chin. Both hands were also heavily bandaged, with only the fingertips protruding.

Fanny grimaced at Adrienne as she entered the room.

"Oh, those terrible articles, Adrienne, will they never stop? You've received another mention in Mr. Stauffer's column today. He makes you sound as if you are a—a—" Fanny groped for words.

"The most scandalous woman in New York?" Adrienne asked bitterly. "Yes, I suppose he does. Oh, I wish I hadn't slapped him! He is my enemy, Fanny. He hates me, I know he does. He'll say anything bad about me that he can."

She walked to the room's one window and stood looking down at the alley which ran behind the boarding house. Four trash barrels sat along a rickety fence. Among them a stray cat poked delicately at the leavings from Mrs. Muldooney's table.

"Well, it's true that you shouldn't have slapped him, honey," Fanny said. "That was certainly a very foolish thing to do. But aside from that, I suppose it's all part of being a star. Great actresses have always had to put up with such publicity. It's a part of their lives they must accept."

Adrienne felt rebellious. "*I* won't accept it!"

"You'll have to. Do you like to see the crowds lined up at the theater waiting to buy tickets? To know that all the seats in the house are full and that people are begging for standing room?" Fanny could not suppress a sigh. "When I was in *The Black Crook*—oh, I would have given anything to be a star, notorious or not."

Adrienne hesitated. She bit down hard on her lower lip. "But I'm not *really* a star, Fanny," she said at last. "Not in any way that counts. Everyone knows that, even the newspaper men. That is why they hold me in such contempt."

She narrowed her eyes at the cat in the alley, seeing it jump gracefully from one barrel to the next. What she had said to Fanny was true, humiliatingly so. It had been only publicity and gossip that had made people want to come to see her. Even William Stauffer, she thought bitterly, had been a help in that respect.

She realized that her friend was speaking.

"Adrienne," Fanny said slowly, almost reluctantly, "there is something I've been wanting to say to you. Somehow, you've been changing. Oh, I know it has been hard for you, all of the ugly things in the newspapers, the gossip, the whispering. But you mustn't let those things affect you."

Adrienne stared at her friend, at the determined look on Fanny's face, so different from its usual cheerful friendliness.

"What do you mean?"

Fanny bit her lip. "I mean, Adrienne, that I would have had to have been deaf not to hear all of the rumors about you! The girls here at the boarding house have been full of them. How you'd been drinking that night I was burned, how that was what made you fall. I've smelled it on your breath when you've come to visit—" She stopped.

Adrienne's cheeks reddened. "I don't drink very much. Besides, I can stop whenever I wish—"

"Can you?" Fanny hesitated. "Perhaps I have no right to say this, but . . . Well, my father was a doctor in Grand Rapids, and once he told me about a group called the Washingtonians. He had been in correspondence with them. It seems they were very much interested in helping those who drank too much—"

"Yes?" Adrienne felt her cheeks grow even redder.

Fanny, too, flushed. "Well, Papa said that the Washingtonians believe that a person cannot *control* his drinking, that he must stop entirely. Alcohol is like a sickness with some people, they cannot take even one sip without trouble. Drinking for them is like stepping off the rim of a cliff—once even one drink is taken, there is no choice but to fall."

"I'm not like that!" Adrienne cried indignantly.

"Perhaps not. I hope not." Fanny looked uncomfortable. A little silence fell into the room, punctuated by the boarding-house noises, the echo of laughter in the corridor, a snatch of song as someone rehearsed a music-hall number.

Adrienne shook her shoulders, as if to push away the sudden heavy mood which had fallen upon her, as thick as dark molasses.

"Well," she said brightly, "why must we discuss me and my affairs, when you are the one, Fanny, who is sick? How are you feeling now? Are you getting better? I've been so worried about you!"

Fanny seemed to relax.

"Oh, I'm improving every day. The doctor has come several times to give me exercises for my hands. When the bandages come off, I'm to squeeze a satin ball every day to keep my fingers limber. As for the scars on my neck and chin—" Fanny's mouth grew suddenly bleak. "Well, nothing can be done about them. I must try to hide the scars with high collars."

"Oh!" Adrienne rushed across the room to fling her arms around her friend. "Oh, I'm selfish, so selfish! To think only of my own problems when—I just wish this hadn't happened to you. I'd give anything if it hadn't."

"But it did happen. And I must accept that, whether I want to or not." Fanny stared downward at her bandaged right hand, flexing the fingertips slightly. "I know I'll never act again. I'm finished wtih the theater. I'll have to go back to Bedesco's now, and hope that they'll hire me."

Adrienne's heart sank. What if the department store

refused to hire her? What if she could get no other job? There had been collections taken up for her, and the proceeds of a benefit performance of *Melissa Charles* had gone to her, but those funds would not last forever. What would Fanny do then?

"I don't want you to go to Bedesco's," Adrienne said at last. "I won't let you."

"Then what do you expect me to do? Take in washing?" Fanny's voice was almost a choke. "I suppose I could do that if I had to—God knows I'm a hard worker!"

"You will not take in washing! I never heard of such a foolish idea!" Adrienne's voice was sharp. "Fanny, I swear to you that won't have to happen. I—I'll think of something. I know I will!"

Half an hour later she was back at the theater, seated in the small cubbyhole that William Mancin used as his office. The room contained a pigeonhole desk stuffed with papers and piled high with old playbills and playscripts. A hole had been knocked into the wall at eye level so that the occupant of the room could peer into the backstage area.

"Well, Adrienne, and what brings you here?" Mancin was a tall, thin man in his early thirties, with lank, dark hair and a strong-thrusting jaw.

"It's Fanny, of course."

"Fanny Pepper?" The stage manager had been making notations in his promptbook with a pencil, and now he put aside his work with a swift gesture. "How is she?"

"Her fever has gone down, and she is on the mend. But she needs a job," Adrienne went on quickly. "She can't work as an actress any more, and I am afraid that she won't be able to get her job back at the department store. I was thinking . . ." She hesitated, then plunged on. "Fanny is very clever with make-up—everyone, even Kristian, has said so—and she is a good seamstress. I thought perhaps you might be able to use her backstage."

Mancin scowled. He pressed his lips together. "We'll have to see."

"But—but she has been a part of the cast—we can't just desert her. . . ."

Mancin's jaw had knotted. "Do you think I am a monster? Of course we won't desert her—haven't we staged a benefit for her? We'll put on another one. And I'll hire her—if she can work, and if there is a job suitable for her to do. But I can't make any promises, Adrienne, and you know it. The theater isn't a charity, it can't afford to be. Every person must carry his own weight."

"And Fanny will do her fair share!"

"I hope she can, Adrienne. No one hopes it more than I. But I have seen burn patients before; my brother was badly injured at Gettysburg and nearly died of his wounds." Mancin's eyes held pity. "Don't get your hopes for her too high, Adrienne."

Three

Chapter 21

"Try, Fanny, try!" Adrienne begged.

"But I can't—my hands are so tired, it seems as if I've been squeezing this wretched ball forever!"

"Then do it some more," Adrienne pleaded. "William Mancin has promised you a job—well, almost promised—if only you can get your hands to work properly again. Oh, do please try!"

"Very well, if you insist, Adrienne. You are the most cruel taskmistress I've ever had. You make old Mrs. Carlson seem like a babe in arms!"

Yet Fanny was grinning at her, and Adrienne knew that once more she would go on with the hand exercises which were so painful and frustrating for her. Fanny, Adrienne had had to recognize over and over again, possessed courage of the best sort.

It was 1873, late afternoon of a hot July day at Saratoga Springs, the famous New York resort. Adrienne supposed they should not have come. Yet New York had been sweltering under a massive heat wave, and little Barrie, now a year old, had been suffering from blotchy heat rash. Awnings put up to shade windows from the glare of the sun served only to close in the occupants until they felt like bread baking in an oven. Wooden fans, suspended from ceilings, only stirred the hot air, making it more unbearable than ever.

So, one scorching afternoon, Adrienne had telegraphed to Saratoga for reservations. Then she had bundled her family and Fanny Pepper onto the train. A painfully small bequest from Barrett's father had come just in time to finance the trip. The old doctor had died in London of apolexy, the same malady which had felled his son. There would certainly be no more remittance checks. Yet gladly Adrienne had seized upon the money, for her dressmaker's bills had been high. And at Saratoga were famous medicinal springs. Perhaps the waters would help Barrett's condition. And they might even aid Fanny, for whom Adrienne felt a consuming responsibility.

Besides, wasn't Kristian at Saratoga Springs as well, working on his new play? She had to admit that that had much to do with her decision to come here. She longed to see him again. And she wished to ask him about his play. Surely, oh, surely, there would be a starring role in it for her!

They had made a strange entourage, Adrienne knew, for such a fashionable spa. Barrie, now a year old, was a solemn child who looked more like her father than ever. If she possessed Barrett's salt-and-pepper mustache, Adrienne reflected wryly, she would look exactly like him.

The little girl walked now, could speak dozens of words in a clear, piping voice, and had taken instantly to Fanny Pepper.

"Fa-nee," she would crow, deserting Adrienne to toddle toward Fanny. Adrienne, watching the two, had to suppress an odd surge of jealousy. Before now, Barrie's attentions had always been for her mother alone. It was Adrienne for whom she cried in the night, Adrienne to whom she brought crumpled little bouquets of daisies and dandelions.

Didn't Barrie ever realize the revulsion Adrienne sometimes felt, she wondered, the moments when, shamed and miserable, she felt as if she could barely stand to touch her daughter?

To care for Barrie, Adrienne had brought the little maid, Annie Smith. And then there was Fanny, of course; dear, practical Fanny. During the past months, Fanny had lived with them, recuperating from her burns. What would she have done without Fanny to laugh with?

And Barrett . . . His condition had worsened. He

was paler, his mustache now more white than gray. His gait was more lurching than ever, and his speech even more slurred and unclear. He had began to insert nonsense words into his conversation, seemingly without realizing that he did so. Adrienne suspected that he suffered another, smaller stroke.

And it was also, she reflected dully, as if he hated her for the successful run of *Melissa Charles,* for the road tour which had followed, the adulation she had received in the newspapers, the flowers and admirers, the crowds which had gathered each night at the stage door.

"You gave it all up, didn't you, Adrienne?" he had said to her one night shortly after she had returned to New York. He jabbed with his forefinger at an opened copy of the *Mirror,* where one of the scathing columns of William Stauffer was visible. "Stardom—real stardom—you gave it all up for a few bouquets of flowers and some newspaper drivel. Crowds! Admiration! Do you enjoy making a spectacle of yourself?"

"Barrett, I don't consider that I'm doing anything of the kind."

"You are, my dear. Oh, yes, you are. And that acid-tongued columnist is helping you to do so. Does it give you pleasure to know that housewives all over New York and Brooklyn read avidly about you? Discuss over teacups the clothes you wear and even that accursed jewel which you display on every possible occasion?"

Her hand flew to her neck where, as always, she wore the Passion Star.

"Why?" she whispered. "Why do you hate me so, Barrett? I am the one who supports you, who—"

"Enough!" His left hand, flinging forward, swept the newspapers to the floor. "Yes, Adrienne, you support me. Do you think that I like that? *I* was a greater actor than you will ever be. *I* could bring audiences to a hush in their seats. I was a superb Uncle Tom. I got twelve curtain calls when I played Hamlet, I—"

His mouth was trembling.

Adrienne felt a flash of pity. Was this the man who had once terrorized her aboard the *Thermopylae?*

And now that tyrant was gone, to be replaced by this

shambling, pathetic invalid, a man whose only power now lay in hurtful words.

"Are you sorry now that you offered to teach me to act?" she asked suddenly, without knowing why she did so. She thought dully of that long-ago night in London, that other, bold Adrienne who had dared to ask a stranger to take charge of her life.

Barrett nodded. "I did wish to teach you once, God knows why. Was it some monstrous act of ego? I wished to prove that I could make a great actress of anyone, that my powers were supreme—"

He picked up one of his canes and brandished it at her.

"Go, woman—get out of my sight, will you?" Barrett's voice had risen with each hoarse, slurred word. Now, with a vicious gesture, he hurled the second cane at the wall. It hit with a frightening bang.

"Damn you, Adrienne! God damn you and curse your grasping, opportunistic little soul to the furthest reaches of hell."

And now they were here at Saratoga, enjoying the view of the Union Hotel's huge and lushly green inner park. She and Fanny sat on a pair of circular, backless stools which had been installed on the grass for the convenience of ladies with bulky hoop skirts.

Adrienne could not help feeling that the two of them made a pretty picture—two women in white tulle, their skirts spread around them like flower petals. And certainly they were as well dressed as any other women at the famous resort. Yet no one had spoken to them since they had arrived here two days ago, save for the hotel employees, who of course did not count.

Now Adrienne narrowed her eyes as a trio of ladies, fashionably dressed in white muslin, strolled up the walk toward them. All three looked pretty and pampered, their voices rising in restrained giggles.

In the warm July air, she caught snatches of their conversation.

"Adrienne Gill, the actress, my dears . . . it's said

that she deliberately slapped him, and, worse, that she—"

The voices lowered, and the youngest of the women stared curiously in Adrienne's direction. The three had been headed directly toward Adrienne and Fanny, but now, as they came nearer, the elder suddenly grasped the elbows of her friends and steered them firmly away.

She and Fanny had been snubbed.

Adrienne flushed, staring downward at her hands, encased in soft kid gloves. She could feel the blood beat painfully through her temples.

"Well!" Fanny was offended. She gave the satin ball an extra-hard squeeze. "The least they could have done was to nod to us! Who do they think they are?"

"Never mind, Fanny."

"But they cut us dead, they acted as if we didn't even exist—"

"For them perhaps we don't."

Adrienne tried to quell her anger, smoothing down the folds of her elaborate "watering-place costume" trimmed with Malines lace. Beside her, Fanny was dressed similarly, the high collar of her gown concealing most of the burn scars which marred her chest, neck, and chin.

"Well," Fanny said philosophically, "at least we're here, aren't we, and that's something. Have you ever seen anything like this place? Why, there are diamonds flashing everywhere, and gambling! They say things happen here, amours, dalliances, which could never go on in a proper city like New York or Boston—"

Adrienne was barely listening to the other's chatter. When, she wondered, was she to see Kristian King? When she had first arrived here, she had sent a message to him, but thus far she had received no reply.

A soft breeze had sprung up, and from the direction of the Union Hotel's dining room wafted the smell of roasting beef and pork. A thousand guests could be served there at once, crammed in rows at long tables.

Everything seemed to happen on a large scale here at Saratoga Springs. The resort's biggest hotels—the

Union and the United States—faced each other across Broadway like two giants. The Union, now in the process of remodeling, covered seven acres, and its two huge wings enclosed the park in which they now sat. Three times a day there were concerts on the long piazzas of the hotel, languid strains of violin and a cello rising like smoke into the hot July air.

And, at Congress Spring or High Rock Spring, under a wooden pavilion, male attendants ladled up the medicinal waters in glasses to the elegantly clad ladies and gentlemen who gathered there.

Fashion. That, it seemed, was the real watchword here. There were women—and men, too—who spent nearly all day preparing their costumes for the afternoon promenade, for the evening fish fries and hops and balls and horseraces.

And, Adrienne had to admit, there was something in herself which enjoyed all this, which reveled in the glorious clothes, the diamonds and rubies so casually displayed, the air of leisure and wealth.

Now, thinking of the promenades, Adrienne stirred restlessly. She was tired of sitting here, watching the world stroll by. She wanted to be up and doing. She wanted to see Kristian, and she intended to do so.

She had brought a small bag outdoors with her, stocked with writing materials. Now she pulled out a sheet of pale cream vellum and scrawled a hasty note.

Kristian, why didn't you answer my letter? It's been more than two months since I've seen you and I can't wait any longer. Please, please, let us meet for dinner tonight. Love, Adrienne.

She finished the letter and folded it. Then, seeing a bellboy hurrying down the graveled walk in the direction of the hotel's little chapel, she jumped up and raced after him. She thrust the letter and a coin into his hand.

"Please, could you deliver this to Mr. Kristian King? He is staying at Phineas Magruder's cottage."

The middle-aged bellboy kept his expression carefully neutral. "Yes, ma'am." He touched his hat.

"And hurry," she urged him.

"Yes, ma'am."

He trotted off again, and Adrienne watched him go impatiently. Then she returned to her stool, and to Fanny.

"This damned satin ball," the other said ruefully. "Do you think I'll wear it out with my exercising? Or merely squeeze it to death?"

Adrienne tried to laugh. "If you squeeze it to death, I'll sew you another one. Anyway, it has helped, hasn't it? You have regained most of the use of your fingers, except the small ones. And when we return to New York and Kristian's new play is in production, I'll get a place for you backstage. William Mancin has just about promised it to me."

Fanny was frowning. "Adrienne, I saw you send that note. Are you sure—I mean, are you really positive that there is going to be a role for you in Kristian's new play?"

Adrienne froze. "Of course I am. Who else could possibly get it? After my successful run in *Melissa Charles*—"

Fanny looked dubious. "But, Adrienne, the theater world is a business. You haven't seen Kristian in nearly two months. Suppose he has someone else in mind for the part? I read in Stauffer's column that he is considering Kate Claxton for it."

"He isn't!" Adrienne snapped. "And if that's the way you are going to talk, Fanny, then I suggest we go back to our rooms at once. I want to dress my hair and take a bath before I go out to dinner with Kristian!"

The drive to Lake Saratoga was four miles, the wide dirt avenue shaded with giant elms and crammed with the equipages of the wealthy: surreys, tally-hos, Victorias, dog-carts, sulkies, and buckboards. Among them cantered riders on horseback, men in natty riding costume and women turned out in riding habits which showed off sleek bodies.

Kristian handled the reins of the rented surrey with easy confidence.

"Well, Adrienne, you managed to find me, didn't you—and to command imperiously that I escort you to dinner!"

Adrienne tried to smile charmingly. "Command? But I thought you would wish to see me, Kristian!"

"I didn't reply to your first letter immediately, because I was busy. My play has been giving me many problems. As for your second letter—"

She turned to look at him, stung. "Then—you don't want me here?"

"Of course I do. God, Adrienne, you must know that I do. Still—" Kristian was staring straight ahead at the road, his mouth twisted. His eyes were the color of the afternoon sky, intensely blue.

"Still, it's Primrose Magruder who gives your face such an angry look, isn't it, Kristian? She is here at Saratoga, too, isn't she? And you don't wish her to find out about us. That's why you didn't answer my letter, isn't it? That's why you hesitated to see me."

"Yes."

For long minutes they rode in silence while Adrienne struggled to regain her composure. Traffic swirled about them, the occupants of well-equipped carriages eyeing them curiously.

"Adrienne, Adrienne," Kristian burst out at last. "Don't you realize just what a problem you present for me? You are lovely, the most beautiful woman I have ever known. You are exciting to me—desirable, you'll never know how desirable! And yet I fight being with you. I struggle against it."

"But—"

Savagely he cut her off. "No, you listen to me. You are married, you little fool! Married! Wed to an invalid, to a man helpless to defend his honor against me."

Adrienne sat numbly. "You always wish to make our love seem wrong and tawdry," she whispered at last.

"No, Adrienne. Our love isn't tawdry, and never will be. But you must admit that there has been a lot of ugly newspaper publicity about the two of us in the past year. And a good deal of gossip too scandalous to print."

"William Stauffer has been the cause of most of that! He'll do anything to hurt me."

Kristian scowled. "Well, if he does hurt you, it'll be

because of that quick temper of yours. My God, girl, it's as if you were a small, private cyclone, sweeping up people and events into your whirlwind. You're beautiful and flamboyant and desirable and greedy. And what I should do right now, God help me, is to stop this surrey, help you out, and keep right on driving."

"What?" She sat bolt upright, stiffening her spine in shock. "You wouldn't do such a thing! You couldn't, not here in the road in front of all these people!"

Kristian's smile was ironic. "No, Adrienne, I am speaking only figuratively. But you are bad for me, you know that, don't you? Disaster lies ahead for us, I can feel it. And without you, life would be so much simpler for me. I could—"

"You could marry Primrose Magruder, couldn't you? That's what you really mean!" Anger made her voice shake. Hurt had begun to choke her, filling her throat like a wad of cloth.

He was silent. It was admission enough.

Again, for long moments, they rode without speaking, a part of the glittering promenade toward the fashionable lake. Adrienne blinked back the tears that stung her eyes. Bitterly she thought of what Barrett had said on that long-ago day in London. *You don't long for silly, romantic love, then, Miss Gill? For some handsome man who will come along and sweep you up into realms of ecstasy?*

And her own reply, foolish and confident: *No, I don't want love, I don't need it.*

She sat enduring the ride, her hands clenched together in her lap, pressing fingernails against flesh.

At last, unwilling to reveal to Kristian just how deeply he had hurt her, she forced herself to chat of the sights they passed, as if nothing had happened. Another surrey overtook them, its two women occupants staring boldly into their own vehicle. A diamond glinted on the hand of one of the women, and more precious stones caught the sunlight at her throat.

Adrienne, putting aside her anger at Kristian, nodded to her and smiled.

The woman did not smile back.

"Why?" she demanded as the surrey surged on ahead of them, boiling up a cloud of dust. "Why do they snub me? It happened earlier today, too—and yesterday, as well!"

Kristian's mouth twisted. "Because you are not one of them, my dear. You are only an actress, and a notorious one at that."

"But I'm dressed as fashionably as they! My gown is modeled after one in *Harper's Bazaar*. I spent a lot of time choosing my parasol and bonnet—"

Kristian looked pitying. "It doesn't matter. You aren't a part of their world and you never will be, nor will I. Oh," he added, "you will certainly be accepted in certain quarters, by men who wish to be seen with a famous beauty. But as for the true society, the *haut monde*, that is a closed world for those who do not belong."

She lifted her chin. "Let them snub me, then. Let them do as they please. *They* are the ones with the dull, stuffy little lives—not me!"

Lake Saratoga, glittering through the trees, was a breathtaking sight. Far out on the waters an excursion boat basked in the sunlight. Flanking it were smaller fishing boats. It was an idyllic scene of peace and contentment, and even in her state of agitation, Adrienne felt herself drawn to it. She could almost forget about these haughty people in their Victorias and surreys, the women with the diamonds dripping from their fingers. . . .

"There is a restaurant on the lake called Cary Moon's Lake House," Kristian told her. "They serve wonderful fish, and the view from the hill is superb. Shall we stop and stroll in that direction?"

"Very well."

They tethered the horse to a tree trunk and then began to walk among the trees which lined the water's edge, finding a well-worn path which led up a hill and through a grove of oaks and elms. The warm, scented summer afternoon enfolded them, colored with bird songs and the hum of insects.

When Kristian pulled Adrienne off the path and into a leafy thicket, she did not resist. His arms went around her, pulling her tightly to him, and his mouth sought hers.

For long moments they kissed, lost together in the sweet blue-green of the afternoon.

"Kristian . . ." Adrienne whispered at last, pulling away from him, her anger and hurt now forgotten. "Oh, it's been weeks since I've seen you—weeks! I've missed you so!"

"And I've missed you, God help me. Adrienne, what is happening to me? To us? I desire you. I want you so fiercely that it seems I can think of nothing else but you. I've thought about you all day, ever since I got your letter."

"I've thought about you, too."

She clung to him, feeling the desire grow in her, the soft, sweet aching of her loins. And when his hands found the buttons at the back of her gown, she did not resist.

They spread her petticoats upon the grass for a makeshift blanket and then sank down, to find each other, and in the loving of their bodies to while away the long afternoon.

It was dusk when they finally pulled apart and stood and helped each other dress. Kristian laughed softly at the grass stains on Adrienne's petticoats, the leaf which had become entangled in her hair. It was as if their conversation in the surrey had never taken place—as if each of them had vowed grimly to forget it.

Adrienne reveled in the fact that she had held him close to her. He loved her, he desired her, hadn't he told her so? And she loved him. Since that was so, surely all their other problems would resolve themselves—somehow.

They finished dressing, and Adrienne fumbled in her small bag for a brush with which to repair the damage to her hair. Then, hand in hand, they found their way back to the path and began to walk slowly toward the surrey.

It was Adrienne who first spotted the branching-off of the path, the leafed-over little trail which led uphill through a grove of perfect wineglass elms.

"Kristian!" She tugged at his hand. "Kristian, oh, let's follow this little path and see where it leads."

"Darling, it's getting late. Barrett must be wondering what has happened to you. Damn, how I'd like to forget that you have a husband!"

"I'd like to forget it, too. Well, let him wonder!" she replied gaily. "Oh, come on, Kristian. Let's explore!"

It was a small brick cottage, perched on the summit of a hill overlooking the lake, shielded from view by a screen of oaks and elms. It had warm red bricks and black shutters. Stained-glass fanlights over the first floor windows caught the fading sunlight. There were porches, towers, cupolas, a widow's walk, and all of it was prettily done on a small scale, as if this were a house built especially as a hideaway for one person.

Adrienne stared at the house, transfixed. What would *Maman* think of such a perfect little place? And was there not a lilac garden to the left of the house, with a summerhouse lovingly constructed of intricately pattened cut-out wood? And climbing its trellises were rose-bushes, their blooms an exquisite pale pink.

"Kristian!" She caught his arm. "That house—it's lovely! Who do you suppose owns it, all hidden away here on the lake?"

"Who knows?"

"I'd like to own a house like that," she said musingly. "It would be wonderful to be able to come here, to get away from New York, from crowds of people following me wherever I go, to be able to escape from everything whenever I wished."

"You couldn't afford such a place, Adrienne. Rumor has it, my darling, that you spend money like water, that you are perpetually in debt to your dressmaker and your grocer and your milliner—"

"Well, I'm not!" she cried angrily. "Yes, I do spend money on clothes—but it's necessary for my profession. I'm an actress, Kristian! People expect me to wear the latest in fashions, and I can't disappoint them, can I?"

Kristian grimaced. "You always do look lovely, I will admit that. Well, I suppose we had better find the

314

Lake House and have something to eat before we go back to the hotel. I've a play to write, you know, and, as I told you, I have some problems with it."

The play which Kristian had come here to Saratoga to finish. . .

It was as if the cold water of reality had drenched over Adrienne. *Are you really positive that there is going to be a role for you in Kristian's new play?* Fanny had asked.

They turned toward the main path, and regretfully Adrienne let the charming little house slip from view behind its canopy of trees.

"Kristian . . ." She steeled herself to speak. Unconsciously her hand had gone to the Passion Star which she wore at her throat. "Kristian, I want to ask you something. About your play——"

"Yes?"

"What are you going to call it?"

He hesitated. "The Passion Star," he said at last.

Silence ticked between them, a little winged beat of seconds. She forced herself to go on.

"Will there be a part for me?"

"No, Adrienne." He said it heavily. "No, there won't be."

"But——" She stared at him. Her throat seemed to close, her belly muscles to squeeze together. She could not believe that she had heard him properly.

"But why not?" she whispered.

Kristian looked uncomfortable. "I didn't make this decision, Adrienne——Phineas Magruder did. There is another actress whom he wants for the lead."

"Who?" she demanded.

"Her name is Kate Claxton. She——"

"Kate Claxton!" Adrienne repeated numbly. So Fanny had been right.

"Yes. Adrienne, don't look so shocked. She is a well-known actress, one of the best, and physically she is more what I had in mind for the part." Kristian's face was savage. "Did you think that because you and I are lovers, you would get special privileges? I was swayed by you

315

once before, darling, and I can't let it happen again. My career is too important to me."

She felt betrayed.

"Your career! What about mine?" she cried.

"Adrienne, you are a lovely woman, you are beautiful, everyone knows that. But physically you are not right for the role of Fatima in this play. You are a blonde, and Fatima must be dark. You are a small woman, and Fatima is larger, magnificent and imposing—"

"I can be imposing on the stage! I'm an actress, Kristian, I can be anything I wish!"

She stared at him, the furious tears welling in her eyes. How dare he do this to her? The part belonged to her—wasn't she the one who had told Kristian the story of the Passion Star?

"Kristian," she cried, "Isn't this my play, too? I mean, you have just told me that you are calling it after the Passion Star—my stone, my very own star sapphire!"

"Yes—"

She unclasped the stone with a quick gesture and held it out. Its surface caught the last rays of sunlight, the six-legged star mysterious within its blue depths.

"Look!" she commanded. "Look at it! See how beautiful it is!" She thrust the jewel at him. "Do you really think, Kristian, that you can stage a play named after such a fabulous jewel and not use the real stone? Do you really think that a sapphire made of paste will impress audiences?"

She thought of Xenos Shane, using any device he could to impress audiences, to awe, to dazzle.

She plunged on desperately. "You are a modern playwright, Kristian—but I am certain that you want to make money. Doesn't your backer, Phineas Magruder, expect it of you?" As Kristian nodded, she went on. "Then you'll have to use the real stone, not an imitation. It will be of great box-office value. Its worth in publicity will be enormous!"

"Perhaps," Kristian admitted.

"It's so." She paused dramatically, as she knew Xenos Shane would have done. "But there is something else. You need the Passion Star, but you also need me. *I* come with it, *I'm* a part of the bargain. If you want to display the sapphire, then you must display me as well!"

Kristian scowled. "Blackmail, Adrienne? Ah, but this time you have failed. You see, in this case, I am not the one who makes the final decision. Unfortunately, it is Phineas Magruder. And he, my love, is not a man you can easily sway."

He is not a man you can easily sway. Adrienne arrived back at her hotel, feeling depressed and desperate. She wanted the part of Fatima—it was hers, really, hers by right. It was unthinkable that anyone else should play it.

The hotel suite was quiet. Barrett's door was closed, and Annie and the baby were already asleep in the small room they shared. Fanny Pepper had left a note saying that she was downstairs in the reading lounge.

Adrienne sat down in her room and began to pull a brush through her pale gold hair. She thought of Phineas Magruder as she had seen him last, at his mansion in New York. She recalled the feeling of power which had emanated from the financier. It had been plain that the man could buy and sell a hundred actresses, even a thousand. Yet . . . hadn't his eyes traveled over her own body with interest? Hadn't he called her a "lovely little piece of womanflesh?"

And, she recalled with growing excitement, Magruder's daughter, Primrose, was here in Saratoga. Hadn't Kristian told her that? Perhaps, then, Magruder was here, as well. And if he were. . . .

Without stopping to consider further, she dropped the brush and began to separate her hair into the long strands which were the beginning of the fashionable coiffure she liked best. Swiftly she looped her hair and pinned it, twisting curls at her temples and at the nape of her neck. Then, like someone possessed, she flew about the room, flinging open the clothes closet to riffle through the gowns which hung there.

The blue silk . . . no, that one was too sober. The

317

gray faille . . . perhaps it was not flattering enough to her figure. Yes, the yellow tulle was better, and its cut, with a low, plunging neck, would show off the smoothness of her skin, as well as the splendors of the Passion Star.

Tonight, of all nights, she and the sapphire must each look their best. . . .

Twenty minutes later she was ready. She paused to face herself in the mirror, seeing there a woman of bold beauty, her eyes sparkling with feverish excitement.

Downstairs in the hotel lobby she fled past the door of the reading lounge—the last thing she wished was for Fanny to see her now—and sought out the nearest bell-boy, a youth of about sixteen with fresh acne eruptions marring his cheeks. She pulled him aside to a corner, where a bank of rubber plants, arranged in pots, provided a semi-shield from curious eyes.

"Phineas Magruder, the New York collar manufacturer, is staying somewhere here at Saratoga Springs," she told him. "If you can tell me where he is, and do it quickly, I will pay you well."

The boy looked at her in awe. "Are you Adrienne Gill, the actress?"

"Yes, I am, but—" She bit her lip, trying to curb her impatience. "Do you think you can find Mr. Magruder?"

"Oh, I 'spose so. But it's pretty big here. There are hundreds of guests at the hotel, and then we have the cottages, too . . . ."

She fished out a bill from the small purse she carried. "I just want you to find him," she whispered. "And please do it right away. I don't want to wait, I wish to see him now, tonight."

"Very well, ma'am. I'll try."

She paced up and down the lobby, ignoring the stares of the few guests who lounged in chairs or read newspapers, becalmed in a backwater of dullness here in this resort village where most guests socialized in the evenings.

But she was unaware of them, and continued to pace, her hands clasped nervously in front of her. What if

Magruder were not here in Saratoga? What would she do then? If she did not move fast, then Kate Claxton would be hired as the female lead in *The Passion Star*, and it would be too late.

Please, she prayed. Let Magruder be here, and let him like me. Let him see that I am the only one who could possibly play Fatima.

In less than half an hour, the bellboy came hurrying back with the news that Phineas Magruder had, as she had suspected, taken one of the apartments which were semi-attached to the hotel.

Adrienne questioned the boy sharply. "Is Mr. Magruder there alone? Who is with him? And which cottage is it?"

Stammering, the boy informed her that the entire Magruder family, including wife and daughters, was here, and had been in great social demand. He gave her the cottage number.

"Oh—"

Disappointment poured through her. Magruder was here—but with his family. How was she to see him alone?

"Do you wish to send a note, ma'am?" The boy's face reflected his hopes of a large tip.

"Yes. No! Oh, I—I don't know!" She gave the boy a handful of coins. "Thank you for your help, and please don't tell anyone, anyone at all, that I asked about him."

"Yes, ma'am." The boy bounced the coins in his palm, then closed his fingers over them. "Yes, ma'am!"

Adrienne lifted her skirts and hurried toward the main door of the hotel. She felt sick with dismay. Magruder was here, but in the company of his wife and three daughters, and thus virtually unapproachable. How was she ever to speak to him?

Nevertheless, she found herself hurrying along the graveled paths of the hotel's inner park in the direction of the cottages, drawn there by desperation. And she was rewarded by the sight, as she emerged again onto the side street, of a group of women coming out of the door of the end cottage to board a sumptuous victoria, its black finish gleaming with polish. A uniformed driver stood at stiff attention, breaking his pose long enough to help each woman climb inside.

It was, she was sure, the Magruder cottage. And these were the Magruder women.

Adrienne stood near the shadow cast by a large clump of bushes, her heart pounding. She waited for Magruder to come out of the front door and join his family. But he did not.

She narrowed her eyes at the lights still glowing in the windows of the cottage. Was Magruder still at home? Or had he already left? The lights in the windows, she knew, meant little. Servants could have been left at home to await the return of the family.

The women were now safely loaded into the victoria, their skirts tucked down on the seat in a billow of fabric. They laughed together, and Primrose's giggle rose above them all, flute-like and infectious. If Primrose were not in love with Kristian, Adrienne might even have liked her, she found herself thinking unwillingly. As it was . . .

The driver swung onto his perch, and the victoria pulled away. Adrienne wondered what to do next. Should she knock at the door of the cottage in the hope that Magruder was still at home and would talk to her? Or should she simply give up and go back to her room?

Suddenly she was startled to see another vehicle, a light buggy, being brought around to the front door of the cottage. Its driver hopped down, hitched the horse to a post, and trotted up to the cottage. In a few moments, the front door pushed open and a dark-suited figure was silhouetted against lamplight.

It was Phineas Magruder, bound for some exclusively male pleasure of the evening. Of course; it had to be.

Adrienne did not hesitate. She rushed forward, out of the shadow cast by the bush.

"Mr. Magruder! Oh, Mr. Magruder! You're making a terrible mistake! There is something which you absolutely must hear!"

"I don't make mistakes, Miss Gill."

He had dismissed the man from the livery stable and had pulled her upward into the buggy. Now they rode down Broadway Street, past the gas lamps which cast yellow circles of light into the summer darkness, attracting zigzags of moths. Lanterns glowed from passing carriages, and somewhere ahead of them, Adrienne knew, must be the victoria which contained Magruder's wife and daughters.

But for now, by lucky chance, she had him to herself. And she must make the most of her opportunity.

"Why," she said as calmly as she could, "it's about the role of Fatima. You are making a terrible error if you give it to Kate Claxton. *I* am the actress who can play the part as Kristian meant it to be played—with excitement and dramatic tension. I am the one!"

Her hand went to her throat, touching the gem which she wore there.

"Kate Claxton is well known and has a large following. And physically she is right for the role."

She stared at the financier. He was ugly, really, with his short, squat body, his thick neck, the fringe of hair surrounding a bald spot, the small eyes. Yet there was an aura of power about him. And because of that, his appearance did not really matter. Nothing did, save the diamond-sharp intelligence in those eyes which now looked her over, missing nothing.

She heard his voice plunge on.

"But it's a terrible mistake to hire someone like Kate Claxton! She doesn't have the feel for the role that I do! And if you hire her, you will have to use a paste jewel to stand in for the Passion Star. Paste, Mr. Magruder— when, if you use me as Fatima, you will have the real thing."

Magruder's laugh was harsh. "Do you realize, Miss Gill, that I can go to any jewel broker in New York and buy a pendant to use on the stage? A real jewel every bit as flashy as the one which you wear now?"

"You can't buy this one," she insisted stubbornly.

"I can buy anything I please—including you."

She flushed. "You can't buy the Passion Star, for I own it, and there is no other stone like it. It has a fabulous story, Mr. Magruder, a true story which can't be faked. Audiences will thrill to that story, they'll love every word of it. And they'll want to come to the theater to see the real stone. They'll pay well for that."

"Perhaps you're right." The financier's expression was speculative. "Then sell me the Passion Star, Miss Gill. That's what you really want, isn't it? I'll pay you well. You can live for many years comfortably on your profit. You'll never have to work again."

"No, I don't want to sell it!" Her voice was a cry. She calmed herself. "No, Mr. Magruder, there is only one way you can get possession of the Passion Star, and that is to let me play Fatima."

There was a silence. A very long one. She could hear the rhythmic clop of the horses' hooves, the jangle of bridle and trappings.

"Very well," Magruder said unexpectedly.

She could not believe she had heard him properly.

"Then—" Her hands flew to her neck, found the cool smoothness of the sapphire. "Then you'll let me play Fatima? You'll use the real Passion Star onstage?"

"Yes, I will." Phineas Magruder grinned at her, his teeth a flash of white in the summer dusk. "But, since you have set a condition for my use of the Passion Star, then I feel free to set a condition, too." His grin widened, and for the first time she felt a stab of fear.

"And my condition is this," he went on. "That you will let me use you."

"Use . . . me?"

"You know what I mean, Miss Gill. I don't think you're so stupid as all that. Why else would you have come to me as you did? Let us turn the buggy around and go back to my cottage. We'll have privacy there. All the privacy we need."

"Well, good evening, dear wife—or shall I say good morning?"

Barrett's slurred voice accused her. She had hoped to steal into her room unseen, but had met her husband sprawled on the couch in the sitting room of the suite, his two canes propped beside him. She could smell, too, the fruity odor of whisky.

"I . . . I couldn't sleep," she replied rapidly. "I was out walking. I—I didn't realize how late it was."

"A likely tale." Barrett inclined his head in her direction bitterly. "Would you like to hear about *my* day, Adrienne? My exciting and fascinating day here at Saratoga Springs? I went to drink the waters. Some of the waters are more efficacious than others, I've found, and some are downright cathartic in nature."

Adrienne turned away. After Phineas Magruder, she felt soiled, dirtied beyond belief. All she wished to do was to go into her own room, strip off her clothes, and scrub her body until it was raw and clean.

"Listen to me!" Barrett ordered. "Did you know that I learned some interesting facts while the attendants were ladling out that foul-tasting stuff?"

She was silent.

"They are all gossiping, it seems. You see, there is a certain actress who is staying here at the Springs. An actress with a fiery temper and pale yellow hair, who—"

She found her voice. "I don't care to hear about it, Barrett."

"Well, you *will* hear. It seems that this actress—we all know who she is, don't we?—has come here because of her lover, a certain playwright who has taken a cottage, one of those little hideaways so popular here at Saratoga where certain . . . liaisons . . . can take place without adverse publicity."

Adrienne swallowed hard against the knot which seemed to fill her throat. She felt like laughing wildly, like running into her own room, slamming the door behind her, and sobbing until she could weep no more.

"Barrett, you've been drinking too much," she said dully. "And I am not referring to the mineral waters."

"The pot calling the kettle black?" His mouth twisted. "Yes, my dear. You are right. I have been drinking, and I'll continue to drink. Whisky soothes pain, did you know that? But of course you do."

She began to back away in the direction of her own room.

"Pour me another glass," her husband ordered.

A thought came into her mind of her father, Jack

McGill, as she had seen him late one evening. He had been hunched at an old table in front of the stove, staring into a bottle, tears running down his cheeks. How many times had her father tried to stop his drinking? And was she herself to be like him, constantly searching for the surcease from pain, the soft, warm, easy blurring of sensation which was to be found only in a bottle?

Despair overwhelmed her.

"Pour me another drink," Barrett repeated.

"Very well."

A flask of whisky sat on a table, and beside it were several small glasses. Blindly Adrienne stumbled forward and splashed liquid into a glass. Then she filled a second glass for herself.

She took Barrett his drink and returned for her own, downing the alcohol as if it were a penance—closing her lips against the harsh burn which seared its way down her gullet.

Almost immediately the gray veil slipped down over her mind, blocking out the image of Phineas Magruder's slug-pale, pudgy body, slack and soft . . . .

She found that she was shaking uncontrollably.

"Well, dear wife, I see that I am not the only one who appreciates a little tot of forgetfulness."

"It's only one drink."

Barrett laughed. His chuckle was somehow terrible. "Yes, I said that once, too, long ago in London. *I* didn't need the stuff. *I* didn't crave it, I could spend an entire evening without it, perhaps even a week or a month."

He tilted up his glass and drained it. "Well, I was wrong, as my family could have informed you. I did require my whisky. I needed it a great deal and I still need it. I know all about what needing is, my dear. I'm an expert at it." His eyes raked hers. "Perhaps you are learning, too?"

"No—"

"Oh, yes, you are. Pour me another, will you? Or better yet, bring me the flask. I'll do it myself."

Silently she did as he asked.

Again he drank. When the whisky was almost gone,

he suddenly lifted his glass high, waving it at her in a hideous, crooked toast.

"To you, my dear wife. To your career. May it last longer than a *meringue glacée* in hell—"

And then Barrett began to laugh. Hard, uncontrollably, until tears ran down his cheeks, and he had to take another glass of whisky, and another one after that.

She was to have the part of Fatima. Kristian sent a note to her hotel room at nine the next morning, informing her of that fact.

Victory is yours, my flamboyant and determined Adrienne. You are Fatima and the Passion Star is mine— for the duration of the play, anyway. May we be glorious partners. Love, Kristian.

Adrienne sat in her room, clad in a blue woolen wrapper, rereading the note and wondering why she didn't feel happier. This was what she had wanted, wasn't it? The chance to play the lead in *The Passion Star?* To show the world what she could do, what she had been born to do?

And yet—

Her head was throbbing, her mouth tasted dry and sticky. She fancied she could taste something else, too, the sweet brandy which Phineas Magruder had pressed on her until she thought she would be sick with the cloying flavor of it.

I know all about what needing is, my dear. Perhaps you are learning, too.

The words taunted her. But resolutely she pushed them away. She wouldn't think about what Barrett had said, or about Magruder, not now, not just yet. She had won, hadn't she? She would play Fatima. And surely that was all that mattered now . . .

An hour later she had dressed and breakfasted and was hurrying down the broad expanse of Broadway Street toward the shops which offered their lures to the promenaders. Whenever she felt upset, a tour through a department store or shop could soothe her. Seeing beautiful things, touching them . . . . She could never tire of it.

The dry-goods shop was small and cluttered. It smelled deliciously of lavender and heliotrope sachet, of the stiff new odors of dry goods, of tulle and *peau de soie* and tarlatan and faille. Adrienne browsed among the bolts of goods, savoring the feel of the cloth against her fingers. *Maman*, she reflected, would love to own a gown made of such soft, silky stuff.

There were two other customers in the shop. One, a slim, middle-aged woman, dickered with the shopkeeper over the price of a roll of ribbon. The other was a young girl who leaned near the front window of the shop, her face turned dreamily in the direction of the fashionably dressed people who thronged Broadway.

"Primrose!" The mother's voice was sharply reprimanding. "Primrose, would you please stop staring out of the window and come and give me your opinion on this ribbon? It is, after all, for your gown."

The girl was Primrose Magruder. Adrienne felt her heart sink. She longed to turn, to flee from the shop without making her purchases.

But before she could do so, the girl turned from the window. Her eyes widened as she saw Adrienne.

"Oh! Miss Gill! Is it really you?" Primrose's pretty mouth had fallen open, revealing small, even teeth. Her skin, Adrienne noted, was as creamy-pale as custard.

"Yes, it is I," she heard herself reply calmly. "I have come to Saratoga to escape the worst of the heat in New York."

"Yes, it was hot, wasn't it? I was so warm that the moisture ran down my sides beneath my gown, and Mama said—"

"Primrose! How many times must I remind you that it is not ladylike to speak so openly of such things! And to someone in a shop, of all places! You must pardon my daughter."

Gloriane Magruder gave Adrienne a cool look. She was tall and slim, and even the wrinkles etched on her forehead were elegant. Adrienne wondered what she would think if she knew that Adrienne had been in her cottage last night, had lain on her bed, and struggled beneath the body of her husband . . . .

"We must finish our selections," Gloriane Magruder said dismissingly. "I hope you will pardon us, Miss . . . "

"Miss Adrienne Gill." Then something made Adrienne add defiantly, "Perhaps you saw me in *Melissa Charles*? I am also to star in Kristian King's new play, *The Passion Star*."

"Indeed. I pay little attention to my husband's business activities." Icy tones, meant to dismiss.

Gloriane Magruder turned away, and Adrienne made her selections hastily, choosing a bolt of fabric to be delivered to her hotel, not caring about anything save that she should be out of this shop.

Five minutes later she was hurrying down Broadway, pushing her way among the groups of promenaders: men, women and children gawking at each other's costumes, or simply enjoying the morning sun.

"Miss Gill! Oh, Miss Gill, do please stop!"

Adrienne turned to see Primrose Magruder running in her direction, her skirts lifted as if she were a twelve-year-old in pursuit of an errant puppy. Yet the girl ran with such easy grace that, instead of seeming childish, she was more charming than ever.

Adrienne stopped. She could feel her hands go suddenly moist.

"Yes?"

"Miss Gill, I want to talk with you for a moment!"

"But what of your mother and the shopping?"

"Oh, *Mama!* Mama is looking at faille again, she has it in her mind to buy me another ball gown to add to the dozen I already have and hate!"

Primrose's laugh was flute-like and infectious. Again Adrienne was reminded of a frisky twelve-year-old. She felt her throat twist. Oh, how could Kristian be attracted by such a childish girl? Surely he wasn't, not really. He had only admired her beauty, that was all. Any man would pay attention to that. . . .

With a start she realized that the other girl had fallen into step beside her.

" . . . and so, Miss Gill, you've got to tell me how I can get into the theater. I want to be an actress! It's what

I desire more than anything else—well, almost anything!"

"You, an actress?" Adrienne was startled.

"Yes. Oh, Mama would die if she knew that I was thinking such a thing. She wishes me to be sedate and ladylike and marry some doddering old man and have a dozen babies. But ever since I met Kristian that day in Central Park—oh, he was handsome, don't you think so, Miss Gill? A real actor! And a playwright, too! Mama doesn't approve, naturally, but . . . "

Primrose continued to chatter, and Adrienne had no choice but to accompany her toward the two giant hotels which faced each other across Broadway, flags flying from atop their long porches.

Primrose bubbled on. "Mama mustn't know of my ambitions, of course. And I daren't tell dear Kristian—how he would scold me! Worse, he might tell Mama of my plans. Kristian considers me only a baby, he doesn't realize that I'm almost eighteen, a woman grown!"

Or did he? Adrienne wondered dryly. Did this young girl realize just how very appealing she was?

"Perhaps Kristian—Mr. King—would be right to discourage you," she said carefully. "Do you know just how much hard work is needed to go on the stage? It is a difficult life. And the road tours are very tiring and grueling. I should know, I have just returned from a tour of *Melissa Charles,* and I don't think I ever wish to see another train station or dirty hotel again as long as I live!"

"But it must be so exciting to travel!" breathed the girl. "Oh, Miss Gill, I'm sure it must be! And I was so thrilled to meet you on the night of *Melissa Charles*'s opening. You were so brave to save that woman from being burned!"

"Oh—I suppose—"

"Kristian says that you are a very kind and quick-thinking person who would risk her own life in order to help others," the girl chattered on. "He assures me that all the gossip about you in the papers—well, most of it, anyway—is just a lie. Of course, you did slap that newspaperman, everyone knows that, but Kristian explained—"

Kristian. Almost every sentence Primrose uttered contained his name.

"Kristian King talks entirely too much!" Adrienne snapped. They had reached the main entrance of the Union Hotel, and she stopped. "Well, Miss Magruder, I really must be getting back to my room. My little girl will be awakening from her morning nap and I must take her for a walk."

Primrose's eyes widened. "You have a little girl?"

"Why, yes." Adrienne felt stung somehow by the surprise on the other's face. "I have a child a year old. Her name is Barrie."

"Oh—Why, Miss Gill, I never thought—I mean—" Primrose floundered. "Although I do know, of course, that you are married, and act under your maiden name. Your husband is very old, isn't he? And an invalid as well . . . ."

"My husband is—none of your business!" Adrienne glared at Primrose, then gathered her skirts and fled into the hotel. She had startled herself with her rudeness.

Yet how dare Primrose Magruder stare at her as if she were a settled matron well past the age of beauty?

Chapter 22

Adrienne pulled her mantle about her shoulders and shivered. A chill rain poured out of the bleak November sky, turning the paving stones in front of the Olympic Theater into a slick, shiny surface which reflected back the glow of the gas lamps. Ten weeks had passed. It was now November, 1873, and *The Passion Star* would open in two days to a packed New York theater.

And the audience, Adrienne reminded herself with sick fear, would include such people as Phineas and Gloriane Magruder, Primrose, Barrett, and of course, all the important New York critics. It would also include her old enemy William Stauffer. How eagerly he would wait for her to fail again!

A cab waited for her at the curb, and Adrienne hurried toward it, lifting the hem of her full skirts so they would not brush the wet pavement. She could hardly wait to get home and put her feet up, or perhaps soak in a warm tub of water.

The rehearsal, ending only minutes ago, had been grueling. Kristian, caught up in pre-production nerves, had been at his temperamental worst. He had shouted at the prop man and the stage manager, and at the thin, weedy boy who ran the gas table. He had been sarcastic to Bettina Smithe, who, much to her joy, had been engaged to play Raji, Fatima's friend. He had finished by flaring up at Adrienne.

"Are you an actress, Adrienne, or just a music-hall

comedienne?" he had demanded. "This is a serious play and a realistic one, and I certainly don't want Fatima to be played as if she were the heroine of some foolish melodrama!"

"And I'm not playing her that way," she had snapped.

Kristian's eyes had blazed at her. "Well? What are you all standing about for?" he had said, turning to the cast. "Take ten minutes, will you? Go on, get out of here, all of you!"

When the cast had trooped down the narrow stairs which led to the greenroom, Adrienne had turned to face Kristian. "You needn't vent your temper on me," she said tightly. "I won't stand for it!"

"And I won't stand for your taking a drink before you come to a rehearsal of my play."

She stared at him. "A drink? But—"

"Don't try to pretend with me, girl. I know you too well. You have come to rehearsal three times now with more than a few drinks in you, and on those occasions you fluffed your lines and missed your cues. I won't put up with it. And neither will Magruder."

Adrienne lifted her chin. "I love the part of Fatima, and I love your play," she told him quickly. "Do you think I could ever to anything to spoil it? Do you think that I ever would? Oh, Kristian, if you think that, then you don't know me very well!"

His face had changed.

"Perhaps. Oh, God, Adrienne, I don't know any more. All I know is that we are nearly ready for the dress rehearsal and we're still beset by problems. I want this play to be right. It must be right!"

"And it will be," she assured him, touching his arm and wishing that she could caress him more openly. "Everything will go splendidly, I promise you, and that includes my drinking!"

Now, hurrying across the paving stones in the rain toward the waiting cab, she was no longer so sure. Her drinking was easily stopped, of course. But *The Passion Star* was a complex play, a drama on many levels. It required much skill and devotion from its cast. As it was, it was sure to cause much controversy—

Rain pelted her cheeks. She half-started to run toward the cab, noting as she did so that a man had taken shelter under the advertising kiosk in front of the theater. He stood hunched over, one hand at the brim of his hat to protect it from the driving rain.

The hack driver hopped down from his perch, and waited to assist her. The man standing by the kiosk had turned, his face a white blur in rain-wet darkness.

A blur, she saw with a swift shiver, which held a certain familiarity. An odd prickle seemed to touch her nerve ends.

"Where to, ma'am?" the cab driver asked.

Automatically, Adrienne gave him the address of the brownstone.

As the cab pulled away into the street, Adrienne glanced back at the man by the kiosk. She saw that he had turned and was now striding down the street in the direction of a corner saloon. His reflection, magnified in the wet paving stones, made him seem taller and thinner than he really was.

Yes, she thought, catching her breath. There *was* something familiar about the way he walked, the very swing of his big hands. Surely she knew him.

Xenos Shane. The name popped into her mind unbidden. Xenos's thick, gnarled fingers, fastening the Passion Star about her neck. That squat body, pushing and pumping over her own smaller one . . .

Dear God. She swallowed back sudden sour bile. Glasgow was an ocean away, in another country. Surely the man had been only what he seemed—some passerby who had stopped to take shelter from the rain.

Nevertheless, as the hack rattled toward the corner, its horse's hooves clopping on the wet paving stones, Adrienne felt a shiver take possesion of her. It was almost as if she could hear the magician's voice, thick, muttering.

Drink! Drink, damn you, you little harlot. That hair of yours—like sunlight it is. Wherever on God's earth did you get it? Ah, you thought you could get away from old

Xenos, did you? Thought you could escape him . . . well, you can't, my sweet rose. You can't. . . .

"Do sit still, Adrienne, or my hands are going to slip, and I'll get eye-blacking all over your cheeks!"

Fanny laughed, low in her throat. Although her hands were ugly with scarring, they had healed well enough for her to work, and William Mancin, true to his word, had found a job for her backstage at the Olympic.

"All right." Adrienne tried not to let her voice shake. "Oh, Fanny, how can you be so calm? It's opening night! They're out there, all of them—like vultures, waiting for me to fail. Oh, how they'd love to see me fail, I really think they would. How they'd all like to laugh at me!"

Opening night. The night they'd all worked for. And especially herself. She had struggled to master the role of Fatima, laboring long hours on her own after the scheduled rehearsals were finished, until she would fall into bed with exhaustion. Never—never again—would she suffer the humiliation she had on the night *Melissa Charles* had opened!

"They won't laugh," Fanny assured her. "You'll be good, Adrienne, the very best. But, remember, honey, this is Kristian's night as well. His play is very controversial, and the love scene in the sultan's palace is quite daring. I am certain he has his own worries tonight.

"Yes, of course."

Flushing, Adrienne accepted the rebuke. Fanny was right, of course. This was Kristian's night—even more so than hers.

Fanny's scarred hands dusted a rabbit's foot in rice powder, then rubbed it over Adrienne's cheeks. Carefully she began to smooth on the carmine rouge, blending it into Adrienne's high cheekbones until they were even more dramatic.

"There." Fanny stood back to admire her work. "You look lovely, Adrienne."

"Do I?"

The mirror—it was a tool almost as important to an

actress as the costumes she wore or the rouge she applied to her face. Adrienne leaned toward the glass, then drew a quick, startled breath. She looked exotic, foreign. Her skin had been darkened, her cheekbones artfully made more prominent, her eyes heavily outlined in black. Her gown, sewn by Fanny with a circular pattern of beads on heavy flounces, dipped low at the neckline, exposing the fullness of her breasts.

Yes, she was beautiful. No one had to tell her that.

Still, if only she didn't feel so frightened! Worse, half an hour previously, an incident had happened which filled her with a superstitious foreboding.

Quince, the stagehand, had stopped on her way down to the dressing room.

"Miss Gill—Miss Gill, I've been watching you, I hope you don't mind."

There had been an urgency about the way the man spoke. "You've worked harder than anyone, I'll admit it, and you could be stunning as Fatima. But there's one problem. Stage fright. I can smell it on you, Miss Gill. I can smell it plain as smoke."

She had recoiled from him.

"Nonsense, Quince, I—I'm only a bit nervous, that's all, and surely it will pass."

The man's eyes had regarded her in sympathy and pity. "I didn't mean to scare you, Miss Gill, you know I wouldn't want to do that. But you're so pretty and all, I just wanted to warn you—"

She had fled past him, not listening to whatever else it was that he had to say.

Now she sat in her dressing room, trying desperately to relax. From outside in the corridor came frantic back-stage noises. William Mancin scolded someone for being late. A dog yapped; it was the little terrier who would appear briefly in the second act. A door slammed. Footsteps sounded on the stone floor. High, nervous laughter rose from the greenroom, to be quickly stifled.

Adrienne felt as if she could hear, too, the frantic pounding of her own heart. It beat in her chest like a trapped bird. Her mouth was dry, her tongue a thick, unwieldy rag. And——desperately she cleared her throat—— wasn't she growing hoarse? Her voice, instead of soaring to the very back of the theater, was going to be cracked, a donkey's bray!

Fanny put down the rabbit's foot.

"I think you're finished now." Her cheerful voice jerked Adrienne back to reality. "I've done all I can. Do you want to put the Passion Star on now? I'll fasten the clasp for you."

She reached into Adrienne's trunk and pulled out a small box, removing the gem from its linen wrapping. In the light of the gas fixture, the sapphire glimmered mysteriously.

"Three hundred fifty carats," Fanny murmured, holding it up. "Even though I've read all about the Passion Star in the newspapers and on the theater playbills, I still can't believe it. A stone so big, so rare——why, even Queen Victoria would be proud to wear such a jewel! All the women in the audience tonight will be breathless with awe."

"Yes."

Fanny fastened the sapphire around Adrienne's neck.

"There," she said.

Again Adrienne narrowed her eyes critically at her own reflection. Yes, without the sapphire she had been beautiful. But now, with it gleaming at her throat, she had acquired the proud, passionate bearing of a queen.

"Well," Fanny said, "I have to go and mend a rip in Kristian's robes——William Mancin is nearly frantic about it. So I'll leave you now, Adrienne." Hands reached out to clasp Adrienne's own. "I don't need to wish you good luck, do I? As far as I've been able to observe, you're very good at making your own."

Adrienne threw herself into her friend's arms.

"Oh, Fanny! Am I good at making my own luck? I don't *know*——"

After Fanny had left, Adrienne sat alone in her dressing room. In only a few minutes, she knew, the callboy would rap at her door. And in fifteen minutes after that, she would be standing in the wings, waiting to go on.

Nervously, she rose and began to pace up and down the small room. An arrangement of pipes served as a clothes hanger and from this her street dress hung, looking forlorn. She had nailed her Turkish hangings to the wall and spread the colorful rug on the floor. Once she had considered these her good-luck pieces, small bits of beauty to cheer her surroundings. Now, they seemed only to mock her.

You're destined, daughter. Destined . . .

Adrienne turned sharply on her heel and began to pace in the other direction. Anxiously she cleared her throat, testing her voice. She clenched her fists, unclenched them.

She had failed once as Melissa Charles, failed miserably. It could not happen again—it must not.

Turning again, she almost caught the hem of her long, flowing gown and stopped to steady herself on the corner of the opened theater trunk. That was when her hand felt the hardness of glass.

The whisky flask, its flat sides embossed by the maker, protruded its neck from among the welter of lace and cambric, wigs and hats which filled the trunk. Had she placed it there?

Adrienne caught her breath.

Well, she decided quickly, it wasn't important how the flask had got there. She wasn't going to have any. She had made a promise to Kristian.

She wheeled away from the trunk and paced to the mirror again, painfully conscious of the noises outside the dressing room. Kristian calling impatiently to someone. A gust of nervous female laughter. The slam of a door.

Adrienne swallowed hard. She felt as if two mad, frightened squirrels chased each other through her belly . . . .

This time, when her pacing took her near the theater trunk, she stopped. It was without surprise that she saw her hand reach out for the amber flask, cradle it, and then wrench out the cork.

Only one quick drink, she assured herself. One

wouldn't harm her performance. She only needed enough to moisten her tongue and throat, to relax her before she went onstage . . . .

"Curse you, Adrienne, what are you trying to do? Ruin my play?"

Kristian's voice was full of fury. He had knocked on her dressing-room door, then thrust it open so quickly that she had not had time to conceal the bottle. Now she stood frozen, in full wig and costume, the amber flask still in her hand.

"I . . . I was nervous . . ." She felt her throat convulse.

"Nervous! We all are, you little fool! Every last one of us, and that includes a big stage crew and a cast of twenty. But none of the rest of us are holed up in our dressing rooms nursing a full flask!"

"I was just going to have one drink—"

"One drink is too damned many!"

In his loose white costume as Ahmad, Fatima's lover, Kristian looked tall and barbaric, a blond pirate ready to do murder. He snatched the bottle from her hand and dumped its contents onto the floor. Whisky splashed and gurgled, making a puddle which spread slowly onto the Turkish rug.

"Kristian!" Her voice was a gasp. "You've ruined the rug—"

"Your rug be damned!" His hands grasped her upper arms, squeezing her flesh so hard that she drew a sharp breath of pain.

"Let go of me!"

"No, I won't. Damn you, Adrienne, damn your beautiful, wilful hide!" His voice had gone husky. "Why do you do such things to me? Don't you know that I risked losing Magruder as my backer in order to get you this role? Do you think that he gave it to you because of anything you did? God, no. I had to stay up until all hours with him, to fight him, to swear you'd be a thousand times better than Kate Claxton—"

"I didn't know," she whispered. "I thought—" She stopped.

"Well, it's true. I fought for you, you little fool. And

now you repay me by risking my play merely because you need a drink!"

She glared at him. His anger was almost a physical force, a magnetic charge leaping from him to her, connecting their bodies. She knew with a sick certainty that she desired him. If he approached her, if he moved one inch closer to her, she would melt into his arms. She would sink with him down onto the whisky-wet floor of the dressing room; she would be helpless in his arms; she would do anything he wished . . . .

"Don't look at me that way, girl. You can't charm me tonight. Tonight I don't know you and you don't know me, we are only two actors doing a job. And that job had better be done right, do you hear me? Or you'll never set foot on the New York stage again."

"Kristian!"

His eyes narrowed at her.

"I mean that. I may love you—and God help me, I never wanted to do that. But I won't let anything stand in the way of my career—or of yours. *I want you to be superb, Adrienne. I want it to happen for you. And for me.*"

"I'll be good, I swear it," she said dully.

"Very well. Then I'll see you onstage."

Kristian slammed out of the dressing room and was gone.

Chapter 23

Whisky. Longingly she thought of it, of the soft glow it could spread through her veins, like gossamer silk, soothing away all tension, all fear.

She wanted a drink. Very badly, she wanted a drink.

Adrienne stood behind the "practical door" of the *Passion Star* box set, staring blindly at the jacks and stage braces which supported it from behind. She could hear the rattling whirr as the curtain lifted, the expectant hush of an audience settling down for the evening.

I want you to be superb, Adrienne. I want it to happen for you. And for me.

"Adrienne!" Fanny's voice hissed behind her. "It's time! Adrienne! You must go on!"

"I . . . I can't."

"You must. They are waiting for you."

"But—" She swallowed and gulped. "I tell you, Fanny, I . . . I don't think I can."

"But of course you can. You must. Sorry, honey, to do this—"

A hand smacked Adrienne's cheek. The blow was hard, stinging, taking her utterly by surprise. She wanted to turn on Fanny, to cry out, to express hurt. But before she could do so she felt Fanny's hand again, shoving in the center of her back, pushing her onstage.

Then the footlights were in her eyes, bathing her in pitiless light.

There was no more time to think, or to be frightened. She heard the collective gasp of the audience as they saw the Passion Star about her neck, gleaming, flawless in its beauty.

Then—abruptly—she was no longer Adrienne Gill. She was Fatima, running onstage to meet her lover in a secluded corner of the king's garden.

"Darling, oh, darling, he mustn't find us here or he will be angry.

I don't care if he is angry. I don't care about anything except you.

But, Ahmad—

Act One. Scenes One and Two and Three. The lines they had all worked over, struggled to polish and perfect. And it was happening, this time, the magic. With each scene she could feel her rapport with the audience grow stronger. It was as if a thin, strong cord connected her to the people sitting beyond the footlights. With her voice, she could pull the cord tighter and tighter, until the whole theater vibrated with the tension.

She controlled her audience, she alone.

And they were a part of her, all of those men and women sitting out there. She was a part of them. She existed only for them . . .

It was over.

At last, it was over.

Breathless, almost weeping with fatigue, Adrienne stood at the apron of the stage taking her curtain calls, curtseying low as Barrett had taught her. One . . . two . . . four . . . six . . . it seemed to go on endlessly, the wild clapping and cheering, echoing against gilt-encrusted wall decorations and crystal chandeliers and sumptuous gas fixtures.

Flowers showered onstage. Hothouse roses, singly and in bouquets. Daisies, jonquils, carnations. A man leaped out of the audience. He jumped precariously over the footlights and their guard chain, and presented her with an enormous basket of pink and gold roses.

She was laughing, she was crying. The blurred rows of faces swam at her.

What must William Stauffer think of her now? Surely he would *have* to give her a good review! As the curtain rang down for the last time, the thought surged triumphantly through her. Now Stauffer would have to admit that she had been good—he would have no choice!

"Adrienne, you did it, you did it! You were wonderful!" Fanny's voice was jubilant. "It was worth smacking you, it was worth everything!"

"Fanny is right, you were superb!" Kristian was there too, to sweep her up in his arms and whirl her about so that her feet did not even touch the floor.

She gasped and cried out joyfully and clung to him, forgiving him everything.

"Darling, darling!" Again he hugged her. "We must go out and celebrate our victory! Where do you want to go? And what do you wish to have? Champagne? A magnum of it, a dozen magnums! None of it would be enough. Adrienne, you were just what I had envisioned. You held the audience in your palm, you grabbed them and never let them go until the final curtain—"

Crowds of people had pushed their way backstage, to cram the narrow corridors outside the dressing room and greenroom area. They shoved each other good-naturedly in an effort to get closer to Adrienne and Kristian.

"There she is—it's Adrienne Gill—wasn't she wonderful?"

"My dear, have you ever been so shocked before in your life? That love scene, I have never seen anything like it! But Miss Gill was tremendous, didn't you think so—"

"Oh, look at her, Sophie, that hair of hers, why, it's as pale as corn tassels. What do you suppose she does to it?"

Adrienne heard snatches of comments, was alternately amused and delighted, and felt herself floating on a high, pink cloud of euphoria. Kristian took her to a famous chophouse, a small, dark, smoky restaurant crowded with theater people.

They dined on lobster, on broiled lamb chops and fried potatos and apple tarts smothered in thick cream. They drank wine, a bottle of it between them, and she would never remember how many bottles of champagne, rich, bubbly, heady. But none of its intoxication could match the wonderful bubbles of triumph which fizzed through her veins. *The Passion Star* was a success. She, Adrienne, was a success. She drank, she laughed, she felt so happy that she could fly.

Afterwards, when the waiters began to eye them crossly, for it was closing time, they went to Kristian's rooms. Was she drunk? Was he? It didn't seem to matter. They laughed, clinging to each other. They half-supported each other up the outside stairs, and then fell down upon his bed to make wild love. They tore into each other's bodies, savoring each other until it was as if they had become one mindless, enjoying creature. As if they had melted together until there was no pulling them apart, or ever would be . . . .

People crammed backstage. Men in expensive suits, women in flowing, full-skirted gowns, well-wishers, backstage dandies, theater buffs for whom the world of Union Square was excitement of the highest order. They filled the dressing rooms and spilled out into the corridor, chattering and laughing.

Members of the cast, still in makeup and costume, moved among them like exotic birds. Bouquets of flowers filled Adrienne's dressing room and had been arranged in the corridor, sending out a heavy perfume. Someone had sent champagne, someone else a huge box of chocolate candy. There were four scrawled invitations to supper.

Adrienne, too excited to change out of her costume, as she usually was after the performance, paced about, examining the flowers and reading the cards.

To a lovely actress, possessor of the world's most intriguing sapphire. The Passion Star is haunting me. As are you. From Martin Greggori.

That card had been attached to a giant bouquet of yellow hothouse roses, at least five dozen blooms arranged in a sterling silver vase.

"Well, and aren't we something!" Bettina Smithe snatched the card away from Adrienne to read it herself. "Look at the flowers from Martin Greggori, of all people!

And that vase—it's solid silver. You could pawn it, Adrienne, and fetch a pretty penny. I wish the man would send me flowers in expensive vases. I'd know what to do with them!"

"Martin Greggori? Who is he?" Adrienne felt dazed. *The Passion Star is haunting me. As are you.* What an odd thing for the man to have written.

"Why, he's just one of the richest men in New York, that's all—if you can stand to look at him. He's a total cripple, a little wizened-up man who has to go around in a wheelchair. And if he wants a woman he has to pay for her, that's the only way he'll ever get one."

Bettina's titter was ugly. "He's been in the audience every night, can you imagine that? Perhaps he's in love with *you*, Adrienne!"

Adrienne turned away, feeling both repelled and uneasy. Why should such a strange man be so interested in the Passion Star? Or herself? But she brushed aside the questions. What did it matter? All actresses received attention from backstage admirers. She should settle down to enjoy her success. Hadn't she worked hard? And wasn't everything happening almost as *Maman* had dreamed?

Maman, I am a star, she wrote in neat pen strokes as she had been taught at the Catholic school. *I never thought it possible. But it has happened. My reviews were wonderful, and even William Stauffer admitted that I did a superb job. Oh,* Maman! *The theater has been packed every night for two weeks. No tickets are to be had in the city. Kristian says the play will run here in New York and then have a road tour. He says that we are all going to make a quantity of money from it, that I am going to be rich.*

Her pen paused, and she stopped to clean it on the pen-wiper before putting it down. Her eyes focused on the street outside the brownstone where a glazier's wagon rumbled slowly past.

She frowned, took a swallow of whisky from the tumbler which sat on the table beside her, and began to write again, more slowly this time, as if the words came with difficulty.

Maman, *there is also something else which I must tell you . . .*

Carefully, almost too carefully, her pen formed the words. Two weeks after the opening of *The Passion Star,* her fears had been realized. After Barrie's birth, her monthly periods had been irregular, and she had not been surprised to find her flux delayed. But one night after the performance, she could no longer deny the facts.

Her menstrual period was more than a month late. Further, she had experienced tenderness and swelling in her breasts, tiredness in the evenings, and nausea in the mornings and at other times of the day as well.

She was going to have another child. And this baby would not be Barrett's, but Kristian King's.

He would be beautiful, she was sure of it, as handsome and arrogant as his father, as filled with the same quick-silver creative spirit. This, she knew, would be a baby she could love wholly. A child for her to worship, as she had once worshipped her little brother, Devin . . . .

She finished the letter to *Maman* and—as always—tucked in two ten-dollar bills, a fortune to *Maman.* Then she found the sealing wax, heated and sealed it. Seldom did she receive a reply from *Maman;* her mother was busy in Glasgow with her perpetual struggle to rear children amid poverty. Yet she knew that *Maman* read her letters and treasured them. At least one McGill was fulfilling a dream.

That night she struggled through the performance, feeling sick and wan. She munched dry crackers between scenes and brushed off Fanny's anxious comments.

But her mood, swinging sharply these days between joy and gloom, took a sharp downward turn as she left the theater for the hack which would take her home. A baby! As the carriage rocked and swayed in the darkness, she could not hold to her pleasant anticipation about bearing Kristian's child.

What would a pregnancy mean to her now? In order to continue in the play, she would have to conceal her condition for as long as possible. Thank God that Fatima's robes were mostly loose, her gowns voluminous. But what would she do when her bulk became too obvious even to hide in that way? What of the tour which was planned for later?

The worry still consumed her as she paid the cab driver and hurried up the steep steps into the brownstone.

"What is wrong with you?" her husband demanded as she emerged from the upstairs dressing area wearing a robe. Her face, she knew, was pale, and she felt as if she might be sick at any moment.

"Oh, I suppose it's the grippe," she replied.

"The grippe! That's likely!"

"You should be in bed, Barrett," she went on after a moment. "You know the doctor said you must take as much rest as possible, or you will weaken your health even further."

Barrett's mouth twisted drunkenly. He smacked one of his canes on the floor.

"That doctor is a charlatan! All doctors are, even my father. Could Papa mend my knee? Could he cure the women who came to him with tumors, could he help even my wife who died twelve years ago of consumption? Can anyone cure me now of this damned paralysis which ties down my tongue?"

"I . . . I am sure something might still be done." She backed away from him toward the door of her own bedroom, hoping to slam it behind her and lock it. Not in months had she seen Barrett quite so malevolent as he was tonight.

"We'll go to other doctors here in New York," she assured him hastily. "They say, also, that there are good doctors in Boston."

"Doctors in Boston be damned! You are not thinking of physicians for me. No, my dear, you have other things on your mind than that!"

Slurred, thick words malformed by the effects of his stroke. Yet there had been an unmistakable malice to them.

"What . . . what do you mean?" she whispered.

"I am speaking of your pregnancy, Adrienne."

She stared at him, stunned. His eyes were glittering with hatred.

"Don't look so surprised, dear wife. Do you think I am an utter fool? You are nauseated in the mornings, tired throughout the day. There have been no 'womanly rags' to be rinsed out in some time, Annie informs me."

"Annie!"

Barrett inclined his head in a mock bow in her direction. "Annie, it seems, relishes a small tot of whisky even as you do. It is a boon which I have been happy to provide her—in exchange for other services, of course."

Adrienne felt something clutch at her belly, hard, ugly. Barrett knew of her child. Knew, too, that he could not possibly be the father. And he had been using the maid, Annie, as his spy, and perhaps for other things as well. A shudder convulsed her.

"Yes," she heard herself admit, drawing her strength from some unknown source. "I am expecting a baby. You are not the father, but it will bear your name."

Barrett laughed hoarsely. With difficulty he brought his good arm up and made the ancient gesture which meant "cuckold."

"But what will you do, dear Adrienne, if I deny paternity? If I decide to tell the world what you really are, to brand you as adulteress?"

"You—you wouldn't do that, Barrett. You can't!"

"And why can't I? Who is to stop me? Surely *you* aren't threatening me, Adrienne?"

"No, of course, I—"

"Because if you are, then there is a step I could take. Something which I could reveal. And if I do, your lover, your Kristian, might find it very uncomfortable."

Hatred. Again that malevolent hatred in Barrett's words.

Adrienne could feel perspiration spring out on her forehead. "There's nothing you could reveal about Kristian!" she cried. "He is an honorable man."

"Is he?"

Night noises: horses' hooves sounding hollow and lonely as a carriage rattled by in the street. A dog barking. A floorboard creaking on the stairs as Annie climbed upstairs to her small attic bedroom. Annie, who had spied for Barrett.

Adrienne stared at her husband, at the hatred so plain on his face.

"Tell me," she demanded. "Tell me what you know about Kristian. I am sure that it cannot be anything very serious."

"Are you indeed?" Barrett's eyes gleamed at her. Planting his canes with difficulty, he supported himself into his bedroom. He poured another drink from the flask he kept there, downing it quickly.

"Would you like some, too, dear wife?" he asked Adrienne, who had followed him. "A swallow or two of solace and forgetfulness?"

"Yes. I'll have some."

"I thought you would. I fear that liquor, my dear, isn't good for an actress. Eventually it will ruin your voice."

"Nonsense! My voice is fine, as you would know if you had read any of the reviews of my performances in the papers."

Barrett grimaced. "Yes, I've read them. According to the *Sun*, there has never been an actress like you. Your skill is consummate, your presence undeniable." He raised his glass and scowled into its depths. "What, I wonder, would your adoring audiences think if they knew that you had taken as your lover a murderer?"

"A murderer!" Adrienne could hear her voice crack. "Barrett, whatever are you talking about? Surely you can't mean—"

"Can I make it any plainer? Your lover is a killer. He is wanted in Stratford, England, for the murder of Paul Hampton, the son of the Earl of Cunliffe."

"You lie!" she whispered.

She staggered backward, catching herself against the edge of a walnut dressing table. She could feel it press painfully into her flesh.

"No, my dear, I do not lie. I am telling the plain truth, as I will shortly prove to you."

Barrett put down his glass. Then he extracted a key from his pocket and, with difficulty, unlocked the top center drawer of the dressing table.

"But—it can't be! Kristian can't possibly be a—"

She could not even say the word. Coldness swept through her, a vicious chilling of the flesh. Nightmare, she thought wildly. This is only a nightmare, and I'll wake up soon.

And yet images, scraps of conversation, kept flashing in her mind. Kristian, as she had first seen him on the *Thermopylae*, his eyes shadowed and somber. *A dawning is a symbol of hope,* he had said to her then. *And at this time in my life I am drawn to every possible semblance of hope.* Strange words for him to have spoken.

She thought, too, of the anger he had shown when she had called him by the nickname Kris—as if it reminded him of some unpleasant part of his life. The violence which she had sensed in him, brooding beneath the surface . . . .

Oh, but surely it was not possible that Kristian was a murderer! Kristian, the man in whose arms she had known such joy.

And yet—

Oh, God, she thought. *Dear God.*

Dazedly she watched as Barrett pulled out a sheaf of papers from the dressing table.

"Proof." His forefinger tapped the papers. "All the proof I need is right here."

"What is in those papers, Barrett?"

"This is the report of a detective agency. I hired them three months ago to discover what they could about your friend Kristian King. They did their job admirably. I was very pleased with their work and gave them a bonus —out of our joint funds." Barrett's nod to her was mocking.

"You . . . hired detectives? To spy on Kristian?"

Her voice had risen. She felt stunned. Using *her* money, Barrett had hired men to investigate Kristian's background!

"I knew there was something wrong about the man the moment I saw him aboard ship," Barrett went on. "I never liked him. He was standoffish and secretive—"

"Let me see those papers!" she demanded.

He handed them to her, and feverishly she leafed

350

through them. The report, penned in a clerk's precise copperplate hand, was detailed. A young man of twenty-eight, Christopher Kingsley (*Chris,* she thought in despair. *Oh, God, Chris . . .*) had been hired as tutor to the six sons of a well-to-do Earl. The oldest boy, Paul, seventeen, was scholastically slower than the others, a large and surly youth who had been expelled from several private schools for his ugly temper.

According to the local magistrate, on the night of October 1 the pupil, Paul Hampton, came to meet with his tutor after having been drinking heavily. When requested by Mr. Kingsley to read aloud in translation from Julius Caesar, the youth refused. Whereupon the tutor, Mr. Kingsley, picked up a heavy walking stick and beat his pupil to death . . .

Adrienne stopped reading. She felt stunned with horror. Kristian, beating a boy to death . . . .

"No!" she cried out. "No, Barrett, this isn't true, it can't be! It's all a pack of lies!"

"It is true."

A heavy sickness swooped in her belly. Bile rose in her throat, hot and metallic.

"No, no! I refuse to listen to such lies about Kristian! Do you think that I would believe such accusations without further proof? How do you even know that Kristian and this—this Christopher Kingsley are one and the same man?"

Barrett's slack mouth twisted.

"Because the detectives were very thorough, my dear. They searched your lover's rooms. In them, they found newspaper clippings, and certain other papers which connect the two men."

Angry strength poured through her.

"A mistake has been made somewhere, then. I know it has! Barrett, how could you do this? How could you? None of this is true, somehow you've managed to twist things—"

Furiously she ripped at the papers, tore them into jagged shreds, ripped those shreds into further scraps. Then, snatching at them by the handful, she hurled the

351

scraps into the fireplace. She watched them burn, her breath coming fast.

"Do you think that will change anything, Adrienne? That childish display of temper? Do you think that burning papers will change facts?"

She whirled on him. "That report wasn't true. I know it wasn't. Barrett, I hate you, do you hear me? I hate you! I wish you were dead! Oh, how I wish it!"

Over the crackling of the small fire, and the odor of scraps of paper going up in smoke, Adrienne and Barrett glared at each other.

Adrienne lay in her bed, tossing and turning fitfully. Her head whirled with a thousand conflicting images. Barrett's eyes narrowed at her with hatred . . . Kristian, lifting a walking stick to strike at a helpless boy . . .

She sat up in bed and reached for the glass of whisky which she had placed on the bedside table before going to bed. She swallowed, barely tasting the fiery liquor.

What did it matter what the stuff tasted like, she asked herself dully, so long as it did its work? Barrett had been right. Whisky *was* forgetfulness, it was soft, gray gauze, winding itself around and around her mind, softening the hard corners of her thoughts until she could bear them.

Kristian a murderer . . .

Abruptly she pushed away the glass and swung her feet to the floor. She stood up, swaying slightly, holding onto the edge of the table for support. She didn't know where she wanted to go, or what she wished to do. She only knew that she couldn't stay here in bed any longer, wondering, tormenting herself. She had to know.

It took her more than an hour to reach Kristian's rooms. She had to walk eight long blocks in the cold November air before finding a dozing hack driver who agreed to take her the rest of the way.

He eyed her curiously, and she knew that he smelled the liquor on her breath, and saw the disheveled state of her hair and clothes.

"Kind of late for you to be out, isn't it, little lady?" The driver leaned close to her, leering suggestively.

He thought her a prostitute, Adrienne knew with a sick despair. Only such a woman would be out alone at this hour.

"Please—just take me where I wish to go!" she snapped. "My little girl is ill and I must fetch the doctor for her."

The man gave her a long look, then did as she asked. The hack rumbled through the deserted streets, past gas lamps glowing on corners, a pack of stray dogs ravaging a heap of garbage, a lone drunk reeling into an alley.

"Want me to wait outside for yer, ma'am?" the driver asked when they had reached the house where Kristian lodged, a four-story brick building equipped with striped canvas awnings on all windows. The awnings, neatly folded now, rattled in the early-morning wind, making an eerie sound.

"Yes," she told him. "If you wait here, I will pay you well."

The driver settled back onto his perch, pulled his hat down over his eyes, and slumped down as if for a snooze. Adrienne gathered her skirts and hurried toward the right side of the house where there was an outside flight of stairs for the use of servants. She and Kristian had used this entrance many times. Now she could only pray that the outside door had not been locked.

"Well, hello."

Kristian answered his door calmly, as if he had not been asleep at all, although she was sure that he had been. He wore a blue silk dressing gown. How handsome and arrogant he was! she had time to think wildly. His face was rugged, his cheekbones bold, his mouth sensually carved. Yet, as always, there was a somber look to him. A shadowing about the eyes, a tense line to the mouth.

Barrett had been right in a way, she thought now. There *was* something about Kristian, some violence, some dark force, in the way he looked and moved.

"Hello, Kristian," she said. Her heart gave a little jumping leap inside her. "Or shall I call you Christopher?"

"So you really think that I am a murderer, Adrienne." Kristian's face was expressionless. It was as if he were a stranger to her.

They sat in a pair of chairs near the window of Kristian's room. A small oil lamp cast fitful shadows. A pearly dawn light had begun to stream into the room, and outside they could hear the sounds of the city waking up: the rumble of a milk wagon, the clatter of carts and drays beginning their morning deliveries. Somewhere a dog barked persistently.

She twisted her hands in her lap, thinking disjointedly of the child she was to bear.

"No, Kristian—it's just that I had to come, I had to find out! You see, Barrett hired a detective agency—"

"He did what?"

"He hired detectives. He said they came here and searched your rooms and were able to connect you with . . . Christopher Kingsley."

"And you believed their report?" She could not have imagined that Kristian's voice could be so cold.

"No! Of course I didn't believe it! I—I just wanted to find out from you. . ."

Her voice trailed away. For long moments Kristian sat silently, his eyes bleak, fixed on the roof of a building across the street as if he were not even aware of her presence.

"Adrienne," he said at last, slowly, "it's true that Paul Hampton did die as a result of my actions. I did kill him. But I did not murder him intentionally. Strange as this may seem, at his young age Paul was an uncontrollable drinker and had been expelled from a number of schools for his violent episodes of temper. He was a big youth, very strong for his age, and once a girl was hurt badly. His father had to pay dearly to cover that one up."

Adrienne nodded. Parts of this story were familiar to her from the report.

"One morning Paul came slamming into the class-room where I taught. The moment I saw him, I knew that he was in an ugly mood. The other boys sensed it, too; he often bullied them and they feared him.

"When I asked him to translate from the Latin, he refused. He had been out walking along the paths of the estate, and carried a large oak walking stick with him. When I turned my back to help Jeremy, his younger brother, with a Latin verb, Paul suddenly sprang at me with the walking stick."

In the half-darkness, Kristian's eyes seemed to glitter with a chilly fire.

"I took it from him. He was angry, and leaped at me, and I brandished the stick, intending only to scare him. I swear I did not mean him any real harm. But Paul lunged at me, and the stick hit his temple. The blow was stronger than I thought. He fell to the floor and I knew that he was dead."

Kristian sat now with his head in his hands, his voice muffled.

"I killed him, Adrienne. Whether I intended to do so or not, it doesn't matter. The act was done. As I stood there over Paul's body, a hundred thoughts raced through my head. He was dead. I had killed him. Three of the younger Hampton boys were witnesses to it. The fact that I had thought only to scare him would mean nothing in the courts. The Cunliffes were a powerful and wealthy family.

"I decided to run, Adrienne. Perhaps it was a mistake. Perhaps I should have stayed there in Stratford and fought. But I did not."

Kristian licked his lips. "Can you understand? There was so much I wished to do, so very much. Plays I wished to write, characters and scraps of dialogue floating around in my head ready to be written down. I had to give myself a chance to do that writing. I had to."

Adrienne nodded. She thought of Kristian as she had first seen him aboard the *Thermopylae,* his features tight with tension, haunted.

"I have paid well for fleeing England," he went on hoarsely. "There isn't a day when I do not think of Paul

Hampton, not a day when I do not wonder what might have become of him if I had not raised the walking stick to him. But it did happen, and I cannot erase it now."

He paused. "There is a small boy in Stratford, the son of a hod-carrier, very quick and intelligent. I am paying to send him to school. Paul's family does not need money, there is nothing I could do for them to make amends. But young Philip—he needs me, and so there has been an anonymous donor . . . ."

Kristian's voice stopped. The morning light was brighter now, touching the crisp curls at his temples, giving him the look of some grieving medieval warrior.

"Kristian," she whispered. "I'm so sorry that I doubted you."

His eyes were bleak. "There are many moments when I have doubted myself. Moments when I wonder if I should not have stayed in England to face whatever waited there for me. Someday, I am going to write a play, Adrienne. A play about Paul and me. Perhaps that will help to make up for what happened, I don't know."

Again silence settled between them. For long moments they sat, Adrienne's hand on Kristian's. How seldom it was that they shared such closeness, she thought. Always between Kristian and herself, it seemed, there was conflict. It was as if they were drawn together like filings to a powerful magnet—yet another magnet, equally powerful, strove to separate them.

Which magnet, she wondered, would win in the end? The force which drove them together, or the one which pulled them apart?

She was trying to think of how to tell him about the child—his baby—when her glance touched upon the small pigeonhole desk where he did his writing. Papers were stacked there in orderly piles. Atop one of the piles was a letter plainly addressed to Miss Primrose Magruder.

Primrose.

Abruptly the moment of peace which she and Kristian had shared was gone.

"I see a letter on your desk," she blurted. "It's addressed to Primrose."

Kristian had stiffened.

"That silly little creature, what can you see in her?" Adrienne heard herself go on tightly. "Why, she's nothing more than a foolish girl who wants to become an actress!"

Kristian smiled sardonically. "*You* are an actress, aren't you?"

"Yes, but—but it isn't the same! You know it isn't! And—and her name," Adrienne rattled on. "How silly and affected it is. *Primrose* is bad enough, but when you add *Magruder*—why, the two hardly fit together at all. It's like combining a flower with . . . with a turnip!"

"It's not the name that counts, but the girl," Kristian replied slowly. "Can't you see that, Adrienne? Primrose is young and shy and eager, as charming as the flower she's named for."

"Indeed! Is she?" Adrienne felt hot color flood to her cheeks. Instantly she forgot her reasons for coming here, even the news of the coming baby. She only knew that Kristian was speaking of another woman in that soft, fond voice.

"Is she so charming that you prefer her to me, then, Kristian? Oh, I've heard the gossip! Fanny keeps me well informed of that. Even Barrett knows you're seeing Primrose! I'm merely your mistress, your plaything, your t-toy—"

Kristian sprang from his chair, scowling. "A toy? My God, Adrienne, if that is so, then you are the most dangerous toy a man could ever own," he said coldly. "Now, I think that our interview has come to an end, don't you? As long as you've seen fit to wake me at dawn, I think I'll finish some correspondence. Shall I see you downstairs?"

He was dismissing her.

"Kristian? I'm sorry, I didn't—"

"I'll see you to the stairs, Adrienne."

"Very well!" She spat out the words, wishing that she dared to slap him again, to smack that cold expression off his face. "If that's the way you wish to treat me—"

"Yes." Kristian's tone was abruptly tired. She

357

thought he glanced toward his desk where his letter to Primrose waited. "God help me, it's the way I plan to treat you, the way I must. I wish I didn't love you. How I wish I didn't."

The hack was still waiting for her when she emerged from the building where Kristian lived, the driver asleep on his perch. Quickly she roused the man and gave him her address, then settled back in her seat, feeling sick at heart.

She had not even told him about the baby. And they had parted in anger. *I wish I didn't love you,* he had said. His words echoed over and over in her mind. *I wish I didn't love you.*

It was full daylight now, and the city was well into its morning hurry. Men in workclothes walked to work, or ran after horsecars. Housewives, in pairs and threes, were on their way to market. A beer delivery wagon nearly collided with a van loaded with raw lumber.

She arrived back at the brownstone to discover a dismaying and frightening scene. A crowd had gathered about the stoop of the brownstone which she and Barrett shared. Some were seated on the steps, others milled about. Most were women, many of them carrying string shopping bags. A pair of small boys chased each other, while a fat old woman hawked apples from a tray about her neck.

"This the place?" The cab driver turned to grin at Adrienne, as if he had expected nothing less than this from her.

"Yes . . ."

"Busy, ain't it? You'd think it were a holiday, or somethin'." He smirked at her.

She fumbled for some coins and paid him, then descended from the cab in mounting dismay. What were all these people doing here?

"There she is!" someone called "There's Adrienne Gill!"

Heads turned, and the crowd began to surge in her direction.

Fans, Adrienne thought. These were fans, come to

stare, and to beg for autographs. That was all this meant; she had experienced similar scenes a hundred times before.

Yet it was so early in the morning, and there was something strange about the expression of the women with the shopping bags, something avid and devouring.

Then, to her shock, she noticed that among the crowd were several policemen, tall men clad in long blue coats with double rows of buttons. And, she observed in mounting horror, the columnist William Stauffer was also present.

The newsman had pushed his way toward a policeman and was talking with him now, while a newspaper artist squatted nearby, sketching the entire scene.

An icy feeling had begun to gather in the pit of Adrienne's belly. *Something has happened,* was her first frantic thought. Had there been a fire? A robbery? Had something happened to Barrie? At the thought of this, her heart gave an ugly and wholly unexpected little squeeze.

A woman in the crowd had shoved her way closer to Adrienne. She was plump and red-faced, clad in rumpled black, and lived, if Adrienne was not mistaken, two doors down.

"That's her," the woman called. "That's Adrienne Gill. And just look at her, arriving home past dawn just as chipper as you please!"

Voices rose in a hubbub.

" . . . her hair all mussed up, why, you'd think she'd have some shame in her, wouldn't you?"

"They *say* she takes lovers, and I wouldn't be surprised if . . . "

" . . . notorious . . ."

Adrienne lifted her chin defiantly high and hurried across the pavement toward the brownstone. Its stone steps and wrought-iron railings were identical with the others in the long row of dwellings, distinguished from them now only by the crowd which surged in front.

"Please," she murmured as a trio of women blocked her progress. "Please, let me by."

The women smirked. Adrienne saw that the columnist, William Stauffer, was grinning at her. Was there triumph on his face? She felt another stab of fear. Why should Stauffer, who hated her, look so victorious?

What had happened?

As she reached the base of the steps, the front door of the brownstone pushed open. From it emerged a policeman, and, sagging from his arm, limp and pale, was the little maid, Annie Smith. Annie's reddish hair was more frizzy and wild than ever, her apron crumpled.

The crowd whispered and gasped. Adrienne pushed forward.

"Annie!" She ran up the steps. "Annie, what is wrong? You must tell me!"

But Annie, instead of replying only turned her face away.

"Annie! Why are all these people here?"

"You know what's wrong, Miss Gill. You know it better than anyone," the frizzy-haired maid muttered.

"What are you talking about? Annie! O, please, Annie, I tell you I don't know!"

But Annie did not reply. Instead, she allowed herself to be escorted down the steps, where a black police carriage awaited.

"Annie!" Adrienne screamed after her. "Annie, what is wrong? *Annie!*"

But Annie, now being half-carried by the policeman, seemed to be on the verge of a faint, and had to be lifted into the carriage.

"Miss Gill? Miss Adrienne Gill? I'd like to speak with you a moment, if you please."

The man was tall and wore a drooping blond mustache. Although he was dressed in a plain black broadcloth suit, with high, proper collar, Adrienne did not need to be told that he, too, was a policeman. Authoritatively he took her arm, dispersing the crowd and escorting her inside the front door of the brownstone.

"Who are you and what is happening?" she demanded to know as soon as they were in the vestibule. She shook herself free of his arm.

"I am Chief Detective James Kelso. Come into the

parlor, Miss Gill, if you don't mind me making free with your house. We'll have our interview there. Surely there is no need for you to see—" He stopped.

"For me to see what?" she cried. "What is wrong? Why won't anyone tell me? Why are all those people out there? Why are the police here? Why—"

"Do you mean to tell me that you really don't know?"

"No, I don't!" she shouted. "How should I be expected to know? I came home and there they all were, gathered outside our steps as if I were . . . one of Barnum's curiosities." Her voice faltered. "What has happened? It isn't my . . . my little girl, is it?"

"It is your husband," the detective told her in an even voice. "He is dead."

"Dead!" Adrienne stared at the combed blond mustache, the florid face and careful eyes. She felt stunned, as if she had been slapped.

"Dead?" she repeated. "You can't mean that."

"Yes. Your maid, Annie Smith, discovered him sprawled upon the floor of his bedroom this morning when she went in to take him his coffee. She summoned us immediately."

The Chief Detective was staring at her grimly.

"But . . . but why the crowd?" Numbly she let him lead her to the parlor. She slumped down in one of the stiffly upholstered chairs as if her backbone had lost all of its strength. "When—when I left Barrett last night, he was fine. He was well."

"*Was* he fine?" Again the detective eyed her. "Your maid told us that she heard raised voices last night. She heard you shout to your husband that you hated him and wished him dead."

Adrienne felt a wash of fear.

"But—but my husband and I were merely having a quarrel. We fought often. He was an invalid and . . . and we did not get along."

The policeman's eyes examined her as if she were a butterfly pinnned to a board. "Annie told us that. A doctor has been summoned, and he has examined the

361

body, of course. Later there will be a post-mortem, and we will know in greater detail exactly what it was that killed him."

Slowly Adrienne straightened her spine. She clenched her hands in her lap, fingers pressing into each other.

"His apoplexy killed him," she said. "He has had several strokes in the past, as his physician can inform you. His death, I might add, could have come at any time."

"We shall see. In the meantime, your maid claims that you shouted to your husband that you wished him dead. By some strange coincidence, the very next morning, he is found dead. Just what explanation can you offer for that, Miss Gill?"

"I've told you——"

"And perhaps you can also explain what you were doing out all night."

She flushed, thinking of Kristian. "I . . . I'd rather not say."

"You arrived here in a cab, Miss Gill, we do know that. We can find the hack driver." Kelso moistened his lips. "He will tell us what we want to know."

"Then ask him!" she cried. "Ask him anything you wish, if that will please you! My husband was alive and well when I left him—can't you understand that? I didn't kill him, I didn't have anything at all to do with his death!"

Kelso inclined his head, his expression dour. "And what of your maid? The fact that she heard you say you wished him dead?"

"Annie is a foolish and jealous girl who made much of a simple marital quarrel," Adrienne replied coldly. "As for me, I think that I have answered enough questions for now. Will you please take me to see my husband?"

The detective nodded. "Very well. They have laid him out temporarily in the back sitting room."

She crouched beside the body of her husband. Someone had pulled away the sheet which had been placed over his face, and Barrett's eyes gazed sightlessly up at her.

In death, his features had softened. His mouth hung slightly open, the lips looking now soft, almost vulnerable. The hatred, she saw, was quite gone from his expression, as if it had never been. Now his features wore only a puzzled look, as if death had caught him by surprise.

For long moments she stared down at him. Behind her, the police detective shifted his feet uncomfortably. Adrienne leaned forward to take Barrett's hand. It was very cold.

"Barrett . . . " she whispered.

Then she stopped. What was there to say to him now? She had lived with this man, had used him for her own purposes, had taken knowledge from him freely. She had endured his hatred, his abuse. There had been a moment or two, brief segments of time when they might have communicated. But they had not done so.

Now it was all over. She was free of him at last.

"Goodbye, Barrett," she whispered. She stood up. "I am going upstairs to my room now," she murmured to Chief Detective Kelso.

"Very well."

"I will appreciate it if you will complete your investigation as quickly as possible, as I . . . I am very tired."

"We will try, Miss Gill, but I cannot guarantee anything."

"And," she added wearily, "if you could summon an undertaker for me . . . "

Upstairs, in her room, she began to take off her crumpled gown, moving automatically, like a puppet. Burning-eyed, she watched from the window as the body of her husband was loaded into a police van.

Half an hour later she found the note from Barrett. Written in the crabbed, sprawling, nearly illegible handwriting of the stroke victim, it had been thrust into the box where she kept the Passion Star, as if he had intended that she should find it. It had been written, she surmised, shortly before his death.

May you rot, you and your child and your murderer lover. May all three of you rot in hell.

Chapter 24

Somehow she managed to endure the rest of that long day. The crowd remained outside the house for most of the afternoon, gradually dispersing until there were only a few children left to jump on the steps, to giggle and stare up at her bedroom window as if she were a freak.

Adrienne forced herself not to watch them. She felt as if she were struggling in the midst of a vat of sticky molasses. Her body seemed to move unnaturally slowly, and all of her muscles felt very heavy.

Dully she prepared a noon meal for Barrie, sitting at the kitchen table while the little girl ate, gazing at her mother with the wide gray eyes so like her father's.

"Men, Mama? Men?"

What did the child mean? Adrienne tried to rouse herself from her lethargy. "They were policemen, Barrie."

"Daddy? Where Daddy?" At eighteen months, Barrie was a precocious talker, and spoke each word with high, clear precision.

"He is dead," Adrienne replied stonily, for she could not think of any soft lies to give the child. Had not she herself been forced to face her brother Devin's death with cold reality? Let Barrie do likewise.

After that, mother and daughter spoke little. Barrie slid down from her chair and began to play on the floor with a set of wooden blocks, her face screwed into an expression of fierce concentration.

Adrienne, watching her, shivered. Did the child even understand death? Did she know?

At four o'clock the undertaker arrived to discuss the funeral and Adrienne dealt with him as best she could, feeling removed, unreal from what was happening. Then she put Barrie to bed and went upstairs herself to take a nap.

Like an old friend, the bottle of whisky she had drunk from on the previous night still sat on the bedside table. Adrienne picked it up and poured herself a strong drink. Her hands shaking, she raised it to her lips and drained it.

She stood rigid, waiting for the familiar surge of numbness to travel along her veins. Solace, Barrett had called this. Forgetfulness.

Well, she thought, whatever its name, I need it.

Needed it more than ever before.

It was dusk when the pounding at the door began. Adrienne had been lying on her bed in a half-stupor, only partly aware of the passage of time, or of the fact that at some point in the afternoon, Barrie had crept into her room to sit playing on the floor with a worn rag doll.

"Mama! Mama!" She felt small fingers pluck at her shoulder.

"Barrie, go away, please. Let me sleep."

"Mama!" the child persisted. "Mama . . . man at door!"

Adrienne pushed away the insistent hand. Her head felt thick and strange, and there was a cottony lump in her gullet which seemed to extend all the way down her gullet. Worse, her belly had begun to cramp, as if she were about to begin her monthly cycle. But of course, she assured herself, that wasn't possible. She was pregnant, expecting Kristian's baby . . . .

"Mama!"

"Oh, just tell him to go away!"

But now Adrienne could hear the insistent knocking at the door, and then the sharper rap of a walking stick being pounded against solid wood.

"Mama—*man!*"

"Oh, bother!" She drew a deep breath and managed

to sit up in bed. The room was spinning about her. She put her hands to her temples and began to massage them, wincing at the throb. She glanced frantically about the room at the shadows lengthening in the corners. Why, it was nearly dark! How long had she been lying here?

The events of last night and today began to flood back to her in all their horror. Barrett's voice raised in accusation. The coldness on Kristian's face. The crowds gathered at the brownstone. The sad and ugly moment when she had crouched beside the corpse of her husband . . .

"Mama! Man!"

"Oh, very well, if he won't go away——"

It must be Chief Detective Kelso, Adrienne thought bitterly, come to plague her with more questions. She lowered her feet to the floor and waited until the room stopped whirling about her.

To her left, something moved. Dimly she realized that it was her own reflection in the gilt-encrusted mirror which hung over her dressing table. She turned her head to stare at herself.

Adrienne Gill, the actress. Oh, surely this could not be she, this distraught woman clad in rumpled blue silk, the bodice of her gown stained with liquor. Her yellow-white hair was lank, long strands escaping from pins and ribbons to stream onto her shoulders.

And her face——

Horrified, Adrienne caught her breath. Her cheeks, in the heavy shadows, looked almost hollow. And weren't there bags beneath her eyes, a smudged, tired, despairing look to them?

With a shudder of rejection, Adrienne jerked away from the mirror.

The banging on the door was louder now, more insistent.

"I'm coming!" She rushed to the pitcher on her bureau and poured tepid water into a basin. With a linen cloth she bathed her face. Then she creamed her skin with camphor cold cream and rinsed it again, scrubbing with the cloth until her skin glowed.

Quickly she took the pins and ribbons from her hair, brushed it, and pulled it back from her face in a simple knot, securing it with a garland of silk flowers. On tour, she had made many rapid costume changes, and now her fingers moved deftly.

She flew to her closet and pulled out a dove-gray walking suit, a smart outfit she had bought only the previous week. Five minutes later she was dressed.

During this time, the pounding at the door had not stopped. If anything, it had grown even louder, punctuated by the insistent bang of the walking stick against wood.

"I'm coming, I'm coming!" she cried. She ran down the stairs to the vestibule.

"Well, Miss Gill. I knew you would come to the door if I waited long enough."

The voice was triumphant. It was the columnist William Stauffer, sleek hair combed back from his face, his expression alive with curiosity and victory.

She could tell by the look on the man's face that her hasty toilette had been successful.

"What are you doing here?" she demanded.

"I wish to interview you, what else?" He grinned, twirling the walking stick, and with a lurch of fear she remembered what he had said to her once: *I am going to make you the most notorious woman in New York.*

She faced him.

"But surely there is little about me to interest your readers. My husband is . . . is dead, probably of apoplexy, as I am sure a doctor will soon determine. He had been an invalid for some time, and had had several strokes."

Stauffer's eyes moved up and down her body. Again he twirled the walking stick. "If that is all, then why were the police here today?"

"I—I don't know."

Stauffer shrugged. "Well, aren't you going to invite me in? Surely you do not wish to conduct the interview here on the stoop like any common fishwife from the Five Points!"

"Very well," she replied angrily. "Come in, then, if

you must. But please don't feel that you are welcome here, because you're not!"

The parlor, a small room with narrow windows overlooking the street, was still untidy from the events of the afternoon. A vase of flowers had been knocked askew, a chair moved out of place, a drape pulled aside. Stauffer looked about with sharp eyes. Then he sat down, uninvited.

He propped the walking stick beside him.

"Why is it, Miss Gill, that the police *did* take such a great concern in the death of your husband if, as you say, there was nothing suspicious about it?"

"Because I'm an actress, of course. I'm a public figure, an object of curiosity, that's all."

"Is it?" The ferret eyes glinted at her. "Well, I for one am very curious about something else. Where were you the night your husband died? I saw you arrive home past dawn, your face pale and your hair unkempt. A lot of other people saw you, too."

Adrienne felt a fresh stab of fright. Stauffer was her enemy. Whatever she said now, he would surely use against her, either in the newspaper, or in the theater gossip mill. She thought of Kristian, of the ugly story of the death of Paul Hampton. The papers must never learn of Kristian's past—it would ruin his career. Thank God she'd had the sense to tear up the detective's report and burn it in the fireplace.

"Where were you last night?" Stauffer was repeating.

She pulled herself out of her frantic thoughts and told the first lie which popped into her head. "My daughter, Barrie, was ill. She has always been delicate, and her cough was bothersome. I—I was out in search of a druggist's which might be open, so that I could mix an infusion for her."

Stauffer looked skeptical. "All night long?"

"Yes!" She was defiant. "I—I was worried about her. I got in a cab and I drove. I—"

"I don't believe you, Miss Gill. And I don't think any of my readers will believe such a flimsy story either."

"Then let them believe anything they wish!"

"Belief? Truth? *Stage truth,* Miss Gill!" Spittle flew from Stauffer's mouth. "That's all you can offer, isn't it—that and the smack of your hand across the face of any man who happens to displease you!"

She stared at him, at the bitter, twisted mouth, at the eyes which raked over her body. He was attracted to her sexually! Why, oh, why hadn't she seen it before?

"Mr. Stauffer, I must ask you to leave now," she said as calmly as she could. "I think our interview is at an end. To come here to taunt me on the very day my husband has died——"

Stauffer's face darkened. "Indeed! How very sorry I am for you, Miss Gill. To think that you have lost your husband this very day. And here you sit in your parlor, immaculately dressed and coiffed, and smelling very strongly of liquor."

Smelling of liquor.

"Why *do* you drink, Miss Gill? Don't you know just how very shocked the good wives of New York would be to learn that you indulge in such a vice?"

She found her voice. "Get out! Get out of here this moment, Mr. Stauffer, before—before I slap you again!"

He rose. "You'd love to do that, wouldn't you? Oh, yes, you little hell-cat, you ache to do that. But I don't think you will. No, I don't think that you'll ever raise your palm to my face again."

He had moved closer to her, was groping toward her. Then she felt the pressure of his hands at her waist.

"Please—Mr. Stauffer——"

"You little devil, flouncing about, mesmerizing men with your voice, with your witch-ways. Did you think that I would be immune to you? Did you think that any man would?"

"Please, Mr. Stauffer, you have no business touching me——"

"God," he muttered. His hands crawled over her body. "You beautiful slut—I know you. You are no more the great lady from Scotland than I am the King of Spain. And someday I'll prove it, too. I'll make them laugh at you. Some day——"

"No!"

Her hands groped beside her, to the walking stick which Stauffer had propped beside his chair. Her fingers closed about its sturdy wood. She lifted the cane and smacked it, as hard as she could, against the man's ankles.

Stauffer jerked backwards, groaning in pain.

"Get out, Mr. Stauffer," she told him tightly. "Go and write anything about me that you please. What does it matter? It will all be lies, won't it? Just go!"

Stauffer had left.

I know you, he had said. *You are no more a great lady from Scotland than I am the King of Spain.*

Reeling with shock and fatigue, Adrienne sank wearily into a chair. Her head was throbbing and her belly was tight with the cramps she had felt earlier.

She did not know how long she sat there in the gathering dark, staring sightlessly at a gleam of light reflecting off the gas fixture which hung on the wall. Barrie was still playing upstairs in her bedroom. She must get up, see to the child, fix her supper.

But Adrienne made no move to light the lamp, or to see to Barrie. She simply sat, letting the ugly thoughts whirl through her head. Barrett . . . Stauffer . . . Kristian . . . the baby she carried . . .

Somehow she found that a bottle of whisky sat beside her on the table, with a full glass beside it. A little thrill of fear lifted the skin on her arms. Had she poured it for herself? She could not even remember having done so. How long had she been sitting here, unaware of the passage of time?

But she pushed away the unease and lifted the glass to her lips, swallowing quickly, eager for the relief to come.

Like an old friend, the whisky smoothed its way into her mind. It was like soft, warm oil, blurring the agony of her thoughts until they were almost bearable . . . .

She heard the precise rapping of the brass knocker, a sound both polite and determined.

"Adrienne!" Fanny Pepper's voice called. "Are you home? Please let me in!"

Slowly, dully, Adrienne got to her feet. She went to the vestibule and opened the door.

Fanny was clad in a brown poplin gown with looped ribbons on its flounces, her hands concealed in kidskin gloves. In the darkness the raised scars on her neck were scarcely visible.

"Adrienne, I just heard about Barrett's death. How terrible! I came over as quickly as I could. Why didn't you send for me? I know you'll need help with Barrie, and you'll have to have someone here. You can't be alone at a time like this."

The two embraced. Adrienne, pressed against the body of her friend, felt tears burn at the backs of her eyes. How much she loved Fanny, and depended on her!

"The police were here, Fanny," she said at last, her voice dulled. "They think I had something to do with Barrett dying so suddenly. They . . . they implied unspeakable things."

Fanny made a dismissing gesture. "Oh, the police are fools, and this only proves it. You are a famous actress. You attract attention, and people love to have something to talk about. If only you hadn't been foolish enough to hire that girl, Annie—"

"Annie?"

"Why, yes." Fanny looked away from her, and Adrienne wondered if she could smell the whisky on her breath. "It has already been in the evening papers, all of it. Haven't you seen them yet? Annie swears that she heard you and Barrett quarreling last night, just before he died."

Adrienne stared at her friend, at the concern written on Fanny's face. She thought of the reporters she had seen in the crowd today, the artist who had been sketching . . . Dread seeped into her throat like acid.

"The story is splashed all over the papers," Fanny went on. "Miss Adrienne Gill, the well-known actress from Scotland, under suspicion in the death of her husband—oh, it's very ugly."

Adrienne could say nothing.

"Well, I know it isn't true," Fanny said heartily. "Come, Adrienne, come upstairs and wash your face.

Where is Barrie? Have you made her supper yet? And have you had any yourself? You look so very tired."

Clucking sympathetically, Fanny took over. She cooked a light supper and saw to it that both Adrienne and Barrie ate something. She put the child to bed and sent a message to the theater that Miss Adrienne Gill would not be in. An understudy would have to be used.

By eleven o'clock the pains in Adrienne's belly were severe enough so that she had to mention them to Fanny, and by midnight she was lying on her own bed with Fannie in attendance, perspiring with pain.

"God help us, it's a miscarriage, and no mistake about it." Fanny produced a glass filled with amber liquid and held it toward Adrienne's mouth. "Here, drink this. It will help with the pain."

Her hands shaking, Adrienne drank.

Pain . . . She was losing the baby she carried, the one which was to have been born of Kristian's love and her own. The baby which was to have been a son, a boy filled with Kristian's quick-silver creative spirit . . .

A numbed, leaden despair filled her. First Barrett, and now this. Was this miscarriage a punishment for the way she had led her life? For the lies she had told, the child she had already borne with so little love? She tossed and turned on the bed, twisting from side to side, caught up in a pain which was both physical and mental, huge, crushing, all-encompassing, so that she did not know where the one began and the other ended.

"A-another drink," she begged, her voice thready. "Please, Fanny."

Fanny hesitated. "Very well. I suppose you need it—"

"I do, I do," Adrienne wept. "Oh, God, Fanny, oh, God, I do—" She clung to her friend.

"There, now, it shouldn't be long," Fanny soothed. "Go ahead and cry if you wish, Adrienne—that will help. Grief brought this on, it was Barrett's death which did this to you, the shock of it."

"I wanted this baby," Adrienne heard herself weep.

Fanny's scarred hand found hers and squeezed it. "I know, honey, I know. But remember, you still have little

Barrie. There are still some blessings left for you to count."

"Blessings," Adrienne whispered bitterly. But the whisky had already begun to take its effect, dulling the reality of her pain, softening the torture of the iron claws which dug at her belly . . . .

Chapter 25

Barrett's funeral took place on a sunny, brisk November day. A blue sky arched overhead, punctuated by harbor gulls which wheeled and dipped in the air.

Adrienne stood beside Kristian King, gazing downward at her husband's bunting-draped casket as it rested on its bed of earth. She wore a black *peau de soie* dress trimmed with narrow pleats, and a black sealskin mantle, the only black garments she owned, for she had always possessed a horror of the color. Black was a hue worn frequently by the poor women of Glasgow, and for Adrienne it would always symbolize squalor and despair.

Anyway, it did not matter what she wore on this day. For today was a day of public mourning for her husband and private grief for the baby she had lost. That ache—for the child of Kristian's seed—throbbed dully through her entire body. She had not realized that she could feel such pain, such a tearing at her heart and throat.

She stood at the gravesite and, with shaking hands, adjusted the black net veil which concealed her face from the crowd of curiosity-seekers who had gathered at the cemetery. Housewives, shopgirls, delivery boys, horsecar drivers, the ragamuffin children known as "street arabs," had badgered the funeral procession as it left the church. Now they were here, to stare, to giggle, and to whisper.

"Damn them!" growled Kristian. Tall and handsome in a black sealskin coat, he had attracted many stares himself. "Damn their souls for coming to gawk. It's as if you were a sideshow, Adrienne, a circus attraction!"

With effort, she pushed away the heavy, dull pain.

"Perhaps I am," she murmured beneath the veil. "Certainly Mr. Stauffer has made it seem so."

Kristian's mouth twisted. Since Barrett's death two days ago, Stauffer's column had vilified Adrienne. Overwritten, full of innuendo, his writing had stuck to facts—but colored those facts in a way that left little doubt of his beliefs.

Although it was determined by autopsy that Barrett Kendall did, in fact, die of apoplexy, it has never been denied that a family servant, Annie Smith, overheard Miss Gill quarreling with her husband on the eve of his death. The fact remains that Miss Gill does lead her life in what one might call the "new and free" mode of womanhood—or shall we say actresshood?

Adrienne, after reading that column, had wanted to storm down to the newspaper office and confront Stauffer with what he had written. It was only Fanny Pepper who had persuaded her not to go.

"Do you really think, Adrienne, that that will do any good? The man is your enemy! You can't control your temper when you are around him, and he loves that, can't you see? He *wants* you to fly at him! Then he can hate you all the more and write even more wicked things about you!"

Angrily, drained by her miscarriage and by the shock of learning of Barrett's death, Adrienne had crumpled up the newspaper in which the column had appeared and hurled it into the fireplace.

"But it's so unfair, Fanny! Merely because I'm an actress—"

"But you are an actress." Fanny patted her arm. "You *are* in the public eye, Adrienne—as actresses have been for centuries. You are being talked about and noticed—which, for someone on the stage, is better than obscurity, isn't it?"

Now, as Adrienne stood trembling by the gravesite, the crowd surged forward, their voices plainly audible.

"That's her—there she is!"

"Look at her, just as cool as she can be."

"See what she's wearing, she must have paid a pretty penny for it. All those pleats, you'd think she was dressing for a fancy ball, not a funeral—"

Kristian, hearing that last remark, glowered. "Your fans are critical, aren't they? Come, take my arm, and act the part of the bereaved widow. At least we can give them a good show."

And a show it had been. Most of the cast of *The Passion Star* was there, to collect their own share of stares and whispers, for they, too, were a part of the exotic theater world, as outlandish as colorful tropical birds. Fanny Pepper, dressed in black velvet, hung on the arm of William Mancin. Bettina Smithe, in daringly low-cut black, seemed to relish the stares she received.

"I saw the picture of you in *Harper's,*" she remarked to Adrienne after offering condolences. "My, but that artist must have had fun with that drawing! Why, he depicted you with a wine glass in one hand and a cigarette in the other. He made you look like one of those females they show in the *Police Gazette!*"

It was true. Adrienne turned away, thankful that her black veil hid her expression. She was filled with an angry, helpless dismay. It was plain that even the people with whom she had worked all these weeks believed the newspaper slander.

Clods of earth flew onto the casket. Adrienne pressed her hands together inside her sealskin muff, squeezing until her flesh hurt. She was free now, she told herself dully. Free of Barrett's demands, his sarcasm, his hatred. Free, too, of his advice. She could do as she wished now.

Involuntarily she turned, lifting her face to the tall man who stood silently beside her. Kristian. Ever since the moment when she had seen him on the *Thermopylae,* a man both somber and tormented, she had loved him. He was the only man there would ever be for her.

Now she could not help dwelling on a new hope. With Barrett gone, why should they not marry? What could stop them now?

They rode home in a buggy which Kristian had hired from a livery stable. A few clouds had blown up from the horizon to mar the purity of the sky, and Adrienne sat silently, letting her body sway with the motion of the carriage. She wondered if it would rain later tonight. It was November now, and the rain would be bone-chilling and bleak.

At last she forced herself to speak the words which she knew must be said.

"There is something I must tell you, Kristian."

"Yes?" He sat stiffly on the seat, managing the reins as if his thoughts were far away from her.

"I was expecting your child. But I lost it on the night after Barrett died." Her breath caught. "I—I didn't want to lose it. I wanted to bear it, Kristian, for you."

"Oh, Adrienne. Oh, my darling."

Kristian's hands slackened on the reins. His eyes glistened. "A child," he said hoarsely. "You can't know how I've wished for one, how I've longed to add something to the world to make up for having taken a life from it."

She drew a deep breath. "I wanted that baby, too. But there is no reason, Fanny says, why I can't have another one. We could get married, Kristian!" Her words tumbled on. "It would be wonderful, so wonderful! *The Passion Star* will soon go on tour, and we could be married by then. The tour could be our wedding trip—"

"Adrienne." Kristian's voice sounded strange. She looked at him. He was staring straight ahead as he drove the livery stable gelding, his mouth a somber line. His eyebrows were beetled together in a scowl.

"Oh, Kristian, ever since we met on the *Thermopylae* I've loved you—and you've loved me. I realize I've been bold, proposing to you as I have. Perhaps that has made you angry, and if so, I'm sorry—"

"No, Adrienne," he said gently. "Don't humiliate yourself like this. It's too late."

"Too late?"

She could feel her heart skip and turn in her chest, and then begin to pound in slow, heavy thumps.

He spoke with difficulty. "I have already proposed to

Primrose Magruder. Her father has approved our marriage. We are to be wed in one month."

"But you can't! You can't marry her, not Primrose Magruder!" Adrienne's voice rose, choked with sobs. She beat her fists against the black *peau de soie* which covered her knees, crumpling the funeral veil into a small, moist wad.

"I am sorry, Adrienne, so sorry. I wouldn't have hurt you, I swear I never meant to do that—not this way, anyway. I asked Primrose to marry me two weeks ago, long before Barrett died. You weren't free then. I didn't know that you ever would be."

She stared at him, feeling betrayed.

"But why? Why didn't you wait? I *am* free now!" she cried. "Barrett is dead, I'm a widow, there's no reason now why we can't be married!"

"Adrienne, don't . . ."

"There's only one thing to do. You must break it off with her."

"I can't do that."

"But why not?" Her voice was a cry.

Again Kristian scowled as he negotiated a busy intersection. His face was a grim mask.

"There are several reasons. First, an innocent girl would be hurt. Primrose loves me very deeply, and has done so for a long time, ever since that day I first met the Magruders in Central Park."

"*I* love you," she told him painfully.

It was as if the heavy horse and carriage traffic had drawn all of Kristian's concentration. "And secondly," he added, "Phineas Magruder is my backer. He finances my plays. Did you know that he and his friends among them own five of the theaters in New York, including the Olympic, in which *The Passion Star* is playing?"

"Oh, what does it matter?" she stormed. "Can't you get your money from somewhere else?"

But even as she spoke, Adrienne remembered the night she had spent with the financier at Saratoga, the raw power which the man exuded. What, indeed, would Phineas Magruder do if Kristian were to jilt his daughter?

Kristian, she realized, was still speaking.

"It isn't a question of getting someone else, Adrienne. There are other rich men in New York, I know that. But Magruder is a dangerous man to have for an enemy. Not that I would back down from facing him. You know I would not do that. Still, the real truth is that I can't hurt Primrose, and I won't. I've proposed marriage to her. I won't back out of my obligation now."

"But what about me?" Her voice rose in a wail. "I love you! I've always loved you! And you love me, you've said it yourself."

He was silent, the squeak of iron buggy wheels against the brick pavement seeming unnaturally loud.

"Yes. I've loved you. But I've also told you that I wish I didn't. Can't you see, Adrienne? You are an opportunist, an utterly determined user of men. You'll do anything, won't you, to get the fame you crave? To get whatever that damned sapphire, the Passion Star, symbolizes for you?"

"No—that isn't true—"

"Isn't it? Didn't you cold-bloodedly marry Barrett Kendall in order to use what he knew? Weren't you absolutely prepared that day in Detroit to get an abortion? To scrape Barrie out of your body as if she were garbage, merely so that you could continue as an actress?"

"No," she whispered. "It wasn't like that. I wouldn't have done it, I'm sure I wouldn't. Not really . . ."

"And that accursed jewel you wear about your neck —didn't you use it as barter in order to get your role in *The Passion Star?* To get the part of Fatima, didn't you seduce me—and Phineas Magruder?"

"M-magruder?" she stammered. She could feel the inside of her mouth go dry. So Kristian knew about that. She stared downward at her lap, using her fingers to pleat the thin fabric of her black dress into folds.

"Adrienne." Kristian's eyes were bleak. "Didn't you know that Phineas told me about that a long time ago? He laughed about it, you little fool. Laughed and told me you were the best roll in the hay he'd had in months."

She sat rigid.

"I did it because I had to! Kristian, surely you can understand that. I—I had to have the part. It was *mine*, it was meant for me, it would have been a crime to let any other woman have it—"

"So you whored for it," he told her quietly. "Well, Adrienne, I loved you in spite of that, I loved you because I had to, because you were as essential to me as opium to an addict. But there are times when drugs must be thrown away and old habits broken. I think that has happened with us. I have to break away, girl."

She could feel the fury rise in her. It pounded at her temples, unbearable.

"So! You'll marry that simpering little Primrose, then! A sweet, pretty, empty-headed doll of a girl!"

"Perhaps she is those things. Nevertheless, I can lead a normal life with Primrose. I can have a family, Adrienne, and children, perhaps give back to the world something of what I took from it. We have set the wedding date, and I don't back out of my promises.

"Now," he went on. "I would suggest that you smooth out that funeral veil and put it back on again. You are supposed to be a grieving widow, remember? We are nearly to your house, and unless I am mistaken, another crowd will have gathered to welcome you back."

Nightmare. Of what did it consist? Was it wild dreams filled with disturbing scenes? A baby crying for its mother, its voice faint and far away? Kristian and Primrose, standing together at the altar, Primrose clad in a gown of white brocaded tulle, Kristian somber and handsome? Or herself racing into the church, trying to stop the wedding, only to look down at herself and discover that she was naked?

Or was the worst of it the waking nightmare, the sodden times when she lay in her bed, the whisky flask conveniently at hand? She barely bothered to pour the golden liquid into a glass before downing it quickly, as if it were medicine. Or her salvation, a shield which could protect her from pain . . .

The ceiling of her bedroom was done in elaborate molded tin, and she lay there studying it for long hours,

381

memorizing every curve and swirl of its design. At times the ceiling seemed to loom down toward her, as if it could crush her. At other times, she felt as if she were lying on mounds of soft clouds. Floating, floating, totally out of control . . . .

She slept long, deep sleeps that seemed to go on from dark to dark, until she woke up confused, not knowing whether it was night or morning. Several times a day she staggered out of bed to use the commode in the hall bathroom. At these moments she would stop to gaze into the walnut-framed mirror there.

A frowsy, sodden stranger would stare back at her, eyes red-rimmed and mute with grief.

Voices punctuated her nightmares, and impatiently she tried to shake them away. One of them belonged to Mary O'Callahan, the maid whom Fanny Pepper had hired after Barrett's death to look after Barrie, do the housework and cook. Mary was a dumpy little woman of fifty, with streaked gray hair pulled back to the nape of her neck in a knot.

Daily Mary carried trays of food upstairs to Adrienne's room, leaving them on the bedside table. Hours later, Adrienne would awaken to find the food congealing on the plate. She would doze off, to awaken at some later time to find another full tray.

Sometimes, if she were awake and her mouth did not taste too foul, she would try to eat something. Most of the time she did not bother. Once she awoke after a long, dead sleep to discover the tray upturned on the rug, roast beef and boiled potatoes scattered all over the floor. She had knocked it over in reaching for the bottle.

Several times she struggled out of bed, fighting dizziness, to rummage in her purse for money to give Mary to buy more whisky.

"Ma'am, oh, and are you sure it's what you wish?" the woman inquired. "Whisky and all, it's fine for the gentlemen, I'm sure, but for a fine lady such as yourself, a lady who's been a countess and all— You been saying some frightening things in your sleep, ma'am, oh, you've scared me—"

"Please, just go and buy it, Mary. I'll pay you extra if you will."

"But, ma'am, you're so sick already, your play had to close for a while, and Miss Fanny Pepper told me——"

"I don't care what Fanny said! I've no one to buy me the whisky but you, Mary, and I need it. If you don't, I—I'll fire you!"

"Very well." The Irish woman's lower lip stuck out mutinously. "But I think it's a crying shame, ma'am, if you don't mind me sayin' so. Yer so pretty, that you are, and so famous, why, the whole city loved you in that play. And here ye are, ruinin' yourself. Do you know what you look like? This has been goin' on for days now, weeks! And Miss Fanny Pepper says——"

"Oh, damn Fanny Pepper!" Adrienne snapped. Her voice slipped a bit over Fanny's name, and carefully she made sure that she pronounced it correctly. "Please, Mary, just go and do as you're paid to do."

"Yes, ma'am. Yes, *ma'am!*"

Fanny came to the brownstone, to see to Mary's duties and to scold Adrienne roundly.

"Adrienne, I'm really ashamed of you," she said one morning. "Thank God the theater has been dark these past weeks on account of Kristian being so busy with his wedding plans."

"I don't care," Adrienne muttered. It was a bleak day, and even the December sunlight which penetrated into the room seemed almost gray. Adrienne blinked her eyes at it, and then buried her face in her pillow.

Fanny sprang forward to grasp the bottle which sat at Adrienne's bedside. Angrily she marched with it across the room and flung it into a drawer.

"Just look at yourself, Adrienne Gill! If your fans could see you now, why, they wouldn't even know you. You look like some frowsy street woman from the Five Points. Or worse! Your hair is straggly, and your complexion is the color of old tallow. And you stink of whisky. Do you hear me? You stink!"

Adrienne was silent. She screwed her eyes shut and buried her mouth in the pillow ticking. She could feel the room whirling about her, dipping up and down like a silent, eerie carousel.

"Did you hear what I said?" Fanny snapped.

"Yes."

"Then what are you going to do about it?"

Tears come, like slow, hot oil, to squeeze down Adrienne's cheeks.

"I don't know. I don't know," she wept. "He's marrying someone else, Fanny. He's marrying Primrose!"

"Let him, then."

Adrienne saw that Fanny was staring at her, the other woman's lips pressed together.

"I . . . need another drink," Adrienne muttered. She struggled to sit up in the bed. "Where . . . where did you put the bottle? I need—"

A hard slap stung her cheek. Then another one.

Adrienne stared, stunned, at Fanny. "F-Fanny! What did you do that for? You slapped me!"

"Yes, I slapped you, Adrienne, and I did it hard. I hope it hurt, because you deserved it. And I'm not going to get you another drink. I won't let you do this to yourself any more."

"Please, Fanny, you don't understand. Barrett said . . . it's solace, forgetfulness . . . ." Adrienne's voice was incoherent. She sank back upon the rumpled pillows, her body shaking convulsively.

"Get up!" Fanny ordered.

"No . . . I can't."

"Adrienne, get up now. I'm going to have Mary draw you a cold bath and I want you to soak yourself in it until you're sober and halfway presentable. And we'll brew plenty of coffee; you'll drink that until you're afloat!"

Adrienne moaned. She turned over in the bed and pulled the pillow about her ears. "No . . . I won't . . . Just leave me alone. God, leave me alone."

Another slap burned her cheek. Even through the pillow cover it hurt.

"No, I won't leave you alone! What's more, if you're not out of that bed in five minutes, I'm going to send Mary out with a message to Mr. Kristian King. And do you know what I'm going to say in my note? That you are in trouble and need him to come here immediately. He'll come, all right. And what will he see when he gets here? Well?"

Adrienne froze. Her mind, which had been spinning dizzily, seemed suddenly to stop. She thought of Kristian, staring down at her with revulsion. He would see that same stranger she had glimpsed in the bathroom mirror, that woman with the tangled hair and red-rimmed eyes.

And was Fanny right? Did she really . . . stink?

Shame filled her.

"Fanny," she whispered. "You wouldn't really do that, would you? Send for Kristian?"

Fanny's voice was very crisp. "Yes, I would. You don't know me very well, Adrienne Gill, if you believe that I would not."

"Oh—oh, damn you, Fanny!"

Chapter 26

She got up. She staggered into the white-painted, utilitarian bathroom to bathe in the tin tub, allowing Mary to pour buckets of cold water over her shoulders until she thought she would weep with the shock of it. She submitted to a hairwashing with Fanny's special egg-and-beer shampoo.

Fanny watched all this with judicious eyes. She saw to it that Adrienne drank cup after cup of bitter black coffee. She made ice packs and applied them to Adrienne's eyes.

"That's to shrink those terrible big bags you have," she announced. "All I can say is thank God the newspapers haven't found out about your—your illness yet. Do you realize what William Stauffer would say about you in his column? If he's well enough, that is. He was attacked in the street going home from the newspaper office a few weeks ago and was quite badly beaten. His nose was broken, they say, and his face is still black and blue."

Adrienne closed her eyes. "Perhaps someone else didn't like what he wrote about them," she said bitterly.

"Perhaps. At any rate, you're lucky he hasn't found out about you. Oh, I asked Mary to prepare you a big plate of roast beef and dumplings. You must begin to eat properly again." Fanny made a face. "Whale bone corsets are a marvelous invention for the female figure, but even boning can't help when a woman is too thin. You must put some fat on your bones, or invest in a good set of padding for your petticoats!"

So, grimly, Adrienne ate what was set before her. She submitted to Fanny's ministrations with rice powder and carmine. She stood rigid while her friend rummaged in her wardrobe for clean petticoats and corsets, for a freshly pressed gown.

"There," Fanny said. She held up something.

"Not black," Adrienne muttered. "I won't wear black, Fanny!"

"And you won't have to. I know you too well for that." Fanny lifted out the stylish dress made of striped camel's hair in golden brown shades, elaborately trimmed with silk, embroidered braid, and fringe. It had been another of Adrienne's extravagances.

"Put this on," Fanny ordered. "We're taking a trip."

"A trip?"

"Yes, I think we'll go to Saratoga. It's off season, but the waters will be as good as ever, and perhaps their medicinal qualities will help you. God knows you need all the help you can get."

Adrienne stared at her friend. It would be quiet at Saratoga—quiet and peaceful. She could get away from the crowds which still came to peer into the windows of the brownstone, to whisper and giggle and speculate about the notorious actress whose illness had caused the closing of the most talked-of play in town.

"But what about Barrie?" she asked Fanny. "And the play, the tour? What about them?"

"*The Passion Star* will go directly on tour as soon as you are well, Kristian told me yesterday. Contracts have already been signed. As for Barrie, we'll take her with us. Mary can come along to care for her. And I'll go, too, just to keep an eye on all of you."

"Very well." Adrienne sighed deeply. "I'll go. What does it matter where I am or what I do? Saratoga will be as good a place as any."

Saratoga at this time of year was bleak, populated almost entirely by the ghosts of summer residents. Adrienne felt that if she looked very hard she might see them, the women in elaborate white tulle watering-place costumes, strolling up and down Broadway, or the ghostly children romping near the fountains and the Opera House. Phantom men rode swift geldings along the road to Lake Saratoga, or clustered in the street to talk horse-races.

There was the ghost, too, of Kristian, tall, somber, his curly hair blowing in the wind. *My God, girl, it's as if you were a small, private cyclone, sweeping up people and events into your whirlwind. You're beautiful and flamboyant and desirable and greedy. What I should do right now, God help me, is to stop this surrey, help you out, and keep on driving . . . .*

They spent their first two nights in a small hotel near the main promenade. Their rooms were cold and damp. At night Adrienne would huddle down under three thick blankets, to battle the nightmares which came nightly to plague her: Kristian and Primrose at the altar; Kristian lifting Primrose onto a bed, stripping off her garments until the girl lay naked and lovely, arms wide to receive him . . . .

By the third day Barrie was coughing and sniffling with the beginning of a cold, and Fanny announced that they would find a cottage to rent for the remainder of their stay.

"I think I know of one," Adrienne said suddenly. She thought of the small house she and Kristian had seen that day at Lake Saratoga, hidden behind its shield of oaks and elms. That day the cottage had seemed like a hideaway, and now it seemed even more appealing.

"Well," Fanny said. "I'm glad to hear you voice an opinion about something, anyway. I was beginning to think that you had given up on life, Adrienne!"

The next morning Fanny made inquiries and sent a series of telegrams. The following afternoon they hired a buggy and drove out to Lake Saratoga. It was a cold but brilliantly sunny December day, the sun reflecting like dagger points off the choppy water.

They stopped the buggy and Fanny and Adrienne strolled up the path she and Kristian had followed before. The leafed-over trail was somber now, drifted over with dead leaves. The wineglass elms were bare, their branches jagged. Here, Adrienne thought with a twist of the heart, she had walked with Kristian in the carefree aftermath of love . . . .

They came upon the cottage suddenly, its bricks gleaming through the bare trees. Adrienne caught her breath.

"Oh, Fanny!" She grasped her friends's arm. "It's just as lovely as I remembered it!"

The cottage's warm red bricks and black shutters were as charming as ever, the stained glass fanlights over the first floor windows catching the sunlight. Adrienne stared at the cottage with possessive eyes. Yes, there were the porches and cupolas, the widow's walk. Even the lilac garden to the left of the house kept a faded summer charm, and the summerhouse, with its elaborate trellis, was in perfect condition, waiting for June and July.

"It is pretty, I'll grant you that," Fanny said. "And we did get it at the off-season rate. I'll send Mary out to buy food and provisions, and we'll move in tonight. There is a good view of the lake, and the fresh air should be fine for you."

"Oh, I know it will be!" Adrienne was soaring with the first enthusiasm she had felt in weeks. "Fanny, I think I'm going to buy this cottage."

"Buy it? But, Adrienne, you have been spending so much—"

"Oh, I know I can afford it, there will be money from the tour. I feel as if this place belongs to me, as if it has been waiting here for me to come."

Fanny laughed. "I'm sure it hasn't been, but if it will make you happy to think so—"

Adrienne was abruptly serious. "Yes, I do like to think so. This house is going to be my hideaway, Fanny." Her hand went to the sapphire which she wore always at her neck. "I'll come here when I'm tired or sick, or when I no longer wish to go on living."

The days passed, like wooden beads on a string. Each day Fanny bundled Barrie up in sealskin coat and muff and took her for a walk along the lakeshore. Usually Adrienne accompanied them, lagging a step or two behind the russet-haired, cheerful woman and the little girl. She felt lonely, trapped behind the barricade of her thoughts. Bleak thoughts which she could not stop, no matter how she tried . . . .

The isolation of the cottage fitted in with Adrienne's mood, although the Irish maid, Mary, complained that she got lonely here with no one to talk to. Twice Mary claimed that she had seen a man hanging about the path. When she had tried to see who he was, she had added, the man had melted into the trees and was gone.

"Oh, nonsense!" Adrienne told the woman sharply. "It's probably just a local man out hunting for raccoon or rabbit. Or one of my fans, come to stare. Or even a newspaper man, here to get what information he can. And he won't get much by loitering about that path, will he?"

All the same, she cautioned the others never to go for a walk alone. Mary was a stolid, unimaginative woman, and if she said she had seen a man, then she had seen one.

But the days went by, and the man was not seen again, and after a while they forgot him.

One morning Fanny drove the hired buggy into town, to return with a New York newspaper and the disquieting news that Kristian King and Primrose Magruder had been married in an elaborate ceremony attended by more than one thousand society people. It had evidently been one of the city's prime social events.

Adrienne skimmed through the article. There was a heavy, hurtful, squeezing sensation in her chest, as if her windpipe had closed up.

Kristian and Primrose, married now. Husband and wife . . .

She swallowed hard, wishing desperately for a drink. One swallow of whisky, just one, to smooth away the pain and make it bearable—

"Perhaps it's all for the best," Fanny tried to cheer her. "If he would marry another woman, then he was not meant for you, Adrienne. It's as simple as that."

Adrienne was unaccountably angry, with a raging

fury that boiled up in her and could have no outlet. For was it Fanny's fault that Kristian had rejected her to marry Primrose? Was it Barrie's, or Mary's, or anyone's? Yet did Fanny have to say such a thing to her? Didn't she know how deeply it would wound?

The days passed, and Adrienne sank into a routine in which she found refuge. First came breakfast, then a brisk tramp around the lake, bundled up against the December chill. Luncheon, then a nap or reading from the stack of novels which Fanny had packed in her trunk.

In the late afternoon, they would take the buggy to town and go to one of the wooden pavilions which housed the medicinal springs. Usually they took Barrie with them on these excursions, and obediently the little girl would drink the water she was given, her gray eyes fixed trustingly on Adrienne.

"See?" Fanny burst out once, half-angrily. She wiped Barrie's mouth and scooped the child up into her arms. "See how this child trusts you? Why, she'll take the waters only from your hand, Adrienne. And she imitates you. Haven't you noticed that? She'll sit on the floor for hours, playing with her dolls and talking to them exactly as you speak, catching almost exactly your tone of voice. She is a very good mimic. And she walks as you do, like a grand lady, picking up the hem of 'her skirt with exactly the mannerism you use."

"Does she?"

Adrienne had asked it uneasily, for she herself had noticed no such thing. To her Barrie was—simply Barrie. Anyway, she assured herself, in a month or two she would have more time to give to her daughter. Once they were touring, she could take Barrie to museums, to tea rooms and for walks. And perhaps then she could look at Barrie in a new light. If only the child did not have her father's eyes and nose and mouth. If only she did not serve as a reminder of the ugliness of her conception. A child born of rape and ugliness . . .

Adrienne was conscious of Fanny's sharp look, a look which seemed to miss nothing.

"That little girl loves you! She always has, ever since

she was an infant. And you choose to ignore it. You barely notice that she exists!"

"Come, Fanny, you exaggerate." Adrienne tossed her head. "Don't I support Barrie? Don't I see to it that she has the prettiest dresses that any child could wish for? Don't I bring her to the theater with me whenever I can, and see to it that she lacks for nothing?"

"Yes, You certainly do all those things." Fanny was tight-lipped. "I cannot fault you there."

"Then why do you look at me that way?"

"If you don't know, then what good will it do for me to tell you?" her friend snapped, turning away.

Six weeks later they were in Philadelphia, in the midst of a grandly successful tour of *The Passion Star*. It was February, 1874, with temperatures hovering at freezing, so that, even bundled in her sealskins, Adrienne shivered as she rushed from carriage to theater. Finally she ordered her dressmaker to sew her some heavy woollen underwear to wear beneath the diaphanous Fatima costume.

They played at the Arch Street Theater on 6th Street, a new and dignified theater only ten years old, its façade adorned with a sheet-draped Muse, and, at the roofline, a gargoyle head molded in plaster. Discreet play-bills on either side of the main entrance advertised the play, proclaiming that it starred the "renowned Scottish actress, Adrienne Gill, wearing the fabulous Passion Star, 350 carats of sapphire beauty and the talk of the entire nation."

In Philadelphia, too, crowds came to cluster about the stage door, to stare, to gossip, to throw flowers or pass scribbled notes. Men gazed at her with covetous eyes. Women whispered and pointed.

"That's her, that's Adrienne Gill! They say she was involved in the death of her husband, it was quite a scandal! And look at her face, at her chin so high and proud. They say she's a born lady, that she comes from the Scottish nobility . . ."

It was in the city of Philadelphia that Adrienne received the surprise of a second bouquet from Martin

Greggori. Once more the yellow roses arrived, a huge five dozen of them, this time arranged in a Waterford crystal vase, each facet of cut glass a work of art.

You are unforgettable, Miss Gill. Your face haunts me, as does the sapphire you wear. Adrienne read the card and dropped it, her hands trembling, although she could not have said why. She had received many such admiring backstage notes—they were a part of the theater world and always had been.

But this time Mr. Greggori himself had accompanied his bouquet backstage and was waiting for her, a wraith in a wheelchair, when she emerged in her street clothes. A uniform attendant had come with him to push the chair.

"Miss Gill . . ."

"The roses are lovely, Mr. Greggori." She stared downward at the man, remembering Bettina Smithe's cruel comments about him. Martin Greggori must once, she thought, have been a handsome man with well-cut, precise features. But it was as if his entire body had been crushed, smashed, and then awkwardly put back together by someone who did not know what he was doing. His legs were limp and wizened, and one arm twisted awkwardly toward his chest. His face was thin almost to the point of emaciation, his jaw muscles prominent. But his mouth was sensitive, and his eyes, a pale blue, were fixed on hers with an intent expression.

"It was a carriage accident which made me this way, Miss Gill," Greggori said softly. "Please don't waste your time pitying me. I have long passed beyond the need for anyone's pity."

She flushed. "I—I wasn't—" She floundered on. "The roses were beautiful, I adore yellow roses. And the vase was exquisite. But you shouldn't have done such a thing. It was much too expensive."

"But I wished to do it."

"Then . . . then I must thank you."

Greggori's eyes rested on her with an intense stare, as if he saw something in her which deeply moved him. Involuntarily, Adrienne's hand went to her neck where she still wore the Passion Star, beneath her mantle.

"And thank you, my dear, for giving such a stunning

394

performance. I am one of your most ardent fans. But I am wondering, Miss Gill, if you can tell me more about the Passion Star. I am aware, of course, of its romantic history—the newspapers have not been able to stop talking about that. But, tell me. What is the real story of the stone?"

Adrienne took a little step backward, drawing in her breath sharply. "The real story? Why, the articles in the papers are all true, Mr. Greggori!"

The man in the wheelchair inclined his head thoughtfully. "There was once such a stone in my family. But that was long ago."

Adrienne lifted her chin, feeling a sudden angry possessiveness for the sapphire.

"Well, sapphires are common enough!" she snapped. "But the Passion Star is special, it is the finest of its kind in the world. It once belonged to a king!"

But before she could finish, a group of women clattered in their direction, demanding autographs, and Greggori nodded and motioned to his attendant to wheel him away.

Adrienne let Martin Greggori, his cards, flowers and expensive vases slip out of her mind. How dare he imply that the history of the Passion Star was all a lie? She refused to think of such a thing.

Most of the cast and stage crew had accompanied them on the tour. Thus backstage life seemed to go on much as ever. William Mancin leafed distractedly through his promptbook or scolded the call boy. Quince, the aging flyman, carted Barrie about on his back, making her giggle.

"This child is a treasure, Miss Gill," he said to her once. "She'll be a beauty one day, God willing."

Fanny performed her usual chores as wardrobe mistress and make-up woman, her scarred hands moving with deft skill. Kristian, too, was much as usual, moving through his dual role as playwright and actor with ease. Crowds gathered to see him, as well, to exclaim at his good looks, to envy the well-tailored suits which covered his rangy body with such flair.

The only abrasive note which had been added to the tour was Primrose. Small, as shyly pretty as the flower for which she had been named, Primrose had at last fulfilled her ambition to become an actress. Kristian had given her the small role of Mara, one of Fatima's maids.

"It will please her," he said. "And audiences will like her, too. She has the appeal of naivete and innocence."

It was true. Clad in flowing robes, Primrose made a charming picture as the doe-eyed young maid, and received enthusiastic curtain calls. But—much to Adrienne's irritation—the other girl's voice was soft and breathy, and often not loud enough to carry through the entire theater. Although she never forgot her lines, she spoke them off-rhythm, or she changed words and phrases, so that the meaning of her speeches emerged differently. Adrienne could not understand why Kristian did not object to this. Did he not see what she was doing to his play? Didn't he even care?

Worse, Primrose daily lorded it over the crowds which gathered at the stage door, enjoying the attention, her laughter high and gay. If a man threw her flowers, she would pick up the nosegay, pluck out one of the blossoms, and thrust it into her hair to wear there until it wilted.

But Primrose seemed entirely innocent of any knowledge of Adrienne's dislike for her.

"Oh, Adrienne, I'm having such fun! I never knew that being an actress could be like this!" A trilling titter of a laugh, both pretty and charming. "I love it—I love it all. I love having the people come to talk to me afterwards, they have been *so* nice to me!" Again she giggled. "You know, Mama is totally shocked that I am on the stage now. But Kristian encourages me in it. He wants me to be happy."

"He—he does?"

"Oh, yes, and he has promised me all the help I need. Perhaps you will have time to assist me, too, Adrienne? There is so much that I don't know, and I would so love to work with you! You are so good, Adrienne, you can hold an audience in the palm of your hand. And you are famous! Everyone knows who you are. Even my Papa keeps asking about you!"

Phineas Magruder. Adrienne fought back the urge to tell Primrose exactly what had occurred between her father and herself.

"After the play they are actually fighting sometimes to get in at the stage door," Primrose continued gaily. "And I know it's mostly because of you. Kristian has said so. Mr. Mancin has had to post a guard there at the door to keep mashers away!"

On and on her breathy voice chattered, until Adrienne had all she could do not to turn and walk away. Couldn't Primrose see how she felt about her? How on earth could Kristian have married a girl like this? Primrose seemed barely old enough to go to bed with a man. Yet she was married, had the privilege of sleeping every night with Kristian.

At last Adrienne could stand it no longer. One night Kristian asked her to stay late after the performance in order to work on the timing of an exit in Act Two. They were in the greenroom, the actor's lounge with its battered tables and wooden chairs, its dirty spittoons, yellowed business cards stuck into the gas fixtures, scribbled notations on the walls. It was a dismal room, drafty and cold, but Adrienne barely noticed her surroundings as she confronted Kristian.

"Why?" she demanded. "Why did you give her a part? She can't even get the lines properly! She changes the meaning. Don't you know that she is no more suited for the role of Mara than—than Barrie is suited to play Hamlet!"

"I know that." Kristian had lit a Havana cigar and now sat tilted back in a chair, staring at the blue smoke as it spiraled upward.

"Then why? She is disruptive to the part, she irritates everyone with the way she gets us off rhythm, she—"

"She is happy playing her bit part. And she certainly isn't that ruinous to the performance. I hadn't noticed anyone in the audience complaining about her."

"Of course not!" Adrienne raged. "Why should

they? Especially the men! They wish to look at her because she is pretty and soft and fashionable!"

"As they like to look at you," Kristian commented dryly. "Anyway, Adrienne, why should it matter to you if I give Primrose a few short months of pleasure? She is enjoying her little fling as an actress—so let her have what fun she can."

Adrienne stared at him. "What do you mean?"

Kristian blew out a plume of cigar smoke, his eyes distant from her. "Don't be stupid, Adrienne. She is expecting a child, of course. And after that I hope there will be other children—a good many of them. So her stage career, as you can see, will be short-lived. And I plan to let her enjoy it exactly as she wishes."

Adrienne thought of Primrose giving birth to a child. It would have Kristian's features, of course, his curly, honey-colored hair, his handsome, arrogant ways. Primrose would be privileged to hold that baby in her arms, the two of them encircled in Kristian's love. . . .

She felt sick.

"You don't mean it," she faltered. "Kristian, you can't mean it. Not—not so soon."

His eyes, deep blue, met hers with sudden compassion. He reached out to put his arm about her shoulders.

"Yes, Adrienne, so soon. I am sorry. I had no idea she would quicken so fast. You can't know how I've longed for a child—"

"*I* could have given you one," she could not help whispering.

"Don't, Adrienne. Don't do this to yourself. You're hurting yourself—and you're hurting me."

"Hurt you? Oh, will anything hurt you?"

Her voice was an abrupt, angry shout. She jumped to her feet and rushed out of the greenroom, slamming its door behind her with all of her strength. The slam made a loud, echoing boom in the faulty acoustics of the theater's backstage.

Then, feverishly, she rushed to her own dressing room and her theater trunk. She tossed out garments and wigs until she found what she was looking for—a half-bottle she had hidden, once, in a side pocket.

Sobbing, she wrenched out the cork. Then she tilted the bottle to her lips. She drank, long and thirstily. Then she lifted the bottle and drank again. It was the first drink she had taken in weeks.

"Adrienne, what are you doing in there? Adrienne, for God's sake, don't you realize you've locked the door?"

Kristian's voice was loud and angry.

Adrienne opened her eyes to discover that she was sitting, knees drawn up to her chest, upon the Turkish rug she had bought long ago during the tour of *Uncle Tom's Cabin,* and which she had carried with her ever since to adorn her dressing room. The whisky bottle lay on its side near her, amber liquid a dark blotch on the rug. Light from the room's two gas fixtures was reflected in the dirty mirror, dusted with ancient rice powder from a thousand other women who had used these quarters.

Ghosts, she thought, her mind whirling. Ghosts were present in the Arch Street Theater, in every theater, the presences of actresses who must struggle to survive, doing what they could or what they must. Her own spirit, she thought dully, would someday haunt this theater, too. It would be a sad phantom, racked with painful sobs. . . .

"Adrienne! It's been nearly two hours! What are you doing in there? Open that door immediately!"

Adrienne shifted her position on the Turkey rug. Painfully she blinked her eyes, noting that each time she did so, the room seemed to spin. The whole world, she thought dully, was spinning.

Or was it only herself? She, Adrienne Gill, spinning alone, always alone? Addie McGill, the little girl from Glasgow whose father had been a drunk, whose husband had been a drunk, and who was now a drunk herself?

She allowed herself a genteel little hiccup, the sort of hiccup a lady might use.

"Adrienne, answer me, dammit! Or I'm going to break the door down!"

There was a heavy banging, followed by a crash as the lock hasp broke and the door exploded inward.

Kristian burst in.

"Adrienne! My God, what are you—"

He stopped, staring downward to where she sat on the floor. His nostrils flared, and she knew that he smelled the whisky. She saw, too, the way his eyes darted around the room, seeing the spilled bottle, the opened trunk, the disarray.

"Hello, Kristian," she whispered.

Kristian scowled at her. With his curly hair and his bold bone structure he looked at this moment like some avenging warrior, she thought wildly. A warrior ready to do battle, to storm battlements. But this, she knew with a sick pang, was a battle he did not know how to fight.

"My God, what happened?" he demanded. "I left the theater to go home. I was angry, my God, I was angry at you! But I couldn't do it. I had to come back here to make sure you were all right, that you'd managed to get a cab. At first I didn't think you were still in the theater. Then I found that the door of your dressing room was still locked. I heard a sound—"

"I was weeping." She said it bitterly, getting to her feet. "And I was drinking, too. I will admit it."

For long moments they stared at each other, their eyes locked. Kristian's gaze was dark blue fire, burning at her.

"I'm going to see to it that you get home," he said at last. "Then I'm going to send a message to Fanny Pepper. I'll have her come and take care of you, stay with you until you're—" He hesitated. "Until you're well again."

Well. He meant sober. Adrienne felt a pang rip at her throat. A yearning possessed her—a hunger to hold Kristian, to feel his body, his nakedness, close to her own. If she could only touch him, if they could be physically close . . . perhaps then it would be all right again between them.

"Kristian," she whispered. "You can take me home, you can do anything you wish, but not—not yet. Oh, please, not yet."

She flung her arms around him and kissed him, her mouth desperate, open and searching.

For a moment Kristian stood stock-still, his body stiff, unyielding. Then the muscles in his arms and chest relaxed as he responded to her hungrily.

"God," he muttered. "What am I doing? You're a witch, a whirlwind!"

As if her weight meant nothing, he carried her to the corner of the dressing room where there was a battered couch, its upholstery ancient. He laid her down, covering her body with his own.

"Oh, God, Adrienne, my darling—"

Her voice was husky. "Kristian. Make love to me. Please. I'll make you forget Primrose, I'll make you forget everything else, there'll be nothing but me and you. . ."

"Yes."

He tore at her clothes, caught now in the same fever which possessed her. She could feel fabric pull, buttons fly, and then she was naked and so was he.

It was a lovemaking the like of which she had never experienced before. Wild, abandoned, almost a rape, almost a battle, yet none of these, for always there was love. They tore at each other, demanded—and gave. His hands possessed her, his mouth owned her. And she owned him. Feverishly they pressed together, breast, belly, thigh, and groin, until she did not know which flesh was his, which hers, and did not care.

They were one, they were joined, they were incandescent.

Chapter 27

It had been a secret moment, her time with Kristian, a stolen hour quickly disappearing into the endless chain of train schedules, shabby hotels, poorly cooked meals, and the struggle to keep clothes clean.

Touring. It was exhausting, exhilarating, challenging. But this time the tour was different. No longer was she with *Uncle Tom's Cabin,* an obscure traveling company which attracted little notice save in the small towns where it played. This time the play was a popular one, and Adrienne was a star.

They played the big cities: Philadelphia, Boston, Chicago. And everywhere the crowds came, to gawk at the sapphire which she wore always about her neck, to stare, too, at Adrienne herself.

And feverishly she played up to their admiration. Before the tour left, she had visited her dressmaker and ordered eight new gowns—lavish creations of faille and India silk and cashmere and moiré striped wool. She spent her money recklessly, as if something drove her, buying box after box of fashionable bonnets trimmed with ostrich feathers, with surah ribbon and filigree buckles and *crêpe lisse* ruching.

Then she turned to Barrie, buying the little girl dresses, petticoats, and bonnets as fashionable as her own. Barrie, she vowed, would be every bit as pretty as any little girl shown simpering in the pages of *Godey's Ladies Book.*

And the purchases paid off. In each city, they arrived grandly at the train station accompanied by twenty trunks crammed with gowns, hats, shoes, and accessories —just as Adrienne had once dreamed that she would do.

At each train station, crowds of onlookers pushed close.

"There she is—look at that dress she's wearing! See the ribbons and trim! Why, Mary, you could add that kind of trimming to my old satin, if you'd only try—"

"Doesn't she look pretty? But temperamental, I'd say. Look at her, so fine and haughty, they say she's a grand lady—"

"Isn't the little girl lovely? And her gowns, why, the *extravagance*—"

Newspaper reporters would meet them at the train station as well. The newsmen would be wary, yet ready to be charmed.

"Are you enjoying your tour, Miss Gill?"

"Why, yes, I am." A toss of her head so that the ostrich feathers on her bonnet would shake entrancingly. A brilliantly flashed smile. "I am quite thrilled with the city of Syracuse, and am only sorry that I cannot stay longer. I hope all of your residents will come to see us in *The Passion Star*. It is a wonderful play by a wonderful playwright, Mr. King."

The reporter would press closer, his eyes avid. "And the Passion Star itself, how many carats would you say it weighs?"

"More than three hundred-fifty carats, and it is a perfect cabochon cut, without peer in this country," she would reply automatically.

Yes, they attracted attention, and in a way Adrienne reveled in it. Hadn't this been her dream? To arrive accompanied by dozens of trunks, by servants and entourage? To sweep regally onto the platform, exactly as the spirited Adrienne LaRivière might have done, while hundreds stared hungrily?

Yes, it was a dream come true.

Yet more and more often now she felt isolated from the crowds which flocked to see her. The dream was turning out to be empty. She wasn't really a Scottish actress from the nobility; that story was a creation of her imagination. No, she was only little Addie McGill from Glasgow. Lonely, often uncertain of herself, often reaching for a bottle to help herself endure one more night.

What would happen if her fans ever found out who she really was?

True to Kristian's prediction, Primrose's tour as the maid Mara did not last more than two months. Kristian's young wife was having a difficult pregnancy. Even Adrienne had to feel pity for her as, racked with nausea, she sat huddled on a bench in the train stations with the rest of the cast.

Always small and slim, Primrose had lost weight. Now the pretty, oval face was marred with violet shadows beneath the eyes, and the bubbly laughter was often absent.

"I'm all right," she would insist, brushing aside expressions of sympathy. "Really I am. Please—just don't tell Kristian I was sick again this morning. I don't want him to be worried."

Fanny Pepper visited an apothecary's for the ingredients and brewed a concoction which was supposed to combat the nausea.

"I'm not pleased at all with the way that girl is doing," she said one morning to Adrienne. "She is fragile and not suited to childbearing. In fact, I've told Kristian she should return home to New York to be with her parents. Of course, she will hear nothing of it. The little fool, she wants to be with her husband."

Adrienne swallowed back envy and hurt. If only Primrose *would* go back to New York! Then she could have Kristian to herself. She might not be married to him, but at least she could be his mistress. Her pride—what little of it now remained—had completely flown now when it came to Kristian. She would accept him on any terms at all.

But Kristian had rejected her.

"Primrose is my wife," he told her one night. They were backstage, near the heavy sandbags used to counterbalance scenery flown high overhead. It was the familiar, drafty, chilly, paint and hemp-smelling background she knew so well.

"But, Kristian, *I* love you too——"

"I know you do. But like it or not, I'm obligated to be faithful to her, especially in her condition. My God, I owe her that, Adrienne."

Adrienne, thrusting out her jaw obstinately, did not reply.

"Adrienne!" His hands gripped her shoulders with fierce strength. "We were both carried away by passion, my darling—and it can't happen again. Poor little Primrose. She's feeling so sick right now, and I just can't hurt her."

"And what about me?"

She clung to him, almost begging, heedless of whether any of the flymen or stagehands saw them.

"I don't want it to end like this. Oh, Kristian, I love you and I know you love me! That night in the dressing room only proved it. We can't just let each other go . . ."

His hands caressed her hair roughly. "We can and we must. And there is another thing, my darling. You must stop your drinking. Don't you know that it is a poison, seeping into your life, and mine, to destroy both?"

She stared at him.

"You have been drinking again before the performance, haven't you?" His voice had grown harder. "Fanny, of course, is too loyal to tell me, but Bettina Smithe has no such compunctions. You have fumbled your lines on more than one occasion, Adrienne, and others have had to pick up your cues for you. Last week in Pittsburgh you nearly appeared onstage without your Fatima wig. Two years ago such a thing would not have happened."

Didn't Kristian understand? Adrienne wondered helplessly. Didn't anyone? The need she had, the desperate need, for the soft, easy shield of the whisky, to dull pain, deaden grief and despair until she could endure them?

"I didn't fumble my lines that much," she whispered. "As for the wig, I . . . I mislaid it. Fanny couldn't find it, and finally rushed it to me at the last moment."

Kristian pressed his lips together. "We all know how important wigs and costumes are—that is why we're all so careful to organize our theater trunks so that we can find anything at a moment's notice. Adrienne, you're getting careless. Not just in your costumes, but in everything you do. It's as if you no longer care."

He walked away from her, to stare upward into the flies, where stored segments of flats and unused scenery hung in grotesque shapes.

"Adrienne." His voice was so low that she could barely hear it. "I love you, I always will, God help me. But disaster lies ahead—I've felt it for a long time, and now that feeling is stronger than ever. And if you don't stop your drinking . . ."

He let his sentence trail off, leaving the rest of the words unsaid.

Days passed, long, hectic touring days punctuated by train trips, by boiled and fried meals in hotel dining rooms. Sometimes, in newspapers purchased in train stations, they read of events in the theater world they had left behind in New York. Fanny Davenport, plump and accomplished, was playing Lady Teazle in *School for Scandal*. Dion Boucicault's play, *The Shaughraun*, was an enormous success, and Kristian predicted that it would have a long run.

One night in Buffalo, after the final curtain had been rung down, Fanny Pepper surprised them all by announcing that she and the stage manager, William Mancin, were to be married.

"Married! But, Fanny! You?" Adrienne could not conceal her shock.

"Yes, and why not me?" Fanny was laughing. "Adrienne, I'm thirty-nine years old. I'm no longer fit to be an actress, and, frankly, I wish some of the good things a marriage can bring. William is a good man, and I think that we can be happy together."

"But—but, Fanny—" Adrienne felt oddly bereft, as if Fanny had done something she had no right to do.

But her friend's russet eyes were sparkling. "Cheer up, Adrienne. Do you begrudge me a bit of happiness?"

Involuntarily she glanced down at her scarred hands. "God knows I've waited long enough for it."

Adrienne was penitent. She threw her arms around the other. "Oh, Fanny, I'm sorry. It's just that I'll miss you. I don't want things to change."

Fanny looked at her strangely. "Everything changes, Adrienne, didn't you know that? Life goes on, carrying us with it whether we like it or not. But I'll always be your friend. I'll always be Fanny, just as usual."

Washington, D.C., in April, 1874, was hot and muggy. The spacious streets were filled with dust from the extensive building and street renovation which was going on. Debris left over from the Civil War was still being carted away, and horsecar lines lengthened. Hundreds of miles of wooden pavements had been laid and, in the humid climate, were already beginning to rot away.

The Passion Star was playing at Ford's Theater where, nine years previously, Abraham Lincoln had been shot. Adrienne, Fanny, and other members of the cast amused themselves by peeping into the Presidential box with its moveable partition, its dark-red figured wallpaper and yellow satin drapes overhung by Nottingham lace curtains. The greenroom and dressing rooms were located in the north wing, a four-story L-shaped building equipped with narrow stairways barely wide enough to accommodate a woman's full skirts.

After the first day's matinee performance, Adrienne emerged from the stage door into the public alley, Barrie at her side, to meet the usual crowd of onlookers.

They were a mixed group, many of them black, for this was a city filled with thousands of former slaves. The women had come to stare enviously at Adrienne's gowns, while the men had come to gawk at the actress well known for her aristocratic background, her beauty and fiery temper, the scandals connected with her name.

"Look," someone whispered excitedly. "There she is, she has it on beneath her mantle—the Passion Star—"

Adrienne, smiling, was in the act of gripping Barrie's hand to escort her to the public cab which waited only a few feet away when she saw Xenos Shane.

She stopped short, her throat closing in a convulsive gasp. The magician was standing at the back of the crowd, half-concealed behind an enormously fat black woman. Yet it was unmistakably Xenos Shane, almost exactly as she remembered him. Only inches taller than she, the magician wore a black suit tailored in a flamboyant cut. His gray-white hair—whiter now, she saw—was combed back from his face in a dramatic crest. His nose was as hooked as ever, his lips red, moist.

Xenos Shane!

Memories tumbled back to her. Xenos and his spectacular magic acts, the Magic Palanquin, the Cassadaga Propaganda. His assistant, little Elijah, small, coffee-colored, dextrous. The rich, theatrical voice which could boom out through a theater, pulling audiences into its spell. Herself locked in the prop room, the gnarled hands forcing a whisky bottle toward her lips . . .

Xenos Shane! How had he found her here? And what did he want?

"Mama . . ." Barrie's voice at her side pulled Adrienne out of her fright. She looked downward at the little girl. Barrie was pale, all of the color drained from her face save for two feverish red spots on her cheekbones. "Mama, I don't like that man."

Adrienne looked again at the magician, who had edged further back in the crowd, almost disappearing now from view, so that, if she had not glimpsed his face, she would never have known he was there.

Why? she wondered desperately. Why had she been so foolish as to think that Xenos could not follow her to the United States? She had not even bothered to change the name of the sapphire. The jewel had received extensive publicity. It had been written up in the New York newspapers, in the papers of a dozen other cities. It had been depicted in sketches which had appeared in *Harper's Weekly* and in *Frank Leslie's*.

Her thoughts tumbled on feverishly. Was Xenos the man whom she had seen outside the Olympic Theater last year? Was it he whom Mary had seen outside the cottage at Saratoga? If so, why had he not come forward then?

What did he want?

"Mama—" Barrie begged. "Mama, I have to go to the bathroom. Mama . . ." Insistently, the little girl tugged at Adrienne's hand.

"Barrie—oh, very well."

Distractedly, barely aware of what she was doing, Adrienne waved away the cab and, turning, went back into the theater.

Twenty minutes later, with Barrie taken to the bathroom and then put safely in the care of the stagehand Quince, Adrienne sat alone in her dressing room. In front of her was a glass half filled with whisky and water. She had needed the drink to quell the fright which had pushed up into her throat like some choking, foul-tasting rag.

What did the man want after all these years? What *could* he want?

Involuntarily, she glanced at her own reflection in the dressing room mirror. At her throat, as always, was the Passion Star, gleaming, opulent. Her fingers went up to touch it. Did Xenos want the Passion Star back? If so, why had he not approached her long ago? Why had he not informed the New York police that she was an escaped felon, that she had stolen the jewel?

Questions tormented her. What had Xenos been doing all of these years? Was the boy Elijah still with him? What of his wife, Frances, the woman who had once stained the red silk gown with the perspiration born of fear?

And what should she, Adrienne, do now? Should she keep quiet and hope that Xenos would go away, that all would be well?

That, she assured herself, taking a burning gulp of whisky, was a foolish hope. Xenos was here for a reason. He would not leave easily.

There was a tapping at her door and then Barrie burst in. The redness in her daughter's cheeks, Adrienne noted dully, had faded to a more normal color.

"Mama, Quince and me are making a doll house. and he is going to take me out for tea! And cakes! He promised me, Mama, he promised!"

Adrienne caught her breath. At two, Barrie was a

fragile and precocious child, with huge, wide gray eyes much like Barrett's. There were brief moments when Adrienne could almost see beauty in her. Then, like the shifting of clouds on a rainy spring day, the loveliness would be gone and there would be only Barrie again, small, big-eyed, intense.

"Of course you may go," she said at last, pushing aside her fear with an effort. The child would be safe in the company of Quince, who loved her. "Tell Quince you may have milk and cream and jam, as much as you wish."

"I want cakes!" the child piped up. Then her face seemed to change, her lower lip to quiver. She rushed to her mother and threw her arms about Adrienne's legs. "Mama? Who was that man? That nasty man who looked at us?"

"Why, he—he was someone I used to know a long time ago," Adrienne faltered.

"He was a bad man. I didn't like him."

"Go, Barrie." She gave the child a little push. "Go and have tea with Quince and forget about the man we saw. He was just someone come to see Mama after the matinee, that's all. Haven't a hundred men come to bring flowers and to stare?"

But still Barrie clung to her. "Mama—the man is bad—"

"Barrie! Go, I said, and have your tea. I want to be alone, I have to think, can't you understand that?"

Adrienne tried not to see the hurt look on Barrie's face as she trotted out of the dressing room.

Two hours later she was back at her hotel, and had given a replete Barrie over to the care of Mary, when a bellman delivered a note to her room. A certain Xenos Shane was in the hotel's lobby lounge, and wished to see her immediately.

Adrienne's heart gave a rabbity jump. Her first impulse was to say no, to crumple the note, fling it in the bellman's face, and slam the door.

But what good would that do? she asked herself

quickly. Xenos could find her any time he chose. After all, *The Passion Star*'s performance schedule was a matter of public record. Sooner or later she would have to face him. So why not now?

With cold hands, she fumbled in her small personal trunk for the bottle she kept there. Quickly she removed the protective wire, uncorked it, and splashed whisky into a small tin cup.

Just one quick drink, she assured herself. One or two swallows for courage, for a little protection against the panic which simmered in her belly like water just come to a boil.

On her way out of the door, she paused at the mirror to adjust the gold chain which supported the Passion Star. Touching the gem, she lifted her chin defiantly. She had stolen the sapphire; he knew it and she knew it. So she would wear the Passion Star downstairs to meet Xenos. Let him make of it what he would!

"You wear that stone well." The voice, flamboyant, theatrical, was as she remembered it.

Xenos was waiting for her in the hotel lounge, a comfortable, high-ceilinged room strewn with wicker chairs and potted plants. The lounge, Adrienne noted with relief, was almost empty save for an old man snoozing in a chair with his mouth open.

"Do I?" She swept toward him, surprised at her own steadiness. "I would advise you, Mr. Shane, to keep your voice down, unless you wish the entire hotel to know of our business."

The magician's black eyes were fixed on the sapphire. "What? One old man?" he murmured. "Ah . . . it is still as beautiful as I remembered it. A stone reeking of passion, of fiery desires."

Now that she could view Xenos at close range, she could see that the man had changed since she had first seen him in Glasgow. Then, he had had a sort of bold magnificence. Now his skin had broken into hundreds of tiny lines, like parchment, and red veins webbed his cheeks and nose. And, seen at close quarters, his theatrically cut suit was shabby, its cuffs frayed.

"With that sapphire about your neck, my dear, you look quite stunning." Xenos's laughter was bitter. "I must admit that I never expected it of you."

She gazed at him uneasily, not knowing what to reply.

"But look at you now, my sweetmeat. Fashionably dressed, sweeping into the room as if you were the Queen herself. One would hardly realize that you are not the great lady the newspapers claim you are. But I know better, don't I?" Xenos's laugh was threatening. "You are not a lady at all, are you, Adrienne Gill? You're really a little thief. A girl from the filthy dung-heaps of Glasgow, an escaped felon!"

Adrienne felt the color drain from her face. The lobby seemed to swirl away from her, its colors to grow clouded. It was only with the greatest effort that she held herself erect.

Xenos Shane was wrong—and he was right, too, in a twisted, horrible way. She was a supremely successful actress, but she was also little Addie McGill, from the slums of Glasgow, claiming a nonexistence aristocratic heritage. She had stolen the Passion Star in desperation and hurt from the man who had raped her—but the British police and the public who now adored her would not know that. If Xenos were to expose her, she would seem no better than a common thief.

Against Xenos's lies, her wrong would count for nothing—certainly not with William Stauffer, who would delight in anything that might blacken her reputation. If her account of herself and her past to Barrett, to Kristian, to Fanny and the public, had been even reasonably near the truth, it might have been possible for her to weather this storm. But she had chosen to live a lie, and could not survive its exposure.

"What do you want with me?" she whispered. "For God's sake, what do you want?"

The magician's laugh was booming and oily, the most frightening sound that Adrienne had ever heard.

"Come." He took her hand and she nearly recoiled from the feel of his skin, at once moist and rough. "Come and sit down, my sweeting, in one of these charming wicker chairs the hotel has been thoughtful enough to provide. We have much to talk about."

"What must we talk about? Why are you here? Why have you been following me?"

"Sit down and I will tell you."

"Very well." Adrienne sank into one of the chairs and folded her hands in her lap, trying to quell their shaking. Xenos selected the chair beside it.

"So you are wondering why I am here."

"Yes, you know I am! Please, tell me!"

He leaned backwards in his chair and suddenly extended his hands, fingers spread wide.

"Look. Look at these."

Fascinated, she stared at the hands displayed before her. Xenos's fingers were like ancient tree roots, the knuckles enlarged, the last joint of each finger twisted at strange side angles. They were pitiful, witch-like hands, gnarled and deformed.

"Arthritis." The magician's voice was harsh. "I'm crippled with it, and there is nothing to be done. I have been to a dozen doctors in the past year."

"Oh. I'm sorry. . . ."

"Do you know what such crippling means to a magician? Have you the remotest idea?"

"Your tricks!" she faltered. "You—I suppose you need your hands to accomplish them."

"Yes, my Adrienne." Xenos's voice was full of sarcasm. "Hands are to a magician what feet are to a dancer. Of course, I have Elijah—thank God for that, anyway. Elijah is bright and quick and has been my mainstay ever since the arthritis attacked me. My mainstay in more than one way," he added with a twisted smile.

Elijah. Adrienne thought of the black youth as she had last seen him, a winsome thirteen years old. Now he would be seventeen. She shivered, although she did not know why. What had the years with Xenos done to the boy?

She listened as the magician went on with his story. His slave "wife," Frances, had died of a tumor of the female parts only months after Adrienne had run away. Of the four black men who had been his assistants, one had run off, one had died, and one had had his pelvis broken in a carriage accident. Only Elijah was left, and many of the acts had had to be altered.

Xenos now practiced "spirit feats" involving an enclosed box and the help of Elijah and some wires strung from the flies. With these acts he had drifted about the music halls of London—Collins', the London Pavilion, the Marylebone, and others. The crippling of his hands had begun, and he had gradually drifted to the smaller towns. As the music halls had grown shabbier, so had his acts.

A fortuitous marriage to a widow had enabled him —with the aid of her savings—to sail to New York in the early months of 1873, in the hope of making a success there. It was in that city that he had picked up a newspaper and found in William Stauffer's column word of Adrienne Gill.

"At first, my sweetmeat, I didn't even realize that it was you. Then I saw the mention of the Passion Star, and I knew. My God, it had to be you, it had to be! How I'd looked for you, girl! Searched and cursed and looked some more, until I was half insane with it. I'd hired detectives, I'd sent telegrams to every pawnshop in Glasgow and London. I'd even searched for you myself in the brothels of London, which was where I was sure you would eventually end."

Adrienne stared at the man. A sick feeling possessed her as she remembered the prostitute in the green dress she had seen outside the music hall in London the night she had met Barrett.

Yes, Xenos had been more accurate than he knew. Only Barrett, and her own quick wits, had saved her from becoming exactly like that girl—a whore.

Her hand went protectively to her neck, her fingers touching the smooth oval which rested near her collarbone.

"Are you after the Passion Star, then?" Her voice deepened with the last shreds of her courage. "Because if you are, Xenos, I won't give it to you!"

415

"What? You won't?"

His eyes danced at her—with amusement? Somehow she felt more frightened than ever.

"No, I won't. I—I don't think you have any right to this sapphire, Mr. Shane. I don't think it belongs to you any more than it does to me. I think you stole it, too!"

The magician laughed. His crippled hands slapped at his knees. "Ah, my sweet, you have caught on, have you, to the sham and trickery of this life? You stole the sapphire from me, I stole it from a man in Paris who had been in an accident—poor devil, he was crushed beyond belief—but why go into that now?"

The deep, theatrical voice went on. "The truth is, my dear Miss Gill, that there is an endless chain of greed and passion eminently suited to a stone with such a fascinating name. Which, by the way, I made up myself, along with the story."

"You . . . made it up?"

Her voice was the barest of whispers. She stared at the magician, barely able to contain her shock.

"Oh ho! Did you really think that there was a lovely young queen? Did you really think that she wore this gem"—He pointed mockingly—"to be beheaded?"

Adrienne, stunned, felt her mouth drop open. "But the girl—her lover—" she stammered. "You said—"

Xenos chuckled. "I said a good deal, and evidently you believed every word of it. People love romance, my dear girl. Their lives are dull and so they crave life and color, they respond to a good, dramatic tale. I gave them the story they wanted, that's all."

Adrienne's hand had crept again to her throat. "I . . . I don't believe you."

It was as if her world had splintered apart. A play had been written around the history of the Passion Star. The gem had been real to her. It had been her symbol, her talisman. And now she had learned that the story of the Passion Star was false. There was no lovely girl, no vengeful king. There was nothing—only a stone dug out of a mine and polished.

Xenos inclined his leonine head mockingly.

"Believe me or not, as you wish. What does it

matter? The truth is that the entire world is a game of sleight-of-hand—and the winners are those who can play it best."

The magician reached into the pocket of his suit and removed a thick envelope. He tapped on it with a twisted forefinger.

"In here," he told her. He tapped again. "In here you'll find it all."

Adrienne tensed on the edge of her chair. "What's in that envelope? What are you going to do, Xenos?"

The black eyes regarded her unwinkingly.

"Why, I'm going to blackmail you, of course."

Chapter 28

It was two o'clock in the morning—or perhaps three. Adrienne had no idea of the time, and she did not care. She tossed and turned on the lumpy hotel room bed, caught in a maze of frightening nightmares from which there was no exit. Dreams in which Xenos's laughter mocked her, in which his hands, gnarled, twisted, hideous, grabbed for her. . . .

She moaned and awoke for the dozenth time. Above her head the high ceiling was streaked with a bar of moonlight which streamed in through a crack in the heavy window drapes. Outside she could hear the clatter of cart wheels in the side street, a sudden burst of laughter from a room farther down the hotel corridor.

Noises. Night noises.

In the room next to her own, there was a sudden whimper as Barrie awoke and then was soothed to sleep by Fanny. She thought she heard the opening and shutting of Fanny's door. Now from the corridor came dimly the sound of someone sobbing. Had there been a marital quarrel, some young bride who had argued with her husband?

Did you really think that there was a lovely young queen? Did you really think she wore this gem to be beheaded?

Why, I'm going to blackmail you, of course.

The words blended with the faraway weeping, and seemed to fill the entire hotel room, occupying all of its shadowy spaces.

I'm going to blackmail you.

Slowly Adrienne struggled out of her bed. She stumbled to her trunk and, in the darkness, groped for the whisky bottle. She had not wished to drink—she had ordered herself not to, had vowed that, for once, she would face a shock without the aid of liquor.

But tonight she simply could not help it.

She took one swallow, closing her eyes against the familiar burning. Then, quickly, she swallowed again. If she drank enough, perhaps she would be able to blank out the memory of that scene in the hotel lounge.

Xenos, she remembered, had leaned back in his chair, looking about the lobby with confidence. The old man still snoozed, snoring loudly. A maid, clad in a black uniform with white apron, hurried past. An elderly couple peered into the lounge, then shuffled in the direction of the front desk. A bellman went past lugging a trunk.

Life in the hotel was normal. No one could possibly guess the ugly words which Xenos spoke to her now, almost under his breath.

"Adrienne Gill, you stole that sapphire from me. I have the proof right here in this envelope, the complete story of the theft, taken straight from the newspapers of Glasgow and London. I clipped everything, you little fool. I have the detectives' report on you, the efforts they made to find the stone. Everything is right here."

She could only stare at him.

Xenos moistened his lips. "There is another report, too—one which I am glad now that I had the sense to have made."

She found her voice. "And . . . and what is that?"

"I sent a detective to your flat on High Street, Miss Gill. He interviewed your mother—and talked to your father. He wrote fully of what he found there."

Adrienne could feel the pressure inside her head, pushing against her temples. She wanted to scream. To jump up from her chair, to run out of the hotel lounge and into the wide, dusty streets of Washington, to keep on running and never stop.

A detective had gone to their flat in the Close on

High Street and seen everything. He had seen the dank, tomb-like Closes with their mildewed stone walls cutting off nearly all light. He had seen the wynds, alleyways not even wide enough for a cart, with drains running down their centers for the transport of sewage, of slops and human excrement. He had seen—and smelled—the animal dung-piles with their choking stench.

He had seen the children playing in the Closes because there was nowhere else for them to go, the disillusioned men, the prostitutes entertaining customers at the back of a filthy stairway.

He had seen *Maman* in her shabby housedress, mended so often that the seams would no longer stay together. He had seen *Maman*'s hands with the sores that would not heal, her tired face. He had seen the eight children all crammed into two cluttered rooms, the stove blackened with soot and grease which no amount of *Maman*'s scrubbing could clean.

He had seen, too, her father, Jack McGill, drunken, unshaven, reeling down the wynd, perhaps stopping to urinate against a stone wall.

Shame coursed through her, a deep and hideous shame.

William Stauffer, her mind went on with sick clarity, was her enemy. He hated her for rejecting him, for slapping him. If Stauffer were ever to learn of the contents of Xenos' envelope . . .

Dear God, she thought in rising panic. he must not know! If the columnist learned her real story he would be sure to publish it in his paper—and to pass the worst details on to the others in the theater by word of mouth. Then the whole world—her world—would know. Would know and laugh at her.

Her life, her pride, her career, would come tumbling down around her ears. No longer would the crowds flock to see her. A former countess was romantic—a dirty little street girl from Glasgow was not. A grand lady dressed in fashionable clothes was someone to command envy. A fugitive thief was not.

Adrienne swallowed hard against the lump of tallow

which seemed to fill her throat. Worst of all, Kristian himself would learn of the filth she came from, and pity her. And she could not bear his pity.

She sensed Xenos' sharp eyes on her.

From somewhere she found the strength to rise from her chair. She drew herself up to her full height and walked with dignity to the window. Here the hotel management had painted on the wall, in leaden green, a climbing wisteria to twine about the window. The effect had been intended to augment the garden look of the lounge. Now her eyes focused on the painted vine without seeing any of it.

"Very well, Mr. Shane," she replied in the full, rich, well-trained voice which was partly inherent in her and partly her legacy from Barrett. "You have made your intentions plain. Now I would like you to tell me this: what are your demands? Surely you must have some. Do you wish the Passion Star back?"

She turned to see the magician's lips open in a smile.

"No," Xenos Shane said. "I thought about that for a long time—it's one of the reasons I took so long to approach you. I don't want the Passion Star back, because it's the goose which laid the golden egg."

His shrug was expressive. "If your play closes, what good will your sapphire do me then? That stone is well-known in this country now. Any pawnbroker or agent would recognize it immediately. No, I don't care about the Passion Star itself. It is merely a mineral. An inert piece of earth with little value save that which men put on it."

"Then"—She struggled to keep her voice even—"just what is it that you do want?"

"Why, the *value* of the stone, of course! All of men's desires eventually translate down to money. And that is all I want, my dear. A nice income to keep me in comfort when my hands have grown even more crippled than they are." Xenos made a face. "Sooner or later my boy, my Elijah, will flee me. Then I will be entirely alone. At that time I'll need the cushion your money can give me."

"Money . . . a cushion . . ." She stared at him in mingled dismay and fear. "But I don't have extra money, Xenos. Do you think that I am rich? I have been extravagant—my dressmaker's bill is very high—"

Her fingers plucked at the fabric of her walking-suit in growing agitation. It was true. She *had* been extravagant. She had bought what she pleased and when, without thinking of the consequences. The cottage at Saratoga, her hideaway. Gowns. Liquor. There had always been the Passion Star, hadn't there? Money from performances flowing in regularly, plus the prospect of a tour, the occasional gifts that came to her backstage from admirers. She had bought as she pleased. She had not thought of the future.

"I am sure your dressmaker's bill *is* high," Xenos commented with a wry look at the gown she wore. "It will be less high in the future."

"But you don't understand. The money has come in, yes, but I have spent most of it—"

"Then from now on you will spend whatever you have on me." Xenos rose from his chair. "You have very little other choice, do you, Miss Gill? If you do not give me the funds I ask for, then I will go to that newspaper columnist who seems to dislike you so violently, and I will tell him everything I know. I'll tell him that you are a harlot, that you stole the Passion Star from me—"

"No!" The cry tore out of her. "No, please don't!"

Xenos smiled. "I want to live comfortably, my sweeting. Elijah and I are most anxious to have a taste of the same luxury in which you indulge. Elijah would like a new suit. He is a pretty boy, and would look very elegant if he were properly garbed."

Adrienne stared at the magician in horror. She remembered the charming child of the Brittania. Ugly pictures had begun to form in her mind. Elijah. Xenos's gnarled hands on that smooth, young body . . .

"Do you mean that I—" Her lips had gone paper-dry. "I must support Elijah, too?"

"You must support both of us You must do it quietly and without fanfare, and you must do it regularly. Or—"

Xenos lunged. His gnarled hands traveled the distance to Adrienne's neck with swift, snakelike ease. His twisted fingers fastened about the chain which held the Passion Star. He yanked it toward him until the metal chain cut into Adrienne's flesh.

"Ouch!" she could not help crying out. "Please— that hurts—"

"Does it indeed? It could hurt more. If I do not get the money from you, then I will exact my payment in other ways. I will take the Passion Star back, and sell it abroad. And I will also take something else. Perhaps that pretty little girl who was clutching you so sweetly in the public alley today. What do you think of that? She, Elijah, and I—what a team we would make, eh?"

Horror coursed through her—a horror she had not known she could feel.

"No! No, you can't do such a thing—not Barrie, not my daughter—"

"I would do anything, Adrienne Gill. Anything at all. Surely you must know that by now."

Xenos's fingers released the chain. The stone dropped back onto her breast.

"I will return, my sweeting, in the morning. At that time I will expect my first payment. I trust that you will be ready."

Now, thinking of what Xenos had said, Adrienne sat in bed with her whisky, forcing down one gulp after another, until the hotel room whirled sickeningly about her.

What was she to do?

Until this time, money had not been much in her thoughts. But it was true that she was exceedingly short of cash. She had bought the cottage at Saratoga, paying a recklessly high price, for the old couple who owned it had been reluctant to sell. She had bought trunkfuls of clothes, had outfitted Barrie as magnificently as herself. She had purchased a pearl bracelet and a small diamond tiara to wear in her hair. She had spent money, too, on restaurants and chop-houses, on whisky, and on all the good food which she had not had a chance to eat during

424

her childhood. She had also sent large sums of money to *Maman.*

Now she would have to pay Xenos what he asked. She had no other choice. For Barrie's sake, if not for her own. . . .

The Passion Star lay on the bedside table. Dully she stared down at it, at the six-legged star gleaming against its backdrop of blue. Shining, cold, empty.

She picked up the pendant and squeezed it in the palm of her hand, fighting the urge to hurl the sapphire at the mirror over the dressing table.

If she threw it, the jewel would slam into the glass, splintering it into a thousand glittering shards. Perhaps the sapphire itself would be damaged, its opulent finish spoiled, the six-legged star ruined forever.

Then she let the gem drop from her fingers onto the surface of the bureau. It lay there, seeming almost to mock her as if it were alive.

Somehow, some way, she must find a way to pay Xenos his money.

She was awakened by hands shaking her shoulders, jolting her from disjointed nightmares of Xenos Shane.

"Adrienne, wake up! Wake up, will you? My God, have you been drinking again? And at a time like this—" It was Fanny, her voice agitated.

Adrienne turned over and buried her face in her pillow. "No . . . don't want to wake up. What time is it?"

"It's nearly dawn. And drunk as you are, that can't be helped now. You must awaken quickly. Primrose is having her baby and, God knows why, she is calling for you."

Adrienne squirmed under the covers, clapping her hands to her temples against the headache which throbbed there. Primrose? A baby? What on earth was Fanny speaking of? She felt as if she had wandered into someone else's dream where nothing made sense.

Fanny shook her again, more violently this time. "Adrienne, you little fool, wake up, I tell you! You stink

425

of whisky, the smell is very strong. What will Kristian say when he sees you? I just hope you can manage, because you've got to come right away. Primrose is crying for you, and she won't be denied."

"But—Primrose—why should she—"

Adrienne struggled to awaken. Her mouth tasted foul, and her tongue felt thick and dry and furry. The gaslights were flickering, sending strange shadows up and down the walls of the hotel room. She must have fallen asleep with them on, she thought confusedly. And now she could hear sounds coming from the corridor. Shrieks, a low, terrible sobbing—God, what was it?

"I don't *know* why Primrose would want you!" Fanny's fists pummeled into her side. "Damn you, Adrienne, you would have to pick tonight to get tipsy, wouldn't you? Come on, girl. Hurry!"

This was a nightmare, a whisky dream, not even real. Adrienne tumbled out of bed and stood swaying.

"Here," Fanny ordered. "Get into a gown—any dress will do, just hurry! The doctor says there isn't much time. She keeps asking for you."

Adrienne looked longingly at the bottle which still sat on the bedside table, an inch of liquid still remaining in it.

"Oh, no!" Fanny snatched up the bottle. "No, you don't, Adrienne Gill! You already stink of that stuff—enough is enough!"

The hotel suite which Primrose and Kristian shared was similar to the one which Adrienne now occupied. It had two large rooms filled with heavy furniture and Turkish rugs in jewel colors. A pair of tall, narrow windows looked out on a side street. Personal items were scattered about—a silver hair brush, Kristian's walking stick, an extra cravat, a froth of petticoats slung over a chair.

Yet these were not the things that drew Adrienne's eyes. It was Primrose, a small mound in the center of the bed, at whom she could not stop looking.

Once Primrose had been clear-skinned and lovely, her beauty as wild and shy as the flower after which she had been named. Now that beauty was utterly gone. The

426

girl looked like—Adrienne swallowed convulsively—like a death's-head. Her skin was the color of old candles, her eyes enormous staring holes, her mouth a pale slash in the drained face. The brown hair, once softly cascaded in fashionable ringlets, now streamed lank upon the pillow, soaked with perspiration. Primrose's thin fingers plucked at the sheets. Droplets of blood, Adrienne noted with a sinking heart, stained the linen.

Kristian stood glowering at the side of the bed, his eyes fierce, as if by anger alone he could defy what was happening to his wife. At the bedside table, the doctor, a harried-looking man of forty with a thin, wispy beard, rummaged in a black leather bag.

As Adrienne entered the room, the doctor extracted a vial of yellowish liquid and came hurrying toward her. His mouth showed distaste as he smelled the whisky on Adrienne.

"So you are the Miss Gill my patient has been calling for?"

She nodded shamefacedly.

"Well, you can't stay long. Her labor has reached an impasse and the hemorrhaging has been severe. I haven't been able to stop it. I've packed her and done all I can, but—" He glanced toward the bed, where Primrose had begun to moan and toss her head from side to side. "The child won't make it, of course. It is being born entirely too early. As for the mother—"

Angrily the doctor looked down at the small glass vial which he held in his hand.

"Useless!" he muttered. "Useless, all of it. Damn, if there were only some way, some good way to stanch bleeding, then she might have a chance—" His lips pressed together. "Well, Miss Gill, see her then, if you must, but make it fast. She hasn't long."

As Adrienne struggled to recover from her shock—Primrose dying!—the doctor bent over the bed and dribbled the contents of the vial into Primrose's mouth.

"Kristian . . ." the sick girl moaned. Her hands reached out and clutched for her husband's. "Kristian, is she here yet? Is Adrienne here?"

"Yes, darling. She just came in."

Adrienne drew herself tall. Her hands bunched into fists at her sides, fingernails cutting into flesh. The pain, like clean, fresh air, revived her. She might have been drunk earlier, but now she was cold sober. The sight of Primrose's death-pale face had done that to her.

She went to the bed and knelt by it.

"It's me," she whispered. "I'm here, Primrose."

The face on the pillow nodded. It looked ravaged, drained of all its life. And now that Adrienne was closer to the bed, she could smell the hot, sweetish odor of blood. Primrose's life-blood, seeping away.

"Good . . . I'm glad . . . glad you came . . . ."

Childbirth! Adrienne fought the desire to be sick, to run away. It wasn't fair, it wasn't! Why did this have to happen to women? Oh, she didn't want to be here and see it. Why, she wondered angrily, hadn't Primrose gone home to New York to be with her family as Fanny had urged? Then none of this might be happening.

She realized that Primrose was speaking again in that soft, dying voice.

"Adrienne . . . want to speak to you alone. . . ."

Beside the bed, Kristian tensed. Fright surged through Adrienne.

"Alone?" She fought back panic. "But, Primrose, surely there is nothing you could say to me that you couldn't say in front of—I mean—"

"Alone," the other girl repeated. "Tell them . . . tell them to leave . . . Kristian and the others. . . ."

Kristian scowled. "Darling, I'm your husband. I wish to stay."

The huge eyes entreated. "Just for a moment, Kristian, that's all."

"Very well, then, if you insist."

Within minutes, the doctor, Fanny and Kristian had stepped into the hotel corridor and Adrienne was alone with her rival. The pale fingers groped for her own.

"Adrienne, I always wanted to be like you . . . did you know that?" Primrose managed a small, wan smile. Then she groaned and arched her back as a contraction racked her body. Tensely Adrienne waited. Thus had she herself struggled in order to give birth to Barrie. But she had survived, and it was plain that Primrose would not. She fought back a wild pity.

At last the contraction was over, and Primrose sank back into the mattress, weaker than ever.

"I'm dying," she whispered, in a voice softer than the beat of butterfly wings.

"No! No, you're not!" Adrienne squeezed the small hand, not knowing what else to do. Again she battled the urge to rush out of the room, to flee from the sight of the suffering eyes.

"Yes, I am, I know it . . ."

"You shouldn't tire yourself by talking, Primrose. The baby—"

The violet eyes had darkened almost to black. "My baby will die, Adrienne. It is being born much too early. I know it's true, I can tell by the look on Kristian's face."

Adrienne was incapable of replying.

"Adrienne . . ." Primrose licked dry lips. "You must marry Kristian."

"What?" Adrienne's surprise was so great that she jumped backwards, dropping Primrose's hand, which fell limply onto the coverlet.

"I said you must marry him. He loves you, didn't you know that? He always has, from the first I knew him. . . ."

Adrienne stared down at Primrose. She felt oddly naked, as if the other had managed to tear away half of her skull and look directly into her soul. "But how do you know?"

"I know." Primrose's lips were curved into a faint smile. "I always knew. I loved him, and I didn't care that he loved you. He spoke of you often. He even cried your name once in his sleep . . . Oh, yes, Adrienne, I heard him. Once he wept—"

"Oh—"

Adrienne sat frozen by the bed, a thousand emotions awhirl in her head. She did not know what to say. All of these months she had disliked Primrose. Had made fun of her name, had looked down on her for being foolish and stage-struck and shallowly pretty. And yet the other girl had been more than these things. She had known that

Kristian loved another woman, had known it and adored him anyway, without demands.

She, Adrienne, had always demanded. . . .

"I want him to have you now." The voice had faded almost beyond a whisper, so that Adrienne had to bend close to hear it. "He needs you, Adrienne. I know it, I've always known it. He doesn't need me, you see. I was the one who needed him. Well, that's done now. . . ."

"Primrose!" Adrienne's voice caught in a sob. "Primrose, you mustn't talk like that!"

"I have to talk." Again the slight body stiffened. "God—another pain . . . oh! It hurts."

Silently Adrienne sat while Primrose suffered. Each twist and arch of the other girl's body was as if it were happening to her.

"Adrienne," the small voice panted at last, "you . . . you must marry him. You're right for him. I was never . . ."

A twitch, an ugly twitch of the frail body. Eyelids fluttered. Primrose's chest rose and fell shallowly. The hot stench of blood filled the air.

"Primrose!" Adrienne was shaking her, shouting. "Primrose! You can't die yet, you can't! Kristian!" She was screaming. "Kristian, Fanny! Doctor! You must come at once! Please hurry!"

An hour later, Primrose was dead, and so was the child she had struggled to birth.

Adrienne found that she could not leave the room, but was drawn, as if she could not help herself, to the scene around the bed. The doctor was glum and preoccupied as he moved about his duties. Fanny Pepper, pale and distressed, attempted to follow the physician's instructions, wiping now and then at a tear which ran jaggedly down her cheeks.

Adrienne, too, felt like weeping. Like giving way to the hard knot which was locked inside her breast, until her grief and pain flowed freely.

Kristian was like a man possessed, lashing out at the harried doctor, even at Primrose herself.

"Live, darling, *live,*" he ordered his dying wife

hoarsely. "Don't give up, you've got to fight it, Primrose! Fight! Life is too damned precious . . ."

He turned to the doctor. "My God, isn't there anything you can do for her, anything? Must she just lie there like that and—and fade away?"

The doctor was angry. "Yes, Mr. King, I'm afraid that she must. Don't you think I've done all I can? Don't you think that if there was more to do I would do it?" His shrug was bleak. "Perhaps in a generation or two, there will be more which can be done to save women from dying in childbed. Meanwhile—"

The look of agony on Kristian's face tore at Adrienne's heart. She stepped forward to the bed, touched his arm.

"Kristian—"

But it was as if he had not even noticed her presence.

He was kneeling by the bed now, his face buried in Primrose's breast.

Her death, when it came, was as soft as a flower petal. The small body twitched once, then seemed imperceptibly to relax. Adrienne, blinking back hot tears, saw that a hint of color had tinged the waxy cheeks. There was a serene curve to Primrose's mouth, as if she had not found any unpleasant surprises in death.

For a moment they all stood silently about the bed.

"It was entirely too soon," the doctor told them grimly, packing away his bag. "There was nothing I could do. She was completely unsuited to childbirth and should never have been allowed to become pregnant. Perhaps if she had had complete bed rest—"

"Oh, God. Dear God." Kristian sat in a chair, his body rigid. He had buried his face in his hands. "*I* did it to her. I wanted a child! And then I compounded it by taking her on tour. The trains, the constant riding in carriages, the unsettled life—"

"Kristian." Adrienne blinked back tears. She reached out to touch his shoulder, wanting to give comfort, but not knowing how. *He needs you, Adrienne. I know it, I've always known it. . . .*

Kristian moved away from her. "Don't touch me

right now, Adrienne. Please don't touch me. I—I must think."

"And I must leave. I have another call to make, a child with belly pains," the doctor announced uncomfortably. He closed the strap and picked up his leather bag. "About my charges. I trust that suitable arrangements will be made?"

Adrienne hurried him to the door, promising that his fee would be paid. Then she returned to the sitting room of the suite, where Kristian now stood stiffly by the window, staring down at the side street where the first early morning horse traffic had begun.

"She didn't deserve to die." His voice was bitter. "She should have lived to be eighty years old, surrounded by her children and her grandchildren. Instead—" He stopped and then went on. "Oh, God, Adrienne, I would have given anything for Primrose to have lived. I would have given up my play, my writing. I would have given up my very life—"

Adrienne stood stock-still, shock pouring through her. She could feel the heat of it in her throat and temples. So, she thought numbly, Kristian had loved Primrose. After all, he had loved her.

Kristian's voice went on dully, as if Adrienne were not even in the room.

"She was beautiful. As lovely as a flower that grows in the woods where there is no one to see it, no one at all. Perhaps she wasn't intelligent, perhaps she was often giddy and silly. But she was full of life and joy. And love . . ."

Chapter 29

"Well? And have you my money, Miss Gill, or must I provide our columnist friend with his best story of the year?"

It was the following morning, actually only hours after Primrose's death, although it seemed to Adrienne as if a thousand years had passed. Primrose's pathetic dying, Kristian's grief—it was nightmare, all of it. And now here was Xenos, like some white-crested Satan, to force her own problems back into sharp focus.

They sat again in the hotel lounge, occupying two chairs near the potted plants and the painted wisteria. A strong odor of brandy came from the magician. This time Elijah had accompanied Xenos and stood at attention behind his chair, wearing a black suit cut as flamboyantly as his master's.

There were other guests in the lobby this morning, and, as Xenos had asked his question, several heads had turned in their direction.

"Please," Adrienne begged. "Lower your voice, Mr. Shane, or everyone in the lounge will hear you and know of our affairs!"

"*Your* affairs, you mean."

Xenos inclined his head mockingly. There was a pause. Adrienne began to chatter desperately, at random, anything to give a little extra time, to put off the moment when money must be discussed.

"Elijah," she said rapidly. "It has been such a long

time since I saw you! Do you remember helping me to put on my stage make-up for the first time? You were only a child then!"

"Yes." Elijah's full lips twitched, and his brown eyes, full of intelligence, stared at her for a moment before looking away. Xenos had been right. Elijah was a beautiful young man. His skin was the color of coffee mixed with cream, and his hair was a tightly-fitting cap of black curls. His body was lithe, full of cat-grace.

The talk went on, brittle.

"Now I am a magician myself, second in skills only to Xenos," Elijah told her proudly. "I am developing my own—"

"Enough of such chattering," the magician interrupted. "I am here for my money, Miss Gill, as we discussed yesterday. I trust that you have it?"

The money. With Primrose's death, there had barely been time to think of it.

She faced him, her hands clenched in her lap. She had put on a dove-gray wool gown, and knew that she looked her best, for the gray brought out the pale blond highlights of her hair, which she had pulled back into a simple French knot, allowing a few ringlets to fall onto her temples and neck. Shaken as she was by Primrose's death, she had still forced herself to dress carefully. She must not let Xenos see her fear.

Now she tried to speak steadily.

"I don't have the money. At least, not very much. It has been difficult. Only an hour ago I telegraphed my banker in New York asking for more funds, but—but there is a problem. You see, my account has grown low, and most of my money has gone to pay bills and to provide for my cottage at Saratoga Springs—"

Her hands twisted in her lap. "I may look wealthy," she admitted. "But all is not as it seems."

Xenos leaned toward her. His black eyes raked over her, and unpleasantly she was reminded of the moment at the Brittania when he had closed the door of the prop room behind her and she had known there was no escape.

She suppressed a shudder of terror. She was no longer a frightened young girl, she reminded herself sharply. She was a grown woman now, an accomplished actress, a well-known one. And this was no isolated backstage room, but the public lobby of a hotel, with plenty of people close at hand. Surely nothing could happen to her here . . .

"You are a star, my sweeting, in one of the major plays of the season, a play which has attracted much talk and controversy," the magician went on. "According to the *Mirror*, you have embarked on a very profitable road tour, with added matinees and benefits. When you return to New York, the play will again have a long run in that city." Xenos's smile was triumphant. "So, please, my little wild rose, do not cry poverty to me."

"But you don't understand—"

"I understand that you are trying to play pretty games, Miss Gill. You, a novice, dare to attempt to play chess with a master. Well, you are being very foolish indeed. There is no way you can hope to win."

She gazed at him. Perspiration was running down her sides beneath the fashionable gown. "But, I tell you, I don't have that much money—not now, not until the end of the tour!"

"You promised it to me, my sweeting."

"Yes, I know I did. And I did telegraph my banker. I'm sure he'll send me what he can—"

"And the rest?" Xenos' eyes fixed her.

She squirmed uneasily in the wicker chair, fear coursing through her. "I'll get it somehow."

"Very well. I will send Elijah to the theater tonight. He can pick up what you have now. Elijah is my boy, aren't you, Elijah?"

Xenos Shane reached up and put one gnarled hand on the youth's arm, patting him as possessively as if he had been an animal. For an instant Adrienne thought she saw a flash of resentment in the young man's eyes. Then it was gone.

"Tonight? But it's so soon!" she protested. "And to send Elijah to the theater will only attract attention!"

"Then you will want to pay him quickly, so that he will go away."

"But—later?" she asked tightly. "It will be difficult sometimes to get payments to you. To what address should I send them?"

"Ah, my dear, it is not necessary for you to worry about that. I will find you when I need you."

"But I won't know how to reach you—"

The magician's eyes were cold. "I tell you, you don't need to reach me. The important thing is that you give me a schedule of the tour, so that I can reach you. And don't forget, my sweeting, about our columnist friend, Mr. Stauffer. Rumor has it that the man hates you because you slapped his face and rejected his amorous advances."

Xenos's chuckle was somehow very ugly. "I am sure he would be delighted, Miss Gill, to learn your full story. Revenge is sweet, isn't it? Ah, yes, very sweet indeed."

Adrienne had the numbed feeling that nightmare had settled down around her shoulders, thick and viscous as molasses. Later in the day, Kristian made arrangements for Primrose's body to be shipped by train back to New York so she could be buried there in the family plot. He himself, he announced, would accompany her. His understudy could take over the role of Ahmad.

"But the play—" William Mancin protested. "The audiences, they expect—"

"Let them expect what they will! Primrose is going home and I must go with her. Surely you can understand that! I need a week and I will take it. The audiences be damned."

Mancin threw out his hands. "But the play, the publicity—"

"Damn the publicity! Damn everything!" Never had Adrienne seen Kristian so coldly furious. "My wife is dead, can't anyone get that through their head? She is dead, and it's my fault."

Adrienne, hearing this conversation, had to swallow hard against the wad of dry cotton which seemed to fill her entire gullet. Yes, Kristian had loved Primrose, that was painfully apparent. Now he grieved deeply for her. And there was nothing that she, Adrienne, could do.

That night, adding to her feeling that life had nightmarishly slipped awry, Elijah was among the crowd which pushed its way backstage after the performance. Adrienne, still in costume, managed to slip away into the corridor which led off the greenroom to the boiler area.

"I don't have much money yet," she whispered quickly to Elijah. "Just this little bit of pocket money, that's all." She pressed it into his hand. "The funds from New York have not yet come. Please, could you ask Mr. Shane to be patient? I—I'll get more, I swear I will."

Elijah's face was carefully blank. His brown eyes flickered to the Passion Star which she wore about her neck. "He told me to get it tonight."

"But I've just told you that I don't have it!"

Elijah shrugged. "Very well, Miss Gill. I'll go back and tell him what you've said. But don't be surprised if he is angry."

Dismay filled her, mingled with a cold fear. She remembered what Xenos had said, about the three of them, Xenos, Elijah and Barrie, making a fine team. . . .

"Please," she begged. She clutched at the black youth's arm. "Please, Elijah, you can talk to him, I know you can. Tell him I'm willing to pay, and I *will* pay. I'll give anything he asks. All I need is a little more time!"

Elijah's eyes looked away.

"Elijah!" Her fingers squeezed into his arm. "Elijah, he has you trapped every bit as much as he does me. Doesn't he? Am I not right? Oh, please, help me if you can. Persuade him to wait. Maybe, oh, maybe there will be some way I can help you. . . ."

An odd expression crossed the black youth's face, and for a fleeting second Adrienne was sharply reminded of the old Elijah.

"There is no way I can be helped now." Elijah said it slowly, his mouth bleak. Then he hesitated. "But, yes, I will talk to him. Perhaps—yes, I'll tell him that you'll give him the money in Detroit. That is two weeks away on your tour. Surely you can manage that, Miss Gill? Surely you have resources?"

She fought back panic. "I—I don't know, Elijah. But I'll try!"

Nightmare. It seemed to go on and on, filling up her life, overflowing at night into choking, perspiring dreams. Her attempts to raise money were futile. Her banker in New York sent word that her account was low, and more funds could not be raised unless she put the home in Saratoga on the market. Unfortunately, it was a poor time of year to sell, and it might take some time—perhaps even six months—to realize any profit from that source.

Desperately Adrienne went to William Mancin, to ask about the possibility of an advance on her salary.

"You're not the only one strapped for cash, Adrienne," he told her. "It seems all actors are profligate when it comes to funds—is it a requirement of the trade? But Phineas Magruder has been emphatic—no advances on pay until the end of the tour."

"But I need it! I would surely pay him back—"

Mancin's eyes held pity. "If you need a small personal loan, perhaps I can arrange something."

"No—no—" She turned away.

"You might try to sell some of your clothing or jewels then, my dear," Mancin's voice called after her. "Surely you don't need twenty trunkfuls of finery, do you? That should be more than enough to pay for your new gowns, or whatever female fripperies you feel you must have now."

"Never mind, it's all right." She said it dully, fleeing to the privacy of her dressing room in order to hide the panic that consumed her. Did Mancin think she was so shallow as to want money merely to buy more dresses or bonnets? Besides, even the sale of all of her possessions would not provide the sums Xenos Shane demanded.

An oddly upsetting event happened one afternoon when Adrienne idly picked up a copy of *Frank Leslie's Illustrated Weekly*. There was an article about the crippled financier, Martin Greggori, a man well-known for his philanthropies. He had been interviewed at length about his life, and part of the article had been devoted to the accident which crippled him.

"As I lay there in the Paris street unconscious and nearly mortally injured, I was robbed," he was quoted as saying. "My wallet, my watch, everything was gone, including a precious stone which had been given to me by someone I loved."

A precious stone. Adrienne put aside the magazine uneasily. For some reason she kept thinking of Xenos Shane's story of how he had stolen the Passion Star from a man severely hurt in a carriage accident. That, too, had happened in Paris.

Was it somehow possible that *Martin Greggori* was the real owner of the Passion Star?

Oh, but surely that was preposterous, she told herself rapidly. She turned her attention to other things, once more pushing Martin Greggori out of her head.

Her malaise seemed to affect the rest of the cast. All missed Primrose, for she had been popular and had made many friends. And now Kristian's absence, like a bad omen, seemed to haunt them.

The part of Ahmad was being played by James Torrenta, Kristian's understudy, much to the dismay of theater patrons, who, in increasing numbers, demanded their money back. They wished to see the famous Kristian King, they told the ticket-sellers angrily, not a mere understudy!

Disaster seemed to dog them. Torrenta's presence subtly threw off the rhythm of the performance. One calamitous night Adrienne, racked with worry over Xenos Shane's demands, actually dropped a whole page of script from one of her speeches. That night the show reaped only perfunctory curtain calls, and there had been heard from the back of the theater, loud, chilling and unmistakable, the sound of booing.

In the greenroom, no one spoke to her. Bettina Smithe and Torrenta whispered together in a corner, Bettina's face bright with malice, the conversation stopping when Adrienne approached. And William Mancin asked her to come to his office.

"You are going to have to watch yourself, Adrienne —and that bottle of whisky you hide in your dressing room," he told her furiously. "Who do you think you are?

Nell Gwynne? The great Rachel? Well, you're not. You are only a working actress, the same as anyone else. And when Kristian comes back and hears about tonight's disaster—"

"Surely you won't tell him?" she whispered, feeling sick.

"I certainly do plan to tell him."

"But, it wasn't as it seems! Oh, I did have a drink before the show, yes, but it was the understudy who threw me off. He missed his cue, and that made me miss mine. It wasn't my fault, I tell you!'"

"I don't want to hear excuses! The fact is, Adrienne, that you dropped nearly an entire page of the script. I know it, the whole cast knows it. No amount of fabrication can change that, for it happened. You were drunk. Drunk again. Admit it."

Drunk again. Admit it.

She felt the deep red flush begin at her breast and travel painfully up to her face. She would not beg. No matter what happened, she would never do that.

"I think I am . . . tired," she said, her voice thick. "I think I will go back to my hotel now, and rest."

"Do that." Mancin reached for the copy of the playscript, a thin, paperbound book, and threw it at her. "And why don't you take a copy of the script with you? You can go over your lines. Word for word, Adrienne. Perhaps that will help—if anything can."

She took the script home—she had sat in bed and cried over it until her eyes were burning and swollen. Then, grimly, she reviewed every line of every one of Fatima's speeches. She would not fail again—she must not! She would drink nothing. She would toss out her supply of whisky and refrain from buying more.

She would be good again, she would be the old Adrienne Gill, forging a tight, thrilling bond with her audience, a bond which could not be broken . . .

"*She* seems a bit under the weather today, don't you think? Or, rather, under the influence?"

A gust of female laughter.

"Well, that's nothing new, is it? Everyone knows

440

she's been drinking like a fish. It's a wonder Kristian keeps her on at all."

"We all know why he does that!"

Another titter, and then Bettina Smithe and Gertrude Wing strolled from behind the back of the *Passion Star* set, leaving Adrienne, who had come onstage to retrieve her shawl, frozen at what she had overheard.

The two actresses disappeared in the direction of the backstage staircase. Their laughter echoed.

Everyone knows she's been drinking like a fish.

Adrienne waited until the sounds of their passage were gone. Then, grimly, she straightened her spine and walked toward the stairs, her chin held high. Let them talk—let them laugh at her! She was working on the Fatima role, harder than she had ever worked in her life, polishing up the part with a determination she had not known she possessed.

In a few days, she would be better than ever. Her performance would leave the audiences breathless in their seats.

She was Adrienne Gill, wasn't she?

A week later, Kristian rejoined the cast. His eyes were bleak, his face fined down and thinner, as if he had not been eating or sleeping well. Yet he was more arrogantly handsome than ever.

Before the performance Adrienne encountered him, in costume, on the narrow, chilly stairs which led from the dressing rooms of the theater to the stage.

"Kristian! You are back!" Despite the worry which gnawed at her, she could not conceal the joy she felt.

"Yes."

"Was the funeral very difficult?"

"Oh, God, Adrienne, you have no idea."

In a dull, flat voice, Kristian related the events of Primrose's burial, his words so vivid that Adrienne could see it all: the gray skies piled high with snow clouds, the somber carriage moving through the sooty streets of New York to the cemetery, the pathetic flower-draped casket.

At the gravesite, Primrose's two young sisters had sobbed bitterly, while Gloriane Magruder, pale and withdrawn in her black funeral garb, had refused the offer of a supporting arm from her husband and insisted upon walking by herself.

Afterwards, at the Magruder mansion, there had been a difficult scene. Gloriane Magruder, her face set, had blamed Kristian for taking Primrose away and making an actress of her.

"You uprooted my little girl and tore her away from where she belonged—this is your fault! Your fault!"

Phineas Magruder, too, had been full of anger, informing Kristian that he should never have taken his wife on tour, that it had been a criminal act for him to have done so.

Adrienne knew the pain this must have caused Kristian.

"Oh, darling—" She advanced a step upward on the stairs, her hands holding to the wooden support rail. "Oh, I'm sorry, so sorry that it all had to happen—"

His voice cut her off. "But it did happen, didn't it? And now, Adrienne, although I know you are sympathetic, there is much work to do before the show tonight. I am calling an extra rehearsal in ten minutes, and I expect you to be there. And to be there sober," he added sharply.

She stared at him.

"Yes, Adrienne, I want you cold sober for a change, so that we can get through a performance without you fluffing your lines or missing a cue. According to Mancin, you haven't been yourself in the past several days. You've been out of control, like a novice instead of a seasoned actress."

She was flushing. "I—I've been upset because of Primrose, and—and because of other things—"

"Upset or not, you've been a burden on the rest of the cast. Your timing has been poor, you've been throwing off the rhythm of the scenes—"

"Who says that?" she demanded.

"Bettina Smithe, for one. And others as well. I've noticed it. So have the critics."

"The critics?" She felt numbed, betrayed.

"Yes, just take a look at these clippings." Kristian fumbled beneath his costume and brought out a folded bit of paper. He held it up. "This is from the Washington paper. *'Miss Adrienne Gill, well-known actress and elegant member of the Scottish nobility, gave a flawed performance last night at the Ford Theater.'*"

"Oh!"

"And here's another one. *'Miss Gill, it appears, missed one whole page of her speech in her rendition of the part of the lovely Fatima.'*"

". . . I didn't see that one," she muttered, barely aware of what she said. A sick feeling, icy and horrid, possessed the pit of her belly. She advanced another step up the stairs, reaching for Kristian, entreating, knowing even as she did so that it was the wrong thing to do. Yet she could not seem to stop herself. "Kristian, I—I'll stop drinking. I promise I will!"

"Will you? You have assured me of that before. And what do I see when poor Primrose is calling for you and begs to see you? You come into her room smelling like a distillery!"

"I—oh, surely I didn't . . ."

She let her voice trail off. She felt stunned by the anger in Kristian's voice, the tormented look on his face. Why, he felt revulsion for her—distaste! Primrose had been wrong, so very wrong. Kristian didn't love her. He felt nothing for her at all.

Tears sprang to her eyes and angrily, proudly, she blinked them back.

"I must go and get ready for the rehearsal, then," she heard herself say.

"A good idea. And, Adrienne, there is one more thing."

She turned. "What is that?"

"I expect your performance tonight to be flawless, do you hear me? Or I swear to you that I will cut you from the part."

Kristian's mouth was grim. "I don't want to do it, and I won't unless it's necessary. But another actress could be brought in to play Fatima. An actress who

443

doesn't find it necessary to drink before the show in order to give herself courage, an actress who can deliver her lines without error. Think about it, Adrienne."

An actress who can deliver her lines without error . . .

How wrong Primrose had been! How very wrong!

Adrienne turned and rushed blindly back downstairs toward the haven of her own dressing room. Kristian didn't need her or love her. On the contrary, he despised her.

She had lost him forever.

Detroit, the riverport city which manufactured steamships, railway cars and stoves, was in the midst of a warm spell. Balmy air melted the last patches of snow which clung to the bricked streets and to the wooden planking which paved Woodward Avenue. A small boy tossed his cap into the air and ran after it, whooping. Fat robins hopped along the horsecar tracks, dodging the occasional vehicle which rumbled along.

But Adrienne could not regard these signs of spring with any joy. She felt numbed, leaden with her heartache and with her worry. Kristian was lost to her—as surely as if he had died. The meaning of her life, the very mainspring of it, had somehow wound down. For it had been Kristian, she realized, always Kristian to whom her thoughts had turned in the bad times, and in the good ones as well. Kristian who had always been there for her, even in the times when she was most angry at him.

Her career was sliding, Kristian was gone, Xenos Shane had made impossible financial demands, and it was only the recollection of *Maman*'s words which now carried her along, giving her the courage to face each bleak day. *You are so like her, full of spirit and temper. Adrienne LaRivière was a real woman, Addie. There was life in her, a spirit that could never be quenched!*

Like an ironic contrast to her despair, it was in Detroit that Fanny Pepper and William Mancin were married by a Justice of the Peace. The ceremony took place in the late afternoon of a melting spring day, and then the bridal couple returned to the theater for the evening performance.

As soon as the final curtain had dropped, the wedding celebration began. Cast members lugged in food from a nearby chop-house: beef and pork chops, fried lake trout, hashed brown potatoes, apple and blueberry pies. There was a wedding cake, adorned with flowers and leaves made of spun sugar, and a barrel of iced champagne. The food was laid out upon the battered table which ran the length of the greenroom of White's Theater, where *The Passion Star* was playing.

"Oh, it looks beautiful, all of it! Every last morsel!" Fanny's eyes sparkled. She rushed to the barrel, demanding that the champagne be opened immediately, so that the cast and crew could begin enjoying it.

Mancin, tall, thin, ungainly, was the same as usual in his good suit, but Fanny looked the prettiest that Adrienne had ever seen her. She had bought a new gown, a pale blue silk trimmed with row upon row of French eyelet lace. A high lace collar concealed the burn scars on her neck and chin. Dainty kid gloves covered her hands.

Her cheeks flaming with excitement, Fanny rushed around the greenroom, throwing her arms about cast members, and urging all to drink more champagne. Actors, grips, flymen, carpenters, ticket-takers, the call boy, and the gas table boy—no one had been left out tonight.

"After all," Fanny cried, "it's my wedding, mine and William's, and I want to celebrate among friends! Come on," she urged, her voice high, as if shaking away the troubles of the past weeks, ."Drink up, everyone, drink up! How many times does Fanny Pepper get married? I want everyone to be happy, happy!"

Happy. Adrienne stood in a corner of the greenroom and watched the merriment, feeling far removed from it all. She didn't belong here . . .

"Mama!" Barrie came running up to her and buried her face in Adrienne's skirt. "Mama, it's loud. The noises are so loud!"

"It's just the champagne corks popping," Adrienne

roused herself to say. "The sounds here in the greenroom are all magnified, it's really nothing to be frightened of—" For a brief moment it was as if she felt a bond between herself and her daughter. Barrie, too, had no place here tonight.

Members of the cast and crew surged past them, laughing, laden plates in hand. Bettina Smithe, on her third glass of champagne, sang a song from *Evangeline,* her voice trilling and perfectly on key.

"Mama—" Barrie's fingers continued to clutch at Adrienne's skirt. "The man, Mama. That man. I saw him again."

Adrienne stiffened. The noise of the party swirled around her, a counterpoint to nightmare, to the climax she had feared for these past two weeks.

"When did you see him?" she asked through tight lips.

"Today. Today in the alley. He was following us, Mama, when we came in the cab. Didn't you see him, Mama?"

"No, I . . . I didn't."

Xenos Shane, come to collect his money. Days had passed, more than sixteen of them, and she had almost allowed herself to hope that Xenos had given up, or changed his mind. What was she to do? Once, she realized dully, panic would have flooded her at the news that Xenos still waited. Now, she barely cared. Nothing mattered now. Nothing.

"Barrie," she heard herself ask calmly, "why didn't you tell me sooner that you saw him?"

The little girl was trembling. "Because, Mama, you were busy. You were in your dressing room and then you told me to go away, you wanted to rest—"

Adrienne flushed. She knelt down and grasped the child's shoulders, gazing into the wide gray eyes. "Barrie, will you promise me something? Swear you'll tell no one about this man, no one at all. *No one,* do you hear me? I want this to be our very own secret."

The little girl's gray eyes widened. "Do you mean that I can't tell Quince? Or Fanny? Or Kristian?"

"No! Tell no one!"

"All right." Barrie wriggled out of Adrienne's grasp and then went running toward the long table laden with food.

Slowly Adrienne rose to her feet. She made her way down the length of the greenroom toward the dressing room doors at its far end. The room was crowded, its usual vault-like chill dispelled by the warmth of many bodies. Women in the flowing robes of *Passion Star* costumes elbowed against grips and carpenters in work clothes.

Someone thrust a glass into her hand.

"Drink!" a man's voice commanded. It was James Torrenta, the understudy. "A pretty woman must not go dry, eh?"

The actor's eyes, she saw, were fastened on her bodice, where the upper part of her bosom peeped attractively through the filmy fabric of her third act costume. The Passion Star gleamed at her throat.

"No, thank you," she began faintly. "I don't want any . . . ."

"Of course you do. This is the very best French champagne, it would be a shame to waste it, would it not?"

Blindly Adrienne reached for the glass he handed her, barely noticing the dry flavor. Torrenta grinned at her, making a little drunken face.

"Good, isn't it? More women should try champagne, eh? Good way to drown your troubles, whatever they are. And you, you are expert at such things, aren't you, my love?"

He winked, as if the two of them shared some secret. Then the actor staggered away from her in the direction of the men's toilet.

Adrienne stood where she was, sipping her wine and letting the wedding celebration surge on around her. Laughter. Noise. The popping of more champagne corks. She felt far away from such gaiety.

It was not that she begrudged Fanny her happiness. Oh, surely she was not that small-minded and selfish! And yet the merriment here made her feel more bleak than ever. Even Kristian, she saw with a sidelong look

447

toward the far end of the greenroom, was enjoying himself, deep in discussion with Arthur Costigan, one of the male cast members.

For a moment she thought that he glanced in her direction, that their eyes met and touched. A curious little thrill ran through her—a small segment of that strong force which once had connected the two of them, as powerful as life itself. But then Kristian looked away, and she decided that she had been mistaken.

She tilted her glass and drank, draining the last of the bubbly wine. A warmth, the old, necessary, familiar warmth, began to spread through her veins like oil. She was drinking again, she realized dully. Yet what did it matter? The performance was over for tonight—and tomorrow was Sunday, a day of rest for the cast. And this was a party, a celebration for Fanny Pepper and William Mancin, who were to be married and happy.

Adrienne went to the long table, where another opened bottle of champagne waited. She refilled her glass. Then, once more, she drank deeply.

It was an hour later. The party was now in full swing, with another case of champagne sent for and half consumed. Laughter, increasingly drunken, echoed in the greenroom. Someone had dropped a glass on the floor, and now everyone had to walk in the crunching mess of spilled wine and broken glass. Quince, sitting in a corner, had quietly taken Barrie onto his lap, where the little girl watched the party with wide eyes.

"Well, Adrienne, too bad this isn't *your* wedding reception!"

Bettina Smithe sat on the end of the long table, swinging her fashionably booted feet. She puffed on an English cigarette, her green eyes narrowed at the smoke. Her eyes sparkled with relish, for actresses in 1874 were among the few women who dared to smoke in public.

"What do you mean?" Adrienne asked stiffly. The champagne had begun to swirl dizzily in her head, and she had difficulty pronouncing the words.

"Oh, don't play innocent. We all know about you and your hopeless infatuation for Kristian King. Did you know that we've been placing bets on whether or not you would win him? I've got my money on not."

Bets. They had placed bets.

Adrienne stared at the plump, blowsy actress.

"I don't believe you. Surely you're joking, Bettina."

"Joking? You're the joke, Miss Adrienne Gill!" Bettina's expression was malicious. "You're nothing but a drunken old has-been, and everyone knows it. See, we're placing bets on something else, too. And would you like to know what that is?"

"Yes," Adrienne said stonily, "I would."

"Why, maybe you already know. We've all made wagers, all of us! It's on the date Kristian King will kick you out of the play and replace you with someone else!"

Bettina's words were like blows to the pit of Adrienne's belly. *The date Kristian King will kick you out of the play* . . .

Humiliation etched her heart like hot acid. Her destiny, if she had ever had one, was gone. Vanished. Now she was nothing more than a laughing-stock, an actress who drank too much, who had lost the only man she could ever love, was soon to lose her leading role.

And soon perhaps there would be something else for people to laugh at, as well—Xenos Shane's incredible story of the girl who had grown up in the filthiest section of Glasgow, who had stolen a precious gem and was now a fugitive thief. . . .

You're nothing but a drunken old has-been. Wildly Adrienne thought of the conversations, recently, which had suddenly stopped as she approached, the sidelong looks from cast members, the whispers. Yes, Bettina was right. They were all laughing at her, snickering behind their backs. Bettina, Torrenta, all of the others with whom she worked, who comprised her entire world . . .

"Well?" Bettina giggled, puffing out a big plume of smoke. "What have you to say, Adrienne? Maybe you'd like to place a wager, too? We have a big pot now—perhaps you can bet on yourself and win it all back!"

"No . . . oh, no!"

It was nightmare.

Blindly Adrienne turned. She fled through the

crowded greenroom, past the clusters of actors and stage-hands jubilant with their celebration. Past Kristian, who, still in deep conversation with Arthur Costigan, did not even see her, or, if he did, chose to ignore her. Past Barrie, cuddled on Quince's lap half asleep. Past William Mancin, half-drunk now with champagne and bride-groom's pride.

We all have wagers on it, all of us ... whether you would win him or not ... the date Kristian King will kick you out of the play ... perhaps you can bet on yourself and win it all back....

Unseeing, her mind exploding with anguish, she ran.

Chapter 30

She fled, lifting the full white gauze skirts of her Fatima costume high so that she would not trip over them. She raced blindly up the narrow stairs, then ran through the darkened, cavernous backstage with its flies hung with the ghostly shapes of curtains and spare sets. Other shapes loomed at her—the back of the *Passion Star* set still in place onstage, a tall paint scaffolding, a gas table with its pipes and knobs and fixtures, the sandbags which weighted down the objects suspended by hemp ropes in the flies.

Her world, familiar and yet strange, mocked her tonight.

A brick wall came at her—the back wall of the stage—and then she was pushing her way out of the stage door and into the alley. Her slippers echoed on the bricks. A dog, rooting in a garbage barrel, looked up to bark menacingly at her. Adrienne uttered a little scream of despair.

She dodged the dog and kept on running. *We've got bets*, Bettina had taunted. *We've all got bets. . . .*

At the far end of the alley, where it opened onto the street, she saw the row of buggies and carriages waiting for theater patrons, and the dark shape of a man.

Too late, she drew up short.

"Well, Adrienne, my sweeting, and where do you think you are going? Surely it is a sin to leave a party so early."

A booming, theatrical voice filled the alley. It was

Xenos Shane, of course. In her anguish she had nearly forgotten about him.

"What . . . what do you want?"

"Why, my money, of course. I would have sent Elijah to pick it up for me, but it seems that Elijah has run away, the ingrate. After all he owes me."

So Elijah had, after all, won his freedom. Adrienne had time for a brief second's satisfaction.

"Money?" She barely knew what she said, heard her own voice blurt out as if it were not a part of her at all. "I've been able to raise only a very small amount, and I—I don't have it with me—"

"Why not? I want it, and I want it now. I have followed you here to Detroit to get it, and I don't give up easily."

The magician stepped toward her, moving surprisingly fast for a man of his age and bulk. Again the arthritic hands, like the twisted roots of trees, reached for her.

Terrified, she jerked backwards.

"Mama! Mama! The bad man!"

The cry, high and piping, came from behind her. There was the sound of a child's steps, and Adrienne whirled about.

"Barrie!"

The little girl, her hair touseled, had toddled out into the alley, her small face screwed up with worry.

"Mama, Mama, the bad man might come, and I don't want him to—" Then Barrie saw Xenos step out of the shadows and suppressed a cry.

Adrienne fought back her own fear. Her voice was urgent. "Barrie, darling, you must go back into the theater at once!"

"You come, too, Mama. The bad man, he'll hurt you, Mama—"

Adrienne caught her breath. Barrie's gray eyes were swimming with tears. At this moment they did not resemble Barrett's at all. Why, perhaps they never had. Barrie was herself, Adrienne had the swift thought. She was not her father, she was not anyone else, only her own self.

Xenos took a step toward the child.

"Barrie," Adrienne repeated, "go back into the theater right now!"

But Barrie, confused and frightened, thrust her thumb into her mouth. Then she ran toward her mother and threw her arms around Adrienne's skirts.

"Ah!" Like a swift old spider, Xenos Shane lunged forward and snatched the child from Adrienne. Barrie dangled from his arms, too terrified to sob.

"Well, Miss Gill?" Xenos's smile, heavily shadowed in the darkness, was frightening. "Now I have her, don't I? And don't you think that this little sweetmeat would make a fine addition to my entourage? There is much I could teach her, ah, yes, much indeed."

This little sweetmeat . . . much I could teach her . . . It was as if a taint of corruption had come from Hell. Horror pounded in Adrienne like the beat of a drum. She thought of Elijah, of herself being raped in the property room of the Brittania so many years ago.

A fierce protectiveness filled her. It didn't matter about herself—what she had suffered was over now. But this was her child being threatened, her own little daughter, a piece of herself.

Instinctively, Adrienne reacted. She lunged toward the magician, her right arm outthrust stiffly, and rammed him in the center of the chest with the rigid palm of her hand.

It was a trick she had learned long ago, in the wild, tumbling days of her childhood.

The magician was caught off balance. He uttered a stifled cry and then he and the child went falling backwards against the brick wall of the theater.

Adrienne ran forward and snatched up her daughter from Xenos Shane's grasp. She aimed a sharp kick at his jawline and heard with satisfaction the sound of his muffled groan. Then she was racing with Barrie toward the stage door. She yanked it open, encountered Kristian standing on the other side, and thrust her child into his startled arms.

"Adrienne! My God, Adrienne, what—"

But she did not wait to hear what Kristian might say. She whirled about and fled into the alley again, the heels of her slippers skidding on the uneven bricks. She dodged past a lunging, bleeding Xenos Shane and raced toward the mouth of the alley. She was free . . . free . . .

Shame drove her, shame and despair.

She did not know how long she ran, only that she pelted down streets and around corners until her breath strangled in her throat, until needles seemed to jab into her ribs, stitching her with pain. There were times when she thought she heard footsteps behind her, the pounding echo of other feet running. Or was it only the frantic echo of her terror?

She paused by a street lamp to catch her breath, sobbing.

Voices clamored in her head, taunting her. *Adrienne, you must marry Kristian. . . . Oh, God, Adrienne, I would have given anything for Primrose to have lived. . . . You have been a burden on the rest of the cast. . . . Another actress could be brought in to play Fatima. . . . Think about it, Adrienne . . . think about it. . . .*

Gradually her breathing slowed. In her wild, headlong run, she had damaged the heel of one of her shoes. Now it had come off so that she could not stand evenly. She slid out of both slippers and threw them into the gutter. She would walk barefoot, she decided dully. What did anything matter now?

She looked about her. She was by the waterfront, she knew, for she could smell water and see, through a gap in a pair of buildings, lantern lights carried on a boat. She gulped in air, rubbing at her sides until the stitches abated. Then, blindly, she plunged on, past frame lodging houses, carpenters' shops and wagonmakers, past warehouses and shipyards bristling with masts, with winches and the darkened forms of paddleboat steamers.

On a corner a saloon had been built into the first floor of a narrow, three-story building. Its lower windows gleamed with gaslight. *Blocker's,* the painted sign said. More signs advised her to try Gray's Ales and "our 20 cent stews."

In the street, carriage wheels suddenly rattled, and Adrienne whirled about to see a public cab bearing down on her. It contained a man in a dark suit, his face in the darkness a blur. Panic pushed through her. What if it were Xenos Shane? He could easily have hired a hack and followed her here, for there had been several waiting outside the theater.

Three men pushed their way out of the saloon. The opened door released the sounds of people enjoying themselves—the high titter of female laughter, deeper male belly-laughs.

The cab rumbled closer.

Adrienne ran toward the saloon and yanked open its door.

Gaslight gleamed off the elaborately carved mahogany bar with its display of polished glasses and bottles. An ornate cash register caught the light. A bartender in shirtsleeves gossiped with a customer. The room itself was crowded with men in workclothes, leaning at the bar or seated at small tables. Two or three women, clad in sleazy, ill-fitting dresses, occupied tables, as well. One of them was smoking a cigarette.

All looked up curiously as Adrienne stumbled into the room. She stood for a moment trying to quell the frightened thumping of her heart, to grow accustomed to the murky, smoky light. Had the man in the carriage been Xenos Shane? She had not seen him clearly enough to be sure. His face had been merely a blur.

She caught her breath and plunged through the crowded room toward an empty table near the back. Nervously she sat down, already wishing that she had not come.

"Eh, and what is it we have here, Bob?"

Two men seated at the table next to hers nudged each other. Their eyes raked over her. They were sailors or tugboat men, she supposed dully, both of them in their thirties, one with a drooping mustache, the other with a full, drooping beard. Both had hard-bitten faces roughened from the outdoors. Her father, Jack McGill, she thought with a strange twist of her heart, had been a man like these.

She sat uncomfortably, not knowing what to do. The

men were staring at her openly, at the diaphanous white gauze costume with its low bodice, its flowing folds of material. Their eyes traveled hungrily over her breasts, over the star sapphire which she wore at her throat.

She looked down at the tabletop, flushing.

"Well, Missy, what'll you have?" The bartender had sauntered to her table and now looked down at her with contempt. She was thankful that her long skirt concealed her bare feet.

"A whiskey," she managed to tell him. "Of the kind made by Mr. I. W. Harper."

"Harper's?" The bartender raised his eyebrows. "Yes, ma'am."

Minutes later she had already downed her first shot, nearly choking on the burning fluid which seared its way down her throat and gullet. Whatever the whiskey was, she knew with anger, it was not I. W. Harper's.

"Well, and ain't you a pretty one? Where did you come from? A fancy society ball? Or mebbe a cathouse?" Laughter roared. One of the sailors, the bearded one, had left his own table to slip into the empty chair beside Adrienne.

"Please—I don't wish company."

"What? On a Saturday night, a pretty like you wants to be alone? Aw, now—"

"Please!" Despair washed through her.

"Ah, you're pretty, you are." The man leaned toward her, his movements fluid. He stared at her breasts.

Adrienne's heart sank. How far she had come from the theater world she knew! Here in this Detroit dockside saloon, she was sure that they had never heard of Adrienne Gill, the actress. Her hard work, the long, grueling hours, the traveling and sacrifices, all were nothing here. In this dark drinking house, her talents and ability had no value.

A chill froze through her, a deep, icy fear. It was as if some vital part of her had been erased, leaving her bereft, leaving her nothing, less than nothing. What had her life come to? What had *she* come to? To be trapped here in this smoky saloon and mistaken for a prostitute

—for surely that was what the man thought she was—was nightmare.

The bearded sailor was signaling the bartender.

"Bring this little lady another drink—she looks like she's mighty thirsty."

The bartender grinned and winked. Then both men laughed loudly.

Her cheeks stinging, Adrienne waited for the drink to arrive. What was she doing here in this murky, sordid place? She should not have come. Yet somehow the prospect of the drink kept her sitting at the table, nervously twisting her hands.

When the whiskey came, she reached for it and downed it thirstily, enduring the burning of her throat and palate for the relief that would come, the gauzy curtain which could soften and dull, making life bearable. . . .

"Thirsty, are you, honey? You downed that one in nothing flat. Want another? I'll buy you all you want, old Bob ain't cheap, is he?"

The sailor looked about him for affirmation, and with a sinking heart Adrienne realized that other men had drawn chairs up to her table—five, six of them, all with weatherbeaten faces and hands roughened by years of outdoor work. A musky smell came from them, comprised of sour sweat, unwashed bodies, beer and cigars.

"Naw—" A short, bandy-legged little man with enormous forearms was at her elbow. "Naw, I'll buy the next one for her."

"*I'll* do it, *I* was the one seen her first, didn't I, Jacko? I was the one spotted her when she walked in, a fine one she is, a jewel—"

Voices bickered about her. A softness was spreading through Adrienne's veins, blurring her senses. She downed the last swallow of her drink, loathing herself, but unable to stop. She had to have this drink—and the next one which was to come. She needed them both urgently, for without them she could not endure.

The saloon was murky with smoke and filled with the shouts of the drinkers. A woman—surely a prostitute in this company—giggled. There was the greasy smell of

457

frying chops and kidneys, the malty, dark odor of beer and ale. The men crowded about her, their laughter suggestive.

Another drink came. Who had finally paid for it? She had no idea, only that it was here, that she was swallowing it as if it were her salvation.

The little bandy-legged man leaned closer to her. He grinned at her.

"Honey? Honey? Do you want . . ."

Somehow another man was at her left, his knee rubbing against her own.

Dimly she was aware of her danger.

". . . if you want another drink, honey, I know where we can get a whole bottle for ourselves—won't cost us nothing, little sweetheart, and there'd be plenty of it, all you could put down. . . ."

The man's voice seemed to come close, then recede. Now, at last, Adrienne could feel the fuzziness grow in her head, the soft, languorous ripples running up and down her veins, dulling her fears.

You're destined, daughter. Destined. Why was it that *Maman*'s voice seemed to speak in her head, mocking her, taunting her? For she wasn't destined at all. She never had been. There was only this, this sordid saloon, these men crowded about her, thinking her easy prey, no better than they.

Adrienne looked about her and was aware of more laughter coming from the door, where yet another drinker had just joined the crowd. From the back she saw that he was tall, like Kristian, yet obviously he belonged here, for he blended in with the bar crowd, clapping his hand across the back of one of the dock workers. Men guffawed, and moved to make room for him.

Adrienne felt herself begin to sway in her chair. Voices buzzed about her.

"Looks all fancy, don't she? Like one of them there actresses. Wonder can she sing and dance, or only do just what any other whore can do?"

"Pretty she is, Jacko, and look—easy it will be—"

Laughter. Loud, suggestive.

The saloon seemed blurred, as if a layer of cotton

batting protected her from what was happening. This was only a dream, she told herself hazily, or a scene from a play.

She felt a hand beneath her elbow. It lifted her to her feet.

"This way, honey, if you want to go and get that other bottle I was tellin' you about. It's in the back room, old Jones the barkeep saves it for me special. . . ."

"I . . . I don't know . . . ."

"Aw, sure you do, honey. I'll give you all you want to drink—"

Hands groped for her, grasping her buttocks, her shoulders, her elbows, half-lifting her from the floor, propelling her toward the back of the saloon.

"No—Please—"

But her protest faded away. What did it matter? What did anything matter now? She had, at last, descended as low as her father, Jack McGill. Now there was nothing left.

The back room of the saloon was used to store empty cases of beer and whiskey. More empties were piled helter skelter against one wall. There was a cluttered pigeonhole desk, and a dilapidated couch was jammed against the other wall. The couch was covered by a soiled blanket, evidently for use by the bartender when business was poor.

It was toward the couch that Adrienne felt herself being carried. Fear had started to penetrate the haze of the whiskey she had drunk, and now she began to struggle and scream, her voice hoarse with a deep, hopeless despair.

"Aw—aw, little lady, don't carry on, we ain't going to *hurt* you, we're only going to *fuck* you—"

Laughter, boisterous and sexual.

"No—oh, please, no! Dear God, I only thought—I didn't mean—"

But they paid her no heed.

She felt herself being flung down on the couch. Hands tore at her bodice, ripping away the fabric of her gown until her breasts were exposed. More hands grabbed the hem of her gown, yanking it up. Only the Passion Star remained, and soon it, too, would be ripped from her throat like a prize.

Now not even the whiskey could dull her terror—nothing could. They were going to tear her clothes off and they were going to rape her, and nothing could stop them, nothing. Hideously she was aware that other saloon patrons had crowded to the door of the storeroom, and were peering in and yelling encouragement, as if this were a bear-baiting or a dog-fight.

You're destined, daughter, destined . . . .

Hands ripped away the last shreds of her Fatima costume, baring her nudity.

"*Maman!*" she shrieked, the cry seeming to come from her very heart. "Oh, God, *Maman*—"

A heavy body pressed down on hers, pinning her to the couch so that she could barely breathe. Male voices rose with excitement and lust. A beer-smelling mouth came cramming down on hers, drowning out her screams.

This was hell, Adrienne thought wildly. It was hell, and she was caught in it; dear, merciful God, this was what her drinking had brought her to—

And then the raucous voices changed. A note of anger had crept into them, thwarted anger. Adrienne was dimly aware that the heavy weight of the man over her body had lifted.

There was a smacking sound, fist on flesh. Someone cried out, his voice full of pain and surprise.

"*Adrienne!* For God's sake, Adrienne, get up, will you? Get up and run!"

It was Kristian's voice.

Adrienne could not believe it.

Kristian was here in this sleazy Detroit bar, his face contorted with savagery as he smashed his fist into the face of the man who had been attempting to rape her, at the same time elbowing another dockworker back.

"Kristian—"

Blood was running down Kristian's cheekbone.

"Don't talk, girl, just get out of here, will you?"

The fuzzy blur of the alcohol was gone now, as if sluiced away by cold spring water. Adrienne gathered her legs beneath her. She snatched at the dirty woolen blanket which covered the couch, pulled it about herself, and ran.

Her bare feet stumbled on the rough paving, and she knew from the pain that they must be bleeding. The blanket flapped from her shoulders like a ludicrous cape, barely covering her. Deep black shadows sprawled across her path, and she uttered a choked shriek and plunged through them.

She ran. Shouts came from the saloon, cries of rage, the sound of smashing glass. Kristian was battling the dockworkers on her behalf. Shame filled her with its hot ire, making her flight even more desperate. For Kristian to have seen her like that—naked, abject, brought lower than the worst of the women in that wretched saloon—

It wasn't to be borne.

She raced on, impelled by her despair, knowing only that she had to run, to run. . . .

Ten minutes later she had slowed to a limping, gasping walk. Her heart, underneath the Passion Star, was slamming heavily. She put a trembling hand to the jewel. It was as if the sapphire, too, were beating with her pulse. *Drunk,* it seemed to accuse. *Drunk . . . failure . . . failure . . .*

Catching her breath, she looked about her. She had passed what seemed like miles of freight cars, and now there were vast stretches of derelict houses and shanties edged along the river. Half-collapsing porches stretched out over the water on pilings, and tiny piers teetered. She could smell the strong stench of rotting fish, of garbage and slops tossed carelessly away. From one of the sagging houses came the low, monotonous sound of a woman sobbing.

Adrienne shuddered and stumbled on.

After a time a light caught her eye and, ahead of her, she saw a long, low building—evidently a warehouse, for a series of heavy log jetties projected from it over the water, and a tangle of ships' masts raked the sky. Crates and piles of burlap sacks were piled on the pier, and a gas lamp burned near a huge winch.

Slowly Adrienne limped toward the light, pausing beneath its yellow glow to rest. Then, slowly, not knowing quite why she did it, she slipped the gold chain off her neck and stood with the Passion Star cupped in her palm.

She held the sapphire up to the flickering light. The stone, with its flamboyant six-legged star, shone up at her. It seemed to pulse and flare with a life of its own. It was almost as if the girl who had once worn it was still present within the sapphire, laughing at Adrienne. . . .

Her hand clenched convulsively over the pendant, shutting it off from view.

There *was* no lovely young girl, or vengeful king, or passionate lover. Hadn't Xenos Shane told her so? The story of the Passion Star was only that, a story invented by the magician. The reality of the stone was much more prosaic. Men had dug it from the earth, had taken the rock and polished it, then had sold it in the bazaar. After that, the Passion Star had been passed from hand to hand. It was no more or less colorful than money.

Yes, the only romance of the Passion Star had been in her own mind.

And—again her fingers squeezed at the stone, perspiring against its cold surface—hadn't her own life been much like the story of the Passion Star? A lie made up to impress and dazzle audiences, and perhaps even herself?

Adrienne began to walk again, limping painfully on her sore feet. She headed out on the log jetty which had been built over the river, its uprights half-rotted from the constant wash of water and spray.

The Detroit river was wide, and its surface seemed almost flat, glittering in the moonlight. Adrienne walked to the end of the pier and stared outward. Across the water she could see a few pinpricks of light—the village of Windsor, in Canada. Gas lights, she thought dully, beacons of human habitation and warmth, of families and laughter.

She sat down on the damp wood, curling her feet beneath her, wincing as the soles of her feet throbbed painfully. She pulled the dirty blanket around her. She felt flat and deadened, as if all of the warmth in her, all of the courage and passion, had been swept away. Now there was only a husk of a woman, a woman who had come down as far as there was to go. A drunken laughing-stock, a thief.

Dully Adrienne stared across the river, toward the pinpricks of light on the other side. Then she looked down at the sapphire, its surface almost black now in the moonlight.

If the Passion Star had a romance, then it also had a real story, she realized slowly. It had belonged to someone before Xenos had stolen it. To Martin Greggori?

But she had not wanted to think about that possibility. She had pushed Greggori out of her mind, for she had not wished to know the real history of the Passion Star. She had clung to the romance.

Now she touched the stone, feeling the smoothness, the enigma of it. She crept closer to the edge of the jetty, her blanket dragging on the damp wood. She stared downward at the water, at the swirling foam which frothed on its surface and washed against the pilings. The Passion Star dangled from her hand, swinging in an arc over the water.

Feeling almost hypnotized, Adrienne watched it swing, glinting in the moonlight as if it still held secrets at which no one could ever guess. . . .

She shivered. She should drop the stone in the water, she thought dully. Bury it forever, all that was false and unreal, all that was ugly and painful and wrong.

All she had to do was to open her palm, release the chain, and let the Passion Star fall. It would drop cleanly beneath the waves, making only a small splash. Then there would be nothing left, nothing at all, to mark where it had been.

"Adrienne!"

A voice stopped her. She heard footsteps behind her, echoing hollowly on the damp wood of the jetty.

"So," Kristian said calmly, "you're here, Adrienne. I've been looking all over for you. Are you all right?"

"Yes, oh, yes!" She jumped to her feet, pulling the blanket about her to cover herself, the Passion Star once more safe in her palm.

"Here," he said. "Take my jacket, darling, it's long enough to cover you."

He came toward her in the moonlight, limping slightly, flexing his hands as if it hurt him to move them. His face looked battered, a flow of blood dark on one cheekbone. His lip was cut and swollen. Yet there was a fierce triumph on his face, and she knew without being told that he had inflicted many injuries in the saloon.

"Kristian"—She accepted the jacket, pulling it on quickly, then wrapping the blanket around her legs— "are *you* all right? I—I heard the sounds of fighting, breaking glass, oh, God—" She was weeping now, the sobs tearing out of her. "Oh, darling, I'm so ashamed, so *ashamed*. I didn't want to face you, I couldn't."

"It doesn't matter." Kristian's arms were hard about her. His reassurances were wordless, a fierce stroking of her hair.

At last they pulled apart.

"How did you find me in that saloon?" she choked.

"From the theater you were easy enough to follow in the moonlight. Did you think that I would just let you run off into the night without trying to help you? The man who accosted you had gone, but even without him, the streets are dangerous enough for a woman alone."

"As are the saloons," Adrienne muttered in a voice barely audible. She felt nearly sick with her shame. To think that Kristian had seen her thus—

". . . it was the third drinking place I'd been to, looking for you," he was saying. "I was about to leave that one when I heard a commotion coming from the back room. Men were crowded about the door, and there was ugliness in their voices. Something made me go and look—" Kristian stopped.

"And you saw me," she whispered. "Me, in that terrible room, with *them*. . . . Oh, my God, Kristian, I'm so ashamed, I . . . I just wish I could die."

"No, darling, I don't want you to die, never that." For long moments he held her, stroking her as if she had been a child.

"I would give my life for you, Adrienne. No matter

what you are, or have been, that doesn't matter to me. I love you. Don't you know that?"

She could only stare at him. "But Kristian—Primrose was your wife, you loved her, you grieved for her. I thought—oh, I thought—"

"Darling, darling!" Kristian pulled her even closer to him. "Don't you realize that there are many types of love? Yes, I loved Primrose very much. To me she was a—a precious thing, a lovely wildflower, rare and beautiful. But you are different. There is something else between the two of us, something raw and powerful. We must always be together, Adrienne. It can never be any other way."

She hesitated, waiting for the words to come.

"I'm not the way you think I am," she began slowly. "I'm not a countess. I never have been. I grew up in Glasgow, in the worst section of the city, in filth and poverty. I—I stole the Passion Star from Xenos Shane. That was why he came to the theater. To blackmail me."

She paused painfully.

"He'll do that no more, I'll see to that. As for you, my darling, I have known for months that you weren't what you seemed. Long ago, at Phineas Magruder's request, I sent a letter to Scotland to verify your credentials. I found that you had none."

"Oh—" She tried to control her tears. "All these years, Kristian, I lived a lie. And now, my drinking—I'm a drunk, like my father, everyone knows it. Everyone, even Bettina Smithe. They've all been laughing at me, placing w-wagers . . ."

She could not even look at him.

Kristian's forefinger was under her jaw, pulling her chin up so that she had no choice but to face him.

"Don't hide from me, darling. What *of* your drinking? *You* are the one who is in control of what happens to you, are you not?"

For long moments she stared into Kristian's eyes, the keen, sharp eyes which searched out her own and would allow no subterfuge, no evasions.

"Yes." She gave a painful little laugh. "I—I suppose I am."

"Well, then?"

"Fanny said something to me once about drinking," she went on slowly. "Alcohol is like a sickness with some people, she said. For them, it's like stepping off the rim of a cliff. Once they take even one drink, there is no choice but to fall." She paused. "I . . . I think I'm like that, Kristian."

"I think you are, too."

"Then . . ."

An odd feeling of joy was pushing through her, a joy which she could not really explain. Was it strength? Was it resolve? Was it perhaps some fierce courage which she had possessed all along but had been unaware of until now? She only knew that this was somehow a changing-place in her life.

Kristian was right. She herself was in control of her life. No one else was, only she, Adrienne Gill.

She could choose not to take that one dangerous drink. She did not have to step off that cliff again—ever.

"Darling . . . darling . . ." She was in his arms once again. "Can you ever forgive me, Kristian, for all I've been and done? For all the pain I've caused?"

"Yes, Adrienne." His arms were firm about her. "You know I can forgive you. I already have. And I'll help you. You are the most important thing in my life, dear heart. Don't you know that? You always have been, and always will be."

Adrienne sat tensely in the buggy, nervousness making her hands tremble. It was May again, May in New York, the streets full of the sweet green of new leaves, the tender pink and white blossoms of cherry and crab and apple.

The buggy rattled down a fragrant Fifth Avenue, past the mansions with their impressive stone fronts, their wrought-iron fencing, their rich frosting of towers and cupolas and balconies.

Adrienne tried to calm herself as they drove, forcing herself to watch the skill with which Kristian handled the reins. How handsome he was, with his firm, well-carved features, his deep blue eyes which held such strength. And how very much she loved him. Loved him—no, adored him—with a passion she had not thought possible.

It was more than a month later. They were back in New York amid the hustle and gossip of Broadway and Union Square, Adrienne's own world. *The Passion Star* had reopened at the Olympic to huge crowds.

Amazingly large crowds, she thought now, dazedly, and friendly ones as well. Men and women had flocked to the theater to see the famous Adrienne Gill who had somehow managed to make a comeback, to give performances flawless in their emotional drama.

Only last night, when she had finished her last, climactic scene as Fatima, there had been a stunned hush in the theater. It had seemed to stretch on and on, almost electric in its intensity.

Then the applause had started, wild, stormy, until Adrienne, taking her bows, did not know whether to laugh or weep. She could only curtsey low, watching in amazement as the flowers began to pelt onstage—little boutonnières, single blooms, extravagant bouquets of hothouse roses. Eight curtain calls—ten—she had lost count when the curtain finally rang down for the last time.

The cast had crowded about her in jubilation.

"You did it, Adrienne, you really did it," Fanny whispered, throwing her arms about Adrienne. "I don't know what it is, I don't know what's happening, but it's different, *you're* different, and they sense it."

"I feel different," Adrienne said. "I feel wonderful."

It was true that there was a joy in her these days, a joy so powerful and all-consuming that it overflowed into everything she did. She was truly gifted, an "extraordinary actress," the *Sun* had said. And even the crusty William Stauffer had admitted that she was the actress of the decade.

She had not taken a drink since Detroit.

"How do you feel, my darling?" Kristian asked now as the buggy jolted along.

"Just a bit nervous," she admitted. "Well, more than nervous. I'm scared. I'm frightened of making a fool of myself."

"This may all be a wild-goose chase. You don't have to do this, you know, Adrienne. No one will fault you if you tell me to turn the buggy around and head for home."

She caught her breath. "But I can't do that. I *must* go to see him, Kristian. I only wish he hadn't been traveling in Europe until now, so that I could have done it sooner."

Martin Greggori lived in one of the more splendid Fifth Avenue mansions, an imposing structure faced with white granite and adorned with marble statuettes and elaborate lawn fountains equipped with reclining cupids.

They were shown inside by a stern-faced butler. Seeing him, Adrienne nearly lost her courage. Surely this was a strange and humiliating errand. Greggori would have every right to throw her out, or worse.

But she had come this far, and she must go on.

"Well, it is a pleasure—a supreme pleasure—to see you again, Miss Gill. As you know, I've long been a fan of yours. One of your most ardent fans."

Martin Greggori was being wheeled toward them, through a doorway enlarged to permit passage of his wheelchair. He was as she had seen him earlier, a wizened, emaciated man whose limbs rested like sticks in the chair. But somehow he was still a person of dignity, his suit well-cut and immaculately pressed. His pale blue eyes were steady on hers. He didn't want her pity, Adrienne remembered.

She could feel her mouth go dry.

"Of course," she heard herself reply. "We have met backstage. And twice you sent me roses in beautiful vases."

"Ah, I should have sent you dozens of bouquets, each one in a vase more lovely than the last."

"Mr. Greggori—" She forced herself to go on, aware

of Kristian beside her. "Mr. Greggori, I haven't come here to pay a social call, pleasant as that might be. I had to come here to tell you— Oh, I'm ashamed, so ashamed of what I did."

"And what have you done, my dear?" The eyes of the crippled financier were intent on her. "But before you tell me, come into my library and have some coffee, won't you both? The library is my favorite room. I can be surrounded by my books, and indeed all the things I love best."

Martin Greggori's library was a gracious room filled with books, art objects, and carefully collected oil paintings. They were seated, and were brought coffee, served on a sterling silver tray with an inlaid design. While Greggori chatted of the theater, and of *The Passion Star,* which he claimed to have seen ten times, Adrienne sat nervously, barely touching her coffee.

At last she could bear it no longer.

"Mr. Greggori," she stammered, "I've come here for a reason, as I'm sure you must know. And my reason is this."

She drew out a small box which she had been carrying concealed in the folds of her gown. She opened the lid and let the sapphire spill out. Its azure face with its six-legged star caught a shaft of sunlight and gleamed incandescently.

"Ah . . ." Martin Greggori caught his breath. "Ah, it's beautiful, even more so than when it is seen onstage. It's as lovely as—" He stopped.

For a moment the stone held them all in its power.

"It's yours," Adrienne whispered. "I'm returning it."

"So. Yes, Miss Gill, I was wondering when you would bring it back to me—or if you would."

She stared at him. It had been only a guess, really, which had brought her here. A guess based more upon instinct than upon fact. Yet now it seemed that her instincts had been accurate.

"But . . . then you knew? You knew that the Passion Star was yours? You knew that I . . . I stole it?"

Greggori's eyes were fixed on hers. "If you stole it,

my dear, then it was not from me. And perhaps you were only taking back what was yours."

The financier's hands tightened on the arms of his wheelchair. His expression was abruptly sad, almost yearning, as if something he saw in Adrienne's face moved him deeply. He turned and gestured to his attendant, waiting until the man had left the room, closing the library door behind him.

"You see, Miss Gill," he went on, "or may I call you Adrienne? It is a lovely, lovely name." Again that strangely sad expression crossed Greggori's face. "It appears that fate has brought us together and intermingled our lives. A fate somehow connected with this stone which you now hold in your hand."

Adrienne turned the Passion Star over in her palm, savoring the heavy, opulent feel of it. Then, reluctantly, she laid it down on a nearby tabletop.

"Is it true that a sapphire, a stone mined out of the earth and polished by men, can still hold a certain magic? A quality about it which cannot be explained by ordinary mortals?" Greggori's voice was soft, speculative. "I have often wondered, and most especially in these recent months."

"What do you mean?" Adrienne whispered.

"I would like to tell you a story, Adrienne. You may not believe it to look at me now"— Greggori made a wry face—"but once I was a young man of dashing good looks. Like many of my generation, I spent a year in Paris, a year of pleasure, of soaking up the joys of that city, before coming home to lead my ordinary life. I especially liked going to the ballet and the theater. I attended the Odéon often, for the plays there were exciting, and—"

"The Odéon?" Adrienne had frozen in her chair. *"Maman* was once wardrobe mistress there."

"Was she?" Greggori's eyes were more intent than ever.

Slowly, he went on. "There was also a girl, an actress at the Odéon. Her name, too, was Adrienne. Adrienne LaRivière."

Greggori's voice had gone low. He did not seem to hear Adrienne's quick, indrawn gasp of shock.

"Adrienne was wildly beautiful, but her looks were not of the ordinary soft, plump prettiness which was fashionable that year in Paris. No, her beauty was full of fire and flash and spirit. She had hair of stunning white-gold, like yours, Adrienne, and high, bold cheekbones. Her face was like a profile on a Roman coin."

Adrienne sat very still, her mind in a turmoil as she remembered *Maman*'s voice long ago in the flat in Glasgow. *She had a hundred admirers, but one in particular, oui, he was special. He was grievously hurt in a carriage accident just before she died.*

Dimly she heard Greggori's words go on. "You look like her, Adrienne. Almost exactly, in every way. The same flamboyant, stunning hair, the same cheekbones. And even the fire in you, the courage . . ."

"She was my aunt," Adrienne murmured. "I was named after her."

But it was as if Greggori did not even hear her.

"We loved each other. Perhaps, if you are very lucky, Adrienne, in your lifetime you can know what that means. It was a love that was not merely physical, although we were passionate lovers. There was something more to it. Something which transcended the body and had to do with the spirit. There was . . . electricity between us, fire. A rightness, a belonging. There is no real way I can describe it. It was simply . . . there, whatever it was."

A silence fell in the library. At last Greggori went on.

"Adrienne had in her possession a beautiful stone, a gorgeous star sapphire which had been given to her by a rich admirer who had recently traveled from the Orient. She loved the stone, was fascinated by it. I was soon to return to the United States. I begged her to marry me and come back to New York with me.

"But she . . . she said that she could not. She was an actress, she insisted, a French-speaking one. The French theater was her life. What would she do in a city like New

York? What could her life be there? She refused to marry me.

"Instead, she gave me this stone—this sapphire—as a token. And that night she scratched her initial on its reverse."

Greggori wheeled his chair forward and picked up the Passion Star from its place on the table. Slowly, with his good hand, he turned the jewel over, holding it up to the shaft of sunlight which streamed in through the tall library window.

"It should be here," he muttered. "Of course, the stone is many years older now, and has been worn often. Perhaps—"

Adrienne leaned forward tensely, her heart slamming in her chest. Beside her Kristian, too, had tensed.

"Ah!" Greggori cried out. "There it is." He held out the sapphire to her. "Do you see it, Adrienne? That mark there on the back, near the clasp? That is *her* initial."

Adrienne stared at the crude scratch on the back of the Passion Star. It was a mark she had seen hundreds of times and had always supposed to be a scratch caused by accident or excessive handling.

It was true, then. The Passion Star had once belonged, however briefly, to Adrienne LaRivière, *Maman*'s sister, her own aunt. It was as if some hugely benevolent force, some magic, had somehow reached out from beyond the grave to touch her. She felt stunned with her shock.

To her surprise, she saw that tears were running down Martin Greggori's cheeks. He made no effort to wipe them away.

"The rest of the story is simple enough," he went on huskily. "That night she refused me, I thrust the sapphire into my pocket and slammed down the steps of her *pension*. I felt as if I no longer wanted to live. I adored Adrienne, she was the center of my existence, the only thing in my world. And she would not come back to New York with me. Blindly I started across the street, not caring where I went or what I did. A carriage rumbled toward me.

"And I didn't even slacken my pace. Did I want to

be hit? Or did the horses suddenly pick that moment to run away? I don't know. I only know that something hit me, something so overwhelming that it was beyond pain, beyond agony.

"I awoke in a hospital—a cab driver had taken me there. My legs were paralyzed, my body crushed almost beyond recognition. I never knew how long I had been lying in the street or what had happened to me there while I was unconscious. My wallet, my money, my watch, my stick pin—everything in my pockets was gone, picked over by one of the thieves who swarmed the alleys of Paris. The sapphire was gone, too, of course."

Xenos, came Adrienne's quick thought. Xenos Shane had been the thief in Paris that night who had robbed the body of an accident victim.

Greggori's voice grew huskier. "A month after my accident, just as I had passed out of danger, my Adrienne died. Rumors sprang up in the theater that she had been poisoned by a rival, but it was all nonsense, of course. She died of poisoning, true, but it was caused by a ruptured appendix, according to her physician. So it had all been for nothing, all of it. She never went to New York with me, but never did she act again on the French stage. A waste . . . oh, God, a waste . . ."

Greggori's face was buried in his hands.

"Oh—please, Mr. Greggori . . ." Adrienne reached out to the man in the wheelchair, taking his hands and pressing them between her own. Tears ran down her own cheeks.

The financier looked up.

"Don't weep, Adrienne. That was all many years ago, and I've learned to live with my grief. Eventually I returned to New York. I learned to live in this new body which the accident gave me." Greggori looked down bitterly at his wasted, shriveled legs. "I was no longer attractive to women, I had nothing left but my work. So I worked. I learned to make money, a good deal of it."

Greggori's shrug dismissed this part of his life as if it had little meaning. "And one day in the newspaper I read of a new play called *The Passion Star*. Its title intrigued me and I went to see it. I came home stunned. There was

473

Adrienne again, my Adrienne ... and, dear God, there was the sapphire, the very star sapphire she had once given me ..."

Greggori's voice cracked. Silence fell again into the library while he struggled to regain his composure.

Adrienne swallowed hard. She picked up the Passion Star and thrust it into the financier's hand. "Take it, Mr. Greggori. The Passion Star, I want you to take it now. I am sure she would have wanted you to have it."

Greggori's smile was fleeting and somehow very sad. "No, Adrienne. No, my darling girl, I don't want the Passion Star any more. What would I do with it? I am rich, a millionaire many times over. Money means little to me. As for the memory of my own Adrienne, I will always have that in my mind, as clear and vivid as if I had just seen her yesterday. I need no physical objects to recall her."

"But—but I've brought it back! It belongs to you! Xenos Shane stole it from you and I ... I stole it from him."

"And the Passion Star somehow got the better of us all, didn't it? No, my dear, the sapphire is yours. You have made it yours with your courage and your dedication. Perhaps it was meant to be yours all along, who knows?"

Greggori hesitated.

"There is only one thing I want from you, Adrienne Gill. One thing only."

Her eyes were brimming with tears. "And what is that?"

"Why, that you allow me to be your friend. I wish your friendship. To see you now and again, just to talk."

Adrienne flung herself toward the man in the wheelchair. "Of course! I—oh, Mr. Greggori!" She threw her arms around him. "You're wonderful, did you know that? No wonder she loved you!"

Martin Greggori held her closely for a moment. Then firmly he released her, propelling her with his good arm toward Kristian.

"He is the one who should be holding you, my dear, and not me. My time for that is long past. He is your man. So go to him, my dear Adrienne. Love him as he loves you. Perhaps it was all written, long ago, in that stone you call the Passion Star."

"Oh . . ."

And then she was somehow again in Kristian's embrace, and she felt herself melt into his arms, knowing that she was completed, in her rightful place at last. *There was electricity between us, fire. A rightness, a belonging. It was simply . . . there. . . .*

Yes, she thought joyfully. *"Yes, oh, yes.*

"There is one more thing I must do," she whispered at last. "Kristian, I must see the press—I must contact William Stauffer and all of the others, and I must tell them everything. I have waited far too long to do that."

Both men started.

"Everything?" Kristian began. "But, darling—"

"No, Kristian. I won't live a lie any more. I'm not a countess, I was born in the poorest part of Glasgow. I stole. I drank too much, I did many things of which I'm ashamed. And now I refuse to be blackmailed by someone like Xenos Shane. Let the people know about me— let them know it all. If they choose not to like me, then . . . then let it happen."

"Darling, oh, my Adrienne."

Kristian was holding her tightly, his arms a bulwark and a strength. "They will like you—they'll love you, they'll adore you even as I do, how could they help it? Adrienne, my darling, my own heart—"

"She is a very brave heart," Greggori said softly beside them. He turned his wheelchair and began propelling it toward the library door.

And then once more Adrienne was locked in Kristian's embrace and felt their love burn around them like a shield and a talisman. And nothing, she knew with joy, would ever come between them again, or ruin the shining fabric of their happiness.

Beside them, on the table, the surface of the Passion Star caught the bar of sunlight, its six-legged star gleaming with cool mystery.

Epilogue

In the small *pension* in Paris, it seemed as if many hours, or perhaps even years, had passed since the dying woman had spoken. But, of course, it had been only a few seconds.

"I couldn't marry him, of course. . . ." The actress's gasps had grown harsher, and there were great long pauses between her words now. "I . . . I could only give him something of mine, something I had loved. I was . . . fascinated by it, for it had a story, that stone . . ."

"Hush, my darling sister. You must not talk. You must rest and save your strength."

"For what? No . . . No time to rest now. The man who gave it to me told me all about it. A king . . . a king once owned that sapphire. And Martin, he never let me finish telling him about it. He was angry, he rushed away before I had time. . . ."

Adrienne LaRivière blinked back tears.

"Sister . . ." Solange, too, had begun to sob in earnest now. "Oh, sister, I don't even know of what you speak. What sapphire? What king? I don't understand . . ."

The dying actress closed her eyes. Her breath came in great gasps, and her lips had gone very blue.

"Doesn't matter now . . . nothing matters now. . . . Only that—there was love in that stone. Felt it when I held it in my hand. Love and . . . and fate. Yes, that's it. Strange . . ."

OUTSTANDING BOOKS FROM WARNER BOOKS

THE GRAY ITCH
by Edmond C. Hallberg   (91-507, $2.50)
You hit middle-age and suddenly realize that you're not going to move up in the company, that your kids don't need you much anymore and you aren't the only focus for your liberated wife. You wonder, Who am I and where am I going? Discover how to handle this almost universal problem with the action plan of solutions that Dr. Hallberg has developed in years of counseling—and begin to enjoy living again.

DISRAELI: A PORTRAIT OF A ROMANTIC
by David Butler   (85-776, $2.75)
Benjamin Disraeli dazzled and shocked British society. His wit, his novels, his devastatingly good looks won him plaudits, but his Jewish origins and scandalous association with succession of the most beautiful . . . and most married . . . women in England was the talk of London. Yet he rose to power in British politics despite overwhelming opposition, won the Prime Ministry and the profound friendship of Queen Victoria. One of the greatest, strangest, and most moving love stories of all time.

FOXES
by Gerald Ayres   (92-156, $2.25)
Sweet Sixteen—it's a great time! All you have to worry about is writing poetry and trading clothes and who your mother is sleeping with and whether your best friend will o.d. or whether her father, the cop, will kill her. And if your friend Dierdre's boyfriends will kill each other. Wouldn't it be great to have a pad somewhere . . . someplace with pillows around and music around and just some people to talk to. Someplace where a girl could do her growing up . . . in peace.

THE BIRDS FALL DOWN
by Rebecca West   (91-189, $2.50)
A drama of beauty and betrayal, of spies and splendor, of manners and cold blooded murder. The Count—betrayed by his lord and ruler but not by his dearest friend. The Girl—beautiful, innocent and possessed of secret information that could prove to be her death warrant. The Informer—his confrontation with the Count could change the course of history. The Spy—does he stalk them all—all those who suspect the truth?

BOOKS OF DISTINCTION FROM WARNER BOOKS

HANTA YO
by Ruth Beebe Hill   (96-298, $3.50)
You become a member of the Mahto band in their sea-
sonal migrations at the turn of the eighteenth century.
You gallop with the warriors triumphantly journeying
home with scalps, horses and captive women. You join
in ceremonies of grief and joy where women trill, men
dance, and the kill-tales are told. "Reading *Hanta Yo* is
like entering a trance."   —New York Times

DEEPER INTO MOVIES
by Pauline Kael   (93-525, $2.95)
Pauline Kael's latest volume brings together more than
one hundred and fifty pieces of criticism from *The New
Yorker*, written between September 1968 and March
1972. The author considers it to be a "record of the
enteraction of movies and our national life during a
frantic time when three decades seem to have been compressed into three years." *Deeper Into Movies* is the only
book on movies ever to have won the National Book
Award (Arts and Letters, 1974).

FAGGOTS
by Larry Kramer   (95-153, $2.75)
It is a novel with precedent. It is an odyssey, not of a
Greek adventurer, but of a fortyish writer, a homosexual
looking for a lover, looking for a permanent relationship.
It is explicit in sexual detail but funny and compassion-
ate, too. "*Faggots*, for all its excesses, is frequently right
on target and, when it is on target, is appallingly funny."
                    —Edward Albee

THE CHANGING LIFE OF THE CORPORATE WIFE
by Maryanne Vandervelde   (91-180, $2.50)
Until recently the answer has been a resounding no! But
women themselves are beginning to change the pattern
to fight for their own identity. Maryanne Vandervelde, a
corporate wife for 16 years, conducted an extensive sur-
vey of the Fortune 500 companies chief executive officers
and their wives to determine current attitudes and pre-
sents the sometimes shocking results.

OUTSTANDING READING FROM WARNER BOOKS

THE CULTURE OF NARCISSISM
by Christopher Lasch (93-264, $2.95)

Have we fallen in love with ourselves? Have we bargained away our future for self-gratification now? With an unsentimental eye, Christopher Lasch examines our society and our values and discovers that we are in thrall in a new enchantment—self-involvement. We live today in THE CULTURE OF NARCISSISM.

HOW TO PROSPER DURING
THE COMING BAD YEARS
by Howard J. Ruff (95-261, $2.75)

Will you survive this round of inflation? You will if you listen to Ruff. Now he tells you what you must do to keep your money intact, be sure of making intelligent investments. "I recommend this book to everyone," said the *Dow Theory Letter*.

PALOVERDE
by Jacqueline Briskin (83-845, $2.95)

The love story of Amelie—the sensitive, ardent, young girl whose uncompromising code of honor leads her to choices that will reverberate for generations, plus the chronicle of a unique city, Los Angeles, wrestling with the power of railroads, discovery of oil, and growing into the fabulous capital of filmdom, makes this one of the most talked about novels of the year.